THE FIT COLLECTION

10TH ANNIVERSARY EDITION

REBEKAH WEATHERSPOON

Books By Rebekah

FIT & CO.

Fit

Tamed

Sated

Wrapped

LOOSE ENDS

Rafe: A Buff Male Nanny

Xeni: A Marriage of Inconvenience

Meegan: A Holidate for Hire

COWBOYS OF CALIFORNIA

A Cowboy To Remember

If The Boot Fits

A Thorn In The Saddle

BEARDS & BONDAGE

Haven

Sanctuary

Harbor

SUGAR BABY NOVELLAS

So Sweet

So Right

So For Real

VAMPIRE SORORITY SISTERS

Better Off Red

Blacker Than Blue

Soul To Keep

STAND ALONE TITLES

The Fling

At Her Feet

Treasure

A Walk In the Park

YOUNG ADULT

Her Good Side

Praise for Rebekah's Work

MEEGAN: A HOLIDATE FOR HIRE

"I don't know that I've ever read a book that's been so unconditionally sexy while also being so, so gentle. Weatherspoon proves again that she's the expert at character-driven romance, and serves us up an intimate, kinky, loving world that we'll never want to leave." — Sierra Simone, USA Today bestselling author

HER GOOD SIDE

"A joyful read brimming with positivity and support, Weatherspoon's romantic YA novel will leave you grinning from ear to ear." - Isaac Fitzgerald, The TODAY SHOW

A COWBOY TO REMEMBER

"In an anxious time, *A Cowboy to Remember* is a weighted blanket of a book." - Maureen Lee Lanker, Entertainment Weekly

RAFE

"'Rafe' is a breeze and a delight, a perfect book to read over and over again."- Jaime Green, The New York Times Review of Books

HAVEN

"...the perfect balance of sexiness, action and angst." - Alexa Martin, author of INTERCEPTED

INTRODUCTION

In the fall of 2013 I wrote a novella and submitted it to a major publisher to be a part of one of their new lines. And at the time I set out to write something that I thought would please those editors. It wasn't my usual style. The couple was straight and white. I know, GASP! Three weeks later I received a rejection and it turned out to be one of the best things that had ever happened to me.

I went back to the drawing board and made a lot of changes, most importantly to Violet and Grant. They became an interracial couple. Their personalities become lighter and more fun. I felt like I had a story I was really proud of on my hands. I talked to a few writer friends who helped me with the ins and outs of self publishing. I put FIT out as a self-published title and the following year, FIT went on to win the Romantic Times Book Reviews Reviewers' Choice Award for Best Erotic Romance Novella. A year later, SATED would would be nominated for the same award.

In the ten years that followed, what some call the Weatherspooniverse came into being. Six novellas and six, soon to be seven novels, connected by family, friendships, a couple gym memberships, an apple orchard, and a particular kinky club.

From FIT to the final notes of Duke and Daniella's love story, I've had so much fun dreaming up these characters and their romantic journeys over the last ten years. I cannot thank you, the readers, enough for all the love and support you've shown them. I'm not fully done with these characters. Daniel won't leave me alone so I'm sure we'll see him and his lovely wife, Keira again soon. In the meantime, please enjoy this special edition with new bonus material. It's all been for you.

Xoxo, Rebekah

Bonus Content

In honor of the tenth anniversary of FIT, I wanted to share a few shorts, deleted scenes, and extras about our friends at Melrose Fitness and their pals at The Club. These shorts were selected with a wee bit of bias (I have a little obsession with Daniel). It made the most sense to feature each scene in chronological order considering by the time we get to Meegan's book people have gotten married and children have been born. Here's a little guide.

Following FIT you will find CELEBRATED, a sexy romp from Meegan's birthday scene starring Meegan, Marcos, and Daniel.

At the conclusion of TAMED you will find ADORED, a turning point in Armando and Nailah's emotional journey.

After SATED, there is BLESSED (not new, but still amazing) where we reunite with Grant and Violet as Violet shares some unexpected news. At Christmas!

And following WRAPPED, there is SNATCHED. A roleplay date night featuring my two favorite switches, Keira and Daniel. I mentioned he won't leave me alone.

I hope you enjoy them all!

FIT

No 1. in the Fit Trilogy

About This Book

FIT
No. 1 in the Fit Trilogy
*Winner: 2014 Romantic Times Book Reviews Reviewers' Choice
Award for Best Erotic Romance Novella*

Violet Ryan loves the delicious food she gets to eat on the reality shows she produces for The Food Channel. What she hates is her expanding waistline. Determined to drop the pounds, Violet hatches a plan to kick-start a fitness regimen. But when her determination isn't enough to get her through even one intense group class without breaking down into tears, she knows she needs a new approach and possibly a new trainer—one with a lighter touch.

Grant Gibson has always managed to mix business with pleasure, but now this trainer by day, and Dominant by night, is bored. Bored and lonely. Even though he owns one of L.A.'s hottest private gyms, his personal life is sorely lacking. After his last submissive tried to kidnap his dog and the contents of his bank account, he's in no hurry to take a new lover under his wing. Not until the voluptuous Violet falls into his lap.

She may be wary of his unorthodox approach of using sexual

gratification as a reward, but even before her initial weigh-in Violet can't seem to stay away from the sexy fitness god. She may have to let Grant show her there's more than one way to get in shape...

This story contains light acts of bondage and a feisty submissive who gives her Dominant a run for his money.

For Steph
#Surfboart

ONE

Day 1

Violet nearly wheezed as she dropped her weights to the ground. She collapsed on all fours, a few drops of sweat beating her to the hard rubber surface. She stretched her hands out, shoulder-width apart. Her knees ached as she raised herself up in a modified push-up. Was it possible to die from push-ups? She didn't know, but part of her wanted it to be true. Sweat ran down her face, between her breasts, and she wanted to die.

Actually, she wanted to kill her friend, Faye. And the people at sharepon.com. Faye had it coming for suggesting they take this all-ladies Pump Fit class together, and sharepon.com deserved a strongly worded letter for offering the class to Faye for free if she brought a friend along to join in the pain. Sure, in reality it was Violet's own fault. She'd spent half their last season on *BBQ Cook-Off* complaining about how much weight she needed to lose, while simultaneously shoving pound after pound of pulled pork into her pie hole.

Faye was a good friend and listened to Violet bitching about the long hours they worked and the high calorie foods they were "forced" to eat on set. Even though Faye seemed to manage the hours and the menus just fine, she listened when Violet confessed that she'd reached her breaking point. Her fat jeans barely buttoned over her stomach the night of the wrap party. It was time to get her body in order.

She'd heard it one hundred and a million times; it takes twenty-one days to create a new habit, and Violet had exactly *twenty-three* days before preproduction started up on their next show for Park Place Productions.

She loved her job as an associate producer. Her company's primary focus was cooking and baking competition shows for The Food Channel. She worked hard and partied even harder, but enough was enough. She had twenty-three days to get on a healthy routine so she could go into the next show with a new diet, a new sleep schedule and, hopefully, a smaller waistline. She envisioned herself taking on this challenge head-on. She'd always been overweight. A chubby kid, turned fat teen, turned fatter adult, but she'd always been somewhat in shape. Pump Fit sounded tough. Still, if she put her mind to it, she could make it through the class. Or so she thought.

"One more minute! Keep going, ladies!" the instructor shouted. Her name was Margaret and even though she was the same height as Violet, she was about ten sizes smaller and carried about seventy-five more pounds of muscle, most of it in the area about the neck and shoulders. Instructor Margaret was from Australia, with an accent so thick her every command would have been hilarious if Violet could find the slightest bit of humor in the situation. Margaret was also a professional Pump Fit competitor. As soon as she offered that bit of information at the start of class, Violet should have run right back to her car.

"Up!" Margaret shouted. "I want twenty burpees! Go!"

Violet struggled to her feet, then dropped back down, extending her legs behind her butt before bringing her knees back up to her chest then springing back up to her feet.

One.

Down again. She could barely breathe. Her lungs burned and that acidic taste, a mixture of burning fat, blood and embarrassment, filled her mouth. Beside her, Faye, with her flat stomach and tight butt, completed burpee three and four. Faye ate her pork too. It wasn't fair.

"Come on, Violet! Keep going! We don't move on until we all finish!"

Right. Great. No pressure there. Violet dropped to the floor one more time, and then again, as Margaret kept screaming.

The buzzer at the front of the room sounded, signaling the end of the timed rotation. Violet had completed six burpees. She'd attempted eight. Margaret frowned at her briefly, but let it go.

"Two hundred meter run! Claire knows the way!" Demon Instructor nodded to a slim redhead, who nodded back then bolted for the open gym door.

"Come on," Faye said, patting Violet's sweaty arm. "You're doing great. Let's go."

Violet kept up as they sprinted down the stairs to the street, but once they hit the hill, the freaking hill that led from the gym plaza to Sunset Boulevard, she started lagging behind. When the second-to-last woman in the class lapped her on the way back, Violet started to cry.

It was gym class all over again. She was the last kid picked. The last kid to finish the mile. The fat-ass who caused the gym teacher's eyebrows to sag down when she even attempted the sit-and-reach. Violet didn't know who she was kidding. She needed more than twenty-three days and her wavering determination. She needed lipo and a miracle.

Violet stopped slow jogging and wiped her face. When she made it back up the stairs, the whole class was waiting for her, jump ropes in hand. They all offered smiles of encouragement. She even got a few "good jobs". When she glanced at herself in the mirror, she could see how red and blotchy her face was. It wasn't the exertion. It was obvious that she had been crying. Violet took the rope Faye had grabbed for her. She fought tears for the rest of the class, but a few managed to trickle out, mixing with the sweat that poured down her face.

*

It was tempting to fall flat on the floor once Margaret called their final time, but Violet had to get out of there. She'd held up the whole class five separate times and actually cried in front of a group of skinny, in-shape strangers, as she tried to remember the proper way to get both feet over a jump rope. She couldn't look at Faye as she wiped off her face and shoved her hand towel into her canvas tote bag. Faye knew Violet wasn't ready for this, but she'd convinced to her to come anyway.

I get it, Violet thought. *You proved your point. You take care of yourself. I don't. You can handle the free production food in moderation. I can't.*

"You ready?" Faye asked. Violet simply nodded, but just as she started to follow Faye out the door, Muscle-Bound Margaret, the self-worth eater, called her name.

"Hey, Violet! Hold on one sec."

Great. Now a pep talk. "I'll meet you down at the car," she told Faye, who took the hint and promptly disappeared out the door, leaving Violet alone with the trainer.

Margaret led her over to the counter at the front of the gym and, for the first time in over an hour, the woman seemed to unclench. She gave Violet a normal smile, full of understanding and lacking false encouragement. "This class isn't for you."

Or not. "Uh, thanks?"

"Sorry, love. I didn't mean for you to take it that way. I'm supposed to tell you that you did awesome and you should come back, 'cause money and word of mouth, etcetera, but you need to scale it back. When was the last time you worked out?"

Violet felt like crying again. "Four months ago."

"And you don't like the yelling either, do you?"

"I fucking hate it, but I need something. I really do want to lose weight."

"That's great, but sometimes you need to start slowly. Your friend's been to my class seven or eight times. Yeah, there's a first time for everyone, but not everyone needs to start in the same place."

Violet swallowed and fought back sudden tears of anger. Was she that far gone that a trainer was telling her she was a lost cause? She kept her mouth shut, confident that she would never set foot in Pinks Women's Fitness ever again. Faye could drag someone else along to suffer through the humiliation.

"I know this guy. Grant. He's a great personal trainer. He has a reputation of being a complete softy, but he gets results."

Despite the fact that Violet kinda wanted to kick Margaret in her muscular shin, the idea of working with a *nice* trainer, someone who would be patient with her, one on one, sounded pretty appealing. It would also be harder for her to be jealous of a guy's body. She wouldn't spend their time together constantly comparing her breasts or her ass to his.

"That might be cool," she finally said.

"I'm going to see him later today actually. You signed in with your info, right?" Margaret looked down at the very sign-in sheet by her elbow. There was Violet's name, right above Faye's. They'd been the first to arrive.

"Yeah." Violet pointed to her name, neatly printed in blue ink. She figured if the staff at Pinks flooded her inbox with class schedules and protein shake promotions, she'd force herself to come back. That was before the second two hundred meter run.

"So you don't chicken out, I'll have him call you. I don't want you to give up, but you will if you're not matched with some class or some trainer who's right for you."

"You're right. Thanks."

After a quick goodbye, Violet left the gym, feeling a little less hostile toward Margaret. But she still had to ride back to Culver City with Faye, who was a little too perky for Violet's liking when she got into the car. Faye didn't even ask what Margaret wanted. She knew. Pat the fat girl on the back. Keep her spirits high.

"We still on for lunch?" Faye asked.

Violet was starving, but she shook her head. "I don't think so. Can you drop me off? I really want to shower and take a nap." Faye looked disappointed, but she didn't argue as she pulled her car out onto Santa Monica. Violet was quiet the whole way back to her apartment, while Faye gabbed cheerfully, refusing to acknowledge that she may have fucked up.

When they stopped in front of her place, Violet came to the conclusion that one workout shouldn't be the end of their friendship. She just needed a little space and some time to feel like herself again.

"Let's get lunch tomorrow and go see a movie or something," she suggested.

"Sure. Let's do it. And I'm sorry. I didn't think it would be that bad. I didn't want you to cry."

"I know," Violet replied. "I just need a few." Faye smiled then offered Violet her signature air kiss before Violet hopped out of the car. By the time she made it upstairs, Violet wasn't upset anymore. Just sweaty and exhausted, and fixated on inhaling everything in her fridge.

✳

After Grant finished his second Beach Bootcamp class of the day, he headed back to Melrose Fitness, where he found Australian Pump Fit champ, Margaret White, waiting for him outside the gym doors.

"Well, if it isn't my favorite Aussie. G'day, Marge."

Margaret laughed, throwing back her head and showing off her chiseled chin.

"It's scary how good you are at that accent. You sound just like my brother."

Grant kept on with the thick impression a moment longer. "Just one of my many talents. What can I do ya for?" He held the front door open, then nodded toward the back office as he kept walking. Margaret followed. Armando was still on the floor, in room two, doing a private yoga session with two of his clients from Beverly Hills, so he and Margaret had the small space, cluttered with Melrose Fitness swag and protein bars, to themselves.

Margaret plopped down into the free chair while Grant dug through his bag for a towel and a clean shirt. He had to shower before his next session.

He looked over his shoulder at Margaret. "What's up?"

"I think I have a new client for you."

"Oh yeah? Tell me about her." He flashed his friend a wicked smile.

"Such a bastard. Her name's Violet Ryan. Her friend brought her into the Pump Fit class I do over at Pinks." Grant grunted as he stripped off his shirt. Pinks provided a female-only fitness environment just a few miles up the road. They were on to something for sure, but intense workouts like Pump Fit weren't for everyone.

"Let me guess. She couldn't finish the class?"

"She finished, but there were a lot of tears. I talked to her after. She wants to get in shape, but she needs someone softer. You know how screaming gives me a hard on."

"I do. Give me her info and I'll see what I can do. You think she's ready?"

"Is anyone ready for *the* Grant Gibson?" Margaret asked, with a smile.

"You have a point."

"I think she's ready. She was just overwhelmed. You've got that soft touch she might need." Grant had no witty response for that. It was part of his reputation. He was a bit of bastard otherwise, but when it came to his clients he prided himself on being able to provide them with a relaxed, pressure-free environment where they could reach their health and fitness goals.

Margaret slipped him a piece of paper with Violet's name and phone number. "Be nice, but not too nice."

"But nice is all I know."

"Right. I'll see you later. I have some kickin' and punchin' to do." Margaret left to join Keira's four-thirty kick boxing class, but not without slugging Grant a solid one in the shoulder. Girl had an arm.

Once he was alone, per standard operating procedure with all referrals, Grant pulled out his laptop and started searching for information on Violet Ryan. It was one thing, meeting a walk-in face-to-face for the first time, but if someone was handed off to him, or Armando, or anyone else on his staff, he liked to be prepared. You'd be amazed what you could discover from someone's Twitter feed or their Facebook page. Picture after picture of high calorie meals littered Instagram and Tumblr. Eating habits, drinking habits, sedentary habits.

Are they posting nonsense in the middle of the night, then complaining about having to be at work first thing in the morning, then having the balls to say they have no time to work out? Are they venting about something going on at work or with family or a significant other? Are they having a hard time finding that special someone? All of these things played into a person's health, whether they wanted to acknowledge it or not, and it was his job to get to the bottom of it all. That's how he kept clients and saw them through to their goals. His blessing and his curse. He could read people. Make them comfortable enough to trust him to help them turn their lives around. He'd built a business to be proud of but, man, was he bored.

It didn't take long for him to find Violet Ryan, but from Margaret's brief description of her and the way she'd crumbled in a class, Grant was surprised by what he found. She was a TV producer, with credits stacked in the online television and movie database. All the producers he knew were cutthroat and cold-blooded. He couldn't imagine any of them bursting into tears in front of a group of people.

He clicked through to her Facebook page and suddenly things slid into place. Violet Ryan, Associate Producer with the Food Channel, was pretty plump. It wasn't a judgment, just a fact. Same as the fact that she was a stunningly gorgeous Asian woman. She smiled in her tiny profile picture, full pink lips below an adorable button nose that was spattered with freckles. She had big brown eyes behind red-framed glasses. Her long, thick hair was doing that black-to-blond thing a lot of women were styling these days.

She managed to be hot and cute and sexy all at the same time.

He looked at her picture again. Well, stared was more like it. He would call her. A client was a client. He'd do what he could to help her out, but other parts of his brain were churning, parts that had been quiet and still for several months now.

He'd been out of the scene for a while. Life as a sexual Dominant had its perks and just as many pitfalls. He'd taken a break, taken some time to pull himself back together, but in the back of his mind he knew he wasn't out of the game forever. The game had consumed too much of his life for him to really let go.

On the flipside, Grant wasn't opposed to mixing his primary business with pleasure. He'd slept with clients before and he was sure he'd do it again. Armando did it all the fucking the time. The two of them had met at a pseudo-bondage party, grew close over their interest in kink and their obsessive dedication to working out, and eventually decided to go into business together. They'd both trained submissives and the occasional Mistress when things got a little routine. They'd both played inside and outside of the gym but lately, at least for Grant, things had been a little slow, even if it was by choice.

Everything had been slow. The classes and training sessions had grown routine, even with the occasional new client thrown into the mix. He had no woman to call his own. His family was three thousand miles away and more than happy with his simple monthly call home. He was bored and, even though it would take a lot for him to admit it openly, outside of this gym he was lonely. He had his friends, his pets, and his co-workers, but not much else. He didn't know when, but at some point something needed to change. He needed a change.

He continued clicking through picture after picture of Violet's smiling face, until Armando came through the office door. An hour of yoga and he hadn't broken a sweat.

"What's up, man?" Armando rummaged through his own things until he produced his cell phone.

"Nothing," Grant said. "Well, new client shit, but nothing."

Armando leaned over the desk and got a better look at Grant's computer screen. "This her?"

"Yeah."

"She's cute, and I assume she can afford you. What's the problem?" Armando asked, his interest in the conversation already waning. He had another class to teach in forty minutes. So did Grant, but his buddy was already thinking about the next group of clients. Grant was stuck on Violet Ryan and her innocent freckles.

"I'm thinking about dusting off the D/s file."

Armando froze in his tracks, then pivoted around to face Grant.

"I know. It's risky," Grant said.

"It's not risky, it's—"

"Risky."

"No, you can handle it. I know you can. I just didn't know you were ready. Is Ariana that far from your head? She was a dick, but I figured you a learned something from that."

"She wasn't a dick."

"She stole your credit cards and tried to steal Max when you broke up with her."

It had been six months since he ended things with his client-turned-submissive. His credit rating and his dog were still trying to recover. It wasn't that he'd slept with her, it was that he'd trusted her more than he should. He was looking for love and she was looking for someone to bleed dry. "You're right, she was a dick, but I think it might be time."

"Good luck, man." Armando looked at the screen again, his expression one of genuine approval. "Could be fun."

Grant clicked through her pictures one more time. Before his imagination got the best of him, he grabbed his cellphone and dialed Violet Ryan's number.

Two

Day 2

Violet pushed back her lunch date with Faye to meet up with this Grant Gibson guy. He'd called her the afternoon before, in the middle of her post-workout, leftover-pizza-induced nap. He suggested they meet at a juice bar around the corner from his gym in West Hollywood. She got there first, ordered herself something loaded with berries and kale, then took a seat outside. The spring weather was perfect. Sunny, but not too warm. She was on the verge of kicking off her sandals to really soak it all in when this beautiful mountain of a man approached her table.

"Violet?" he said, stretching out his hand. Oh, and that voice.

"Hi. Nice to meet you."

"Likewise. I'm Grant."

Violet stood, shook his hand, and did her best not to drool. Grant Gibson wasn't just a trainer. He was some sort of Scandinavian athletic god, tall and perfectly toned. Blue-eyed, with blond hair that was longer than most guys were wearing these days, but thick and styled perfectly back away from his face, cut cleanly along the base of his neck. His beard was thick but manicured, gold with patches of red and brown. And his lips...

He wore jeans and sneakers and a dark-gray hoodie, unzipped, showing off a white t-shirt and the outlines of the tattoos that decorated the broad chest underneath. Somehow Violet kept it together. She didn't babble or stumble over her chair as she moved to sit back down, but the thoughts running through her head? They were messy and very, very dirty.

Grant took the other seat and offered Violet an easy smile. He was dangerous, this one. "So tell me about yourself," he said.

"Well. I've been wanting to get in shape. Actually, I have a goal weight I want to reach. I know it'll take a long time. I can be patient, but I need to get started. I'm sick of looking this way and I'm sure, in some way I'm not seeing, these extra pounds can't be good for my health."

"That's cool. So why don't you tell me about yourself?" Grant repeated. He licked his lips, then smiled even wider.

Violet almost kicked *him* in his stupid shin, but that grin he flashed her melted her reflexes. He was sarcastic. Okay. She could do sarcastic.

Violet leaned forward and mimicked his tone. "Why don't you tell me about *yourself*. I'm fat. I want to pay you to make me unfat. Why don't you tell me how you're going to make that happen?"

Grant sat back and stretched his long legs out beside her chair. She thought about straddling him and kissing that look of satisfaction right off his face. But as fun as the brief fantasy seemed, it wouldn't help her achieve her weight-loss goal.

"I'm not going to make anything happen. It's on you, but here's how I can help."

"I'm listening."

"I believe our outside reflects the way we feel inside, whether that's good or bad, clean-cut or complicated. For some people, it's about our weight. For others it's about the way we dress or the way we sport our hair or the way we accessorize. Buddy of mine won't leave the house without his gold watch."

"That makes sense. So you want to know about my insides?"

Grant chuckled as he shifted in his chair. He had dimples under all that scruff. "Yes, Violet. I want to get inside of you."

"Well, all you had to do was ask. My car is right around the corner."

"Tempting. Really it is." For a moment, Violet thought he might be serious. She might have issues with her weight but she wasn't completely hopeless with men. She knew when a guy was flirting, and Grant climb-me-like-a-tree-and-shake-all-my-branches Gibson was definitely flirting. Or so she thought. He got right back to business.

"But that's not exactly what I mean. I have clients who come to me to lose weight for weddings or movies they're starring in or just to get back at their spouses, but every once in a while I have a client who wants to lose weight for themselves. In order to help you with that, I want to know why you put the weight on in the first place and why you keep it on. That way I can help you take it off and keep it off. Basically, I want to be the last trainer you see."

Oh, he was good. Smooth, honest, and a bit poetic. He could be the last of anything Violet ever had. Too bad he was talking about the circumference of her thighs and not gracing her bed or her backseat with his own gorgeous body.

"Tell me more about your techniques," she said. "Margaret made it sound like you were the Fatty Whisperer."

Grant's laughter sputtered out this time, his eyes alight with humor. "I do have a way about me that people seem to appreciate. I won't deny that, but, really, I would like to get to know you. I need to know what drives you. What you couldn't care less about. What kind of encouragement works on you. What doesn't."

"I'm a sucker for positive reinforcement. I can admit that. And I do better in solo environments. Margaret's class reminded me of middle school gym, and that wasn't a happy time for me."

Grant suddenly seemed to withdraw, like he was thinking heavily on something. Maybe she'd said too much. He was used to socialites and actresses, not East Coast girls with childhood complexes about being the only Chinese kid in their whole school.

"What is it?" Violet asked. "Too much?"

"No, that's not it. Can I ask you something?" Something in his tone set off alarm bells in her head. He was about to say something she had no interest in hearing.

"Sure…"

"What do you know about Domination and submission?"

"Oh, Jesus." Violet shoved back in her seat and clutched her purse against her stomach. The commotion drew the stares of the juice drinkers nearby. "Are you kidding me right now? What is this all about?"

"You said you respond well to positive reinforcement. I'm simply trying to figure out which kind." Violet could sense his confidence was wavering, but he really wanted to see this line of thinking through. Fine. She'd let him take it all the way and then she'd bitch him out and leave. *Thanks a lot, Margaret.* This was not what she signed up for.

"I know a little about BDSM. I've never participated in it though. Do you have any idea how unprofessional you sound right now?"

"I'm sorry." Grant held out his hands, like he was trying to calm a frightened dog. "Please, stay. Just hear me out. Please."

"Fine." Violet eased back into her chair.

"As long as I've been a personal trainer, I've been a part of the BDSM lifestyle, as a Dominant."

"And?"

Finally he gave up and his confidence faltered completed. He leaned forward and scrubbed his face with his large hands, as his whole head seemed to turn bright red. She knew the color of embarrassment well. When he looked up, Violet could see the genuine regret in his eyes.

"Violet, I am really sorry. I read this chemistry between us all wrong." So he had been flirting. Great. Too bad he completely blew it. Still, Violet tried to relax. He'd made a mistake, but at least he was trying to own it.

"It's okay. It's fine. You were saying?"

"Forget what I said. It's off the table. It was never on the table. I promise, none of that will be a part of this."

"So you're saying you can train me without trying to whip me or fuck me?" She let the sarcasm drip. "You're willing to make that sacrifice?"

"Really. I thought I read something in you—never mind. We do a simple on-ramp program. I gauge your current fitness level and we go from there. We'll cover nutrition and then, when you get where you want to be, we'll focus on maintenance."

"And no flogging or chains required?" Violet asked, doing nothing to hide the look of disgust on her face.

"Fuck, I'm such an idiot. No, none of that. I promise." Grant reached into his pocket and pulled out a black business card, then handed it to Violet. She looked at the cream and red lettering.

Grant Gibson Owner/Trainer Melrose Fitness

It should have read: **Dom/Smooth Operator/Professional Buffoon/Can't Read Women For Shit**

"Why don't you think it over? About training with me. If I don't hear from you, I'll completely understand. If you decide you want to, we can get started this week."

Violet glanced between him and the card. She didn't know what was left to consider. He was gorgeous, she couldn't ignore that obvious detail. And it wasn't that she thought consenting adults didn't have the right to get their jollies off in all sorts of different ways, but this wasn't about Grant Gibson's perfect body or his flawless face. Violet had a huge change she wanted to make, and she couldn't do it with someone who was looking to "get kinky". She took his card and slid it into a small pocket inside her bag. She'd toss it in the trash when he wasn't around to see.

"Why did we meet here instead of at your gym?"

"I find that the gym itself is intimidating for people who are just getting started. There's an advanced kick-boxing class going on right now, and I didn't think that would give you the idea that I was trying to ease you into your workouts."

A brutal comeback about trying to ease her into BDSM was on the tip of her tongue, but she let it go.

"Okay, well. I have to meet a friend for lunch." Violet snatched up the rest of her berry-kale drink and stood to leave. "It was... interesting to meet you."

Grant stood as well. A more sincere smile touched his lips this time. He knew he'd fucked up. "It was."

Violet nodded then walked toward her car. She could feel Grant Gibson's eyes on her back the whole way.

∗

Hours later Grant found himself where he wound up on most Sunday nights. Alone on his couch, Lakers on his TV, beer in his hand, black cat at his shoulder and snoring Rottweiler at his side.

He thought about calling Master Philip and seeing if he could drop into The Club, maybe haul some sweet new thing over his knee and teach her a thing or two about patience and obedience. But the idea was immediately chased away by the memory of the grimace of horror that had popped up on Violet Ryan's face the second he'd opened his big fucking mouth.

He'd fucked up. Huge. Was Violet his type? Hell yeah—she was pretty, smart, funny—but he had interpreted her all wrong. She wanted a trainer, they both got that part. But the flirting, the way she nearly stripped him bare with her eyes the moment he sat down at the table? He'd gotten that all wrong. There had been attraction, a mutual one at that, but just because he was looking for more didn't mean she was.

Grant thought Violet would be an amazing submissive, but she wasn't his to test that theory and he'd completely driven her away by suggesting their professional relationship should become even the slightest bit sexual.

He could just picture her now, telling her friends about this pervert trainer who tries to seduce his clients before their first Visa payment even went through. She'd probably give Margaret an earful too, for suggesting this guy who made it seem like he couldn't keep it in pants. Margaret knew all about him so she wouldn't hold that part against him, but she'd rib him royally for making such an ass out of himself. Either way, it was time for him to suck it up and go back to The Club or at least take it to the Internet. He had needs that had to be met.

Just as the third quarter ended, his phone jumped and sang on the coffee table. His cat, Bill, dug his claws into his jeans at the sound. It was probably Armando asking if he wanted to grab some food or a drink before they started their week. But when he picked up the phone he didn't see his buddy's name and he didn't recognize the number.

"Grant Gibson," he said.

Violet Ryan's sweet voice answered back. "Are you a chubby chaser? Like do you just screw fat women as some sort of fetish? Does banging big girls stroke your ego?"

"No." Grant laughed. "It's nothing like that."

"Do you have yellow fever? Do you only date Asian women? Should I tell you now that I'm Chinese, not Korean or Japanese, lest it fuck up some weird nationalist streak you have going?"

Grant's laugh was pretty manic this time. "Whoa. No. And what kind of guys have you been dating?"

"I haven't been dating those guys. I just know those guys are out there. Anyway, you gotta tell me what gives. That was... Yeah, I don't know what the hell that was. I want you to train me, but you have to help me out here. Explain."

Grant couldn't believe she'd called. Pleased that she was even willing to speak with him, he dropped the Don Juan act and told her the truth. "I find you very attractive and I thought we clicked on another level. I can handle being wrong but, no, I don't chubby chase. I'm not an Asian fetishist. My last girlfriend was Greek. This, what I proposed, is all about you and the fact that I genuinely like what I know about you so far."

"Have you done this with your clients before?"

"Yes. Three times. Twice it was mutually causal, just bondage and submission, and once it got serious and turned into a long term, exclusive relationship."

"Why did it end?"

"You're digging right in there, aren't you?"

"Uh, yeah. Three seconds after I meet you, you basically suggest we should fuck while I'm trying to lose weight. I think I'm allowed to ask some questions, so spill it, buster. Why did it end?"

"She was a thief."

"What?" Violet had every right to snicker. It had been Grant's same reaction when he first found out the truth about Ariana.

"She liked to steal. Money, clothing. She maxed out two of my credit cards and then, when I broke up with her, she tried to take my dog as a parting gift." Max whimpered beside him, as if he were recalling the trauma of that fateful autumn night.

"She tried to steal your dog?"

"Yeah. Tried to take his doggy bowl and his toys too."

"What kind of dog is it?"

"Rottweiler. His name is Max. He's still a big puppy."

"Cute. I like dogs. My landlord won't allow them and I work too much to really take care of one, but I like them." This is good, Grant thought. Let's talk more about dogs and less about me being a complete dickhead. "So, did you just approach the others all forward? Or did you at least wait until the second session?"

Grant didn't really know where she was going with this. At first she sounded angry and offended, but now she sounded interested. A little intrigued.

"It just happened. Well, one woman knew about me. She'd heard about my extracurricular interests through a friend, so she brought it up herself. But the other two, it just happened."

"So what about me? Why didn't I get that chance to ease into it? Test where the chemistry could go between us. Do I look that desperate?"

"No. It's me. I'm the desperate one."

"Oh, that sounds great."

"No! No! That's not what I meant. I think you're beautiful, Violet. You're funny as hell. I should have just told you that, but I've never had an adult relationship that didn't involve my kinks in some way. I just got a little ahead of myself. I'm sorry."

Violet was quiet for a long time, a really long time when you're on the phone. He almost asked if she was still there, but he could hear her quietly mumbling to herself. Was she actually reconsidering?

"I've never done anything like that before. I've read about it and I've seen porn, but my sex life has been relatively tame."

Grant tried his most soothing tone. "It's not all about whips and chains."

Violet responded in kind, her voice softening almost to a bashful level. "I know."

"Do you have a boyfriend?" Grant asked. He didn't see a hint of one online, but he should have asked before.

"Polite of you to ask. *Now*. No, I'm not with anyone. My last boyfriend and I broke up two years ago. He wanted to get married and have kids right away, but I wasn't ready." She paused again, her voice taking on that hesitant, almost innocent tone. Grant nearly groaned. She would make an excellent submissive. "Are you seeing anyone else?" she asked. "Are you fucking anyone else, I mean? I know this is Hollywood or whatever, but I believe in monogamy, even if it's casual. If you're screwing all of your clients, we'll have to keep this thing between us to strictly sit ups."

"I'm not seeing anyone, Violet. Sexually or otherwise."

"Okay."

Another pause.

"I need to work out early in the morning, like six, so I can knock it out before I go to work. Does that work for you? I don't know what your schedule is like."

"Six a.m. works just fine."

"Can we start tomorrow?"

"Tomorrow would be great. We can meet at the gym."

"Great. Sounds great. Do I need to wear leather panties under my sweats?"

"No. No leather anything. You just need to show up and I'll handle the rest."

"I'm sure you will." Violet sounded annoyed, but resigned. Grant didn't know how to take her mood. "I'll see you tomorrow."

"Goodnight."

"Night. Oh, and Grant?"

"Yeah?"

"I'm not a big fan of being tied up, but I could be persuaded to try some spanking. Maybe a little light paddling."

Before Grant could respond, Violet hung up.

THREE

Day 3

Violet couldn't believe she was going through with this. She stood outside Melrose Fitness, ten minutes before six a.m.. On a Monday. During a hiatus. No matter how much weight she wanted to lose, she could easily sleep in until noon and then work out. She could also find another trainer. But no. She needed a new routine and some foolish voice in the back of her head told her Grant Gibson, Captain None-Too-Smooth, was the one to help her get her new life on track.

She should have slapped him. She definitely shouldn't have called him, but she did, and now here she was, completely unprepared to live up to her ballsy parting words.

Did she want Grant to spank her after she completed her workouts? Of course she did. The thought of him putting his hands on her body like that, slapping her bare ass until it was pink and swollen had her soaking wet. She shuffled in her new Nikes just thinking about it. Did that make getting involved with him this way a good idea? Sure didn't, but it was too late now. He was walking down the street, straight toward her, with a big dog on a red leash lumbering by his side. She could run, but he'd already seen her. Grant waved. Violet waved back. Oh God. What the hell was she doing?

She did her best not to stare outright as he approached. First thing in the morning he looked just as hot as she remembered. He had on shorts instead of jeans, showing off the tattoos on his left leg.

She glanced at the dog, not sure what to make of the beast.

"This is Max," Grant said.

"Can I pet him?"

"He'd be insulted if you didn't."

Violet reached out her hand a mere inch before the dog shoved his large head the rest of the way under her palm. She gave him a light scratch, as Grant opened the doors to the gym and cut off the alarm. She and the dog followed him inside. Max, with his leash dragging across the floor, took off for the back, while Violet stayed a step behind Grant as he flipped on the lights.

The space was large, deceptively so considering how small it looked from the outside. The main floor was split into two areas. One side, an open space where she imagined they taught stuff like yoga or whatever new aerobics trend was on the rise. Step risers and sit up pads were stacked against the wall. The other half was dominated by weight machines and racks of free weights. The window that faced the street was lined with treadmills and ellipticals.

Violet could see the rear of the space actually had two more doors that led to men's and women's lockers rooms. She'd read on the Melrose Fitness website that both were equipped with saunas.

"Let's head to my office. We're going to go over a few things and then we can get started."

Violet stayed silent, trailing him the rest of the way down a short hallway just to the left of the men's room door. The office was small. Long and narrow. A big table ran along one wall and two rolling chairs, which looked too small for Grant and another to work comfortably, were shoved just a foot or two away, against the opposite wall. A filing cabinet, a tiny printer, another dog bed, and some boxes ate up the rest of the space. Grant shuffled by the first chair and pushed it in Violet's direction.

"Sorry. I don't usually bring clients back here, but I make exceptions for special clients like you."

"Funny."

Once they were seated, Grant pulled a piece of paper, a questionnaire, out of the short file cabinet by his knee.

"First fill this out, we'll weigh you, and then you'll get your first Melrose Fitness workout."

Violet nodded and slipped the pen between her teeth.

"Not a morning person?" Grant asked. She realized she'd barely said a word to him.

"I am, I—just..." She was anxious. When did the whole domination thing start? Had it already started? The gym was completely empty. Were they going to work out naked? "Nothing. Let me fill this out." The questionnaire looked pretty standard. Questions about her physical and mental health, usual activity level, sleep patterns. She filled in her date of birth. Only a few more months until her twenty-ninth birthday.

"What's a hidden disability?" she asked.

"They can vary. ADD, partial hearing loss, epilepsy. Just let me know if any of those apply and we can adjust your workouts accordingly."

"Oh, okay. None of those apply to me. I'm putting birth control down under medication though," she added, to lighten the mood.

The corner of Grant's mouth tipped up under his gold-dusted mustache. "Good to know."

When she finished her paperwork, including coughing up her credit card info, which bound her to Grant's expertise twice a week for the next thirty days and most certainly drained her vacation fund, they left the office and walked over to the scale.

"Okay. Let's do this." She didn't wait for Grant's prompt. She stepped right on the metal plate and stared straight ahead at the digital readout.

The number that blinked into existence was like a punch to her chubby chin. She told herself twenty times it was just a number, but it was a really high number. Still, she could do this. That number would come down.

She stepped off the scale, letting out a deep exhale, and faced Grant.

"How do you feel?" he asked.

"Honestly? Disappointed in myself. I've gained ten pounds in the last year."

"Well, let's get started pulling those ten pounds off."

Violet took another deep breath and braced herself for the part she'd been dreading. The actual workout. That awful class at Pinks was fresh in her mind. She was still a little miffed at Faye for dragging her along. She could taste that acrid bile that accompanied her dry mouth, as she struggled with the burning in her lungs. Grant might appreciate her looks and her wit, but he was about to see just how weak she really was.

"Come on Max!"

"Wait. What are we doing?" Violet asked, confused, as the dog trotted back to them. What did the dog have to do with her workout? Grant picked up Max's leash then nodded toward the door.

"We're starting your first workout. Let's go."

Great. Now he would see she could barely handle a steady jog with his Rottweiler. She might as well get on with it. She followed Grant back outside. He locked the front door and they started walking down the street toward Melrose Ave. The gym itself was on Melrose Place, between some high-end boutique that carried clothes Violet would never be small enough to wear and a coffee shop that was just opening its doors. Her stomach rumbled, thinking about a piping hot latte. She had a feeling she could sweet talk Grant into letting her grab one and then she remembered the number on the scale. She kept walking. Soon, Grant would pump things up and they'd be running. Well, he'd be running or slow jogging beside her while she wheezed and sputtered and begged him to slow down.

"Tell me about your job," Grant said. The sun was up, cresting over the bungalow style homes that ran up the cross street to the next section of retail shops. Violet thought about why she moved to L.A. in the first place. She'd pictured things differently, her life and her work.

"I'm an associate producer for Park Place Entertainment. We shoot stuff for The Food Channel. Have you seen any cooking competition shows? Cupcake Champions? Third Course?"

"I haven't *watched* them, but I know what shows you're talking about."

"That's what our production company specializes in. We're shooting an edgier show for this new men's network in a few weeks. We just finished a barbecue competition show. I know I gained eight of those ten pounds on that show alone."

"Do you enjoy it?"

"Yeah. It's a lot of work, but I love my crew. We have a great time." Violet went on telling Grant more about the wacky adventures she'd had behind the scenes on various cooking competition shows. They kept walking, stopping momentarily to let Max sniff some bushes or an errant piece of gum. Before she realized, they were back in front of Melrose Fitness.

Grant turned to her, as he looked at his watch. He pressed a little button and it beeped. She hadn't noticed the first time he'd toyed with it.

"You, Miss Ryan, just walked three miles."

"Really?"

"Yeah. Wasn't too bad, was it?"

"No, actually it wasn't." She didn't feel like she'd worked out at all, but she had really been on her feet for fifty minutes and not once did she ask Grant if they could slow down. A small victory, but she'd take it.

Back inside the gym, another man was setting out a yoga mat. Grant introduced him as Armando Vasquez, co-owner of the gym. Max, free off his leash, wandered over to a doggy bed beside the weight rack. Three miles was plenty for him. They left the dog and the yogi and went back to the office.

"So you want to shoot for Thursday?" Grant asked.

"Yeah. Monday, Thursday should work."

"Good. In the meantime, you have homework. I want you to write down everything you eat and drink this week. Everything. You don't have to count calories, but try to get everything down and be exact. If you have a pint of ice cream, say you had a pint. If you eat one slice of pizza, write it down. If you eat three large pizzas, write it down."

"Got it. Write it down."

"Good. We're almost done here. Close the door."

Violet flinched. "Excuse me?"

Grant stood, pushing back his chair. His arms moved smoothly as he crossed them over his broad chest. He repeated himself. "Close the door. And lock it." Violet hesitated a moment longer. She'd agreed to this. She hadn't forgotten, but as their hour together wore on she almost thought Grant had changed his mind. He'd been so normal during their walk. He dialed back the flirting and just talked to her, like a normal person who had no plans on getting into her undies. From this new look on his face, though, he hadn't changed his mind about anything. Violet swallowed. Neither had she.

She stood and slowly walked over to the door, closing it then turning the big locking mechanism above the knob. She turned back to face Grant.

"Good. Now come here and sit down. Right here." He

pointed to a spot he'd cleared on his desk. Right between his legs. Her legs carried her back to him. She hopped up onto the smooth metal surface and sat down where he instructed her to. Her feet dangled a few inches off the floor.

"Spread your thighs." She pulled her knees apart, making room for him to step a bit closer. "Wider." Her hips obeyed his order, opening up to accommodate his large body. He came closer, towered over her. His gaze was so focused she doubted she actually wanted to know the dark thoughts that were on his mind. Her imagination had gone back to that dirty, messy place. She'd barely broken a sweat, but her skin was damp from their long stroll. Usually she would have asked for a chance to hop in the shower or even a second to run to the restroom to splash some water on her face before he touched her, but the way he looked at her now, like she was the sexiest thing he'd ever seen, made her think the shower could wait.

In the next moment, he leaned forward and his lips were on hers, soft and somehow firm too, and completely seductive. Violet melted into Grant, kissing him back, meeting his tongue with her own when it gently teased her bottom lip. She could feel his arm above her head, bracing his body against the wall, but she wanted more of him. She wanted to feel his whole body against hers.

Violet reached out and ran her hand over the bulge in Grant's shorts. She barely got a sense of its girth before he gripped her wrist and took her hand away.

"Uh-uh, Miss Ryan. You have to earn that," Grant breathed against her lips. He kissed her again, releasing her wrist. Her pussy was wet now, throbbing, aching against the cotton between her legs. She needed some friction, something more. She was on fire. Kissing Grant wouldn't be enough. His knuckles grazed her left breast a time or two through her thin jogging jacket, driving her even crazier. He was good, a thorough tease. Violet enjoyed this slow burn, the build, but she was about two seconds from turning the tables and mounting Grant on the plaid doggy bed in the corner.

His hand slipped between her legs. Violet's lips slipped from Grant's as she moaned. He took the opportunity to kiss his way across her cheek, nipping her chin before he moved lower to her neck. Violet's moan was loud and desperate and just in time for her to remember Grant's fellow trainer and probably a whole class of yoga students were right outside the door.

"Can they hear us?" she said, panting for the air she needed to fill her lungs.

"We're fine. Don't worry about Mando," Grant replied. "Just be here with me."

Easy, Violet thought. Too easy with his fingers pressed against her clit like that.

She moved with him, grinding shamelessly as his hand moved harder against her body, pressing along her aching pussy through the layers of her clothing. It had been ages since she'd had herself a good dry hump, but the thighs and the clothed cocks of her old boyfriends had nothing on the bold force of Grant Gibson's single hand.

Violet came, whimpering, gasping, mouth wide open as Grant's teeth caught the tender skin where her neck met her shoulder. He let her down with softer strokes, easing up bit by bit with his fingers as his lips made their way back to hers. He held the back of her head with both his hands, digging into her ponytailed strands, holding her steady as he kissed her senseless once more. She'd reached her peak, but she was far from satisfied. She wanted more. Much more.

Grant pulled away with a final caress to her lips with the pad of his thumb. She could barely see straight and there was a ringing in her ears. She wasn't safe to drive. He leaned against the wall just across from her, his arms taking up residence again across his chest.

"That was for completing step one. You showed up. No leather panties required."

"I see. I'll be sure to show up next time." Violet slid to her feet and readjusted her yoga pants and her underwear. She definitely needed a shower now. She checked her pockets. She had her keys and her phone. Her hour with Grant Gibson was up. Without another word, she nodded to Grant, the corner of her bottom lip clenched between her teeth, and then she practically ran to her car.

Four

Day 5

Violet slowly walked beside Faye, as they made their way down the beer aisle. Faye was talking about her boyfriend Patrick. He'd done something funny that morning before he left for work. Faye was reliving the moment. Violet was thinking about Grant. Or more appropriately, she was thinking about the moment her life had become so pornographic.

Violet was far from a prude. There had been one night stands, backseats, movie theaters; she even let one boyfriend find his way up her skirt in a crowded bar. She'd had good, and bad, and adventurous sex, but she'd never been with anyone like Grant.

Technically, they hadn't even had sex. He'd kissed her though. She been kissed well before, but Grant? His lips were dangerous, a trap, a tricky temptation that could cause a woman like Violet to follow him willingly down a very precarious path. A guy like Grant could make her foolish. She knew it but, for now, she wanted to enjoy it.

He'd kissed her stupid, fingered her over her clothes until she was a weak-kneed, breathless dolt, and then he claimed that was her reward for showing up. What would he do when she ran her first mile or completed her first real sit-up? Top off, down the pants, anal? Would he marry her and give her a muscular baby when she reached her goal weight?

Violet forgot herself and snorted, covering the hideous noise with her clenched fist as the thought crossed her mind.

"What's so funny?" Faye asked.

"Nothing. Was he late for work?" She'd sort of been listening.

Faye chuckled. "No. He called in to his first meeting and then he left. I'm all for morning sex, but he needs to calm down with the acrobatics. He almost broke both our necks."

"Yes, please tell him to be careful."

They rounded the corner into the frozen food section. Violet hung by the cart while Faye walked back and forth in front of the ice cream.

Violet had been really good the last two days. She wrote down everything she ate. It was a lot, but she made sure to record every morsel. In the mornings, she woke up at six and walked around her neighborhood. She didn't clock the distance, but she logged the time. Sixty minutes round trip. Additional movement wasn't a part of her assignment, but if she was going to commit to this weight loss, she might as well keep up with the exercise portion in between her meetings with Grant. She wasn't touching another burpee as long as she lived. Walking, though, she could do.

Faye opened the freezer door and analyzed the arrangement of Ben and Jerry's. "You know what I want?" she said, over the hum from the industrial motors. She turned to Violet. "YogurtTown."

Violet groaned. "Why'd you have to say that? You know I love YogurtTown." The franchise that featured an array of self-serve flavors and double the choices in toppings was one of Violet's many weaknesses. It was fattening and overpriced, and Violet went there every chance she got.

"Come on. Let's finish up here and then we'll go to Yogurt-Town. My treat."

Violet winced dramatically. "I don't know."

"Come on. We can head back to Pinks tomorrow. You'll sweat it off in five minutes." Faye was kidding, but a slice of anger heated Violet's face. That experience at Pinks had been one of the lowest moments in her adult life and Faye had been there to witness it. Violet couldn't find the idea of reliving that humiliation for the sake of some frozen yogurt funny. She hadn't mentioned Grant to Faye yet. She wasn't in the mood to talk too much to anyone about her weight loss attempts, but it was time to let Faye know.

"I'm actually working with a new private trainer now. We have our second session tomorrow."

Faye's genuine surprise didn't help the situation. "Oh! How'd this come about?"

"Margaret, your friend over at Pinks, recommended him to me. That's what she wanted to talk to me about."

"That's cool. Do you like him?"

I like the way he kisses. "Yeah. He's great."

"Well, if you're already back in the workout game, some YogurtTown won't kill you. Come on. Let's do it."

The NO was on the tip of Violet's lips. Faye kept on with her rationalizations. "You don't have to eat *all* the yogurt. Just get a little."

"Clearly we've just met." Violet patted her stomach. "I am all yogurt."

Thursday morning, Grant beat Violet to the gym. He woke up a bit earlier, took Max for his real walk then jogged the half mile between his condo and Melrose Fitness. He was eager to see her. He couldn't or wouldn't put it into words, but he knew that feeling; the charge in his chest that sometimes migrated to his stomach when he was starting to feel something for a woman. Though he'd managed to completely fuck up his initial proposal, he'd been right on the money about Violet and her capacity to submit.

He started slowly, watching her closely for signs of fear or reluctance, but when he'd given her the simple order to close the door and the command clicked in her mind, he saw the spark in her eyes. She was nervous, a little unsure about what to expect, but she was down for the moment. She was present and ready. It took all his control not to take things further, especially after she responded to his kiss. Violet was hot, a physical force. Grant knew when they finally had the sex he'd been dreaming about, she would rock his world. It would be a test of his patience to wait for that moment, but he would wait until he absolutely knew she was ready. He would wait as long as she wanted.

The thought startled him. Not because he was some sort of sick fuck who couldn't control himself. It caught him off guard because Grant realized how long it had been since he had to step this gingerly around a woman who held his interest. Ariana was wild, out of control with her desires. He loved that part of her. The women before her were just as eager. They were trained submissives, ready to respond to him with practiced moves, or women who pursued him because they knew what he had to offer. Violet knew what she wanted. She wouldn't let Grant take her anyplace she didn't want to go, but he was honored to be the first to receive her submission. He wanted to work to keep her trust.

The prospect of it had changed him. Grant often didn't realize how much time he spent with people he couldn't stand. His clients paid him and they paid him a lot. He cared about the collective health of his clients, but they were just that. Clients. In the one session he'd spent with Violet he also realized just how routine things had become around the gym. He knew. He felt the depth of boredom but, really, he'd only scratched the surface. Walking with Violet, listening to her talk about the TV shows she worked on, he felt his outlook shifting when he was around her. Not that he'd been an asshole around the gym or anything, but Violet had definitely lifted his mood. Even Armando said something about the way he was acting when he walked by the office and overheard

Grant singing to himself. It had been a while since he'd burst out in song.

Yeah, Violet was different and Grant wanted more of her in his life.

Her silver Jetta pulled up just before six o'clock. Violet looked tired when she climbed out of the car, but the moment she saw him, she smiled. That smile seemed to wipe every hint of exhaustion from her face. They exchanged their hellos. Grant wanted to kiss her, but instead he led her inside the gym. She followed him to the gym floor and sat down beside him on the polished wood. He'd take her back to the office. Later. After.

"Did you do your homework?"

"I sure did." Violet unzipped her bag and pulled out a small blue Moleskin and a pen.

"You got a notebook. Good," Grant said, as he took it from her hand. He flipped it open and looked over the food Violet had consumed in three days. He didn't see anything alarming. She liked her assorted coffee beverages and she seemed to skip breakfast and sometimes lunch, making up for it with snacking and heavy dinners. She liked her pre-packed foods and she liked to eat out. Right on par with most working adults.

"I found an app, but I thought it would easier this way," Violet said. "Things are easier to remember when I actually put pen to paper."

"That's excellent. I want you to do this for two full weeks. You'll see two things. One, you'll notice that you have eating patterns. We all do. I eat the same thing for breakfast almost every day. I save my alcohol intake for Sunday nights. You'll notice when you eat certain things and then you can start working out why, and then you can think about how to change those patterns." Grant flipped back through the pages to see if anything else caught his eye, but nothing stood out.

"That doesn't sound so hard."

"It is and it isn't. What's hard is trying to change everything you've been doing most of your life overnight. Habits are hard to break, but you're trying and that matters." He handed the notebook back to Violet. "Well done, Miss Ryan. You ready?"

"Wait." Violet took the notepad and pressed it against her face.

"What's up?"

"Uh..."

Grant knew that tone. She was hiding something. "Is there something you want to tell me?"

"I didn't write everything down."

He took the notebook back, flipped it open then scooped up her pen. They would amend this now. "What's missing?"

"Yesterday afternoon, I got YogurtTown with my friend, Faye. And then last night we got drinks. This new bar on Hillhurst opened and we wanted to check it out."

Grant flipped to the day she'd titled Wednesday in her cute feminine handwriting and prepared to add his own practiced script. "How many drinks did you have?"

"Three. No, four?"

"Mixed drinks? Beers? Shots?"

"I had a mojito, this fancy pear thing, and two cranberry vodkas. And a shot of Patron." He scribbled them down and steeled himself to keep all hints of judgment off his face. This woman could drink. This explained why she looked so tired, but he was surprised she was even upright.

"I hope you didn't drive."

"No. We had a DD."

"Anything else?"

"No, that's it."

"So five drinks. What did you get from YogurtTown? They measure in ounces right? How many ounces do you think you had?"

She sighed like she was about to confess to an extramarital affair. "Fourteen, maybe? And I had gummy bears on top."

"Okay. That's it?"

"Yep. That's it."

Grant closed the notebook and handed it back to Violet. Once she slipped it back into her bag, he took her hand and helped her off the floor.

"Am I in trouble?" she asked, as she stowed her stuff in a cubby by the entrance.

"Yup. But not the way you're thinking. Let's go." Grant almost laughed at the look on Violet's face. She had no idea what he had in store for her. He called for Max and the three of them headed out for another walk. They'd go further this time, another .2 miles, and they'd do it in the fifty minutes they had, but he wasn't going to tell Violet that until after they returned to the gym. As they walked down the street, by the storefronts that wouldn't open for another few hours, Grant focused on subtly varying their pace, using Max as an excuse to include a bit of jogging across streets and between a few of the shorter blocks.

Violet babbled. She was worried about what was coming. He loved this part of the game. The harmless fear and the anticipation. She didn't know it, but she was getting herself worked up, readying herself for him. All he had to do was walk.

By the time they'd circled back, Grant thought Violet was going to talk herself into a stroke. She'd told him what he was pretty sure amounted to her whole life story. She was adopted as an infant and became the youngest of three to a family from Connecticut. Her brother was a doctor. Her sister was back in school getting her law degree. She'd had a baby at a young age, but her new husband and her had worked things out so she could chase her dream of upholding the law. Her mom's name was Wendy. Her dad's name was Arnold. Growing up, she had a dog named Taffy. She'd picked out the name because she loved Laffy Taffy so much. Faye was her best friend and her co-worker. They did everything together, but Violet didn't think they should come to Melrose Fitness together. Grant agreed.

Somewhere in the middle of all that, Violet said she regretted the trip to YogurtTown. She said it wasn't worth it.

Grant checked his watch. They'd tacked on an extra minute, but Violet had extended her distance.

"Three point two miles. How do you feel about that?"

She seemed to snap out of her ramble mode. She smiled. "Good. I know you snuck in that jogging on purpose, but it wasn't so bad. We should go further next time."

"We can do that. We can add weights too."

"Whoa. Whoa. Slow down. No one said anything about weights."

"Oh there will be weights, but we'll go slowly. We have one more piece of business to attend to. Go." The words yanked the smile right off Violet's face. Her expressive shifts were so sudden and comical, she'd teach him more about his own poker face than years at The Club. He needed to maintain the illusion of control. Still the look on her adorable face had him cracking up inside.

He ushered her past Armando doing his morning routine, and into the office, locking the door behind them. Violet stood against the wall, looking at him boldly, waiting for his next move. He pulled out his chair and turned it around so she'd have to straddle it with the back against her chest.

"Sit."

She sat.

Grant took a mental deep breath. What he planned to do next would tell him a lot about Violet, her likes and dislikes. What he did next could also shut this party they were having together right the fuck down.

With his back to Violet, Grant took off his hoodie and threw the sweatshirt on Armando's chair. It didn't take much for him to get hard. He'd been thinking about fucking Violet for nearly a week. He'd been thinking about kissing her again almost non-stop for the last three days, and when she showed up that morning, he thought about squeezing her ripe tits again as they strained against the confines of her running jacket.

He stroked himself twice over the fabric of his shorts. When he turned back to Violet he was halfway to fully erect. She glanced at his hand, then to his face before looking back down to his hand. Or, more aptly, his cock. Grant saw that look in her eyes, the hunger, the lust. She licked her lips. The rest of his blood rushed right to his crotch.

He tapped the black fabric on the back of the chair. "Put your hands right there and leave them there."

"I've heard it's better if I use my hands," she said, even though she slid her fingers into position.

"We'll manage without them. I promise." Closing the space between them, Grant pulled his cock from his shorts. With his other hand, he took hold of Violet's chin in a gentle grip. He scanned her eyes for a sign of silent hesitation, but when her tongue darted out again and she released a short breath, almost a sigh, he knew she was on board.

He ran his thumb along her bottom lip, where her tongue had just been. Her mouth parted again, just a bit, and she barely made contact with his skin as her tongue flicked out once more. Grant's cock throbbed in his hand.

"If you want to stop just say so, okay?" They hadn't gone over safe words or tap out signals yet. He wanted to keep things simple for her. Violet was embracing her submission, but she understood her control. She wouldn't shy away from letting him know exactly how she felt.

"I don't want to stop."

"Good. Open your mouth." Violet's lips popped open like she'd been waiting for his cock all morning long. Her tongue presented itself, eager and ready.

Grant slipped inside and fought to keep his eyes open as the wet heat of Violet's mouth enveloped him. He moved his hips forward, just slightly, teasing her, teasing himself. As he retreated,

Violet's lips followed, the muscles of her tongue swirling around the crown of his dick. Fuck, was he in trouble. He wanted to take this slowly just as badly as he wanted to grip the back of her head and fuck her mouth until tears of surrender streaked her checks. Violet wanted to use her hands.

Grant looked down as the tips of her fingers grazed his balls. She looked up at him with those big brown eyes as she lightly teased the seam of his sack with her nails. He wanted her to keep going, but commands were commands, and his were meant to be followed.

He swallowed the saliva pooling in his mouth and fixed her with a stern glare. "I told you not to move your hands. Put your hands behind your back and keep them there. Unless you want me to tie them back there with a resistance band." He remembered what she said about bondage, so it was just an idle threat. He'd never tie her up without having a long discussion with her first, but it was threat enough for her to comply. Grant nearly choked on a groan as his cock slipped from her mouth.

"Fine," she said, with an annoyed sigh, but she knotted her fingers at the base of her back. The simple motion thrust her breasts out over the top of the chair. Someday, not today, but sometime soon, he was going to come all over those tits and enjoy every moment of it.

He slipped his dick back into her welcoming mouth and wound his fingers into her hair, just below her ponytail. He moved his hips in sync with the bobbing of Violet's head. She met his every thrust with the perfect amount of suction and a gentle swirling of her tongue. She moaned around him, fidgeting in the chair until the back of it and her breasts were pressed against his thighs. Together they found a perfect pace, not too slow to keep them at it for hours, but not too fast that either of them were over- whelmed. But Violet was enthusiastic, moving her head this way and that, pulling back completely when she could and running her tongue up the length of his shaft. When the position made it possible, she would look up at him, not seeking approval but showing him just exactly what he had gotten himself into. It was all too much. The softness of her lips. The light brush of her breath against his abs. He wouldn't last much longer.

"You want me to come in your mouth?"

Violet made a high-pitched sound of approval and nodded her head just the slightest bit. She sucked him harder, the movement of her head becoming more urgent. He knew that desperation. She wasn't in a hurry to finish, but she wanted to make him come. She wanted the satisfaction of making him finish. That telltale spasm rippled up from his balls, sending that sensation, like lightning, all over his body, until it singed his nervous system. The sound Grant made when he came was a sound that belonged to a man who hadn't come in years. His eyes squeezed shut for just a moment before opening again so he could watch her lick his cock clean.

When she was done, Grant stuffed himself back into his shorts, then reached for a bottle of water in the small mini fridge under Armando's side of the desk. He helped Violet out of the chair and handed her the water. She was flushed and out of breath, and this adorably wicked smile dimpled her cheeks as she took a swing.

Grant couldn't resist brushing that dimple with the edge of his knuckles. "You enjoyed that, didn't you?"

"Maybe. It wasn't much of a punishment."

"Who said that was your punishment?"

Her eyes narrowed, then closed when Grant slipped his other hand between her legs. She was burning up.

"I want you to keep writing down your food and drink intake, and I want you to be honest and thorough. And keep up the walking. You can walk every day."

"And my punishment?"

"Look at me." Her eyes fluttered open. "Your next orgasm is mine."

"What do you mean?"

"You don't come again until I let you. Could be Monday

morning when I see you again. Could be sometime late next week." He crisscrossed his fingers against her tight pants, finding the cleft of her pussy. Violet blinked, but managed to keep her eyes on his face. "I could call you tonight and tell you to finger yourself while I listen to you breathe through the phone. But you don't come again until I say so."

"How will you know?"

"You think you don't have a tell?" He slid his fingers higher, brushing against the cotton over her clit.

"I—I don't."

"You do. Trust me." She was in trouble with him, but that didn't stop him from wanting to kiss her. He pulled her close and pressed his lips to hers. Their tongues flirted for just a moment. He pulled away, though, before he bent her over the desk like he'd been wanting to do all morning long. "Just know that I'll know. Now get out of here," he said. "I'll see you on Monday."

FIVE

Day 9

Violet never gave much thought to how much she masturbated until she wasn't allowed to do it. Actually, she was allowed to touch herself. She could do whatever the hell she wanted, but every time she drummed up the nerve—she didn't need to work up the arousal, as she'd been perpetually horny since the first time Grant had touched her—she could hear Grant's voice in her head telling her no. And, for some crazy reason, she wanted to do what he said.

The food log, the exercise, even the waking up early and getting her day started, that was for her. It hadn't been a full week yet, but she already looked forward to her morning walks. She'd slept in that morning. It was Sunday. She had to give herself a bit of a break. But a little after ten, she woke up, Googled a Starbucks just far enough away from her apartment, then walked almost three miles round trip while she enjoyed her cinnamon latte. Her body was nowhere near where she wanted it. It would take more than a week for her to see any results, but she felt better. She felt better about herself. So yeah, signing up with Grant had been good for her, but the extras? The sex? That was for them both.

Somehow Grant managed to separate and combine the two in way that made her want to work harder for herself and just as hard at pleasing Grant. She had to get him naked. She had to see the rest of that amazing body. She wanted to kiss it, touch it.

The blowjob had been such a tease. Sitting in that chair, her hips rocking back and forth as Grant's beautiful, thick cock slipped in and out if her mouth, while her breasts rubbed against his legs and her pussy ached to be filled. It was torture. And she loved it. She wanted more.

And now she was wet all over again just thinking about it. Grant was right, this was a punishment. She wanted to touch herself. She wanted to come, but more than that release of pleasure, she wanted Grant.

Violet nearly rolled off her couch reaching for her phone. She just barely tipped it off her coffee table into her hand then pulled up Grant's number. If she had to suffer, he was going to suffer with her. She typed out a text then hit send before she changed her mind.

> I'm really horny and you should do something about it.

Grant texted back right away.

> Is that how punishments work?

> I don't know. I've only been a submitter for a few days. I don't know how these things work.

> A submitter?

> Yeah. Someone who submits to their super sexy Dom. You should know the terminology by now, Mr. Gibson. I'm a little disappointed.

> As my submitter you are entitled to a little begging, but as your Dominer it's my job to stand by my convictions. I said no coming, so you're not coming until I say so, Miss Ryan.

> You sure you don't want me to come right now? I'll take pictures.

Would she really? Yes. No. Yes. She didn't have to include her face.

It was a long time in rapid-fire text time before Grant responded. He was thinking it over.

> No. No pictures. Keep all fingers, vibrators, and improvised household items away from your cunt. Next time you come, you come for me.

Of course her cunt tingled as she read the text. She would see him in less than twelve hours. She would be on time with her food log immaculately kept. She'd even logged the two grapes she'd sampled at the farmers' market. He was sure to let her come after their workout, but she didn't want to wait. She sent him another text.

> Don't you get horny? We could help each other.

> Who says I'm not helping myself right now?

She read the words and then a picture popped up. Grant's hand wrapped around his hard cock.

It could have been any dick pic harvested off the Internet, but she knew that cock. She recognized his pubic hair. The carpet matched the beard, golden-blond and red. She recognized the tattoos on his forearm, and in the background was a blurry, but sleeping Max, passed out on a doggy bed near his entertainment center.

Violet pressed CALL so hard she thought she would crack her screen.

Grant's cruel laughter echoed through the phone when he picked up. "Hello?"

"Are you kidding me right now?!"

"What? You don't like my cock?"

"You know I do!"

"You haven't said as much."

"Well, I like your cock. There. I said it."

"You should feel it right now. It's really hard."

Just then her other line beeped in. Violet pulled her phone from her ear and saw Faye's name lighting up the screen. "That's my friend. I'm going to talk to her and then I'm going to masturbate so hard. I'm gonna masturbate all over the place."

"Don't do it, Vi." She almost groaned, hating how smooth her nickname sounded on his lips.

"Bye," she grumbled instead of cursing at him. She was all kinds of flustered when she clicked over.

"Oh, thank god," Faye said frantically. "I thought you'd fallen asleep."

"I got the PJs on, but I'm awake."

"Get dressed right fucking now. Backstreet Boys are giving a secret show at a bar downtown. Well, kinda secret. They tweeted that the first fifty people to respond get in with a plus one and Patrick got us in. God, I could marry him. Show starts in an hour. Let's go!"

Violet couldn't believe it, but she actually hesitated. She looked at her clock. It was already ten and… And she had to get to bed so she could get up at five-thirty and meet Grant.

"Hello? What is wrong with you? Backstreet Boys. On stools. Singing 'I Want It That Way' four feet from your face. Are you in or are you out?"

Violet cursed and pounded her fist against the couch. She'd fully grown out of her boy band phase. The current title holders looked like ten-year-olds she used to babysit, but Backstreet Boys? She could just picture the posters of Nick Carter that used to plaster her bedroom walls. It was her duty as a woman to go to this show. "I'm in."

Still, Faye could tell something was up. "What's the problem?"

"Nothing. I have a session with my trainer in the morning. That's all."

"Oh my god! Fuck him. It's *the* Backstreet Boys."

"I know! I'm getting dressed."

"Good. I'll be there in twenty."

Violet hung up and stared at her clock a moment longer, doing that stupid bedtime math. She'd be back around one. Private show, no opening act. They wouldn't be on that long. There would be almost no traffic back to her part of town at that time of night. Yeah, one. She'd be in bed by one thirty. That would give her four hours of sleep before she met Grant. Then she could take a nap after they worked out. Piece of cake. Violet pushed Grant to the back of her mind and ran to her closet.

Grant waited outside of his gym until six thirty. Fifteen minutes late could mean she overslept. Maybe there was an accident or she hit some strange patch of early morning construction. L.A. was good for that. By six thirty, Grant knew she wasn't coming. No call. No text. For all that could happen, he hoped she'd overslept. At six thirty, he took Max inside. He called Violet's phone, but it went to voicemail. He left her a brief message. Hopefully, when she got it, she'd call him back.

Violet woke up with one of those heart attack gasps. She'd overslept, forgotten to finish a term paper and had eight minutes to run across campus to get to her final. That was the feeling. It had been years, but that's exactly what it felt like when she woke up the next morning, at nine freaking fifteen, and realized she had completely slept through her workout with Grant.

When she tried to swing her legs out of bed, she also realized she was wrapped up in her charge cord, which she'd somehow managed to yank out of the wall. Her phone had been dying before they left the after-show meet and greet. She'd plugged it in right when she climbed into bed. She also set her alarm then put the thing right next to her head so she would be sure to hear it. No dice. The piece of crap was dead. She shoved the cord back into its cube in the wall and waited for her phone to fire up. Two texts popped up right away. One from her sister.

> Saw Faye's pics on Facebook. I was studying for torts and you were cheek kissing Howie. So jelz right now.

And another from Faye.

> Patrick got super laid last night. Call me.

And then a voicemail.

Violet hit play, then buried her face in her pillow.

"Hey, Violet. It's Grant and Max. We missed you this morning. Give me a call when you get a chance and we'll reschedule the session."

His voice sounded strange, like he was trying to play it cool, but he was nervous or angry or something. She was getting to know him, but she didn't know him that well yet. He might be with a client now, but Violet hit his number anyway.

"Glad you're still with us." Oh, he was pissed.

"Shit, Grant. I'm so sorry. Faye and I caught a late show last night and then my phone died and I overslept."

"You went to a concert *after* I talked to you?" He laughed and seemed to relax a little bit. He was a little annoyed, but he wasn't pissed. Violet rolled on her back, covering her face with her arm.

"Yeah…I'm in trouble, aren't I?"

"Oh, you have no idea." The tone she did know was back, all deep and seductive. She'd happily take her punishment this time. But just as she started to smile and offer her own flirtatious response, his voice changed again, became more sobering. "I'm just glad you're okay."

"I understand. I would have freaked out too if you left me hanging."

"What are you doing tonight?" he asked.

"Nothing much. I was going to review some casting tapes for backup contestants for this competition thing, but it's not urgent. Why?"

"Well, I think you've earned another punishment and you have a workout to make up for."

Violet knew she could say no. It was one of the things she liked about Grant. There were rules, but no real pressure. She could put her foot down and knock out some work. Or she could see him.

"I did screw up pretty bad, didn't I?"

"You did. Be here at nine-thirty."

She knew from the company website that the gym closed at nine. Violet swallowed the lump that made a sudden appearance in her throat. She could only imagine what he had planned.

"I can do that."

"The shades will be down, but the doors will open. Let yourself in."

"Okay."

"And while you're home today, don't even think about touching yourself."

"But you sent me such lovely inspiration. What am I going to do with it on my phone all day?"

"Goodbye, Violet."

✶

It was strange pulling up to Melrose Fitness at night. The street was poorly lit, but the trees lining the road were in such full bloom they almost provided a certain coziness to the empty street. She locked her car and walked up to the front door. Like Grant said, the shades were pulled down, but thin ribbons of light shone through where the thick panels failed to reach all the way to the bottom and the sides of the windows. Violet could hear music too, loud rock music muffled by the closed door. She opened it and went inside.

The gym was empty except for Grant and Armando, who seemed to be in the middle of a vigorous workout. Grant. Oh lord bless him, Grant was shirtless, doing an intense set of pull-ups on a bar that ran between the tricep pull-down and the seated-row contraption. Armando was facing the mirrors doing chest flys with what seemed to be fifty pound weights in each hand. He had a shirt on, but the gray cotton was soaking wet and his bronze-brown skin was covered in sweat. Violet stood by, not exactly sure what to do. She thought about grabbing a towel and dabbing both their foreheads as they continued to load her fantasy files.

Grant dropped from the pull-up bar then crossed the room without saying a word to Violet. He grabbed a sit up mat and dragged it to the center of the floor.

"Hi," she said, as he passed her.

He just pointed to the mat. "Sit."

Violet scowled at him, but plopped down on the purple piece of rubber. She was here to pay the piper, but did Armando have to witness the transaction? He must know, Violet thought. Maybe not the full details of their Dominer/submitter relationship, but Grant must have explained what Violet was doing there after hours. And why he was having her sit in the middle of the floor like a five-year-old on time out. Grant turned his back and went right back to his workout. The song ended and some rap song came blaring through the speakers. Even if Grant was in a talking mood, it wasn't like Violet could hear him.

Twenty minutes passed and still nothing. Not a word, not a glance, but Violet realized his intention. Watching him like this, every glistening inch of his hard body as it pushed through exercise after exercise was torture. Being near him and not being able to talk to him or touch added another degree of pain to the burn. Violet wasn't upset about it, just frustrated in more ways than one. Was this part of submission? Or was Grant just being a particular bastard because she'd bailed on their workout? It had to be a combination of both. Grant got off on telling her what to do. She got off on following his orders, so that wasn't an issue. It was something in the way Grant wasn't looking at her. Something was bothering him.

Finally Armando called it quits. He disappeared into the back and when he returned he'd changed his clothes and his gym bag was tossed over his shoulder. He fooled with his keys as he walked over to Violet and squatted down beside her.

"He's been going balls out for over an hour. What did you do?"

Violet frowned and looked between the two men. Grant was still going hard, no sign of letting up, but she thought this was part of their usual night routine. "All because of me?"

"Oh yeah. This is a woman-done-me-wrong kind of workout. He's sweating out everything so he doesn't say something stupid to you at the wrong time."

"Does he ever aim to say something stupid at the right time? 'Cause he's done that already."

Armando laughed and patted Violet on the shoulder. "He's not perfect, but I think you're the right person to get him in line."

Grant stood from his squat position and looked at them both in the mirror. "Don't talk to her," he yelled over the music. "She's not here to socialize."

"Now we're both in trouble." Armando winked at her then slipped out the front door.

Grant paced in front of the free weights. Violet wanted to say something, but what? She decided it was better to wait.

Grant walked into the office then came back out and turned off the music. He locked the front door then held his hand out for Violet. "Come on."

She stood, swallowing her nerves again as he led her into the men's locker room. She imagined the women's locker room had a similar set up, a small restroom area with sinks and a few toilets, lockers lining one wall, a cramped shower area with three shower heads, and then the sauna. Grant started the timer just outside the sauna door, then led Violet over to the one bench in the room that afforded her a view of the showers.

"Sit here and don't move."

She sat, but not without an argument. "Are you planning on talking to me tonight?"

Instead of answering her, Grant started to strip. Completely. All of a sudden, Violet was willing to wait for a reply as he pulled off his socks and finally his underwear. She'd seen his cock already, but naked—butt naked—Grant was something to behold. He turned on the shower and stepped under the hot spray. He then proceeded to wash himself with some manly type body wash he must have stashed in the shower earlier in the day. Violet watched him as he turned, soaping the thick muscles of his arms and shoulders. His ass was perfect, plump and round, stacked above large thighs that were dusted with a mixture of light and dark hairs. If he ever let her near it again, she was going to squeeze that ass. Squeeze it good.

When he turned around, his dick was hard.

Violets lips parted almost automatically, as his soapy hands moved lower, over his stomach then down around his shaft. Grant stroked himself three, then four times. Violet knew then she was going to faint or beg or burst into flames if he didn't do something with her soon.

She gripped the edge of the wooden bench and rocked her hips forward, unintentionally causing her wet pussy to clench on itself. She must have moaned or gasped because Grant suddenly looked over at her. He stared her down, looking at every inch of her face and body as he kept stroking his cock.

"Take off your clothes and get in here," he said with no preamble.

It took a minute for Violet's brain to process what he'd actually said, but soon she was on her feet, peeling off her clothes. Whatever reservations she had about showing Grant her naked body, rolls and dimples and all, went right down that shower drain. She kicked off her running shoes. Her socks went flying over her shoulder. Grant could keep right on with the teasing smile that flashed across his lips, as she almost tripped pulling off her yoga pants. In record time she was nude and crossing the few feet between them. She was going right for his butt, both hands primed, palms open. She was going to leave marks with her nails.

Their bodies nearly collided. Grant's hand gripped the sides of her face, as he tilted her head up to kiss her. She almost shoved her tongue into his mouth as her hands found his butt. He kissed her right back, swirling his tongue around hers, making her moan. The feeling of his cock between them, sliding along her stomach, made her squirm. She leaned in closer, giving his ass the proper squeeze it deserved.

Grant tilted his head back, drawing a tight breath between his teeth. "Jesus, woman." He gazed down at her face and wiped away the wet hairs that were plastered to her forehead. Violet kissed his chest.

"I have no idea what lesson you're trying to teach me," she said, over the sound of the spray. "But please don't stop kissing me."

"Maybe the lesson is that we could have done this this morning if you'd showed up. I was worried about you."

"I know, but I'm here now. You're touching me now. I'm okay with that."

"Right." He kissed her once more, lightly this time, before brushing his lips over the tip of her nose then her cheek. "Please extract your hands from my ass and bend over."

Violet turned and braced her hands against the tile. Grant's touch slid down the small of her back, down along her ass. She felt him grip his cock, his knuckles brushing against her skin. She felt him slip between her legs, the full length of his shaft rubbing against her pussy. She spread her feet wider, giving him more space, giving him permission to go inside.

He teased her instead, simply moving back and forth. She had to respond to him. Her body wouldn't have it any other way. She was so wet, the ache of it nearly painful, as the head of Grant's cock rubbed over her sensitive clit again and again.

He moved back, positioning himself to finally, finally give Violet what she wanted. The sensation was hers to enjoy, just for a moment. He let her feel the crown of his head, the thick smoothness of him, as he entered her. Just barely. And then he pulled away. As in all the way. The heat from his body was replaced by the shower stream

Violet spun around to find Grant rinsing under the other shower head, calm as could be, with his erection jutting out from his hips.

"Go wait for me in the sauna," he said.

Violet blinked the water out of her eyes in disbelief. "What are *you* about to do?"

"Stop touching yourself." Violet glanced down at her hand, which she'd unintentionally shoved between her legs. Her clit was dying for attention. It was a natural reflex. Still, just as simply, she pulled her hand away at Grant's command. "Thanks. Now, go. I'm going to finish."

He turned his back to her and started stroking his cock. He was going to finish himself off without her.

"You are Satan. Actually Satan."

He said nothing, probably thinking the motion of his arm was response enough.

Violet spun around and stormed off to the sauna, grabbing a fluffy white towel off a decorative stand before she slammed the door behind her. She climbed up on the warm wood and waited, thinking of how bad she was going to tell Grant off when he came through the door.

He may be the Dom, but what did that even mean? Nothing. He would come walking into the sauna with his beautiful, naked body and his sexy, rugged facial hair and she would demand that he make her come. If he was spent and needed some recovery time to get it up, he'd just have to get creative. Hands, mouth. She didn't care. She was going to end this orgasm drought tonight.

Finally the sauna door swung open, and stupid, perfect Grant stepped inside. The small space shrunk by half as he ducked his head to enter. His cock was softening, but still partially engorged. She couldn't believe he'd come without her.

Violet made a show of throwing off her towel and opening her legs. Then she ran her fingers over her clit to show Grant she really meant business. "We can do this the easy way or the hard way, but either way I'm coming tonight."

"Okay."

He practically pounced on her, hoisting her legs over the crooks of his arm and sliding her butt to the edge of the wood. Pinning her down with the angle of his body, he used all four of his fingers to swiftly rub her clit and her pussy lips. Violet was so wound up, so sensitive, that the quick flicks of his wrist were all it took for her back to seize up, as her orgasm shattered through her.

She cried out, begging for more. To be filled and fucked, but Grant pulled his hand away, trailing a path of her wetness down her thigh.

"That's all you get tonight," he said. Still he kissed her, in the mind-scrambling way that keyed her up all over again.

✶

Nearly an hour later, they still sat in the sauna. Grant had turned the heat off and the room had cooled, but Violet was still warm, pressed against his body. He stroked her arm, his breath fanning lightly over the crown of her head.

"You know every time you've gotten in trouble, you've been with that friend of yours, Faye," he said.

"She's not all bad. We just make poor decisions together."

"I'm going to say this and I don't want you take it the wrong way and I don't want you to think of it as fodder for a confrontation with your friend either, but as your trainer this is food for thought I need to give you."

Violet sat back a bit so she could see his face.

"Do you think Faye is an enabler? You said she took you to YogurtTown, then out to drinks and then out to a concert last night. You told me yourself that you regretted the yogurt. *I* want to see Backstreet Boys live, so I know you don't regret that, but are there other times that you do things with her that you regret?"

Violet knew the answer immediately, but she hated to say the words out loud. She loved Faye. She was an amazing friend, but ninety-percent of the time they spent together was under Faye's pressure or Faye's insistence.

Their work was hard. They put in long hours for weeks at a time. Some shows stretched on where they wouldn't have a personal day off for a month. When they had free time, and when Faye wasn't with Patrick, Violet felt obligated to hang out with her, even when she didn't want to. Not that she didn't enjoy Faye's company, but there were times she wanted to be alone, just to unwind and veg. Not think about work. Or Faye or her boyfriend.

"She's not an enabler," Violet said. "But there are times I wish I could say no to her."

"Why can't you?"

Another truth that carried a brutal sting. "She's my only friend. So many people out here are so fake. I tried to be myself and make friends when I moved here, but it feels like everyone has ulterior motives. A script to be sold, a headshot to push. People survive out here stepping on each other's necks, but Faye and I met and we stuck together. We helped each other professionally and became friends because of it."

"I get that. I want you to forget about Faye for a moment. Other than your obvious weight loss goals, what do you want for yourself?"

Violet smiled at the first thing that popped into her mind. It was so superficial and silly, but it was something she wanted. She chuckled a little. "A new dress. A few new dresses. I have nice stuff, but the sizes are all over the place and really it's all work stuff. I want a new dress and some cute boots."

"Then that's your homework this week. New boots. New dress. And—"

"And?"

"Don't take Faye shopping with you."

The suggestion should have felt odd, but it didn't. She considered a little retail therapy on her own, without having to talk about work or someone else's boyfriend, or even feeling the odd pressure of having to keep what happened between her and Grant to herself, and suddenly she felt relieved.

Six

Day 11

Grant stepped out of Armando's truck, not even trying to wipe the dumb grin off his face. He managed it when he had to, but it was hard to stop thinking about Violet. As he and Mando made their way to the Whole Foods entrance, her face was all he could picture. The cute way she complained and taunted him was all that played in his mind.

"You're singing again, man," Armando said.

Grant hadn't even noticed. "Sorry."

"Don't apologize to me, but you gotta give me details. I thought you were going to break something last night and now you look like—well, I mean, shit, you're singing."

They walked inside and joined the line at the juice bar so Armando could order this gross beet-celery shit he swore by.

"I don't know what to say, man."

"Is it working out the way you wanted it to? Clearly it is, but the way she was talking, no respect for you at all. Sure she fits in the D/s file?"

"She's destroying the D/s file." Grant laughed. "She's never subbed before, but she's a natural at it, when she's not yelling at me."

"You spank her yet?"

"No. She'll like it too much and she hasn't earned that reward yet."

"You are so screwed."

"Why? Because I'm taking it slow with her?"

"'Cause she has you wrapped around her whole fist. Just look at yourself. You're smiling like a dope and you've only been messing with her for a week."

Immediately Grant wanted to defend their relationship. Instead he told Mando to go grab them a table while he picked out his own lunch. He didn't feel like he and Violet were messing around. Things were casual, in a sense. He hadn't tied her up, gagged her, spanked her, made her kneel in various submissive poses to his satisfaction. She only followed his instructions fifty percent of the time and, fuckin' hell, she couldn't keep from talking back to him. They weren't up all night talking on the phone. She wasn't blowing his cell up with non-stop texts, but there was something there, a connection that extended way beyond their agreement as client and trainer. More than the simple verbal pact they'd made as completely unprepared Dom and shit-talking sub.

Grant loaded up a square cardboard bowl with vegetables from the salad bar then, after he paid, joined Armando at a table by the front exit. They had a little under an hour to get back to the gym. In the meantime, Max was there holding the fort down while Keira taught a cardio barre class.

Armando sat back and scratched his day's worth of stubble. "I can't imagine breaking in someone new at this point."

"Honestly, I didn't even think of that. Having to train her or whatever."

Armando shook his head. He had every right to. Grant was lucky Violet hadn't ripped his nuts off during their first conversation. His tunnel vision was so damn tight and closed off, he skipped several must-do steps when trying to bring someone into the scene.

"Let's not tell Master Philip about this," he suggested. Violet was perfectly safe with Grant and damn near running their relationship as it was, but their mentor would definitely have a thing or two to say about Grant's approach.

"My lips are sealed," Armando replied. "You stupid fuck."

Just then, Grant's phone vibrated and beeped in his pocket. He pulled it out and looked at a picture of Violet standing in some store dressing room, wearing a tight black lace dress. Her cellphone caught the reflection of her hip, cocked out to the side, creating the sexiest silhouette. Her other hand was holding up her mass of thick hair on top of her head. Her full lips were pursed in an expression that was part invitation, part warning. The woman had curves for days. Grant would do anything to help her reach her fitness goals, but that body? His eyeballs almost rolled back in his head.

Then another text popped up.

> Finished my weekly assignment. Bought the boots, but they're in the car. Can I have the D now?

"See. How do I say no to this face?" Grant turned his phone around so Armando could see the picture and the text.

"God damn. She's thick."

"I know."

"Yeah, okay. I'd let her talk back to me. What's this about giving her the D? You haven't fucked her yet?"

"Mando, I said this before. You and I have two completely different styles of dealing with our pets. I like to take my time. You, on the other hand, are impatient and don't see the value in making a woman wait."

"No complaints, yet, my brother. Not a single complaint." Armando handed the phone back, and continued ragging on

Grant. "She ain't your pet. You're hers. If she were *mine*, I would have fucked her already. Shit, I might fuck her if you don't hurry the hell up and get the job done."

Grant squared Armando with a deadly stare that was only edged with humor. "Try it." They'd shared women before, plenty of times, but Grant wouldn't even entertain the thought of sharing Violet.

"You know I'm fucking with you. I know better than to come between you and a woman who makes you sing. That's when I know you're whipped enough to take a swing at me."

Whipped? For some reason, Grant couldn't see a problem with that, but whipped within reason. He might be singing and staking his claim on a woman he'd only just met, but Armando didn't get to see Violet the way Grant did. He didn't get to see the fire in her eyes when she came to him willingly and followed his every order. He didn't hear the way her voice strained when she asked for what she wanted. Yeah he was whipped, to the point where he texted Violet right back. Still, he had to keep up the front, like he really thought he was in control of the situation.

> You'll get the D when I say so.

> Violet replied. That's too bad. I was going to wear this dress for you.

Grant winced and dropped his phone. He was in over his head.

Violet pushed her chair back and stood. Her whole body ached as she stretched. She'd been in that horrible designer chair for almost six hours and from the look of her inbox and the constant ringing of her cell phone she knew she wasn't going anywhere soon. She'd been with Faye, their casting director Jonathan, and their executive producer Dana at Dana's Malibu home all day. It was another few days before their office space would be set up on the studio lot. When crisis arose—that kind of crisis that wasn't actually serious in terms of life or death, but had to be dealt with immediately unless they wanted to answer to the network—they had to meet here.

Three out of the four contestants had up and dropped out of the first episode. Violet and her team had spent all day pleading with them, trying to get them to reconsider. It was all so stupid. One chef from Boston found out he'd be competing against a former coworker and refused to share a kitchen with him, even though appearing on the show would guarantee exposure for his restaurant and possibly earn him a cash prize. The other guy dropped out when he heard about Chef A's exit from God-knows who. He wouldn't be on a show if his arch-cooking enemy felt he was too good for it. The third guy? Flying him out to Los Angeles from San Antonio would be a violation of his parole.

Violet's life seemed so pleasant just the day before. She'd followed Grant's suggestion and taken herself shopping. Well, first she hit the internet and did some hardcore research about where she could find fun party dresses and not bland floral polyester tents in her size. She found two stores that caught her eye, then she took herself shopping, without Faye. No, that wasn't it. It had nothing to do with Faye. It just felt so nice to do something for herself; leave her house when she wanted, without worrying about Patrick's schedule. She teased Grant about getting under that perfect dress she found, but she couldn't wait to wear it out, even if she wouldn't get the chance until the next wrap party.

Violet excused herself to go to the kitchen under the guise of needing a glass of water. When she was alone in the massive space, where she knew Dana didn't prepare a single meal herself, she called Grant. It was getting late, but she had a feeling he would pick up. He did.

"Hello, Miss Ryan. What can I do for you this evening?"

Violet almost whimpered at the sound of his voice. She wanted to be with him.

"You can come save me," she replied.

"What's wrong?"

"Nothing. Just some ridiculous work shit. I'm out in Malibu."

"Having a cook-off?"

"Ha, yeah. I don't think I'll be home until really late. Can we push our workout?"

"Sure. How about we do this? You think you'll have to work tomorrow night?"

"Hopefully not."

"Come by the gym around nine. We'll go for a walk and then afterwards—"

"You'll give me the D?"

Grant's rich laugh came through the phone. "Please stop saying that."

"I'm sorry. How about this? Please, oh please, Mr. Master Gibson. Oh please, will you fuck me? I want you to fuck me so bad."

"Dana said she had some gourmet pear juice we should try," Faye said, as she appeared in the kitchen, scaring the crap out of Violet, who spun around and almost choked on her tongue.

"I have to get back to work," she said into the phone.

"Okay. See you tomorrow?" Grant asked, clearly shocked by the sudden change in her voice.

"Yeah. Night." Violet managed not to be completely rude and let Grant get out his own "Goodnight" before she hung up the phone.

Faye's head popped above the fridge door. "Who was that?"

"Oh, my trainer, Grant. I was just rescheduling our session for tomorrow."

"Cool. He must be good. You look great."

Violet's stomach cringed at the loaded compliment. She'd lost a whole five pounds since they'd started working out together, five pounds that were composed of flushed water weight and maybe some fat in between her toes. When she looked in the mirror the only difference she saw was in her face, and that change had nothing to do with her weight. Her typical scowl, the creases of worry that were a constant part of her appearance because something was always on her mind, was replaced by this dreamy smile. Even early in the morning, she couldn't stop smiling, thinking about Grant. But that smile was gone now and Faye knew nothing about it. Did she usually look like shit? Was she missing some other superficial change in her appearance, or was that just something you're supposed to say when you know someone is getting off their ass and eating a little better?

"Thanks," she said anyway.

"Does he charge a lot? I like Pinks, but I'm getting kind of bored over there."

"Uh, yeah he's a little pricey." Violet told Faye the amount she paid for the month. And maybe she tacked on another two hundred dollars.

"The fuck! Can you afford that?"

"It's a sacrifice I'm willing to make."

"You think he'd give us a discount if he trained us together? Patrick said I can't dip into the Paris fund anymore. We'll be vacationing at his parents' house in Lancaster if I keep at it."

Christ, what did she have to do to get Faye off Grant's scent? "Uh..."

"Finally!" They heard Jonathan screech from the other room. His outburst of triumph saved her from another lie.

"Let's go see what that's all about." Violet grabbed a couple glasses and a large bottle of water, then led Faye, with her pitcher of pear juice, out of the kitchen.

SEVEN

Day 13

Grant was waiting for her on the dark street, backlit by the lights coming through the gym windows. Max was by his side, waiting patiently for them to get his walk started. Violet dragged herself from her car, exaggerating her exhaustion. She reached Grant and leaned against his chest, looking up into his dark-blue eyes.

"Can we skip the walk and go right for the sauna?" she whined.

His free hand rose to the end of her ponytail and he gave her hair a gentle tug, pulling her head back just far enough so he could lay a soft kiss on her lips. "We walk and then I'm taking you someplace special. But if you want the sauna that bad—"

"No. We can go someplace special."

"I figured you'd say that," he said, before kissing her one more time.

They started walking, but in a different direction this time. Instead of heading south toward Melrose Avenue they headed north, up La Cienega. The walk was longer this time, that much was obvious when Violet found herself walking with Grant down Santa Monica Boulevard. The streets were busy, as the streets of West Hollywood were every night. Bars, restaurants, and convenience stores open for business for the inhabitants of Los Angeles who were getting their weekends started a little early. Or enjoying their last night off before they worked the weekend.

They passed by several construction sites, new "luxury" apartments taking over lots, as the population boom and limited space for sprawl caused the city to build up instead of out. Being smack between a mountain range and an ocean would do that.

For a couple blocks here and there they were quiet, just soaking the night in, but most of the time they talked. Violet told Grant more about their casting clusterfuck. Grant asked her how she ended up in reality TV; the million dollar question, since she had moved to Los Angeles to work in entertainment news. She confessed to her childhood obsession with Entertainment Tonight and then went on to explain what she was told about the job security in producing that type of news.

There would always be red carpets and gossip, even when the industry was going through a creative lull, one of her professors at Emerson had told her when she'd disclosed her plans to move West. She told Grant how the only work she could find when she arrived was as a production assistant on an MTV dating show. That's where she met Faye. They'd stuck together, climbing their way up from coffee fetchers to producers in a few short years. Here she was now, producing cooking competition shows and trying to shed the additional weight she'd added to her already chubby frame.

When they circled back down La Brea to Melrose, Violet realized just how long they'd been gone. Her legs were feeling the mileage and she'd developed a nice sheen of sweat in the seventy-degree night air, but she didn't mind. She'd walk around with Grant and his big dog, talking all night long if they wanted to.

On the corner of Kings Road and Willoughby they stopped so

Max could evaluate the trunk of a tree. Violet looked up at Grant. He looked back at her and she felt a sudden urge to hold his hand.

"I don't feel like I'm working out when I'm with you," she said. "Every fitness professional I've ever met is just *Go, go, go. Sweat, sweat, sweat. Cry, cry, cry.* Even when Margaret said you were a softy, I was expecting you to make me cry at least once. How'd you—how are you not a dick?"

"I'll take that as a compliment. I don't know, I guess I just like to treat my clients like people and not dollar signs. I think I got it from my parents."

"They're big hearted fitness experts?"

"No. They run a nursing home in Florida. They're kind of known for actually caring about the people who live there on an individual level. They raised me to respect the process of being kind and patient, you could say."

"So this is how you treat all old people?" Violet said, squinting at him.

"Oh yeah. I had an eighty-year-old in the sauna just last week. I rocked her world."

"I'm sure she's grateful. But yeah, you're pretty cool. I thought I would hate *exercising* with you. I know we have to step it up soon, but I like that you're going slow with me. I honestly didn't know trainers like you existed."

"We do. You want to know how far we've walked tonight? Five point three miles."

She hadn't run a marathon, but Violet was impressed with herself and even happier with the realization that the distance was one she could easily tackle again. She wasn't a Pump Fit champ, but she enjoyed the hell out of these tiny achievements.

"Last time I walked that much, Faye tricked me into doing some 10K fun run. It was not fun."

"You're not warming me up to this Faye person," Grant replied, as his brow knitted together in a frown. "We're about a half mile from the gym. We can head back or we can stop here."

Violet looked in the direction Grant quirked his head, across a short lawn to a four story residential building. It looked relatively new with its boxy construction, brown and green exterior and steel accents. "What's here?"

"My place."

"Don't you need to lock the gym up? And what about my car?"

"Armando is there and your car will be fine overnight, but we can go get it if you want."

Violet was not about to change the course the evening had suddenly veered on to, even if Grant had to drive her to the impound lot later. "No. It's okay. Show me your place."

There was a heavy glass door that Grant opened with a code, a short flight of steps leading down into an open courtyard complete with trees, stone benches, and a small fountain, then another long flight of stairs before Grant brought Violet to the short, private hallway that led to his front door. Max nudged his way past her, as Grant opened it to let them inside.

Violet cursed under her breath. "Okay, clearly I'm in the wrong business."

"Reality TV not paying its weight in gold?"

"Not exactly."

The condo was huge, an open floor plan that joined the kitchen, living room, and dining area into one large space. It was well decorated, for being owned by a single guy in his thirties. Most of the guys Violet knew lived with roommates or their significant others. Their places were either trashed, constantly taking on the look of a frat house with a revolving door or their girlfriends/wives had the run of the joint and feminine influences could be found wall-to-wall. Grant's place definitely had a masculine feel to it. Several pieces of industrial art hung on the walls, rusted metal works crafted from chains, old car parts and pieces of scrap metal. His furniture matched. The dining room set near the kitchen was the same unfinished wood as his coffee table and an oversized rocking chair near the TV. His couch and the armchair and ottoman opposite it were a dark-chocolate leather.

He had other furniture that Violet hadn't quite expected. Like the giant armoire that had its doors secured open, revealing shelves decorated with picture frames and miscellaneous trinkets. And, of course, Violet recognized Max's plaid doggy bed. Blankets of a similar design were draped off the back of the couch and the rocking chair.

She took the glass of water Grant offered her and watched him as he refilled Max's food bowl.

"Armando and I made a lot of smart business decisions. Don't be fooled by the look of the place, though. I didn't do any of it. I had a client who was an interior designer and he insisted on helping me when I moved in last year. He even framed pictures my parents sent me."

Suddenly a sleek, black cat appeared from behind the couch and made its way over to Violet. He wound a path between her feet, purring loudly as he rubbed against her leg. She reached down and gave his head and back a thorough rubbing.

"You have a cat?" Violet said, asking the world's most obvious question.

"That's Bill. I got him and Max the same day."

"It's a lot of responsibility to take on at once. I don't even keep a goldfish."

"Hey, goldfish are hard to keep alive. I went through a bit of a wild streak and my mom told me to get a dog. She knows I wouldn't neglect an animal and it would force me to slow down before I ran off to Vegas or somewhere to do stupid shit. While I was filling out the paperwork to bring Max home, some lady at the shelter was talking about the lone survivor of Bill's litter, so I took them both.

"That's so sweet." Violet abandoned Bill to look around some more. She stopped at what was clearly a gold record plaque for what looked like a five member pop group that had a name she didn't recognize. She also didn't understand what it was doing on Grant's wall. He could have found it at a garage sale. Failed artists were always selling personal treasures to keep their heads above water. But the frame on this piece seemed pristine and cared for, and its position on the wall seemed to be special. Was he that into music?

She looked closer at the guys in the picture and in the middle —she had to blink twice—in the middle, hunched, with his arms around his bandmates, was a lanky, baby-faced Grant. He looked so different without the five or so inches of height, the thirty pounds of muscle, not to mention the full beard he'd grown in the sixteen or so years since the picture had been taken.

Violet covered her mouth to muffle her girl-screech of disbelief. "Is that you?!"

Grant came over and looked at the plaque. "Yes."

"You. Were in a boy band called First Base?"

This time Violet actually stumbled back, her lips still covered, as Grant started to sing.

"My heart, it's true, girl, belongs to you, girl. The days, the nights apart. You don't know what it does to my heart, when I'm not with you. Girl."

Violet couldn't believe her eyes or her ears. It was frightening the difference some well-manicured facial hair could make, but his voice? Grant had one of the most beautiful singing voices she had ever heard.

"I have never heard that song," she confessed. "But wow."

Grant shrugged it off, as if his vocal skills were no big deal. "It was a lifetime ago."

"What happened?"

"I did the whole wanna sing, wanna dance, wanna act thing when I was a kid and then I got sucked into the boy band machine.

Artist development takes a long time. They test you in different markets, swap out band members. We had one hit in Europe, but we just missed the craze here. The record label dropped us and that was that."

"But how'd you go from this to owning a gym? I'm missing something in the gap."

"That just sort of happened." He shrugged again, making Violet want to shake him for downplaying his accomplishments. She worked to pay the rent and stay in the industry, but Grant had stories to tell and she wanted to hear them all.

"Starting a successful business doesn't just sort of happen. Tell me," she said.

"After my career as part two of a five-part adolescent harmony didn't work out, I moved back to Florida with my parents and tried to go back to school."

"Florida didn't hold the cultural appeal of Paris and London?"

"Not really. I wanted to sing, so I moved out here and quickly realized that my dreams of being a white R&B singer were not going to pan out. The group thing was still hot and executives saw me more as a face than a voice."

"So you started turning tricks?"

"Close. I started modeling. Sort of."

"Does that mean you actually did porn?"

"No. I worked for this company that hired semi-nude models to work as living statues and servers at parties. That's how I ran into Armando. And how I ended up being a Dominer."

Violet smiled. "You know you like that word better. Admit it."

"I do, but don't tell Mando that."

"So?" Violet wanted more details.

"We both got hired to be eye candy at this bondage-themed party an actor was throwing. He contacted a real dungeon master to give it an authentic feel. That man, Philip, everything he set up for the guy was just for show. Nothing kinky even happened. Well, with us anyway. Some people fucked in various rooms, but that's typical Hollywood shit. We just had to stand around in leather jock straps and chest harnesses and hold trays, but after the party Philip heard Armando and I talking about wanting to get into the bondage scene for real. He invited us to meet some people, participate in some scenes and, after a while, he was training us both to be Dominants."

"You really have to train for that? It's just extra crazy sex, isn't it?"

Grant stepped closer and wrapped his arms over Violet's shoulders. The contact left her conflicted. She wanted to rip his clothes off and she wanted to hear the rest of his story. If only they could do both. His hand was in her hair in the next second, tilting her head back in a gesture Violet was starting to crave. His gentle control was so freaking sexy. She looked from his eyes to his golden brown mustache as he continued to talk.

"Sometimes it doesn't even involve sex. Mainly I needed to learn how listen to my partner, how to anticipate their needs, when to push, when to stop, when to walk away altogether. Anyone can have extra crazy sex, but if I'm tying you up and whipping you, I want to make sure we both enjoy the experience, and also want to make sure you don't need therapy afterwards."

"Is whipping people your favorite thing to do?" Was that something she was willing to do?

"No. I like control, Miss Ryan. I like controlling where you sit, where you stand, where you lie down, when you speak and when you're silent, when you come and just how hard."

"Oh, I see. You like bossing me around and making me miserable."

"Something along those lines. Are you too tired to play?"

Her body surged with heat and that seemed to be the answer she was looking for. Still, Violet wasn't dumb enough to ignore the words Grant had just said. This BDSM stuff was really serious to him. She was pleased he approached it with such practical caution and consideration, but she wasn't sure how deep those waters truly ran and if she was willing to test them. She exhaled lightly, and took her own cautious step. "What do you have in mind?"

Grant crossed the room and unhooked what Violet thought was a piece of art on the wall. A length of chain uncoiled and two long metal bars slowly dropped from the ceiling a few feet away from the couch. Grant beckoned her closer as he separated the two bars. One he held in his hand and the other still hung from the ceiling.

Violet examined the bar that was still suspended. It looked sturdy enough. Each end had a small metal hook. "Hands up here and...?"

Grant pointed to the floor. "Feet spread apart here." Violet pictured herself tied up just so, naked, she guessed, with her arms suspended over her head and her thighs unable to close. Had it been anyone other than Grant looking at her with those big, sweet eyes, waiting patiently for an answer but silently praying that she would be open to this experience, that she would be open to trusting him, she would have said no. But it was Grant and she did trust him. Though she wished she had called Faye or someone to let them know where she was. If he really planned to, say, tie her up and keep her prisoner or kill her, Faye would at least know where to start looking.

"It's safe, right?" she asked.

"Yes. And I told Armando where we were going. If for some reason I drop dead and you're still chained up here, he'd come by looking for us by tomorrow night, at the latest." She could tell he was teasing about the last part.

"Sure. Let's do it. Can I freshen up a bit first?"

"Bathroom's right through there." He pointed down the hallway. "Just leave your clothes in there."

The pep talk Violet gave herself lasted the length of her super-short shower. Grant liked her. He enjoyed her body just the way it was. He'd already made her come like crazy and hopefully tonight they would finally have sex. It was okay for her to be a little nervous, but there was no need for her to be afraid. This was something new, a new part of this new life she was trying to create for herself. More than just new dresses and a tighter stomach. This new life had long walks and great sex. She was facing something that shined brightly with excitement and she wanted to embrace it.

When she walked back out to the living room, completely naked and dry except for her damp hair, she found Grant had changed into jeans and a t-shirt. Digging through the bottom drawer of the armoire he pulled out a cordless vibrator, two pairs of cuffs and a strip of black fabric.

"You just keep that down there?" Violet said.

"It's not like I have kids. Do your friends come over and dig through your shit?"

"No, I guess not. I just keep that stuff in my bedroom."

"You'll have to show me some time." He placed everything on the ottoman then faced Violet with a clear, but serious expression on his face. "We are going to skip safewords because this is your first time. If at any point you are in pain, extremely uncomfortable, anything like that, tell me. Just say, 'Grant, stop', or tell me whatever you need in that moment. Yes, you are giving up your body for me to enjoy for the time being, but you are in control, do you understand?"

"Got it."

"Okay. Come here." It didn't take much time, maybe five minutes, and Grant had Violet cuffed up in his living room. Her arms were fine, suspended above her head. It almost felt natural. The feet took some getting used to. She wanted to close them, not because she was uncomfortable being bared to Grant that way, but because her body instinctively wanted to put her hands on her hips when her feet were spread apart. She felt like she was stuck mid jumping jack and Grant was just getting started.

When he slipped the black fabric over her eyes, Violet took a deep breath. Everything went dark and she strained to keep her bearings. There was nothing to hear though, nothing to feel but Grant. His lips brushed against her ear. "Are you ready?"

There was something witty she wanted to say, something defiant and smart, but she couldn't find the words. She just wanted Grant to touch her, so she nodded and said yes.

He started with his mouth on hers. In his nearly signature way, her head was pulled back and his tongue slid against hers, soft and slow. The kiss was enough to ease her anxious nerves. Her body went from tight and tense to so hot and wet. The burn between her legs, was heavy and throbbing. She wanted more.

Grant's mouth moved lower, farther from her mouth, but always pressed against her skin, leaving a hot, tingling trail of sensation in its wake. He bit her neck then sucked on the tender spot to ease the pinch of pain away.

She moaned, as he continued on to her left breast and then to the other, sucking each nipple gently before pinching it between his thick fingers and drawing his tongue over the sensitive tip all over again. With every new touch, Violet tried to squirm and move, but it was useless. The balls of her feet seemed stuck to the floor. She was stretched to the point that there was nowhere for her to go. She felt awkwardly off balance. Still, Grant was always right there, some part of his body pressed to hers. His mouth on her breast, a hand on her waist or between her legs, helping her regain her balance. She wanted the blindfold off so she could see his face, but more than anything she wanted to touch him.

So many times she almost asked. He could give her sight back, but the dark was part of the game. It heightened her senses, and drove her mind wild as she tried to anticipate his next move. His hand was on her thigh when she heard the sound of wood on wood then the smoosh of leather. The ottoman, she thought, just as Grant's whole face, wet tongue and all, pressed between her legs. That was the end of her intentional thought for what would turn out to be another hour.

Grant made her come with his mouth in no time. His fingers

helped things along, thrusting up into her wet cunt as her whole body clenched and swayed. After the first time, his lips left her body, but his fingers stayed in place, slowly pumping in and out, pulling back just enough to let her come back to herself while reminding her exactly who was in charge.

And then, just when she thought she could breathe, there was a buzzing sound. Grant pressed the head of the vibrator between her legs, right on the height her clit. She called out this time, almost screaming as he kept his thick fingers still while the toy did its job of making her come all over again. And then again.

It's whirling sound cut off. Violet could almost feel its silence as her muscles continued to shake and tremble on their own.

And then he was back at her with his mouth.

Back and forth between his own lips and the vibrating head, while Violet's feet were still secured to the floor.

"How are you doing? Tell me."

Violet nodded her head and swallowed the drool that was pooling in her mouth. "I'm fine. I'm okay."

"You're sure? Do your wrists hurt? Your ankles?"

Violet tried to focus, to see if she could find any pain. All she found was a soreness in her shoulders and the balls of her feet, but neither ache gave her pause or reason to ask Grant to stop or even slow down. She took a few deep breaths and swallowed again. "I'm fine."

"Okay," she heard his deep voice say, and then his touch was gone. She heard movement, a shuffling of clothes and maybe some plastic crinkling, but she couldn't feel him. She didn't like that.

"Where'd you go?" The panic in her voice was unintentional, but it was there nonetheless.

"Shh, Vi. I'm right here. See." His lips brushed her and instantly her heart rate slowed. "Just give me one sec and I'll be with you."

"'Kay. Hurry."

As promised, his hands returned to her body, but this time he was behind her. With a slight tug backwards, she was bent forward as far as the chain would allow her and Grant was inside of her, the long thick length of him welcome in her pussy, which was beyond primed and ready. She could feel the thin sheath of plastic between them and she knew this time he meant business. Fresh endorphins filled her system as he started pumping in and out. He'd given her just a taste that day in the sauna, but she'd known it would be this good. She knew she would feel this full and even though she'd already come two dozen times, she still wanted his cock inside her when she came once more.

She reached the point then, with that simple understanding. She'd beg if she had to. Her voice was hoarse when she spoke. "Please."

Grant paused, his lips near her ear again. "Please what?"

"Take off the blindfold. I wanna see you. Please." Regret filled her when he withdrew. She wanted to see him. She didn't want him to stop.

He freed her ankles first, another thing she hadn't expected. Then she heard his voice on the other side of the room. "Violet, do me a favor. Pull your wrists forward real slowly, not down. Forward, like you're trying to bring the bar down to your thighs."

She obeyed and felt her arms slowly lowering, but just enough for Grant to reposition her. His legs were between hers, an arm around her waist and a hand on her ankle, guiding her onto the ottoman on her knees and over his lap. Her arms were back, straining above her head.

Then, finally, he took off the blindfold. Violet blinked, and managed to get a fix on Grant's face, mere inches away from hers. He'd dimmed the lights in the room, making the adjustment easier. Still, it took a second.

"Okay?" Grant said with a sweet smile.

"Yeah."

"Good. Now you're going to make me come." He gripped her

hips and pulled her down to meet his cock just as his pelvis thrust up.

✶

Violet was almost surprised when she woke up the next morning, because she was pretty sure she'd died from coming the night before. She rode Grant hard and fast, grinding her pelvis against his with everything she had, until he came and she came twice more. She was pretty sure she'd blacked out and come to again when he slid her off his lap. She'd been in a haze when he carried her to his bed, but not so much of a haze that she didn't comment on his capacity to carry large amounts of weight. He'd kissed her silent, yet again.

Between his soft sheets, he massaged her whole body. Her shoulders, her wrists and ankles, even her thighs and back. He might have explored some other areas, but she didn't know. She fell asleep.

But now her phone was ringing. She peeled her eyes open, heart-warmed to see that Grant had plugged it into a charger for her. It kept ringing. She reached for it and looked at the screen.

Grant's arm moved from its position around her waist. "Answer it," he mumbled against the pillow.

"It's Faye."

"Don't answer it."

She rolled her eyes and hit accept. "Hello?"

"Breakfast. Let's get breakfast. I want breakfast."

Violet groaned and rolled onto her back, closer to Grant's warmth. "No go. I'm out of commission."

"Huh?"

"I'll explain later."

"How about pizza and Netflix tonight? Patrick is spending the weekend with his folks." Naturally.

"Sure, sounds great."

"What are you doing?"

"Nothing. I'll call you later."

Faye didn't like it, but Violet rushed her off the phone, then turned to Grant. He opened one eye and looked back at her. His hand slipped between her legs. "Do me a favor, don't tell Faye and the people you work with about us?"

Violet tensed and pulled away. "Why?"

Grant pulled her back. "Stop. I mean for your own sake. Shit, for both our sakes, I don't think it would be wise for your friends and coworkers to think that you're sleeping with your trainer."

Immediately Violet thought of how it would sound coming from her mouth, even in passing. Like a joke. Like Grant was a whore. Like she was an idiot.

"I don't mind being Grant, the guy you fuck around with, or even Grant, your Dominer, but I'm not interested in being Grant, the trainer you're fucking when you should be exercising. You see the difference?"

"Yeah. I do. Speaking of, it's almost nine o'clock. Don't you have a class to teach or a client to train or an elderly woman to bang in the saunas?"

"My first client is at eleven. I was hoping to bang you before I got ready, but if you're in such a hurry for me to leave..." Grant tossed back the sheets, revealing his awesome nakedness. And his erection. He started to get up.

Violet grabbed his arm and pulled him back down to her. "No, stay. Bang *me*."

"If you insist." His stash of condoms was within reach and once he slid one into place, he slid perfectly into Violet's welcoming pussy.

She managed to make it five whole minutes without mentioning her victory in finally getting the D from Grant Gibson. Dominant/Pop Singer/Epic Wielder of Perfect Penis.

EIGHT

Day 14

"Pepperoni and a veggie masters because I know you're working on your fitness."

Oh, dear Faye, Violet thought. You have no idea. Almost twelve hours later and Violet's whole body was still feeling the effects of being with one Mr. Grant Gibson. Violet grabbed two slices of the vegetable pizza, then leaned back on the couch.

"What happened this morning" Faye asked. "Why were you out of commission?"

Violet froze mid-chew. She put down her plate and turned to Faye. This girl talk was about to get serious. She had to tell *someone* what was going on with Grant or she was going to burst.

"Okay. Please don't tell anyone. Like don't mention it accidentally to Jonathan while you're hanging out at crafty 'cause this is one of those little things that is *not* a big thing, but can turn into a big thing if people run their mouths."

"I swear, no games of telephone. No notes passed in class. Tell me."

"I'm kinda seeing someone. My trainer."

"What?"

"I know. He's also a Dominant or whatever. Like heavy into BDSM. We've been trying it out some."

"What?! For how long and why didn't you tell me?"

"Since we met. We fooled around after our first session."

"Violet!" Faye smacked her leg with a pillow.

"I know."

"I don't know whether to be upset with you or really impressed. You are usually so by-the-book. Court, sex on the third date, meet his parents, all that crap."

Violet hesitated before she responded. That wasn't her at all, but maybe Faye misunderstood the way she usually got to know guys before she got serious with them. "It just sort of happened."

"Is this why you were so freaked about missing your session with him when we went to the concert?"

"Maybe."

"Wow. Okay. So you're seeing him or screwing him? 'Cause there's a difference."

"No. I—Wait. No. We're seeing each other." They walked his dog together. No way Grant did that with his other clients, and he swore to her that it was just the two of them. Monogamy all around. "Yeah. We're seeing each other."

"Has he asked you to be his girlfriend?"

"Guys still do that?"

"Patrick did."

"Of course he did. No, he hasn't asked me to be his girlfriend."

"Okay, so no GF status. What about exclusivity? Is he seeing anyone else?"

"No, I told him no one else or no deal."

"How often do you see him? Has he taken you out or is all this going on during your sessions?"

"Uh... no." It bothered Violet how much it bothered her to admit it. "We haven't gone out anywhere. We've worked out and hooked up. But it's not like wham bam kind of hooking up. Last night he— Last night was amazing. I'll just say that. We did it at his place."

"Where are you doing it the other times? The gym?"

"Yeah." God, she never should have said anything. Faye was making the whole situation sound so seedy and sordid and she was making Violet feel like a complete asshole for going along with Grant's suggestion.

"I hope you know that's fucking gross. You're sleeping together in a gym where people get all sweaty and gross," Faye said. She even threw some extra spice on the sentiment by making one of the most disgusted, yet pitying faces Violet had ever seen. "I—yeah, no."

"What? What are you about to say?"

Faye relaxed against the couch and started picked at a thread that was coming loose from the pillow. "It's just—never mind."

"It's just what? Say it."

"You're trying so hard to get in shape and they always say drastic body changes can be really emotional. Do you really want your weight loss to be wrapped up with some guy who you're paying to fuck you?"

Violet had never been punched in the face, but she was pretty sure, in that moment, she knew exactly how it felt. She almost climbed off the couch and walked right out the door.

"I'm not paying him to fuck me."

"Can I just call it as I see it? Please? You tell me point-blank when Patrick is being a jerk. I'm telling you that you are paying a guy you just met to have sex with you under the guise of him helping you to work out. I'm not sure your being completely on board with it as a part of your workout regime makes things much better. You see him twice a week, but he doesn't take you anywhere. He fucks you at his place of employment—"

"Ugh. He was right. I shouldn't have told you." As soon as the words left her mouth Violet thought jumping out the window might be a better alternative.

"He told you what? Violet, are you kidding me right now?" Faye threw up her hands in surrender, which made Violet feel like she was being even more delusional.

She couldn't think. Everything Faye was saying was bouncing off the walls of her head, smashing into thoughts of Grant's smile, Grant's face, the sound of his voice, his touch, his kiss. She didn't want to give what her friend was trying to tell her an ounce of footing, but little by little her logical words started to crush those pieces of Grant that were starting to move south to her heart.

"So what are you saying?"

"I'm saying do what you want. I know you don't like being single." It was true, but such a small part of the situation. "But maybe try dating a guy without money changing hands. And with someone who *wants* you to tell people. He shouldn't be ashamed to be with you. This sounds like an episode of some teen drama. Hot jock hooks up with dumpy fat girl, but no one can know. Come on, Vi. You're better than this."

Violet started to say a hundred different things, never mind the fact that her best friend had just called her fat, but every exception was matched up with one simple truth. She hadn't even known Grant a full month. They hadn't even spent an entire week together. She knew Faye was taking his plea of silence the wrong way, but Faye did have a point. Grant was getting everything he wanted from Violet, her body, her obedience, and her money and she only got to see him at the appointed times. Did she want more with him? Yes? But at this point she didn't even know if he was that type of guy.

Grant had only mentioned other submissives in his past. No girlfriends or even women who he cared deeply for. Could he even give her a normal relationship? Did the boyfriend title even belong on that little black card? Violet wanted to know, but there was one small thing standing in her way. Grant and the terms he seemed to live by. She could talk to him, but she couldn't change him. That much was true.

✶

Grant had all the pieces in place. It took every moment he had over the weekend, but he pulled together everything he needed to talk to Violet about being his girlfriend. It was almost a foreign idea to him, the idea of asking a woman who lived her life entirely outside of the scene to be in an exclusive relationship, but it was what he wanted. He couldn't change the dominant part of his personality. Bondage and domination and submission were a huge part of his life, but he would present Violet with every bit of information he had at his disposal, he could let her get a clearer picture of what this part of his life really entailed and if she was on board, they could try being a couple. Outside of the gym.

He talked to Master Philip and got permission to bring Violet by his club if and when she was ready. He talked to Armando, who offered any support they needed. He also agreed that Violet should be refunded for the fees she'd forked over to Melrose Fitness. Grant had enjoyed every moment he had spent with her. None of it was part of a business transaction and he wouldn't go any further until she understood that simple fact.

Right at six he left the folder, complete with some reading material and a check for her refund, on his desk and went outside to meet Violet. Her car pulled up the moment the gym door closed behind him. Grant swallowed his nerves and straightened his spine, but his spirit took a nosedive when Violet walked around the side of her car. She was in her street clothes. She still had her glasses on and the look on her face defined grim.

"I need to talk to you," she said. Her tone wasn't too cheery either.

"Okay."

"I don't think this is a good idea."

"What? The working out? Or us?"

"Us."

It was ingrained in Grant not to questions another person's

final decisions, but he had to understand. The last time he saw Violet, they could barely pull themselves off each other and now she was pushing him away. "Do you want to tell me why?"

"When you told me not to tell Faye—"

Grant felt this sickness in his stomach turn into a pressure behind his eyes. Why did everything in Violet's life come back to this Faye woman? "I told you not to tell Faye because you two work in television and so do a nice number of my clients. What we do is between us and I didn't want people coming up to you at work functions asking for the number of that trainer you fucked. And I don't want wanna-be clients coming up to me and thinking this is just something I offer up with every membership."

"What about the others? They live in L.A. too. They probably know TV people too."

Grant closed his eyes and rubbed his beard. This conversation was worse than his entire breakup with Ariana. At least he knew she was little crazy. "They were in the BDSM scene already. They knew how to keep certain things to themselves. Either way, that wasn't about you. That was about your friend, Faye and your coworkers, who I don't know."

"Exactly. You don't know her and you also don't know me as well as she does. I like you, but you're into all this stuff. I don't know where the games end and begin with you. I don't want to get halfway to my weight loss goal and then you decide you're bored with me and then I end up eating my way back to where I am now. I don't want my weight to be wrapped up in my feelings about you at all. I—I..."

Grant waited. He wasn't putting any words in her mouth. He wasn't going to let her force him to say the words that were on her mind, that she had come to him to say, only to be called the bad guy sometime down the road. If she felt she was better off without him, then fine. If she truly believed he was the type of guy to use her, especially after the kind of time they'd spent together, then he wasn't going to beg her to change her mind. If she wanted to cut him off, she'd have to nut up and say the words herself.

"I don't think we should do this," she finally said.

"Okay." That was all he needed to hear. Grant turned to the door to the gym.

"Grant." He hated that tears lined her eyes when he turned back around, but what was he supposed to do? She said what she needed to say and the message has been received and processed in full. When her lip started to quiver, he'd had enough.

"Bye, Violet." He opened the door all the way then, after stepping through, closed it on another chapter of his life.

✱

Violet didn't eat her feelings. She pushed them out in heaping sobs as she cried and cried for nearly two days straight. She went through every stage of regret, denial, partial acceptance, and shame. On the third day, when a check from Melrose Fitness arrived in the mail, she knew she had made a mistake. Yes, what they had and how it started was unorthodox, but it wasn't wrong. Grant wasn't ashamed of her. He had presented everything they did together to her in clear terms and she agreed to everything, every step of the way. And instead of acknowledging what was special about Grant and what they had, she fucked it up.

She took the painful things Faye had said at face value, and dumped Grant before they even had a chance to become something more. Whenever her emotions were running this high and strong, she wanted to call Faye but, instead, Violet blew her off as she continued to wallow in her meltdown.

Grant had wanted to know about her insides, about what made her tick, and in those few days Violet realized that her insides were shockingly hollow. She had her work. She had the time she spent with Faye. And that was it. Grant didn't exactly fill that void, but being without him, and not being able to open up to Faye again, showed Violet how deep that void was. She needed more in her life. She needed more for herself.

Eventually though, she knew she had to talk to her friend. It wouldn't be good to head back to work with any sort of rift between them. When Faye called for the fiftieth time, Violet answered.

"Are we still friends?" Faye asked, after Violet said her hello.

"I guess it's better than being completely alone."

"Violet, I am the worst friend in the world. I shouldn't have said all that stuff."

"It's okay. You were right."

"No, I was a jerk. And I promise I'll never be that big of a jerk again, but you've gotta tell me what's been happening? What happened with Trainer Guy?"

Violet's chest started to ache all over again. "I ended things, but I'm not sure I should have. I didn't realize how much I liked him."

"Neither did I." Faye sighed. "Seriously, I should have at least met the guy or really heard you out before I started dumping all over him and jumping to all of these conclusions about why you were with him. Do you think you guys can work things out? What's his name again?"

"It's Grant."

"Do you think Grant will give you another chance? I can call him. Beg on your behalf?" And that's why Faye was her best friend. They had their issues but, if she asked, Faye would call up Grant and try to set things straight. Faye would make that call in a heartbeat. Maybe that's why her initial words about him carried so much weight. Faye did care about her.

Violet sighed this time. "I'm not sure. I was a pretty big bitch."

"I think we're all a little guilty of that every now and then. Call him and then call me back. I'll buy you a super healthy dinner."

"Throw in some YogurtTown and you have a deal."

NINE

Day 21

Grant's Saturday morning boot camp class was packed. Violet stretched near the wall, watching Grant as he talked with another man. Another heavy woman, blond with flushed cheeks, sat on the floor beside her, lamenting her decision to sign up for the class. Violet nodded, feeling the exact same way for a completely different reason.

Grant saw her. Fifty different emotions flashed across his face the moment she walked through the door, but he wiped his expression clean just as quickly and started greeting people with smiles and hellos. Everyone but Violet. He started the class with a brief description of the workout for the new people, then led everyone through some quick stretches. He looked so good in his gray Melrose Fitness T-shirt. Violet missed those pecs, the thick biceps and that butt. How she missed his butt. She got a good look at it when he directed them out of the front door.

When Violet had signed up for the class under a fake name and slid the cash to Armando early that morning, she hadn't exactly thought the plan through. She tried calling Grant a bunch of times, but each time she got his voicemail. She had to see him or at least talk to him before she had to get back to her grueling work schedule. Short of showing up at Grant's house at five a.m. and praying one of his neighbors would let her into the complex, showing up at his first Saturday group class was the next best option. She would see Grant. He would be angry, but he wouldn't completely blow her off. He'd be professional. But there was something else Violet forgot to take into consideration. The actual workout she'd have to get through to squeeze in a word with him. She didn't think of the running.

After the first quarter mile it was obvious that Grant was slowing down the whole group so she and the blonde woman could keep up. He jogged back to them and smiled at the woman who was clearly in pain even though she managed to stay a step ahead of Violet. "Great job, Shana. It's not a race. You don't have to beat anyone. I just want you to finish." The woman nodded, wheezing as she went.

Grant fell back another step beside Violet. She could almost smell how pissed off he was.

"You're doing great. Just a little further. Keep on pushing." Grant delivered the generic encouragements, still refusing to look at her. Violet appreciated it. She'd missed his voice and hearing it take on that pleasant tone she hadn't meant to deprived herself of kept her mind off the fact that her lungs were bleeding and actually trying to climb out of her body via her mouth. She swallowed the sour bile down and glanced up at Grant again, as he turned to run back to the front of the line.

"Grant. Please," she puffed.

He slowed down to her pace, but his gaze fixed her at a dead stop. "We can't talk about this right now. We absolutely cannot. Not now."

"I get it. I understand, but after. Please. There's something I have to say."

After another bloated pause, he nodded. "After." He took off to finish the class as its lead and not the focus of Violet's stalking.

Violet pushed herself a little further until she caught up with the other woman. Shana, if she'd heard right, glanced at her. "I don't know why I signed up for this. I'm going to die," Shana said.

Violet's chuckle sounded more like a cough. "We can die together."

Shana stuck by Violet the whole class. Violet would have been grateful if her single-minded focus had been on executing the exercises and not counting down the minutes until the class itself was over so she could get to Grant.

Oh, but was it torture. Squats. Lunges. Push-ups. They did this awful thing with bags of sand and she learned two new things you could do with a kettlebell. And they did burpees. She must be falling in love with Grant if she was willing to do burpees. She didn't cry this time but by the end of the hour Violet wasn't exactly sure she wasn't going to die. Her whole body hurt and, even as the rest of the class took their turns saying goodbye to Grant, even after a superficial promise to see Shana at the next class, her whole body screamed at her, wanting to know why. Why?

Grant was why. She had to see him. She had to get him back. Or at least try.

Eventually Grant came over to her. He nodded toward the door. "Let's step outside."

Right. The office was for special people who didn't trash his character and treat him like crap. They walked two blocks, down to a residential corner. Saturday was a busy morning for Melrose Fitness and they didn't need an audience. When Grant stopped and turned to her, she didn't wait for a formal invitation to start groveling. She wiped away the sweat that would not stop pouring from her forehead and launched into her speech.

"You asked me what I wanted for myself. Well, I want you."

"You told me I was exactly what you didn't want. What's different now?"

"I don't know how to say this without sounding outstandingly creepy so I'll just say it. When I was with you I felt like I was a part of a healthy couple. I felt like I woke up in the morning and got to see my boyfriend and I got to tell him about my day and we walked his dog together and then, after, we had the sex I have been wanting to have my whole entire life.

"And then when we were apart, I couldn't wait to see you again. Faye said some things that were right, that would have been right if she was talking about someone who wasn't you. And if she knew you, she never would have said those things and if I had just trusted the wa..."

Violet had way more to say, but suddenly her own words were slurring in her mouth. Her body was also sloping a little to the left.

Grant caught her before she hit the ground.

"Whoa. Whoa. Here sit." Violet couldn't see clearly, but she tried to sit up when the cold asphalt on the curb met her butt.

Violet could hear Grant talking on his phone as he wrapped his arm around her. It felt nice to have him so close again, but she was more concerned about the ringing in her ears and the way the trees in front of her were blurring together. Just as quickly as she'd almost toppled over a protein bar appeared in front of her face. Keira had brought the food, probably sprinted down the street on her muscular legs, but Grant held the sustenance up to her mouth. She took a bite and then a sip of water Grant urged her to drink. Next was a segment of an orange and another bite of the protein bar.

"Did you eat before you came to class?"

"No. I was kind of on a mission." She really needed her head to stop spinning.

Grant muttered something under his breath, but Violet continued to focus on getting the food in her mouth.

"Better?"

"A little."

"I'm going to take you back to my place. I'd drive you home, but I won't make it back in time for my next class."

"I'm not arguing, only because your voice has a really neat echo right now and I'm not sure that's right."

Violet let Grant and Keira lead her back to her car and she handed over her keys. In no time they were at his condo. Grant helped her inside, out of her sticky clothes, into his shower, and then into his bed. Violet didn't know where Keira disappeared to, but she would be sure to thank her the next time she could. Throughout the whole awkward situation, Violet still felt light-headed and a little off. Grant pulled the covers around her and it was some of the coldest contact she'd ever experienced. He left her for a moment then came back with a glass of water and bag of granola that he put on his nightstand.

"I have to get changed for my next client, but I'll be back a little later. Just rest. Eat some of this."

"Thanks."

Violet closed her eyes as Grant dipped into his closet. She tried to relax and pull herself together as she felt the mattress dip at the foot of the bed and he put his sneakers back on. But she failed at finding a single semblance of calm as she heard the front door close and lock behind him. When she knew he was gone, Violet started to cry.

✱

When she woke up, she had a wicked case of dry mouth. Still, Violet felt much better. Never again would she set foot near a group class of any kind. Even if the fate of her heart was at stake. She rolled over to reach for the water and realized Grant was sitting on the bed, right beside her.

"Hi," he said, handing her the glass.

"Hey. Thanks." She took it and chugged the water down.

"How are you feeling?"

"Much better. Thank you."

"Violet, I know I should have just kicked you out of the class, but what were you doing this morning?"

"Being an idiot. But really? I was backpedaling," she said. Then she spit out the rest, just in case she had to pass out again, this time from embarrassment. "That's what I'm doing. I thought one thing and I was wrong, and now I'm thinking another. I don't want to be your client anymore. I don't want to train with you. You're not the guy I want to help me lose weight. You're the guy I want to be my boyfriend. I would like us to date."

"I charge more for that, you know."

Violet almost sighed with relief. It wasn't a yes, or a you're forgiven, but a small smile was trying to creep out from under that blond mustache. "Figured you would. Grant, I'm so sorry. My entire life has been work and people from work. I forgot what it was like to have a life of my own."

He sighed and lay down on the bed beside her. He lightly brushed his lips across her forehead. "What am I going to do with you, Miss Ryan?" he whispered.

"Miss Ryan? Does this mean you forgive me?"

"No. I'm still pissed."

"Oh."

"But I think you must be pretty serious to go through that intense of a workout just to talk to me."

"I was. I am. I've never jumped into something with a guy this way. I guess I almost expected something fishy under the surface, but that's not your fault and it wasn't fair for me to act like it was."

"You're not all wrong. I think I should have courted you."

"Really?"

"Yeah. I should have set you up with Armando. He'd train you just as well as me. And then I should have asked you out. And then I should have asked you to be my submitter."

"Would there have been any singing involved?"

"All kinds of singing. You know that day you kicked me to the curb, I was about to ask you out. I talked to Master Philip about how to make my interest in bondage and submission easier for you, and I even told Armando what I planned to do. You got the check?"

Violet wanted to crawl under the bed and die. "Yes."

"I had it ready in the office when you showed up. I was going to give you your money back because I didn't want to charge you to spend time with me when I was more than happy to start my day with you." Grant's lips brushed her forehead again and Violet knew this was exactly where she belonged.

"Will you please forgive me and be my boyfriend and boss me around? You can tie me up whenever you want. I won't complain too much, I swear."

"Miss Ryan, you can complain all you want."

TEN

Day 43

The minute their AD called lunch, Violet nearly vaulted over the back of her chair and ran out of the tech trailer. She power walked down the clanky metal steps then hit the button on her walkie-talkie and called for the office production assistant.

"Go for Brenna," a soft voice answered.

"Hey, Brenna is my one o'clock here?"

"Yes. He drove on a few minutes ago. He said he'd wait for you outside the elephant doors."

"Copy."

Violet made a U-turn around a forklift that was still haphazardly parked outside of the trailer and made straight for the soundstage doors. They were only in their second week of filming *Perfect Cut*. It had been a rough one. Problems from every department. Cast that she wanted to murder and production meetings that ran longer than they had any right to. But every night, when she left the studio lot, there was Grant. They tried to take things slowly, going on actual dates, trying to space out their time between seeing each other, like normal people do, but that didn't work. She was at his place every single night. And when he could get away during the day, he came to her.

They continued to work out together and, so far, Violet managed to shed a few more pounds, but now she was focused more on her overall wellness, not just her weight. Grant helped with that too. They managed to talk out their differences. Violet admitted her eagerness to learn more about being a submissive, but she hadn't worked up the courage to go with Grant to his club. Still, he was patient with her and she was starting to love him for that patience more and more.

Violet rounded another hedge and that's when she saw him, standing by the elephant door. Talking to Faye. She walked right over and plucked the paper bag out of his hand. They didn't need to stop talking for Violet to enjoy her lunch.

"Nice to see you, too," Grant said.

"She's an ungrateful asshole. I wish Patrick would bring me lunch."

Violet scoffed. "He's taking you to Paris. Let me have my sandwich."

"As if this one wouldn't take you to Paris. As if!" Faye winked at them both then wandered off to join the line at catering.

Violet automatically stepped into Grant's arms, perched up on her tiptoes so she could greet him with the tender affection he deserved. She realized it was a huge mistake the second their lips met. She had another six hours of work ahead of her, but all she wanted to do was drag him to the closest empty room and repeat what they had done in the bathroom, and the kitchen, the night before. Her inner thighs were still sore. He smelled so good and even though it was easily eighty degrees outside, she felt warmer when they touched.

Grant pulled back a bit and kissed her nose. "You want me to take you to Paris, Miss Ryan?"

"No. I want you to take me home. There's this chef from

Boston in this episode and he's driving us all up the wall. I just want this day to be over."

"Well at least I brought you a healthy lunch. All your veggies and chicken on wheat bread so whole it was just harvested, and a salad."

"Thank you. They're having beef tacos again. I couldn't do it."

Grant had to leave soon, and she had to eat and get back into the tech trailer for the second half of her torturous day, but she still took the time to walk him back to his car. She held his hand. "Do you want to know what I have planned for this weekend?" Grant asked. "Or do you want it to be a surprise?"

"Surprise. Just tell me what shoes I need to wear. Sneakers, heels, sandals, wellies?"

"Yeah, wellies. No, wear some heels. And do you still have that lace dress?"

"I sure do."

"You should bust that out."

"For you, baby." She leaned up and kissed him one more time. "Anything."

The End

CELEBRATED

Daniel checked everything one more time. The implements he needed, the lube and the condoms. He was stretched and ready, choosing to do this scene without his prosthesis. He wasn't arrogant, but he'd earned his reputation as a skilled switch, able to give and receive with the use of only one hand. He double checked that the camera was ready to go, battery fully charged. They might be at this for a while and his Domme wanted to see every frame, proof that he had completed the task he was charged with. He crossed the perfectly lit space to the submissive he'd gladly gone to all this trouble for.

It was Meegan's birthday and she deserved the best. Their Mistress, Evelyn was out of town for the day, but she'd be back over the weekend to celebrate with the rest of their kink family and the membership at The Club. There would be a public flogging and definitely some public fucking, but today was for the birthday girl.

Daniel glanced over at Marcos, clad in his studded collar and leather jockstrap, his pup tail plug shoved firmly up his ass. The chain leash connected to the D-ring stopping him from running all over the room. His friend and fellow plaything belonged to

Mistress Evelyn's husband, Master Philip. Marcos pinched his lips together, trying not to laugh. The man didn't have a serious molecule in his body. Daniel narrowed his glare and Marcos straightened right up. They had some serious shit to do. He focused back on Meegan where she stood blindfolded.

She was stunning. Tall, pale skin, adorable freckles, and long, dark hair. Heavy breasts and legs for days. Daniel knew they were meant to be in each other's lives from the moment they met. Another goofball who only took the amount of sex she loved to have seriously. Meegan was just joy and fucking and mischief all rolled into one package. Daniel was looking forward to giving her her gift.

He stood silently in front of her, sure the blindfold was doing its trick as he took his time looking her up and down again. She was secured in a red leather body harness that wrapped around her breasts and the height of her thighs, still leaving her nipples and the cleft of her pussy exposed. A red collar marking her as Mistress Evelyn's was secured around her neck.

"You ready to play, pet?" he whispered, the bass and arousal in his voice a slight shock to his own system.

Meegan nodded, a smile pressing across her pink lips. Daniel pulled the blindfold off and gave her a moment to take in the room. She glanced down at Marcos where he sat on his haunches, pretending to behave. They'd played in this space on the second floor of The Club plenty of times, but usually Mistress Evelyn was with them, along with a decent sized audience. It was just the three of them now. And the camera.

Daniel took her hand and led her down to the center of the room, where the large platform mattress set up for group play, sat under the bright lights. He helped her up onto the bed, draped in black and waited for her to get comfortable, sitting on the edge.

He took her by the chin and kissed her lightly on the mouth. "Let me go get our little friend."

"Okay," she whispered back.

In the back of the room, Daniel released the leash that was hooked on Marcos's collar and grabbed him firmly by the throat. He lived for it rough. "Do what I say, or you're gonna be in deep shit when Master Philip gets back."

Marcos looked off to the side, probably contemplating if he was in the mood for pleasure or punishment. He glanced back and gave Daniel's forearm a good lick. Daniel rolled his eyes, then stood, swatting him on the ass. "Go."

He looked back at Meegan as she leaned forward, both hands outstretched, waving Marcos over. Her smile widen as she laughed. Marcos crawled toward Meegan with his hands on the floor and when he reached her, he nipped her knee with his teeth before he climbed up her body, kissing and biting at her as he went.

Daniel watched as Marcos paused long enough to give both of Meegan's taunt nipples the attention they needed. He continued his way up her body, kissing between her harness and doing the best to kiss her neck and her cheeks before they were face to face. Daniel was already hard, but watching the two of them together had his erection pressing against the fly of his jeans.

"We're supposed to wear you out, but I think we should tag team him and wear him out. You wanna?" Marcos said. Meegan laughed, nodding before Marcos playfully tackled her to the bed, kissing her deeply on the mouth. Daniel shook his head as he walked and grabbed a paddle, the crop, and some lube off the nearby table. They had permission to kiss and touch, but they both knew he was in charge. Somehow Marcos just couldn't keep his mouth shut. Daniel was gonna paddle his ass his ass into next week when he got the chance.

Still, Daniel stood by and waited, knowing how much Meegan liked this kind of gentle attention. He didn't interrupt as Marcos kept kissing her, rolling slightly as he slipped his hand between Meegan's legs. She closed her thighs around his forearm, squirming as her sexy little moans filled the air.

Finally Daniel had done enough waiting. It was time to give

Meegan her real present. He moved to the side of the bed and set everything he needed down before he joined them at the foot of the platform. Carefully, but with a good amount of force, he shoved his fingers into Marcos's hair and gave it a firm tug, bringing the kissing to stop. He pulled hard enough that Marcos had to sit all the way up. Meegan followed, a playful look still on her face as she looked at them both.

"Did you say something about wearing *me* out?" Daniel said gruffly.

Marcos tried to shake his head, but couldn't move more than an inch. "No, I was just joking."

"That's what I thought," Daniel replied and then leaned down, tipping Marcos's face up so he could kiss him deeply on the mouth. Marcos was such a little shit, but an amazing kisser, good with his mouth in all kinds of other ways. Daniel's cock stirred as he thought about putting that mouth to use for Marcos's eventual punishment. Daniel released him, then moved over to Meegan, cupping her cheek.

"We're gonna have some fun, yeah?"

"Yeah," Meegan smiled up at him. Daniel brushed his thumb slowly across her bottom lip, before he slipped the single digit into her mouth. He had to force himself to stay on task as her tongue swirled over his skin. She knew exactly what he liked too. He pulled his thumb free after a moment and reached into his pocket for the lube, telling Marcos to stand up.

He handed the lube to Marcos and then helped Meegan stand. He slipped his hand around her neck, tilting her chin up and then kissed her. Deep and raw. They had always been drawn to each other, wild and insatiable, and the pull between them had not gone unnoticed, both by their Masters or the members of The Club.

Daniel felt Marcos step closer and didn't stop the muscular pup from slipping his hand back between Meegan's legs. Daniel shuddered as Meegan whimpered against his mouth begging for more. A moment later he stepped back just enough so he could see what Marcos was doing with his hand.

"You wet for me?" Daniel asked. Meegan nodded in response, biting her bottom lip.

"Let's see if we can't get you wetter. Happy Birthday, gorgeous."

Meegan smiled wider. "Thank you."

Daniel turned his attention to his other submissive of the hour and deftly removed the butt plug from Marcos's ass and tossed it toward the top of the bed where it bounced once and then came to rest on the black top sheet. Then he turned back to Meegan, pulling her closer again with the remaining portion of his right arm. He kissed her again, his other hand gripping her ass firmly. They ended the kiss just as Marcos pulled his jockstrap to the side and began slathering his erection with lube, as Daniel had instructed him to do while they were preparing.

Daniel had Marcos lean back and then he whispered in Meegan's ear. "I want you to sit on it," he told her. "I want you to take every inch in your ass."

Meegan glanced down at Marcho's lap, a bashful look coming over her face like Marcos hadn't taken her that way dozens of times. Then she stepped between Marcos's now spread knees, facing forward. Daniel watched her as she glanced back, reaching for Marcos's erection. With practiced ease, she lowered herself down, moaning as she looked up at Daniel, taking every inch. When she was settled in the curve of Marcos's lap, she steadied herself with a firm grip on his thighs as Marcos held on to her waist, giving her the additional support she needed.

"That feels good, doesn't?" Daniel asked, stroking her cheek.

"Mhmm," she whimpered.

"If you're both good maybe I'll let Marcos come in my ass."

"Yay!" Marcos shouted. Daniel and Meegan both burst out laughing, but Meegan's laugh quickly melted into a moan. She steadied herself, letting out a deep breath.

"Good girl," Daniel said. He left the two of them and walked around to the other side of the platform while Meegan and Marcos both tried not to move. Daniel tucked the crop under his arm, then pulled a chair up to the edge of the platform. He took a seat and allowed himself the pleasure of admiring Meegan's body. Skin blushed as she reclined on Marcos's lap, her wet pussy on display. Sure they were recording this for their Mistress, but Daniel knew he'd watch this scene over and over again.

He scooted the chair closer, feeling Meegan's hungry gaze on him as he moved. Daniel reached up and drew his thumb up the length of her slit. She squirmed just a bit. "You ready, pet?" Daniel asked.

"Yes, please," Meegan replied. Daniel held up the riding crop giving her a clear view of the implement he planned to use on her, one of her favorites. He had to force himself not to smile as she licked her lips.

"You know your words?" he asked her.

"Yes. Red, yellow, green."

"Good girl."

"Green!" Marcos shouted, his engulfed but unridden dick clearly driving him to forget his place. Daniel shook his head at the outburst before he let out a deep breath and refocused all of his attention back to Meegan.

"Let's begin."

After losing the lower portion of his right arm, he spent year learning how to wield a crop, a flog, paddle, anything he could get his hand on with the left. Every time, there was still a part of his brain, the phantom sensation telling him to switch hands, but it only lasted a moment as he was reminded of just how far he'd come. Lightly, he tapped the top of Meegan's cunt, where her soft blushing lips covered her clit. He did it again and again, over a dozen times, harder and faster, watching closely for Meegan's reactions. She squirmed and whimpered with every impact.

Slowly, Daniel increased the intensity of his strokes. Meegan's cries got louder, her breathing shakier. Her pussy was bright pink now and visibly slick. Another strike and she was coming. Daniel didn't stop. He landed more harsh, rhythmic strokes one after the other. Meegan couldn't stop herself from rising to meet each one, each motion of her hips forcing her to ride Marcos's dick as she arched and fell.

Daniel's cock throbbed in his pants as a high pitch moan left her mouth. Liquid squirted from her pussy in short but forceful bursts. Still Daniel didn't stop. He kept on with the same intense rhythm which only made Meegan more frantic, hungry. This was another thing they had in common, the three of them. Always wanting more. Wanting to be pushed, punished, taken, until they had nothing left to give and even then they ached to be pushed a little more.

Meegan was riding Marcos in earnest now. Daniel couldn't see his face, but Marcos was actually behaving himself, keeping a steady grip on Meegan's waist, stopping himself from thrusting up. The spanking continued and so did the squirting.

"Yes," Meegan chanted, her gaze trained down on the top of her own slit. "Please. Please. Fuck. Please."

Daniel knew she was dying to put her own hand in the mix, start rubbing her clit, fingering herself even if it got in the way of the crop. He was proud of herself control. By the time Daniel put down the riding crop on the platform beside her, Meegan was a whimpering mess, her pussy bright red and puffy, soaking wet and dripping. She stopped moving her hips, but her chest still heaved.

"You're still hungry, aren't you?" Daniel asked her. Meegan nodded, her teeth digging into her bottom lip. "I bet you are." Daniel tilted his head to the side and gave her body a thoughtful look before slapping her cunt with his bare hand. Meegan cried out, her body jerking, but he knew she liked it that more than the crop. He slapped it a few more times before he pushed one finger into her soaking entrance. And then another. He stood, turning his body to give himself better leverage as his jean clad shin brushed against Marcos's leg.

"Hmmm it looks like you need more. You want more, don't you?" he asked her as more liquid dribbled out of her slit, soaking his fingers. "It is your birthday so I think we need to give you what you want."

"Please," Meegan replied. A pained sound. Daniel pulled his fingers out and slapped her pussy one more time before he gripped it with his whole hand. Meegan hissed and arched up into his grasp. When he pulled his wet hand away Meegan sunk back down fully on Marcos's erection, making them both moan.

Daniel gave Marcos a few instructions to move further up the platform and settle Meegan with her back more flush against Marcos's chest. When they were in place, Meegan had her feet planted securely on the high surface, giving her more stability to lay back and giving Daniel more access. As they were moving Daniel unzipped his jeans and slipped a condom on to his straining erection. He took a moment to look at them, Meegan spread wide open, Marcos's dick still buried deep inside her, his balls pressed against her lush ass. Daniel couldn't ask for anything more. The best of both worlds, his for the taking with Mistress's Evelyn's blessing of course. He took his hard dick in his hand, climbed over the two of them and pushed his way into Meegan's slick pussy.

"You can move, pup," he told Marcos with a harsh breath and that's when the real fun began. They both fucked her, filled her up until she was sobbing, sweating and limp between them. Daniel could have stayed there forever, but he had to take care of Marcos too, give him a break from the bottom of the pile.

Daniel helped Meegan up, gathering here close as he told Marcos to discard his own condom. Daniel smoothed a few stay hairs away from Meegan's face and kissed her cheeks. "How are we doing?"

"Good. Very good," she said with a drowsy laugh. "Thank you."

"You're welcome, pet."

Meanwhile Marcos tossed the condom he'd used with her and slipped on a new one. After dropping a short kiss on Meegan's lips, Daniel led her to the side of the platform keeping the camera in mind.

"Get me ready," he said to Marcos, but it was Meegan who dropped to her knees and took Daniel's cock in her mouth. Beside them Marcos slathered his dick, waiting a few moments while Meegan went to work before he stepped closer and used his fingers to lubricate Daniel's ass. Daniel had to breathe deep to harness his control. It felt amazing to be buried in Meegan just minutes before, but her mouth and Marcos's skilled fingers at the same time? If edging wasn't his favorite recreational activity, he'd have nutted already.

Eventually, Daniel pulled Meegan to her feet and then bent over the edge of the platform, giving his slicked hole to Marcos who wasted no time pushing all the way to the hilt. Daniel held in a groan of his own, but his leaking cock told on him almost immediately. He leaned into Marcos's strong thrusts, glancing over his shoulder when his rhythm slowed. He wasn't surprised to see that Marcos had gotten distracted, kissing Meegan. Daniel stilled his own hips waiting for Marcos to get back in the game, but it was Meegan who broke the kiss, shooting Daniel a bashful smile. Marcos wrapped his arm around her waist and she rested her head on his shoulder as he continued fuck Daniel's ass.

Soon Daniel let go, white jets of his cum streaking along the black top sheet.

"Come, Marcos," Daniel grunted. "Come inside me."

Another tremor ran through Daniel at the feeling of Marcos's fingers digging into his hip. Marcos came with his own loud grunt and a few "Oh fucks!" Marcos sagged on top of him for a bit before he carefully pulled out. Daniel hated that empty feeling, but he knew Marcos would be up for another round soon, a round they wouldn't record. Daniel stood up and wrung the last drop out of the tip of his dick with his fingers.

"Clean that up," he said to Marcos. Daniel as he zipped himself back into his jeans, his erection almost rising again as he watched Marcos bend over the bed and licked up the whole puddle. Daniel turned to their birthday girl and pulled her closer again, kissing her deeply on the mouth.

"Was that good enough, pet?" he asked as she dropped her head to his shoulder. Meegan nodded, snuggling closer.

"It was perfect."

Daniel had a lot more to do. Cut the video. Aftercare for Marcos and Meegan, a little hydration and a nap for himself before he went back to the rest of the assignments Mistress Evelyn had left him, but as Meegan shivered, burrowing even closer to his warmth, he knew they'd given her a birthday to remember.

TAMED

No. 2 in the Fit Trilogy

About This Book

TAMED
No. 2 in the Fit Trilogy

Nailah Shalaby loves her interior design work almost as much as she loves her family. What she hates is the way her brothers and her father can't seem to stay out of her business. When her current personal trainer and casual sex buddy is exposed in a very public, very scandalous affair—with a client who isn't Nailah—Nailah agrees to switch trainers at her father's insistence. Too bad her father found her another fitness professional whose bright personality and rugged good looks make it impossible for Nailah to see him as anything other than her next conquest.

Armando Vasquez expects a little bit of drama when he agrees to take on the daughter of an acquaintance as a new client. What he doesn't count on is Nailah Shalaby being such a complete ice princess. Always the professional, Armando is determined to ignore Nailah's frosty demeanor while he gets her into the best shape of her life. Their workouts are going as smoothly as planned until Nailah discovers Armando's sexually dominant side and insists he use his knowledge of all things B, D, and S, M to escort her through his world of kink. They can hardly stand each other, but with every erotic encounter neither of them can deny that that thin line between love and hate never felt so good.

This one is for all the Violet fans. Your awesome words encouraged me to write yet another leading lady who takes no crap, even from her Dom.

ONE

Nailah switched the book of samples to her other hand as she stepped out of her car. She almost dropped her phone, but dropped her Prada bag instead. Extra-fucking-late couldn't begin to describe what she was for dinner with her family, but she didn't quite care at that moment. Her day had been a success. She'd landed two new clients through referrals and received some promising news from her brother on a new investment property. Everything was going along just fine until a hiccup with some granite she'd ordered for a client had thrown off her whole afternoon schedule.

As she stepped around the back of her car, her heel caught the slightest tangle of grass and she almost dropped all her stuff again. "Shit!"

"What's wrong?" her assistant Maura asked through the phone.

"Nothing. Dropped my bag on the street and then I almost ate pavement. What were you saying?"

"I was saying if you're going to treat your crazy expensive handbag like shit you should just give it to me."

"I got you the same bag for your birthday, you little asshole! Tell me what Mrs. Levitz said."

"She loved the mock-up, but she was hoping we could change a few of the colors. She thought the brown was a little too dark. She wants you to come by tomorrow."

Nailah quickly thought through her schedule for the next day. She'd been working for herself for a year, and in those twelve months her interior design company, NSL Designs, had taken off. It helped that her brother was a professional flipper, a master of real estate who sent dozens of clients her way, but she'd built a respectable list off her online portfolio alone. Mrs. Levitz, a widow on the mend, had asked her to redesign her whole house. It was Nailah's summer project.

"I have the morning, right? Call her and ask her if 10:00 a.m. is okay."

"Are you excited to see Kalli again?" Maura asked, with a giggle. Nailah's smile matched Maura's giddy tone. It had been two days too long since she'd been with her trainer. Their workouts kept her in great shape. The sex they had kept her sane. Nailah didn't have time to date, but she had to get some quality sex from someone, and who better than from a man she already paid for his other services? The no strings, emotionless arrangement she had with Kalli fit her busy schedule perfectly. Tomorrow they were on for 3:00 p.m. on the dot.

Nailah fished her keys out of her bag and let herself into her parents' house.

"Excited isn't the right word. Let's just say I'll be happy to relieve some of this stress."

"Well are you least going anywhere fun this time?" Maura giggled again. She was engaged, but Nailah knew her own sex life was more exciting than whatever Maura and her fiancé were up to.

"I'm meeting Kalli at the park. Jesus—!" Nailah gasped as her preteen cousin jumped into the hallway.

"No! No, you're not!" the kid sang.

"Is that Aziza?" Maura asked.

"Yeah. It's going to be a long summer. Hold this." Nailah shoved her sample book into Aziza's hands then playful pinched the little girl's shoulder. "What do you know?"

"I know you're not seeing your trainer tomorrow. Uncle fired him."

"What?!"

"Uncle fired your trainer. He fucked up bad."

"Hey, watch your language. Maura, let me call you back." Nailah ended her call with her assistant then shoved her phone into her bag. All the while, Aziza was bouncing back and forth on the balls of her feet.

"Why are you so hyper?" Nailah asked.

"You wanna see?"

"See what?"

"Here. Hold this." Aziza shoved the sample book back into Nailah's hands, then started going through her own cellphone. "That Kalli guy gets around."

Nailah gave up on her armful of crap and put her bag and samples on the floor so she could take Aziza's phone. What she saw was...not good. A picture of Kalli with an older woman. She was bent over an outdoor barbecue, her yoga pants down around her ankles. Kalli's dick was firmly inside of her, that much was obvious. Nailah swallowed the unusual rage that bubbled up into her throat.

"Who is this and where did you get these?"

"That's my friend Ivy's mom. You met Ivy last week. She posted them on Facebook. They're all over Facebook."

"There's more?"

"Scroll left."

Naliah slid her thumb over the screen and saw another and another and another picture of Kalli with this Ivy's mom.

"You showed this to my dad?" Aziza was ten and she had a Facebook page. The terms and conditions stated that she shouldn't even have an account but there she was, doing recon for Nailah's father. Nailah tried to remember that strangling a child was illegal.

"*No*. They were all over Facebook. Ivy was trying to catch her mom in the act. She's been doing it with Kalli for like forever. Auntie knew who it was right away when she saw the pictures. She told Uncle. Facebook already deleted them, but I saved them."

Nailah didn't have time to think about this woman's daughter posting evidence of her infidelity all over the internet, let alone the ridiculous game of connect the dots her parents had participated in. Instead, she sent five of the ten pictures to her own phone. Then she deleted them all from her cousin's cell.

"What are you doing?" Aziza asked.

"You don't need to keep these in your phone."

"Hey!"

"Babies?" Nailah's mother called out. "Come eat dinner."

"Come on." Nailah nudged Aziza down the hall and followed after her. The unmarried members of the Shalaby family joined her parents around the dining room table, including her other cousin, Abasi, and her little brother Haji. They were both busy with their own phones, while her mother set out platters of traditional Egyptian cuisine. Nailah's stomach growled. She was starving, but she had one little issue to attend to.

"Baba, what's going on with Kalli? Aziza said you fired him," she said to her father. Nailah should have never let her father pick up the tab for Kalli's expertise.

Dr. Shalaby took his seat, casually refusing to look Nailah in the eye, something he did when he was knew he was a little bit in the wrong. "He is trash. You'll find someone else." Meaning *I'll find someone else I approve of.*

"Couldn't you have asked me first?"

"Why? You don't need to associate with someone who philanders with his clients."

Philanders? Really, Dad?

Her mother slipped by her and kissed Nailah on her cheeks. "Sit, habebti. Eat."

"Let me go wash my hands."

"You don't need to wash your hands! Eat!" her dad said, gesturing at the food in front of him. Sometimes, her father got so puffed up over nothing. Nailah managed not to roll her eyes and deferred to her mother. She was getting too old for this.

"Om?"

"Go wash your hands then come back and eat." Her father grunted and went on grumbling in Arabic, but Nailah ignored him to duck into the powder room just off her parents' kitchen. She pulled her phone out of her pocket and started texting like mad. She attached one of the pictures she'd taken from Aziza's phone.

> Are you fucking serious with this shit?

They weren't exclusive. They weren't even dating, but Nailah liked to think that Kalli had some scruples, some standards. She was all for equal opportunity, but she was not the kind of girl who liked to share the hot guy she was screwing with women who were older than her mom.

Kalli texted back right away.

> I can't.

"You can't *what*?" Nailah had a habit of getting animated, even if she was talking to herself. "That's not even a complete sentence."

> What the hell? What do you mean you can't?

> I can't talk to you anymore.

Nailah's thumbs worked double-time.

Nailah could find another trainer, one she'd pay for, but Kalli owed her an explanation. And maybe one final bang session. She hadn't decided yet. Kalli's next texts came through rapid fire, one after another.

Her brother? How did Garai even know about them?

Fine, Nailah said in her final text. If Kalli couldn't be man enough to stand up to her brother or have damn a conversation with her, the person he was fucking, she couldn't be bothered with him. After another lovely family dinner, she'd have Maura find her a new trainer. When she had some free moments, Nailah would have to find someone else to fulfill her other needs.

It took a few minutes for Armando to make his way across the semi-crowded bondage club. Known simply as THE CLUB, most in their circle of kink referred to the refurbished warehouse as Philip's, after the man who had bought the place almost thirty years ago and turned it into the den of sin, the home away from home, it was today.

After he greeted some old friends and introduced himself to a few new players, Armando settled into the leather couch and finally shook off the exhaustion from a long week. A long month actually. Melrose Fitness, the high-end gym he co-owned, was going through a lot of changes. Between the on-going debate he had with his team about expansion and the new electronic filing system they'd recently implemented, Armando was stretching himself thin making sure his clientele still received the top-notch service they were paying for.

Not that he should complain. Armando was one of those people who could really look at his life and say he was happy. He loved owning his own business. He had a supportive family and great friends, friends like Master Philip, who really knew how to maximize some free time. That might be his only problem at the moment. Hard work and not nearly enough play. Armando usually flew solo to Master Philip's larger BDSM parties, where a few unattached submissives were invited. He'd find someone to play with for a little while. Maybe someone to take home for the night.

In the meantime, he waited for the show to start. Grant, his best friend, fellow trainer and business partner in Melrose Fitness, was slowly trying to ease his girlfriend Violet into his life of kink. The two of them had been playing for a few months at Grant's condo, but tonight was Violet's first visit to their mentor's private bondage club. Armando was mostly there for moral support. He sat quietly while Violet commented on and questioned everything going on around them.

Grant was more of a Dom's Dominant. He loved loving on submissives. He'd taught Violet a lot about things like orgasm control and obeying some commands. She loved talking back, but it seemed like they'd worked out a pretty good system. She was easing into more and more bondage techniques, but they had yet to try any sort of pain or impact play. That was more Armando's bag.

He was a consummate sadist. If Violet was up for it, Armando could demonstrate a few things. On another bottom of course. Grant wasn't willing to share. Armando didn't blame him. Physically, Armando didn't have a type, but even if he did, he would've still found Violet attractive. Grant was a lucky man.

The three of them waited on a curved leather couch positioned to give the perfect view of another good friend of theirs as he prepared to demonstrate his skills with a good old-fashioned flogger. Daniel Song had lost the lower portion of his right arm in a workplace accident about five years before he and Armando met. Didn't slow him down much though. He'd simply learned how to wield his implements of pleasure and pain with his left hand and gone about his business.

Armando loved watching Daniel work. He was a true professional. Maybe it helped that he was a switch, playing the roles of either Dominant or submissive whenever the scene called for it. Daniel knew both sides of the coin so well. When he was in control, he knew how to read his playthings better than most. Whatever his secret was, it worked.

Armando relaxed some more as Daniel led an older white woman named May over to the cross. Violet was asking Grant questions. What was the wooden X thing called? Was it necessary? Was he going to use a whip on that woman? Armando smiled to himself as Grant answered. He missed the days when he was green and learning. There was something to discover with every partner, but he missed the excitement of experiencing the scene for the first time.

And it had been years since he'd played with someone who was on their way in. He thought he didn't have the patience for it. He liked a woman who knew the limits of her submission, but listening to Grant and Violet talk to each other, knowing what her inexperience did for Grant, how teaching Violet made Grant feel as a Top and a man, made Armando think he'd been limiting himself by sticking to one type of submissive.

Finally, the show started. You couldn't hear what Daniel said to May, but you *could* see the slight shiver that traveled over her body as he whispered in her ear. Daniel tucked the flogger under his right armpit and ran the fingers of his left hand down May's back and over her bare ass.

Violet shuddered then settled further into Grant's lap. May nodded a few times then let Daniel kiss the corner of her mouth. The first blow landed right across May's ass. Her body tensed for a fraction of a second before she relaxed again. Beside Armando, Violet gasped.

*

Daniel went at May for a while, until her ass was glowing a bright red. Afterward, he pulled her down from the cross and took her to a nearby sitting area, where he started in with the aftercare. When they were settled, their captive audience finally let out a sigh of a relief. Armando was completely hard, contemplating what his next move would be. Grant had already made up his mind.

He got up from the couch, pulling Violet with him. "We're gonna take off."

"Sounds good." Armando stood and clapped Grant on the back. The night was young, but Armando completely understood. Grant and Violet could stay and make use of Master Philip's facilities, but why not take the party home to the comfort of their own bed? Armando said his goodbyes to Violet then turned to survey the room.

The real show would start on the main stage in a little while. Still, the place was buzzing with activity. Couples, a few singles, even small clusters, were mingling and thinking of play. A twosome nearby was surveying a bench. A man on his own checked out the set of stocks closer to the beverage area. A small group of ladies gathered around one of the upgraded cage and pole set-ups Philip had added on either side of the main stage. Armando caught the eye of a short black woman standing in front of the cage. She was eyeing him actually, whispering in her friend's ear. They were new to Philip's. At least Armando had never seen them before. It would be impolite if he didn't mosey over and introduce himself.

He made it two steps before Meegan, one of the many pets kept by Master Philip and his wife, intercepted him.

"Mr. Vasquez?"

"Hey, Meegan. What's up?"

"Master Philip would like to speak with you."

Armando followed Meegan's line of vision to the glass window above the main floor. The glass was tinted, but he knew Master Philip stood behind it, looking out over the party, brandy in hand. Armando thanked Meegan, kissed her cheek, then headed toward the hidden exit in the far corner.

Upstairs, he knocked on his mentor's door before letting himself in. Just as Armando expected, Master Philip stood by the window that gave him a view of the whole club below.

"The Great and Powerful would like a word?"

Philip smiled as he turned around. He lifted the tumbler in his hand. "Brandy?"

"No, thanks." Armando didn't like to drink and play.

"How is Miss Violet doing? I saw her and Grant leave."

Armando shrugged and offered his own smile. "She seems to be doing all right. Think they just wanted to be alone. I'll be honest, Grant shocked me with her."

"Me too, but I believe they have what it takes to last." Strong words coming from Philip, but Armando had to agree. "That's not what I wanted to speak with you about."

"I figured. What's on your mind?"

"I need a favor. It's a bit of a situation."

"Okay..."

"Do you know a trainer by the name of Kalli Norwalk?"

Oh, Armando knew him. The world of high-end trainers was pretty small. He'd run into "Kalli" every few months, listen to him brag about his latest conquest and come away glad as shit that he didn't have to deal with a douche like that in Grant.

Armando rolled his eyes. "You mean Clarence Normand? Yeah, I know him."

Philip let out a short laugh. "Personas can make or break your business, I suppose. Well, Clarence has apparently gotten himself into a little trouble with some of his clients and their husbands."

"About time. He's not that slick with his side scamming. What does that have to do with me? Or you?"

"He was training the daughter of a colleague."

"Oh."

"Yes. *Oh*. My friend, Dr. Shalaby, released Kalli from his role with his daughter. She's a little sore about him interfering in her personal life. He's not concerned about them continuing their tryst, but now she needs a new trainer."

"Oh sure," Armando said, feeling relieved. "Send her by the gym. We'll set her up with Keira. She gets along with everyone. Hell, Keira knows Kalli too. Maybe once this girl hears the whole truth about him she'll be glad her dad butted in."

"I think the situation is more complicated than that. His daughter wants a male trainer, I suspect so she can continue with her extracurricular exploits, but Dr. Shalaby wants her with someone who won't give in to her temptations. And honestly, I would rather you looked after her."

Armando knew he was making a face. "Uh, can I ask why? Do I *want* to get involved in this?"

"There's a reason I'm coming to you. Dr. Shalaby, while a brilliant surgeon and an extremely kind man, wants to guide the direction of his daughter's behavior and he wants me to find someone to help him with that guidance."

Armando was definitely making a face now. "How old is this girl?"

"Twenty-four."

Young, Armando thought, but still, she was an adult capable of making her own decisions. He blew out a deep breath. There was more to this, but something told him Philip wanted him to figure it out on his own. Philip waited while he considered all the angles. Finally it dawned on him.

"You don't want me to participate in this at all. You just want her around someone *you* trust."

Philip nodded a bit and offered a slight smile. "What's happening between her and her father is between them, but I'm slightly offended that he thought *I* would happily go along with his plan to keep her under his thumb. After all, she's done nothing wrong."

Armando had to agree. A young woman's sex life and her father's beef with it wasn't something he wanted to get involved with at all, but if her father needed the peace of mind that she was working with someone who wasn't trying to fuck her, Armando had no problem with that. Yeah he had a strong sexual appetite, but the business came first. And even if this girl was completely his type, ready and willing, the drama she would be bringing to the table pretty much guaranteed he would keep his hands to himself.

Armando pulled out his phone. "Go ahead. Give me her number."

Two

Nailah glared at her brother across the half-built kitchen counter. The new property would sell as soon as the renovations were finished, with the aid of Nailah's immaculate staging, of course. That was, if she decided to help her brother again. She was seriously questioning it after the stunt he'd pulled.

"I can take care of myself, G."

"Who said you couldn't?"

"You! Acting like some psycho, showing up at Kalli's house. Why would you do that?"

"Nailah, listen. I know you're a big girl. You're a strong, independent woman—"

"Shut up."

"But I can't have a guy like that making a fool out of my little sister."

"Who says he was making a fool out of me?" Okay, maybe she had been a little foolish, thinking she was the only one of his clients Kalli was fucking, but that was her problem to deal with.

"So you were sleeping with him?"

Nailah's eyes narrowed. "No."

"Whatever. The guy's a dirtbag and he needs to stay away from you, period. Now, my darling sister, will you please come over here and tell me if this will work as an accent wall?"

"I don't know how, but I'm going to make you pay for this."

"I don't know how either. You got nothing on me, sister."

"Oh, there's always Isra." Nailah was just talking now. She was super close with Garai's wife, but the two of them were a solid team, one of those annoying couples who were not only lovers but best friends and were constantly reminding everyone within earshot of that fact. Isra would help Nailah trick her husband with a harmless prank, but nothing more. She loved Garai too much.

"Good luck with that," Garai scoffed. "She thinks Kalli's a loser too."

"You told Isra?" Jesus Christ, who didn't know all her business?

"She's my wife. She's my—"

"Yeah, she's your best friend. You tell her everything. Ugh. I hate you."

Nailah rounded the counter and looked at the mockup on her brother's computer screen. Garai had bought a fixer-upper from a couple who had filed for bankruptcy three days after they started their own renovations. They'd shown Garai the plans they'd set in motion, but he wanted Nailah's opinion on the overall aesthetic.

It took two seconds for Nailah to spot the problem. "Nope. Won't work."

"What's the issue?" Garai asked, just as Nailah's cell phone started to ring.

Nailah reached into the pocket of her blazer and pulled out her iPhone. She didn't recognize the number on the screen. "This is Nailah Shalaby with NSL Designs. How may I help you?"

"Nailah? This is Armando Vasquez at Melrose Fitness. Your father informed me you were looking for a new trainer. I just wanted to reach out to you and see if you wanted to set up a consultation."

Nailah groaned nice and loud into the phone. "Ugh, yeah. What was your name again?"

"Armando Vasquez. Is this a bad time?"

"No, no. Now's fine. We can skip the consultation. I just need to work out. Um, how about Tuesdays, Thursdays, and Saturdays at nine a.m.?" She'd been meaning to switch her workouts to mornings.

"Yeah, we can do that. So I'll see you tomorrow then?"

"Yup, tomorrow." Nailah got the address to the gym and Armando's barely helpful suggestions for parking. Then, she hung up. After she finished with her brother, she had three other projects to attend to. She didn't have time to hang out on the phone.

"Who was that?" Garai asked.

"My new trainer, I guess. Why? You want his home address too?"

Nailah almost growled when her brother burst out laughing. "Not if he can keep his hands to himself." She didn't think that would be a problem. As far as she was concerned, there would be no more mixing business with pleasure.

Nailah was running late. Then, of course, Melrose Fitness didn't have their own parking lot. She had to drive around in circles for five extra minutes until a man, doing his rumpled walk of shame, moved his beat down Altima out of a space right in front of the gym. Even as she stepped out of her car, in her head, she had already moved on with her day. There was work to do at her office, then she had to meet Garai and another client to discuss the hideous condo the woman had just purchased. He'd talked Nailah's talents up and now the client was ready to pull the trigger on some design work.

Nailah considered having Maura come along so she could take

notes and pictures as they walked around the property. That way, Nailah could focus on her client. She sent Maura a text as she backed her way through the front door of the gym. She stopped just on the other side, her thumbs padding out across her screen of her phone.

"Nailah?" Vaguely, she sensed the owner of the voice coming closer to her, but Maura was texting back. She just needed to wrap this up.

"Yeah."

"Hi. I'm Armando." This Armando guy was right in front of her. Nailah sensed the height of him towering over her, but Maura was saying that she couldn't find the camera. Did Nailah have it or had Maura left in her car?

"You ready to get started?" Right. She came there to work out. One last text, just to tell Maura she'd check her trunk. Then, she looked up.

A strange noise came out of her mouth, like a low-grade sort of squawk. Then, she licked her lips as if the sweep of her tongue would recalibrate her brain. "Jesus Christ."

Armando smiled down at her and let out a rough laugh. "Everything okay?"

Nailah jostled her head to clear it. "Yeah, sorry. Sorry, I'm late." She held up her phone. "Just a little client business."

"No problem. You wanna get started?"

"Yeah... I..." Nailah could not stop staring. This Armando guy was drop-dead gorgeous. Deeply tanned skin and a thick goatee. And his eyes, a brown so deep Nailah just knew they held all kinds of interesting secrets. The man was tall, chiseled. His hair was long on the top, but styled back and shaved on the sides. Nailah almost shivered.

"Are you sure you're okay?"

No. She really wasn't. She didn't know whether to laugh at herself or walk right out the door. "Yeah, I just–I don't know what my father was thinking. Calling you, I mean."

"Come on." Armando took her keys and cellphone, placing them in a cubby by the door. Then he motioned for her to join him over by a rack of weights.

Nailah explained, as they walked across the room. "I had some... issues with my last trainer, and considering your overall aesthetic appeal, I'm not sure why he thought you were a better choice."

"Are you saying I'm too good looking to train you?" Even his teasing scowl was sexy. Nailah almost looked away.

"No, no. I–"

"Listen. I wasn't going to say anything, and I'm not assuming anything about you, I just...I know Kalli. I know what he's about. We're very happy to have you here with us, but I'm not that kind of guy and this is not that kind of gym. We'll have a good time. We'll have some good workouts. It'll all be good."

His perfect white teeth gleamed under his perfectly trimmed mustache. Nailah didn't know whether to be pissed off or turned on. He was just so damn attractive, but what the fuck did he know about her and Kalli? Why did he know about Kalli at all? Why'd he have to be so hot?

Nailah swallowed and squared her shoulders. She needed her control back. "I'd appreciate it if we didn't talk about Kalli."

Armando offered her a sobering nod. "Deal. Let's get all your stats down and then you tell me about your goals."

After Armando weighed her in, she filled out all her info on a tablet—their plan to cut down on paper waste, he explained. They talked about the ass Nailah wanted to sculpt and the bit of her stomach she wanted to trim down. Her arm strength was pretty non-existent, so she wanted to work on that too. When Nailah actually thought about it, Kalli didn't train her that well. Their sessions were more like foreplay than actually workouts. She maintained her weight through her own effort, but none of the goals she set when she signed up with Kalli had been met. She explained all this to Armando, and for the fifty minutes that followed, he made her work her ass off.

∗

"Lady, those mini blinds are so ugly. Like real fucking ugly," Nailah said to herself. Everyone teased her about the way she had full conversations with no one else in the room, but she could never come up with a good reason to make herself stop, so she just went with it. Even now, with her office door wide open, her and her brother's assistants sitting ten feet away, she didn't really care if she sounded crazy or not.

"Nope, that's ugly too."

Mrs. Levitz had sent over some ideas for her daughter's bedroom, dozens of links for paint colors, light fixtures, and decor that all clashed or looked flat- out hideous. Luckily, Mrs. Levitz was just trying to be more helpful than insistent. Nailah could use maybe one of her ideas. It wouldn't be too tough to steer her client away from the rest.

"I found him!" Maura shouted from the next room.

"Oh my god, he's cute," Brian added. Garai's assistant was a great asset to Shalaby-Gold Realty, when he wasn't drifting down the hall to play with Maura.

"Nailah, you wanna see? I think we found some good dirt."

That had her attention. "Yeah, yeah! Let me see. Bring it in here."

She absently registered Maura and Brian bolting into her office, chattering on as they came. Nailah finally looked up from her email when Maura plopped her laptop down on the desk.

"That's him, right?"

After their first workout together, Nailah checked out the Melrose Fitness company website and spent a few moments drooling over Armando's picture on the ABOUT US page. She had work to do and beauty sleep to catch up on, but as soon as she got back to the office the following day she put Maura up to further recon.

Nailah scanned over the Facebook profile in front of her before her eyes focused on the profile picture itself. The page most definitely belonged to Armando Vasquez, her new trainer and one of the sexiest men she had even seen up close. "Yep. That's him."

She should have scoped him out before she went over to Melrose Fitness, but she was so busy and still so irritated with her father, she'd simply put the address into her phone and prayed he was at least tolerable enough to spend a sweaty hour with.

Tolerable would have been a blessing. What she got was a complete punishment. He said his only interest was helping her sculpt the body she wanted. That didn't change the array of sudden interests that popped up in her mind. How could she not sleep with him? Not only was he a work of art to behold but everything about him, his voice, his demeanor, his smile, even his eyebrows—which weren't manicured but still managed to be perfectly in control— screamed mount me, do me, fuck me until you can barely move. She had been a fool with Kalli. He was a boy. A pitiful pastime. Armando Vasquez was a man. A man she could really spend some quality time with.

"Okay." Nailah pushed her laptop to the side and pulled Maura's computer closer. "Let's see what we can find."

"Start with his tagged photos," Brian suggested. "You can usually find the best dirt from the people who've tagged him."

Nailah clicked on his photos and saw that Brian was right. Armando had tons of public photos of him with his friends. She recognized his co-workers from the gym, this white guy Grant something or other and a pretty black woman named Keira. A ton of pictures of the three of them being fitness-minded at different fitness-related events. There was a picture of Armando with Kalli at a fitness expo. Nailah quickly moved on from that and clicked on a picture that looked like Armando with his family and some friends. A Javier, Maria, and Connie Vasquez were bunched around Armando, who towered over all of them except for a Mark Vasquez, a taller, older black man who stood behind the girl tagged Maria.

The next picture was of the two older men, Javier and Mark, kissing Armando on either cheek. Nailah ignored Maura and Brian's awwww's of sweetness, but she had to admit to herself that the picture was pretty cute.

It took some clicking, and a solid five minutes of Brian and Maura saying "Click that one. Click that one," but finally things got interesting. The first gem they found was a few years old, a picture of Armando with a different older black man and a younger white girl. Armando was in a t-shirt. The girl was wearing a collar and a corset that pushed her boobs up to her chin. The other man was wearing a leather vest that hung open, revealing some ink on his chest. He looked familiar, but Nailah couldn't place him. The caption read "Sir and I ran into Master Philip at the expo." Nailah read it out loud.

"Hello!" Brian added.

"Is that the kink expo they have down at the convention center?" Maura asked.

"What do you know about it?" Nailah couldn't hide her shock.

"They put a billboard up near my apartment every year."

"Click on the Master Philip guy," Brian suggested.

Nailah clicked through to his profile and found more gilded breadcrumbs. This Philip guy was massively into kink. All his pictures were relatively g- rated, but most of them were taken at some kind of fetish event. Nailah was surprised when she came across pictures of him and a woman named Evelyn Baker, who he'd tagged as his wife, sitting on the beach. But the rest of the pictures? Leather. So much leather.

"Go to his 'about' tab." Brian suggested. "There. Click that."

The URL took them to a fetish site, kinklife.com. "You have to have a profile to view his page," Nailah said as she reached a digital roadblock.

"So let's make one. Here." Maura grabbed her laptop back and flopped into the chair on the other side of Nailah's desk.

Nailah tried to focus on Mrs. Levitz and her home decor, but she couldn't keep her mind off Armando and his interesting group of acquaintances. "I wonder if he's still with her," she pondered out loud.

"With who?" Brian asked.

"Uh, no one." She was thinking of the girl who'd referred to Armando as Sir, Tina something. The jab of jealousy she felt made no sense, but it was there, poking her like a stick.

"Okay. I made you a new email account to register with," Maura boasted, as if she'd just scored Nailah her dream client. She handed the laptop back to Nailah, as she scurried behind her chair.

"Queen_oftheNile? Really?" Nailah looked at the profile name they'd come up with, right next to a picture of a woman's hands holding a set of golden handcuffs.

"It's just for stalking purposes," Maura said, offering a shrug.

"Very subtle." Nailah clicked on the link next to Master Philip's profile. "There's a lot going on."

The man's page boasted over one thousand pictures, a bio longer than Nailah's arm and more personal associations than one could follow. He was in a relationship with a MistresstoherKnight, who she quickly discovered was his wife Evelyn, but his leather family, whatever the fuck that was, was a list of nearly ten people. Nailah clicked on pictures, knowing she'd have better luck finding Armando on sight rather than looking for some silly nickname.

Third row down, second picture in, there he was. Nailah could almost feel the anticipation coming off of Brian and Maura as they looked over her shoulder. He wasn't tagged in the picture, but he'd liked it. His face was clearly visible in a little icon off to the right.

She didn't wait for any comments or directions from the peanut gallery. His page told her a few things right off the bat. He knew how to pose for a good photo. The larger version of his profile picture showed him shirtless, his body half-cast in shadow.

He had tattoos all down his right side and up his left shoulder and left pec. His profile said he was a Dominant and that he was single. So much for the girl from the expo.

Nailah clicked on his pictures.

"Oh my god!" Maura screeched.

"What?!" Nailah's eyes darted back and forth across the screen, searching for the source of the shock.

"That's what." Brian pointed at the screen, at a picture of a very nude Armando where he was sporting a very real hard on.

"Out. Everybody out!"

"What?" Brian said.

"I need a minute and you don't need to be looking at this. Out."

"But I need my laptop to work," Maura said.

"Here." Nailah grabbed her wallet and slapped all the cash she had in Maura's palm. "Go get lunch."

"It's 10:30."

"Go to Starbucks! Take Brian. Tell Garai it was my idea. Go."

"Come on, Maur. She needs some alone time with that picture." Nailah's glare wiped the smirk right off Brian's face as he ran out the door.

When she was finally alone, Nailah let out a deep breath. The nudity wasn't that big of a deal, on its own, but finding this whole other side to the lighthearted man she'd met the day before was a lot to process. She clicked through the whole set of photos, all erotic nudes of Armando displaying different items. A whip, a set of handcuffs, a length of rope. There were more pictures of him at different events.

She recognized Master Philip and that Grant guy in a handful of them. These guys really knew how to have a good time. And then there were the women. Various women in various states of undress, some in leather, some in lace, some completely nude, over

Armando's knee, on their knees at his feet, trailing a few steps behind him as he led them on a leash.

Nailah felt herself growing hot all over. The craziest thing she'd ever done was have sex with Kalli in the backseat of his car. She'd never imagined a sex life like the one Armando was deeply engaged in. She knew it was none of her business, but she had to know more about Mr_V724.

✴

Something was up with Nailah Shalaby. Not that he knew her really at all, but during their first session she'd been pretty talkative. Gruff and direct, but they talked the whole time. Today, she was acting...weird. She wasn't talking much and she was pointedly avoiding eye contact with him. She'd admitted to finding him attractive, but insisted in almost the same breath that she'd be able to put that attraction aside so they could work together.

Their first session had gone perfectly well. His own raging attraction to Nailah aside, he thought she was a great client. He'd looked her up before he'd even called her, as was the unofficial protocol with all referrals. It seemed like something he specifically had to do this time, especially from the way Master Philip presented the situation to him. Her page was easy to find on Facebook. Her interior design company popped up after a quick Google search. Digging up information on her proved to be a good idea. It prepared him for just how hot she was.

Nailah Shalaby was a damn goddess. She was nearly a foot shorter than him, petite in some ways, but she was thick with perfectly shaped legs and an amazing ass. He was a little shocked when she said she wanted to "work on it", but he kept his opinion out of the conversation. She had beautiful caramel-brown eyes and these kissable pink lips, but she was off limits and all business, so that made his job much easier. Or at least it had, before she stopped speaking to him.

During their first session, she joked a little here and there. Complained just enough as he added weights, but stuck it out and pushed through to the end. She even thanked him for pushing her before she took off. Now? He wondered if something had happened. Was she having a terrible day or was she angrier about his knowledge of her relationship with Kalli than she'd initially let on? Did he smell? Finally, he just asked.

"How are you doing today? You're a little quiet."

Nailah nodded, but still kept her gaze toward the floor as she completed another curl. "Yeah, I'm great. I'm just sweating it out. Pumping this iron."

Armando smiled to himself. She probably just had a lot on her mind. Clearly, he was making something out of nothing. "Two more."

She finished her set and they moved on to some heavier weights so she could complete her squats. As soon as they finished up, they had a quick chat about a few nutritional changes she wanted to make in order to reach her goals a little faster.

"You're doing great, Nailah." Armando meant the bit of encouragement. So far her effort and no-nonsense approach made her a dream client. "Do you have any questions for me?" He followed her over to the cubbies, where she grabbed her keys and her phone.

"Actually, yeah." Nailah said. And then, for the first time all day, she looked him in the eye. "What exactly is a leather family?"

Armando almost took a step back, but he managed to keep it together. "Say that again?"

"A leather family. I noticed you weren't a part of one, but some of your buddies are. But I couldn't quite figure out what it was, exactly."

Armando took a deep breath and scrubbed his face with his hands.

"Nailah, listen. I don't know what you think—"

"Oh, I know what I think. I just figured since you were all up in my business with Kalli, it's only fair that we're on the same page. You knew a little bit about my personal life and now I know a little about yours. I'd say we're even, but still—so many questions."

It was rare for Armando to be struck speechless, but he had no clue what to say.

Nailah sighed and rolled her eyes. "I want to know more, okay?"

"About what?"

"Your kinks. Kink. The kinky things you do."

"Why?"

"Why not?"

Armando threw up his hands and started pacing away. Clients for Keira's first class would come walking through the door any minute. He needed to get Nailah out of there. When he turned around she was waiting impatiently, with her hands on her hips, like he owed her an explanation.

"I...can we not talk about this right now?"

"Fine. We'll talk about it later. I usually get home from the office around six, but I'm having dinner with my parents tonight, so let's say you call me around nine?"

The fuck? Armando felt the sentiment written all over his face and it pissed him off even more that Nailah still didn't seem the slightest bit fazed by his shocked expression.

"How about no. If you really want to talk about this, *you* can come by my place at nine-thirty and we can have a real conversation, unless you're not allowed out past curfew."

That got to her. Her nostrils flared as she straightened her spine. "I don't have a fucking curfew. Just text me your address. I'll be there."

"Sounds great."

"Sure does. Bye." Nailah spun on her heel and stormed out of the gym.

Armando stood there staring at the fogged glass doors, wondering what the fuck had just happened.

THREE

Armando checked himself in the mirror one more time before he headed back out to the living room. His place was always spotless—his mother didn't raise slobs—, but he still straightened the cushions on the couch and double-checked the ice maker. According to the text she'd sent a little while ago, Nailah would be there any minute.

Armando straightened his shirt one more time before he grabbed his keys and ran down to the main courtyard. Grant's condo was just across the grass, but he was at the gym closing things up with Keira while Armando saw to Nailah Shalaby and her list of really intrusive questions.

Her black BMW pulled up just as he came through the outer door of their complex. When she stepped up on the curb, he knew he'd made a huge mistake. She looked good in workout gear, but the outfit she had on now was too much. A billowy, see- through white blouse and a skintight blue mini skirt, and some tall, tall gold heels that made her legs look impossibly long. Her hair was down, spilling along her shoulders. He really considered calling it a night right then and there. She had no business setting foot in his house.

The hellos they exchanged were awkward, but her comments

on the architecture and decor of the building broke up a bit of the tension.

"See you found the place okay," he said, when they finally walked into his condo.

"Yeah, wasn't too hard." She reached into her enormous purse then and handed him a heavy bottle with a gold label. "It's Egyptian wine."

"Thank you. That's very kind of you, but we'll save this for another time. Can I offer you some water or a soda?"

"Water would be fine." She sat on the couch and he went to the fridge, then joined her with two glasses of ice water. There was no reason for him to be nervous. He had this under control.

"Alright. Let's get a few things straight first. Your father contacted my mentor Philip and asked him to find you a trainer that he knew wouldn't try to sleep with you. So any beef you have about me knowing your business, you need to take up with your dad. When I mentioned Kalli, I was only trying to be transparent with you. I wasn't trying to humiliate you, which seemed to be your angle when you came at me with that leather family business."

Nailah just looked down at her skirt and pursed her lips, so Armando kept going.

"That said, if you're curious about the lifestyle, I'm happy to share some information. Even introduce you to a few people if you want. I have to have one condition though. Whatever happens, we keep this separate from whatever we're doing in the gym. If you're paying me for an hour to train you, then I'm going to train you. We're not discussing any of this during that hour. Okay?"

Nailah let out a quick breath before she met his gaze. "Yeah, that sounds fine."

"Okay. So, in this digital age, you can find everything you need to know about erotic power exchange online. Do you really want to know more from me, or are you just trying to get back at me?"

Nailah sighed and leaned back against the couch. "I'm not

trying to get back at you. I'm genuinely interested. I did look you up, and I did follow a trail of interesting breadcrumbs to your kinklife page, but what I found shocked me in a good way."

"How so?"

"I've always been...sexual. I think of myself as a sexual person. Some women are into relationships. I like sex. I think that's why Kalli and I got along. But just from the little bit I saw from your page and looking around the Internet—I knew people were into this type of shit, but I didn't really picture it. No, that's a lie. I've pictured it, but what I imagined and what I saw were so different. It's one thing to hear about things like bondage and sadism, but to know someone who's into it? That's different."

"More people are into it than you think."

"And I like that too. I like that it seems to be this big secret, but one that's right there in the open, if you know what to look for. My father knows your Master Philip friend from the hospital. Apparently, they've been close for years, but I know for a fact that my dad knows nothing about this. He never would have asked Philip to find a trainer for me if he'd had even the slightest clue."

"Are you sure about that? Our parents have their own private lives too, ya know."

"No. Trust me. My mom's probably got a little freak in her, but my dad is solidly square."

"Okay. What else? What else shocked you? What else interests you about all this?"

A hint of pink flashed up Nailah's face. "I looked through your pictures. And even though your nudes were pretty impressive, I kept clicking on the pictures of you with other women."

Armando knew exactly what pictures she was talking about. And as Nailah's eyes met his, he felt the air shift between them. She was opening up, and even though he was still kinda pissed at her, he knew if he didn't listen now and give her the proper shoulder to lean on, she might seek out someone else to show her the ropes. Someone who would use her or push her in the wrong directions.

He relaxed a little and adopted a more soothing tone to his voice. "What about them? What was it about those women?"

"I was jealous of them. Actually, envious of them is more accurate. There was one where you were in the middle of paddling one woman and it seemed like she was squirming in your lap, and I felt like I wanted that. I do want that."

It was Tina she was talking about. They'd played together, had some really fucking fun times together for about eight months, but she'd moved for work and they'd both decided to move on.

"What else?"

"There was another one, the same woman, but maybe a different time? The lighting looked different. She was sitting on the floor at your feet, with her arms like wrapped around your legs, and you were stroking her hair, and she just looked so peaceful. I don't think I've ever felt that way."

The image popped into Armando's head before he could stop himself. Nailah naked, leaning against him in a similar way after an intense spanking and a thorough fucking. He swallowed before he spoke again. "So you want to explore impact play— spanking, paddling, flogging," he said. "And you're interested in exploring submission?"

"Yes. I am."

"And you want to do all this with me?"

"Yes."

Armando didn't want to insult her by asking why again. He understood why. He was the only person in the lifestyle that she knew. She trusted him to a degree. And then there was the fact that they were clearly attracted to each other. But he knew what it was like with your first, knew how intense that bond could be. Did he want that with Nailah? He didn't know. At this point, the pros matched the cons, which brought him to the only logical conclusion. Say yes now and deal with the rest later.

"Gimme a second." Armando left the couch and went to grab his laptop.

✴

Nailah didn't know exactly what was happening, but she didn't want it to stop. Over an hour later she found herself on the other end of the couch, pressed tight against Armando's side. Her bare feet were tucked under her butt and his arm was around her shoulders. His laptop was balanced on her thighs. At some point, the tension between them seemed to fade away. He told her to move closer. She joked that he was typing too slowly and now they were here.

She loved the way he smelled. He didn't wear any sort of cologne. It was just his soap and something natural to him. Nailah had to stop herself from nuzzling and maybe licking his neck every time he started talking. He was warm and solid. She was going to have to force herself to go home when their time together was over.

"Go to the submissivehandbook.com and email that link to yourself," he instructed. It was the tenth link he'd recommended that she check out before they got started.

"You're giving me so much homework, I'll be forty before we even do anything."

His chest rumbled with laughter against her side. "You'll thank me. I promise."

They visited two more sites that featured some implements, but it was mostly more reading. Lots and lots of reading. And then Armando took over the keyboard, just for a minute. "Let's watch this. Break up the monotony a little bit. Buddy of mine made this."

The video started with an Asian guy sitting on a couch. He had on jeans and a white undershirt that stretched across his muscular chest. He had pretty buff arms, but the right one seemed to have been amputated just below the elbow. He said something that Nailah couldn't make out, and a second later a woman with deep brown skin stepped into the frame. She was completely naked. Her curly hair was pulled up in a ponytail. She handed him a square paddle and then followed his instructions when he directed her across his lap.

He leaned down and whispered something in her ear. She nodded, turning her face up a bit to look at him, whispering something back. He leaned down further and kissed her on the mouth. The whole time his hand was gently rubbing her ass. Nailah tried to remain calm, but she was aching to squirm around. She held still though. Somehow, rubbing up against Armando didn't seem like a good idea.

Then the paddling started. The woman's body jumped with every smack, even though Nailah could tell she was also struggling to hold still. The man paddled her ass for a long time, increasing the force of impact as the seconds went by. Eventually, the woman was screaming, but for some reason, Nailah didn't think they were exactly screams of pain. They sounded more like cries of frustration. He struck her five more times, just as much as it seemed she could handle, and then he stopped.

The man calmly set the paddle down on the couch. In the next moment, he slid his fingers between her legs and started fucking her with his hand. The woman really started squirming then, and she was crying. The man turned her, cradling the back of her head with his other arm so she was facing the back of the couch. But he kept fucking her. Now, he was kissing her, her lips and her face as she seemed to calm down. It was like she needed to relax before she could come. And did she come, loud and trembling in his arms. Her orgasm went on forever.

When she finally stopped shaking, the man pulled his fingers from between her legs and urged her to lick them. She did it slowly but without hesitation, and after that the man just held her. After a while the man stood up and ended the video. Nailah sat there, staring at the frozen image of the front of his shirt where it clung to his abs. She was afraid to say anything. Her whole body was vibrating, her skin tight and hot. She knew her breathing sounded funny. She'd never felt this way with Kalli.

Armando took the laptop and moved it to his coffee table. Nailah had no idea what he saw when he turned around and looked at her, but she felt raw and exposed.

"Okay?" he asked, flashing her a hopeful smile.

Nailah nodded then swallowed, smoothing her skirt down like it would stop her horny from showing. "Yeah," she said, even though her voice didn't sound right.

"What did you see in that video?"

"A spanking. I mean, a paddling, right?"

"Right. And what else? Tell me about the woman."

Nailah was quiet for a moment, replaying the video in her head. "She wanted the paddling. And she seemed... she changed as the video went on. Maybe nervous at first, but then it was like she had some sort of emotional release."

"And what about him?"

"He was...in control. I'm sure he was turned on, but that didn't seem to matter. He was so focused. Is it always like that?"

"When it's right? Yeah. Let's call it a night."

Before we fuck each other's brains out? she wanted to say, but she kept that to herself.

"Yeah, I should probably get home." She stood and stretched, trying to ignore the hum that still radiated through her body. Armando stood too, and did absolutely nothing to hide the enormous bulge fighting against the zipper of his jeans. Nailah stepped into her shoes, then scrambled to grab her bag and started for the door. Armando walked her all the way down to her car.

"So what now?" What happens right now? What happens tomorrow? Are we supposed to kiss or...?

"I'll probably stay up for a few more hours kicking myself for not asking you to spend the night."

Nailah glared up at him. "Are you flirting with me now?"

"There are rules, but I think flirting's allowed, if you want it to be."

"I'm considering it. But yeah, after you cope with your regret, what do we do?"

"Saturday night, can you be open to the possibility of coming back? Maybe spending the night?"

"I can be open to it." She'd have to come up with an excuse for being gone all night. Her parents would notice if her car wasn't there in the morning, but she could swing it.

"Why don't you come back over around eight. You can tell me what you've learned from your reading and then we can see where things go from there."

"Okay."

"Well, I guess this is goodnight."

Nailah looked up at him again. Armando just looked back. Okay then. Time to go. She opened her door and got into her car. He didn't try to stop her. She started her car and he stepped back up on the curb. She started to drive away. He waved then headed back toward his condo.

At the first red light, Nailah pulled out her phone and fired off a text.

> Did you seriously just NOT kiss me?

Her phone beeped a few moments later, but she couldn't check it until the next light.

> If I'd kissed you, you would have definitely spent the night.

> You say it like that's a bad thing.

> Maybe it is, for me. Maybe I need to pace myself. Now stop texting me and drive.

Nailah didn't know how that made her feel. She wanted to argue with him some more, but for the first time in her whole life she wanted someone else to be right. She was ready for the games between them to begin. Still, when she got home she sent Armando a little something. You couldn't see her whole face, but Armando would know it was her as soon as he'd looked at his phone. He'd regret skipping that goodnight kiss.

✳

Armando was distracted. He couldn't stop thinking about Nailah and the way she made him feel. Or the picture she'd sent him the other night. It wasn't exactly a nude but it was pretty close. She appeared to be naked, with a light blue blanket tucked under her arms as she sat up in bed. It came with a text that said *I could have stayed*. He knew he'd made the right decision, sending her home, but everything that had happened, the way she'd reacted to Daniel's video, the blunt way she spoke to him, combined with the fact that she seemed to really be into it, made no sense. He didn't realize how out of it he was until Keira came up behind him and poked him in the ribs.

"Whatcha doing?" she asked in her usual light tone.

By all appearances, he was standing outside the gym staring aimlessly across the street. "Waiting on Connie. She borrowed my truck." He held out his hands, palms up, as he answered. Keira knew what time it was. They engaged in their daily game of patty-cake. They improvised of course, adding in a few extra moves to spice things up.

"Oh, yay. I love Connie."

Armando remembered wanting to strangle Grant when he first hired Keira. She was one of the most beautiful women he'd ever seen but, after a few days, he'd come to see her as a sister and less of the object of his lust, mostly because she reminded him so much of Connie. Keira and his baby sister were nearly identical in their temperament, even their mannerisms. Both shy at times, then shockingly outgoing when they were in their comfort zone.

Connie's comfort zone was on stage with her guitar. Keira's was in the gym with her small group of kickboxing students.

"You look all zoned out. What's on your mind?" Keira asked, as she flipped his hands over and lightly slapped the backs. He returned the affectionate slap a second later. He wasn't sure how to answer the question. Half of the truth just sort of tumbled out.

"I'm having trouble with a girl."

"Good trouble or bad trouble?"

"I don't know yet."

"I know my sex life is non-existent, but do you want to talk about it?" Keira asked.

"She's harmless, ya know? I mean, she's a smart-ass and not someone I would fuck with intentionally."

"She's no pushover."

"Not even close."

"Good. And?"

"She's a good person, I think. Under all that, I get the sense that she's actually kind of sweet."

"But?"

"I don't know. Harmless and sweet can become danger-ous...hazardous in the wrong situation."

"Hazardous, huh? If she's all of these things, then the only hazardous part of the equation would be you?"

That, right there, was the problem. Armando was starting to like Nailah. They'd texted a few more times since they'd last seen each other. She had questions about her assigned reading. Thoughtful, legitimate questions, but every brief conversation ended with some smart-ass comment, some dig that undeniably turned Armando on. He'd never been with a woman as green as Nailah, but he'd never been with a woman as smart or as inquisi-tive as she was either.

She'd asked him for something pretty specific: introduction and guidance. She would glean what she could from him, and then find a Dom who truly suited her. Or maybe she'd figure out the submissive life wasn't for her. Either way, Armando had a feeling his time with Nailah Shalaby was limited. And he didn't like that.

"Nah," Armando finally said. "I wouldn't do anything hazardous."

Just then, Connie pulled up in his pickup.

"Well, the real question is, do you like her?" Keira asked.

Connie came around the side of the truck, all sweaty and covered in dust. She'd spent the morning helping a friend move. Armando and Keira hugged her anyway.

"Do you like who?" Connie asked, as she handed over his keys.

"Your brother's having girl problems."

"Ah. Well, yeah. That's a good point. Do you like her?"

Best to come clean now so Connie could blab all his business to his family instead of them trying to drag it from him as a group. His dads never bugged him for details if his sisters spilled them first.

Armando sighed and let out the uncomfortable confession. "Yeah, I do."

But the question still remained; did he let Nailah in on the truth? Not now, he thought to himself. Not just yet.

Four

Nailah cleared her weekend. As far as her family was concerned she was cashing in a day and a night a client had given her at a spa in Santa Barbara. Her father didn't like the idea of her going away alone, but her mother insisted she needed a break since she'd been working so hard. Nailah almost felt bad for lying.

Armando was waiting for her outside again. He greeted her with a quick hug, then took her overnight bag and led her up to his condo. The place was nice, new construction. Just enough units to justify the space it took up on the block, but few enough that you could get to know your neighbors, if you wanted to. Nailah loved the open floor plan of his condo, but it needed some work. It was so bland. No decoration at all, just the essential furniture. They'd have to have a chat about it at some point. She couldn't let someone she was associated with live in such conditions.

"You're quiet again," Armando said, as he placed her bag on the counter.

Nailah was nervous. Too nervous. And when she was nervous, she got bitchy. It was a horrible defense mechanism, but it was just a part of her personality. Almost genetic. Her dad was the same way.

She'd spent the last few days learning everything she could about submission and domination, topping and bottoming, different kinds of paddling, flogging, restraints, self-restraint, self-spanking. She was overwhelmed and a little confused about how she and Armando were going to work this out. She was starting to understand the submission aspect better for herself, but what about him? She had no clue what he liked. How was she supposed to surrender to him? What if they were horribly mismatched?

She'd read so much, seen so many things, but Armando seemed different from the leather-clad Dominants she'd found online. Or wasn't he supposed to be wearing a tux or an Armani suit or something? He was throwing her off with his jeans and long sleeve T-shirt.

Armando reached out a hand and pulled her closer. They leaned against the kitchen counter together, side-by-side. "You're overthinking this," he said, his low voice buttery smooth.

Nailah swallowed. "Possibly."

"We don't have to do anything. We can just talk again. This is about you pushing yourself and exploring your boundaries, but it's also about taking the steps that are right for you."

"And what about the right steps for you?"

"I'll let you know if we're crossing one of my lines, but for now, this isn't about me. I know what I like. I know what I want. We're here to discover more about you."

"So how do we do this?"

"You told me you spent a lot of time on kinklife and those submissive forums. Tell me what you learned. Tell me what you liked, what you didn't like."

"I learned that I know surprisingly little about sex. I know how to have sex, obviously, but I didn't realize there was *so* much other stuff. Blood play? What the fuck is that all about?"

Armando laughed a bit, and it helped her relax. Maybe talking before they jumped into things was a good idea.

"I look at things like blood play like this; sometimes you're connected with a deeply sensual side of yourself that craves more and more intense things, or what I feel are kind of nasty things."

"Oh, yeah." Nailah groaned a little. "I saw some of that too."

"The key is mutual consent. If you're alone, or you and two or more people agree to a particular act, something like blood play, and you're conscientious about everything that's happening, you're attentive, you're safe, then blood play it up."

"We're not doing that."

Armando laughed again. "I wouldn't ask you to. But tell me, what *do* you want? What did you like?"

"I liked all the stuff about consent. I think from the outside, everything I've heard about BDSM seemed like it was about forcing people to do things or tricking them into thinking they want to."

"See, that's called rape."

"Yeah, I see that now. I read the submissive handbook's website for hours the other day and she had so many interesting things to say about submission as freedom and choice. It was a little intoxicating. Addictive."

"It can be, yes."

"I like the idea of giving up control, and I do want to be spanked and paddled. I want that, like now. But first we have to..." Nailah hesitated again. She hated being in unfamiliar waters.

"We have to what?"

"We have to define the scene and negotiate."

"That's correct. Good." Armando's smile lit up his whole face. Nailah felt her own cheeks heat up.

She looked down at their shoes. Her peep-toe Louboutins and his crisp white Adidas shell tops.

"Can you tell me what you want?" Her frustration kept

creeping back. "You just know so much more. It'll help me clarify my own desires."

She glanced up at him again for confirmation. Something about his deep brown eyes seemed to soothe her. Armando nodded.

"I want you naked the whole time you're here. I'll want you on your knees part of the time too. I want to spank you with my bare hand while you blow me. And then, I just want to focus on your ass, spanking you until you can't take any more. I'll spank your pussy too. You'll probably come from that. And then I'm going to want to fuck you. After, I'll hold you until you fall asleep. I might want to fuck you again in the middle of the night. Definitely in the morning, before you go. Just depends on how tired you are."

Nailah could barely breathe. He hadn't even touched her and she could feel her pussy swelling just from his words. Just from the sound of his voice.

"Oh, and I want you to keep those heels on the whole time."

Nailah swallowed and made a weird noise, like she'd considered choking for a moment. "We can do all that and I'll keep the shoes on, but there's something else I want."

"Tell me."

"You have to go down on me if I'm going down on you. It's only fair."

"And what else?"

Nailah turned and faced Armando.

"I want you to kiss me." It was something she realized she'd wanted from the moment they met.

"Then I think we have a deal."

His arms were around her waist in the next moment. Then his warm, soft lips were on hers.

✱

The next morning, Nailah lay awake in Armando's bed,

listening as he tooled around in the kitchen. So much was running through her head. She couldn't believe how the night had unfolded. Armando had followed through on every single thing he'd said.

They'd moved from the kitchen to the couch where he stripped her completely down while he kissed her and kissed her. She'd never been with a man who knew how to kiss that way. They could have made out all night and she would have been completely satisfied, but they both had other things in mind. Once she was naked, free of everything but her high heels, Armando moved the coffee table then instructed her to kneel on the area rug in front of his couch. It was a little scratchy, but not enough to distract her from the way his muscular thighs parted inches from her face.

He leaned forward, with his legs still spread wide, and they talked about safe words while he massaged her left breast, and then her right.

She could barely think straight when he asked her questions, but Nailah remembered what she'd read about safe words and paying attention to perceived pain vs the actual threat of injury. He lightly pinched her nipples then asked her to pick her safe word. She'd chosen "backsplash".

There was more kissing before Armando freed his cock from his pants.

She didn't know how he would manage it, but he did spank her while she sucked him deep, his thick cock lightly nudging the back of her tongue as he warmed her up. He gripped her hair to keep her close and, with his other hand, he slapped one ass cheek and then the other, harder and harder with each stroke.

Nailah rolled over in bed, her thighs rubbing restlessly together. She thought about the way she'd squirmed, how tightly she'd squeezed her eyes shut. She'd struggled to breathe through her nose, but she didn't want him to stop. Even as the drool started running down her chin, she never wanted it to end.

The sound of his voice only made things worse. He talked so

dirty, so hot, telling her how good she felt, how pretty her ass looked in the air. He cursed a lot and Nailah liked it.

She'd stopped thinking, stopped worrying about what would come next. Nailah simply let herself feel, let herself be used for Armando's pleasure.

But before Nailah realized what was happening, Armando scooped her up and positioned her on the couch on her knees. It was his turn to hit the floor. He squatted behind her, buried his tongue in her pussy then fingered her as he continued to pepper her ass with harsh slaps.

"Hope you're hungry."

Nailah rolled toward the door to find Armando, still very naked, standing in the doorway with a tray of food. It was still hard to look at him. She was coming to terms with his face, but she needed more time to wrap her mind around his body. Kalli had the stupidest tattoos. Nailah almost always asked him to fuck her from behind so she didn't have to look at them. And he didn't seem to have his shaving/waxing routine in order. Sometimes his chest felt over- lotioned and prickly. She even told him once to leave his shirt on because she didn't want stubble burn on the palms of her hands.

Armando's body was a work of art. Light brown skin, thick dark hair in all the right places, that goatee. His dick wasn't half bad either. It was soft now, but Nailah would never forget how well he used it. Maybe she should stop staring.

Nailah sat up and took the breakfast tray from him so he could join her back in bed. Her ass burned as she slid up the sheets. She didn't do much to hide her wincing.

"Still a little sore?" he asked.

"Yeah. A little."

"Here." Armando took the tray back and placed it on the bedside table. Then he pulled back the sheets. "Lie on your stomach. Please."

"Since you said please." Nailah rolled onto her stomach. Her eyes closed automatically when his fingers brushed over her skin.

"No bruising, but it's still a pretty red. You have a high tolerance for pain."

"You think?" She'd never been much of a crybaby, but she'd never really hurt herself either.

"Yeah. I did *not* take it easy on you, but you didn't come close to your safe word."

"It hurt, but it didn't. So many other things were happening it was impossible to think of you spanking me in terms of pain. Not with your tongue inside me."

"Pleasant distractions help. You want to see?"

"See what?"

"Your ass." He stroked her skin again as he said the words. Nailah's eyes closed again, just for a moment.

"Yeah. Why not?"

Armando reached for his phone. Nailah turned her head while he snapped a couple pictures, then he handed her the phone. Her ass was pretty red. She wasn't entirely sure it wouldn't bruise, but she didn't really mind. She was ready for more.

She moved her thumb to the left and looked at the two other pictures he'd taken. One closer up, of just her ass. There was another from farther away, capturing nearly her whole body. Her hair was splayed out across the pillow.

"I'll delete them."

Nailah shrugged and handed the phone back. "You don't have to."

"You sure?"

"You can't see my face. It's fine. You can post it on kinklife if you want."

"Oh really?"

"Like I said, you can't see my face. Now about that breakfast."

"Oh, sorry. Here you are, your highness."

Nailah took a few bites of the delicious egg scramble heaped together with hot peppers, onions, potatoes, and cheese. She held out a forkful for Armando to keep him busy while he stared at her. She followed that with a bite of the waffle.

"Have any plans for the day?" she asked.

"My buddy Grant and I are having dinner with my dads and my sisters."

"You said 'dads' right? As in more than one?" Nailah asked. She thought of the two men from the Facebook picture who shared his last name, the two kissing his cheeks.

Instantly, Armando's whole demeanor changed and he went on the defensive. "Yeah. My dad and his husband. Is that a problem?"

"No, no. I—when I was being a nosey asshole, I think I saw a picture of them online. I was just wondering if they were the same people. Don't worry. I am all for gay dads. I love me some gay dads."

That seemed to mellow him out. "Oh, yeah. Those are my dads. I try to do dinner with them a few times a month."

"I have dinner with my family all the time. My little cousins are staying with us for the summer, so it feels like the family time has doubled."

"Hey, family's important to me too, but let's get through the first meal of the day."

"And then?"

"I'm fucking you again. Now eat."

Nailah ate, doing her best not to actually shove handfuls of food in her mouth. Then, after Armando slid on some protection, she rode his cock until she couldn't see straight. His grip on her ass left marks this time. She let him take pictures of those too.

✳

Armando was hiding in the kitchen, washing the dinner dishes. That's where Grant found him.

"Still recovering from that probing?" his buddy asked with a chuckle.

"Ha, yeah. I should recover in a few days. I'm gonna kill Keira. I never should have let her tell Connie."

"Is it so bad, man? They just care about you." Grant was right and their Q&A didn't last too long, but he'd gotten grilled, for sure.

What's her name again? What does she do? Where does she live? Are her parents here in LA? Do you think it's a good idea for you to train someone you're dating? Are you two even dating or are you just sleeping with her? Or are you two just tying each other up? That was his personal favorite from Connie. His whole family had a good laugh about that one.

It didn't bother Armando that his family had an idea of his kinks. His dad had met Mark in a leather bar when he first started dating again, so he knew they were up to some freaky shit. And thanks to the lovely tag feature on Facebook, his sisters had found out years before that he'd frequented some bondage events. They didn't care, but they loved giving him a hard time about it. Usually, with his family, he didn't mind the inquisition, but something felt different this time.

It was Nailah. She was different and it was clear as hell to Armando that he was playing on a different field. For the life of him, he could not figure out how to answer simple questions about her or whatever relationship they had. How could he be the proactive, albeit temporary Dom she needed when didn't understand whether he, himself was coming or going?

"What's going on?" Grant asked.

"I'm just thinking about Nailah."

"Miss Shalaby getting under your skin?"

"She asked me to guide her in, ya know. And we've only been together once, but something's bugging me."

"What?"

"In the moment, she was there, like all there. She totally gave herself up. Grant, man, I was rough. It was what she said she wanted, but I was rough."

"And she loved it? Hated it? What?"

"She loved it. She embraced it. And I think I have a pretty good grip on what she needs going forward."

"That all sounds good. What's the problem?"

"I keep thinking about the future. I also keep thinking about how to be right for her. I know what I told my sisters. I know what I told Keira, but I don't even know if I like her or if I'm just drawn to what she's letting me provide for her."

Grant grabbed a dish towel and started drying. "You sound pretty fucking confused."

"Damn right, I'm confused." Armando's laugh was a hair north of hysterical. "One minute it feels like it did with the rest. Catch and release. Catch and release."

"You've been fucking a lot of fish."

"Yeah, tons. I should have gills by now. She's making me want to try dry land for a while though."

"I have no idea what the fuck you're talking about," Grant said.

"I don't know what I want. I don't know what she wants."

"Did you try asking her?"

"I've asked her about, ya know...this stuff, but I haven't asked her about us."

"'Cause it's been two days."

"Pretty much."

"Well. You're fucked," Grant said, giving Armando a hard pat on the shoulder.

"Pretty much. I just can't tell if I need to be prepared to hold on to her. Like, I need to play this whole thing with every intention of it going the distance or if I just need to give her what I can and let her go."

"You wanna know what Violet would say?"

"Fuck no, I don't." Armando laughed, but he was serious.

"What? Violet knows a lot about women."

"I'm sure she does."

"Violet would say—"

"Christ, you're gonna tell me anyway."

"Violet would say you should talk to her. You can't make plans for a future with someone when they have no clue about the plans."

"I'm not in a plan-sharing mood."

"Then keep sulking like a little bitch. I'm sure that'll work out fine. You coming to Philip's on Saturday? He's having that party. Vi and I are going."

"We probably should. I should probably show her that side of things."

"Why not? She can newbie it up with Violet. I'm sure they'll both be into that."

"Grant! You said you brought ice cream!" Maria yelled from the living room.

"One sec! Stop yelling!" Grant tossed down the dish towel and headed for the freezer. "You good here?"

"Grant! Now!" Connie added, and then there was a fit of giggles and his dad's booming laughter.

"Do you want bowls and spoons? Or you wanna eat this with your hands?" Grant called back.

"You need a hand?" Armando asked. He was trying not to laugh himself.

"Nah, I live for this abuse."

FIVE

The party was fine. Perfectly fine. They arrived fashionably late. Nailah got to formally meet Armando's best friend and business partner, Grant. She got to meet Grant's girlfriend, Violet, who was perfectly cool and almost as clueless as Nailah, so they had plenty to talk about.

She also met the infamous Master Philip, director of the medical center where her father did his pro-bono work. She had seen him before, years ago at a holiday party, but they'd never been introduced. He welcomed her with sweet warmth that reminded her of her grandfather, though Master Philip was much younger than the ancient man. He also assured her that her father would never know they had met, officially, and under what circumstances. He then went on at length about how wonderful Armando was and how she was in such wonderful hands.

Blah, blah, what the fuck ever. Armando could shove his wonderfully skilled hands right up his own ass. After he introduced her around–there was still Master Philip's wife Evelyn to meet and then some girl named Meegan who was available to fetch Nailah whatever she wanted to drink–Armando took off.

Sure, he told her not to be shy, but to ask politely before she engaged anyone. There were instructions not to interrupt any play or to let any Dom assume ownership over her for the evening before working out a little scene negotiation. He told her there would be a series of floor demonstrations starting in a few moments and then he fucking disappeared. He didn't leave the party, exactly, but he sure as hell did leave her on a couch with Violet and Grant, as if she'd come downtown to a sketchy refurbished warehouse to spend her Saturday night with them.

There were demonstrations, Grant explained, couples that Master Philip had handpicked to put on little shows of bondage and sadism.

The Asian guy she'd seen in the video, Daniel was his name, brought up some young guy and paddled him purple as he hung helpless in a set of medieval stocks. A little while later Mistress Evelyn brought the Meegan girl up and demonstrated this really interesting suspension trick with brightly colored rope. Grant was nice enough to explain each scene to her, who was who and what was happening, so at least she wasn't completely out of the loop.

As the night went on, three women did a strip-burlesque dance with whips on what seemed to be a main stage. Meanwhile couples or small groups of people all around the place engaged in their own intimate acts. Whispering, kissing, touching, a lot of touching. She saw submissives serving their Masters, Dominants showing their submissives off.

And there she was, with her thumb up her ass, drinking her third glass of sparkling water, while Grant felt Violet up beside her. He was whispering something about wanting to flog her. Then Violet was fending him off with some bullshit, coy responses. Nailah could tell she totally wanted it. She didn't blame Violet. Grant was sexy and he was actually speaking to her.

Armando was nice enough to offer a nod or mouth "How you doing?" whenever they made eye contact, but he literally spent the whole night circulating the room, as far away from her as possible.

First, he was talking to Master Philip, then the Daniel guy. He ducked into some hidden corner, but then reappeared a couple minutes later with something for Master Philip. He spoke to a lesbian couple that had some May-December thing going on. The older of the two had to be twice her submissive's age, but they seemed happy together.

Violet and Grant got up twice, once to dance and another time so Violet could use the restroom, or give Grant a handy-j. Why else would he go with her? Every time Nailah was alone for a second a different man would approach her, ask her if she was new, ask her if she wanted them to show her around. She politely declined each time. And after each time she looked around for Armando. He'd seen it all, but he definitely didn't care. He'd just smile at her, or keep talking, not even missing a beat in his conversation.

At one point, she wondered why she'd even come. Why had Armando bothered to invite her? She was having a nice time in theory, but she could have a nice time by herself or with her own friends. She could have stayed home with Aziza and watched *Frozen* for the four-hundredth time.

Part of the allure of all of this, of her coming clean to Armando about wanting to know more about the lifestyle, was feeling owned and possessed. He seemed to understand that. The first night they spent together she thought they were on the same page, but now Nailah had no idea what he was doing. She wasn't sure he did either.

Eventually, he made his way back over to her. He must have noticed that Grant and Violet were starting to have a hard time catering to their third wheel.

Violet was on Grant's lap and Nailah was pretty sure Violet didn't have any underwear on from the way she was squirming. Nailah almost broke Armando's hand when he placed it on her shoulder.

"How's it going?" he asked, with a bright smile. "You having a good time?"

She stood and smoothed down the hem of her dress. "I'm ready to go."

"Oh. Yeah? Okay."

"I can catch a cab if you're not ready."

"No, it's cool. Let's take off."

"We're going too." Grant stood and oh-so coolly zipped up his fly while Violet pulled down her skirt in the back. Nailah rolled her eyes.

The four of them said a quick goodbye to Daniel and the young man he'd paddled, then Master Philip and Mistress Evelyn. Evelyn told Nailah to reach out to her anytime with any questions. Nailah would appreciate the gesture when she wasn't so busy wanting to separate Armando's testicles from his body. There was another goodbye with Grant and Violet in the alley. Nailah didn't shake either of their hands. And she almost socked Armando when he agreed to Grant's idea that they double. On what fucking planet would she be seeing Armando again?

Finally, they climbed into his pickup truck. As soon as they got back to his place, she was grabbing her car and she was going home.

He must have disagreed with the silent treatment she was giving him, because after a few short minutes of driving, Armando pulled over somewhere in Koreatown. Smart. Very smart, because she was ditching his ass the first real chance she got.

He sighed as he leaned back against the seat, "Let's talk about this. What's wrong?"

Nailah looked straight ahead, but she answered. "I just don't get why you're half-assing this."

"I'm half-assing this?" His display of shock was almost insulting. He really thought he'd knocked this whole evening out of the park.

"Yeah. You give me all this homework. Stuff I hope you've read too, because it would be pretty silly if you haven't. All this reading gives me a certain impression of what's supposed to happen. What

I'm supposed to do. What I'm supposed to expect from you, but it's like you only do part of it."

"Is that right?"

"Yes. The spanking and the fucking you've got down, but the dominating and the possessing? I'm waiting for you to show up. Three dudes tried to talk to me tonight. Is that what you wanted?"

"I wanted you to have a good time. I want you to meet people. I'm not the only Dom on the planet and I don't own you."

"Yeah. Well, that much is clear."

"Oh. Okay. I see."

Nailah could have sworn she heard his jaw crack. Finally, she looked at him. "Do you?"

"Yeah."

"Say it. I know you want to. It's right on the tip of your tongue. You've got something for me when we get back up your place? You're gonna show me a thing or two about how real you can be?"

Armando stared at her for a moment, his eyes narrowing. She didn't care if she pissed him off. He set the bar of expectations so fucking high, but then he seemed to pull the plug or change lanes at the worst possible moment.

She could go on sleeping with him, no problem, but why would he go to all this trouble if he wanted to take things slow, giving her the walking tour that included stopovers at Dominants that didn't interest at her all? He hadn't even been her guide for the evening. He left that to Grant and Violet. What was the point of them going into this together if he wanted to give her an opportunity to do all this exploration with someone else?

"I'm not saying you have to up and collar me or whatever, but for the time being I want you, okay? So don't take me somewhere and leave me with your friends. And don't leave me for other men to try and pick me up. I can do that all on my own."

He faced forward this time. Nailah watched the lights turn

from red to green on the bottom half of his face. His goatee almost glowed. "Yeah," he eventually said. "I hear you."

She turned back around and faced the window. "I just want you." Her voice was a little quieter this time, but she knew he'd heard her.

✱

Armando finally understood the allure of hate-fucking. He'd taken Nailah to one of the most exclusive bondage clubs in the city. He'd introduced her to one of the most experienced, most skilled Dominant couples in the country in Philip and Evelyn.

She'd been waited on and entertained by players that he had grown to love and admire, and here she was sulking like he'd taken her to some third rate hipster dive bar that made her check all her designer labels at the door. He wanted to make her see exactly what he was trying to expose her to—the larger picture, the variety of the community. It was more than the walls of his condo. He wanted to take her home and bang her silly until she stopped being so pissed off at him.

Still, he understood why Nailah was upset. She felt ditched at the party and that had never been his intention. He genuinely thought it would be a good idea for her to get a sense of the scene without him hovering over her shoulder. That wasn't what she wanted. She'd made that nice and clear, but Christ, she knew how to hit below the belt. She basically told him he was failing as a teacher, that he was failing as Dom.

He couldn't stand for that. She may have been mocking him, but he was going to show her a thing or two, way more than she'd bargained for, the second they set foot in his house.

Nailah was quiet for the rest of the ride to his place, but when he parked his truck she let him open the door for her and she didn't give him any shit when he reached for her overnight bag.

She was silent all the way up the stairs. He pulled out his keys, then he turned to her. It was time to fix this.

"Once I open this door you have five minutes to say whatever you need to say, and after that all I want to hear out if your mouth is yes sir, no sir, please sir and thank you, sir. That's all I want to hear until we are through. Are we understood?"

She wouldn't look at him. She seemed unusually calm. "Yes."

"Good."

Armando opened the door and let Nailah walk inside.

"Now do you have anything else you want to say? Anything you want to get out of the way for the rest of the night? Need to make a phone call, send a text?"

Nailah checked her nails like she could not be more bored, then looked him square in the eyes. "I just want you to stop bull-shitting. I'm good with the phone calls."

"Sounds wonderful." He held up her overnight bag, some leather Prada whosy-what that probably cost more than his truck. "You have your lady stuff in here? Lotion, toothbrush and crap?"

"Yes, it's filled with lady crap, like a toothbrush just for ladies."

"Great. Here." He shoved the bag back in her direction. She took it from him with no argument. "Go do whatever you need to do to freshen up. There are towels and washcloths right in the bathroom. Then come back out here. No clothes, no shoes. Those heels look great, but you almost spiked me in the nuts last time." He ignored the hint of a smile that tried to peek from her mouth. "Any questions?"

"No, Sir." She started walking away.

"Where are you going?"

Nailah looked at him over her shoulder. "To change."

"Don't remember dismissing you."

"Sorry, Sir." She retraced the three or four steps then stood facing him. "Was there anything else, Sir?"

Armando leaned down and whispered in her ear. "When you come back, I want that pussy dripping wet. Am I understood?"

When he slid his hand along her neck and up under her hair, Armando felt her shiver. His lips brushed the shell of her ear. "Am I?"

Nailah turned her head so their lips just barely touched. "Yes, Sir."

"Good. Go ahead."

Eight minutes later, when Nailah came back, completely naked, Armando was already busy catching up with email on his laptop. Maria's birthday was coming up and he had to find her a gift.

Nailah stood somewhat patiently in front of him. "Come kneel right here." She sank to her knees between his feet. Armando put his laptop aside, then grabbed the collar he'd fished out of the chest in his closet. She followed his cues and let him fasten the thick strap of leather around her neck.

It's only temporary, he told himself. This is only for tonight. She's not yours. She is not yours.

He closed the buckle then lifted her chin with the edge of his knuckle. "Is it too tight? Too loose?"

"No, Sir. It feels fine."

"Good. Now, what did you learn about submissive poses, about posture?"

"I know some of the positions have names and there are different poses for different purposes, like service and punishment. But I didn't memorize them. Sir."

"That's fine. I'm glad you've got the gist." He lightly drew his finger down her cheek. Her eyes slid closed.

Only for tonight, he told himself again. He kept touching her face, lightly stroking her cheek and drawing his thumbs across her lips. She'd taken off all her make-up and still she looked beautiful.

"I want you to present yourself to me. Right here on the floor. Show me if you can and then we'll make adjustments."

"Yes, Sir," she said clearly.

She started to move and he already saw that even though she had the right idea, he wanted her a different way.

"Uh-huh. Forward, like that. Legs spread, ass up. I want to see your pussy. You have to show me how wet it is. Good. Good girl. Rest your head on your hands. Yes, just like that. Thank you. Now stay."

"Yes, Sir," she said, nearly whimpering just loud enough for him to hear.

Then he grabbed his laptop and went back to his online shopping. He listened closely to Nailah's breathing. There were a few stutters and gasps, but soon she took a deep breath and made herself relax. She dropped her lower back, keeping her ass in the air the way he'd instructed her to. It took the strain off her abs and shoulders.

He only made her wait a few minutes, ten or so, while he picked out an iPad and some accessories for his sister. Nailah was good, held as still as possible, but he could tell this was her first time doing something like this with her body. She was starting to get uncomfortable.

Armando closed his laptop, setting it aside, and then toed off his dress shoes, leaving him in a fancy pair of socks Maria had picked out for him. "You doing okay down there?"

"Yes, Sir. I'm fine."

"Good. I like the view from here. I'm tempted to keep you there all night. What do you think about that?"

"I—" Nailah was brought up short by Armando's silk-clad foot rubbing along her cunt. Not that he couldn't tell from a few feet away, but the touch confirmed it. She was soaking wet.

"I can't hear you, sweetheart. You'll have to speak a little louder." Armando suppressed his laughter as Nailah pushed back against his foot. She whimpered before she answered.

"I don't think you would want that, Sir."

"Is that right?"

"Yes, Sir. I think you'd want to fuck me or spank me, eventually."

"You don't think I could do all that and then some with you just like that? Your ass is in the air, just primed for a paddling, and there are all sorts of ways for me to fuck you just the way you are." His foot was moving the whole time and, shamelessly, Nailah kept rocking against him. He could have told her to hold still, but the rocking of her hips was giving him serious wood.

"I'm going to fuck you in the ass one day. Would you like that?"

"I've never done it before, Sir."

"That's not what I asked."

"Yes, Sir. I would like it. I want you to fuck me in the ass."

"Don't move," Armando said as he rose to his feet. "I'll be right back."

"Yes, Sir." She barely got the words out.

Armando went to his bedroom and stripped out of his clothes. The top of his left sock was completely soaked. When he came back out to the living room, he set the condoms he'd grabbed down on the coffee table and then he leaned down right into Nailah's field of vision.

He ran his hand down her back as he showed her the flogger he'd also grabbed. "Can we continue?"

She swallowed and nodded. "Yes, Sir."

"Good. I'm going to flog your ass with this. Nowhere else, just your ass, okay?"

"Yes, Sir."

"Good." Armando stood, rolling his shoulders. He paced a few feet away from Nailah's prone body. He took several deep but quiet breaths and then he walked back to his girl.

Armando didn't stop with the flogger until her ass was bright red. He could have gone on a little longer. Nailah seemed to like the flogger more than his rough palms, but she'd been in that spread position long enough and there was something more that he wanted. Two more rough strokes, one on each cheek, and each strike met with the same moan and jerk she'd displayed since he'd finished warming her up.

He tossed the flogger onto the couch, and then sank to his knees between her feet. It took nothing for him to flip her over onto her back. She stared up at him, her face bright red, a few tears gathering at the corner of her eyes. He leaned over her and wiped her cheeks.

"Okay?"

"Mhmm." Her voice came almost in a pant. "Yes, Sir."

Armando kissed her long and hard to remind of her what he was feeling for her. To remind her that they were in this together. When he pulled away, he looked down at her gorgeous body. "Hold your ankles."

She did as she as was told and then he started in on her pussy. Light, quick slaps at first, then harder and harder, smacking the delicate folds that covered her clit. She shook and cried out, biting the inside of her cheek to try and contain her pleas.

He smacked until she came, her back arching off the floor. A long stream of swearing mixed with "Oh, god! Oh god! Oh god!" echoed off the high ceilings of his condo. He stopped with the smacks and started rubbing her pussy, doing it harder as she came again. She held her ankles the whole time. He'd see in the morning if she'd bruised her own skin.

Before she could come back to herself completely, Armando yanked her off the floor and brought her over to the couch. He nearly fell onto the cushions, impressed that she managed to get her footing and stand still until he instructed her what to do next. But he didn't have any instructions this time. He tore the condom wrapper open and slipped the sheath on. Then he pulled her onto his lap.

Nailah sank onto his cock, her slick, swollen cunt welcoming him home. It was his turn to moan. He'd been wanting this all week, wanting to be inside her again, wanting her luscious tits with their tight brown tips bouncing inches away from his face. Armando pulled her arms behind her back, gathering both her small wrists in one of his larger hands. She tossed her head back, almost in offering, and it would have been plain rude for him not to accept.

There was no need to slow her bouncing. He could suck her nipples and pound away all at the same time. So he did. First one then the other, pulling each breast deep into his mouth until he knew the suction edged close to pain.

Fuck, the noises she made. The screams and the cries, his name over and over, all jumbled together as she tried to hold on to him. But he had her.

He pulled her closer, his hand buried deep in her hair. Her wrists were still trapped behind her back.

"Is this what you wanted? Is this what you wanted all night?"

"Yes," she sobbed.

Her failed response only made him fuck her harder. "What was that?"

"Yes, Sir!"

"That's what I thought. You wanted this all night, huh? And you were pissed at me because I didn't give it to you right away."

"No, Sir."

"No?"

"No, Sir," she sobbed again. "I just wanted you with me."

"I'm with you now. And I'm not letting you go." Just words, he told himself. Just for tonight. She's not yours. "Are you my girl?"

"Yes."

"Are you my girl? Tell me."

"Yes, Sir. Oh my god. Fuck. Yes. I'm your girl. I'm your girl."

It wasn't time yet, he had miles to go, but those simple words shot down his spine right to his balls and he filled that condom, filled Nailah's swollen pussy with everything he had. Armando knew for a fact he'd never come that hard before in his life.

Six

Nailah could feel Armando's eyes on her as she moved around the bedroom. She had to get home. At the very least, her mother would expect her for Sunday dinner. She also had some work she wanted to knock out. Or so she told herself. Really, she knew she was in danger of developing some serious feelings for the naked man lying a few feet away from her. Being around him was too much, too intoxicating. She had to put some distance between them before she became addicted.

"How do you feel?" he asked, his voice still thick from sleep.

"Good, but sore."

"Sore or in pain?"

"Definitely just sore." Nailah turned around and smiled at him. "I'm fine."

"Come here."

She really had to go and she didn't think it was a good idea to spread her thighs again. That was the sorest part, but she could handle another quickie.

Nailah crawled across the sheets and kissed Armando on the mouth.

"I don't think your family needs to see you in this," he said, as he reached around her neck. She moved her hair so he could unfasten the collar.

"Shit. I completely forgot I had that on. Did it leave a mark?"

Armando looked closer, touching her skin. Goosebumps broke out all over her body. "Nah. It's a little pink, but that's probably just because the skin's so warm."

Nailah swallowed, as if that would clear away the effect Armando had on her. Then she went back to getting dressed.

"So you live at home with your parents?"

"Sort of. I live in the pool house. I like to say it's 'cause my parents don't charge me rent, but really my dad is a bit overprotective and old school, and I'm not ready to have the whole 'I'm moving away' argument with him yet."

"Hey, the free rent part sounds pretty good to me. I sold a kidney for the down payment on this place."

"It's nice, but it could use a little personality."

"Oh?"

"Yeah." Nailah pulled on her bra, then paused to look around. "It's very Spartan in here. Great bed and all. I like the built-in you added in the bathroom, but overall it lacks warmth. You're a warm guy. Your place should reflect that."

"You think I'm warm?"

Nailah shrugged as she scrunched up her nose. "I guess you're okay."

"Thanks. I'll take that."

"I can fix it up for you. At a cost, of course."

"I'm all for the fair exchange for goods and services."

"I'll work something up."

"Great. When can I see you again? Outside of the gym."

Nailah was wondering the same thing. They were sticking with their workouts and, per Armando's request, when they were in the gym it was about the weights and cardio and nothing else. But Nailah thought about him all the time. She liked being around him, even when he pissed her off.

"A bunch of us are going to Vegas next weekend," Nailah said before she could stop herself. "You can be my plus one."

"Driving or flying?"

"Psssht, flying. What kind of peasant do you take me for?" It wasn't a bad drive, but why waste the hours in the car when you could spend them partying poolside?

"I have a few clients on Saturday, but I could meet you up there."

"That works. I'll call you when I know the rest of the details."

"Great." Armando hopped out of bed, still naked as the night before. Nailah turned away to keep from staring at his ass or his semi-erect cock. He dressed in a fraction of the time it took her to get ready then walked her out to the car. He kissed her goodbye again and told her to call him if the soreness turned into anything else. She promised she would.

She got home right as her parents arrived from church. Just a quick shower, she told her mom, and then she'd join them for some lunch. Her mother only had a few questions about her night. Nailah passed the quiz with flying colors, but when her mom told her to hurry and gave her an affectionate pat on the butt, Nailah fucked up and flinched.

Her mother noticed.

∗

Armando was wasting time between sessions, staring at his computer screen. He'd finally uploaded the pictures he took of Nailah two weeks before. She'd decided to stick with kinklife.com, with her fake profile. Their friendship had been confirmed, but so far no relationship statuses added. He was trying to decide whether or not to tag her in the picture, or add a caption. What could he say about her?

Grant came into their cramped office, singing to himself. Armando wished he could be that carefree with his lovesickness.

"You still pouting?" Grant asked. "I thought you guys made up the night of the party."

"Yeah and we've been talking and shit, but I feel like I'm out of some sort of loop. She hates when I flirt with her. Through text, over the phone, whatever. If I even try it she shoots me down."

"She just might not be that kind of girl."

"Yeah, but then she freaked when she thought I wasn't paying attention to her at the party. I can't tell if she just doesn't like being ignored. If she wants me, ya know, just when I'm around. Or if she wants me all the time. Or *how* she really wants me."

"Ask her."

"I can't! When we're not in scene or coming down from one, it's almost impossible to have a normal conversation with her. She's such a..."

"A dick?" Grant laughed. Armando had called Grant's last girlfriend a dick on a daily basis, so he wasn't offended.

"Not like Arianna, but she's kind of a dick and she cuts deep. Even when we're in a scene she talks so much shit."

"And you love it."

"Fuuuuck. I do. What is wrong with me?"

"Come on, man. You know."

He did, but Armando wasn't ready to admit it to himself yet. Not yet. "She won't go for a grand gesture."

"Then skip it. Judging by how pissed she was, I'm pretty sure she's digging you, but if she needs time and her own kind of space, give it to her. Are you in some sort of hurry?"

"No, I guess not. I just don't remember it being this difficult." Grant fixed him with a hard stare. "What?"

"Let's go back. A young Armando age twenty-six finds himself hopelessly in love with a Mistress Cowley—"

"Fuck that. That lady got all in my head and I'd been in the scene for all of five minutes."

"And Nailah's been at this how long...?"

"Man, fuck you with your valid points." Armando hunched

forward on the desk as Grant burst out laughing. He came over and looked at the picture of Nailah on the screen.

"Is that her?"

"Yeah."

"Yeah. Give that woman all the time she needs. From the look of things, she's worth it."

Armando knew Grant was right, no matter what he saw in that picture. She was completely worth it.

✳

What's this guy do again?" Shelly asked. The rest of Nailah's friends were already inside the restaurant. When Armando called from the airport to say that he'd landed, she figured it would be easier to meet him in the lobby of the hotel instead of him picking his way through the crowds to find them. Plus, she wanted ten seconds alone with him before she introduced him to her friends. Too bad Shelly wouldn't let her leave the table alone.

"He owns the gym where I work out. He trains me too. And his name's Armando, not This Guy."

"Calm down. We'll all call him by his name. It is serious or just banging?"

Nailah made a dismissive, non-committal noise. "Don't know yet, but I figured he'd keep me distracted once RJ and Meena get liquored up. Or more liquored up."

"Oh god. Did you see them at the pool?"

"Everyone saw them at the pool."

Shelly offered a dramatic shudder. "Sick." Before Shelly could ask any more questions, Armando came striding out from the bank of elevators.

"This is him." Nailah stood a little straighter, but managed not to fix her hair or smooth down her dress as he came closer. He just looked so good, wearing crisp, dark gray slacks and a matching suit jacket. The white button-up shirt he had on underneath was open, showing off a bit of that chest hair Nailah loved. The sides of his hair were freshly shaved, and long strands on top were perfectly slicked back. Nailah swallowed and forced herself to relax.

"Oh my god. He's hotter than Kalli," Shelly said. "And who was that guy before him?"

"Doesn't matter."

"You are not lying. This one's the hottest by far–Hi!"

"Hey!" Armando said back, even though he looked completely confused by Shelly's enthusiasm. Nailah covered her mouth as she snorted. Then she straightened up once she realized Armando wasn't alone. His friend Daniel was with him. Daniel was kind enough to distract Shelly so Nailah could hug the only person she actually wanted to see this weekend. Still, Nailah wondered why Daniel was there. They did their introductions, then headed into EIG8T, the steakhouse Shelly's boyfriend had picked for dinner.

"Planning to ditch me again?" Nailah muttered, as she let Armando take her hand. He stopped walking and pulled her around to face him as Daniel followed Shelly to the table. Nailah managed not swoon against his chest when he touched her cheek. Damn, she was getting soft.

"There will be no ditching. His mom lives here. He's just tagging along for a bit. Besides, Daniel knows how to take care of himself. I'm all yours."

"Hmm. Okay. You look really good right now."

"Thank you. You look beautiful. As always," he replied with that devastating smile that tore up her insides.

"I would have kissed you back there—"

"I get it. Just meeting the friends. We don't need to suck face in front of them."

"No. This lipstick is just really tacky," Nailah said, gesturing to the red tint on her lips. "It would be all over your mouth."

"I see."

"Later."

"Sounds good to me. Let's go join them."

Dinner went as well as could be expected. Other than Meena blatantly flirting with Armando in front of RJ, and Mario rudely asking Daniel about how he lost his hand. When Daniel responded with, "I'll just say it's never a good idea to play with explosives," that shut Mario right up. But other than those few unnecessarily awkward moments, Armando definitely charmed her friends. Nailah was glad she'd invited him.

After dinner, they planned to go to a rooftop club where RJ had booked a table and bottle service, but there was some debate about killing time with some more pre-partying. Meena had stopped at the liquor store on their way from the airport, but the drinks by the pool and the drinks with dinner and the drinks to come weren't nearly enough. It was still a little early to head to the club. They wanted to wait for the crowd to build a little, so they decided to let their food settle with a few more drinks back at Meena and RJ's room.

"I have something for you in *my* room," Armando said, as they waited for the elevators. "If you want to come with me for a sec."

"Uh, sure."

After Daniel assured them he was in good hands, Nailah told Shelly she'd meet her back at the suite so they could change for the club. They hopped off on ten while their friends continued up to the higher floors. Armando's room was just a short walk down the hall. He keyed them in, then led her right over to the bed where he handed her a small gift bag.

He sat down as Nailah rifled through the bit of tissue paper hiding the goods. She pulled out a little box. It was a remote controlled vibrating egg in "satin black". There was also a little bottle of lube.

"I thought we could have some fun tonight with that, when we hit the town," Armando said.

"Are we on now? Are the games beginning?"

"If you want them to."

"I do." Nailah handed the toy and the lube back. He

unwrapped the small vibrator then told her to go rinse it with some soap and warm water in the bathroom. When she came back, he was flipping the top of the lube open and closed.

"Lift up your dress."

Nailah pulled the black fabric of her dress up to her stomach, showing off the black lace thong she had on underneath. Armando held up the little bottle of lube.

"Do I need this?"

"No, Sir." Nailah had been wet since he called from the airport. It was something about his voice, something about the anticipation.

"Come closer, sweetness."

Nailah closed the small distance between them, making sure she held her dress in place. Armando moved her thong to the side and traced her pussy with his fingertips before he parted her lips. "Wider, babe. Open your legs. Good. Watch me." It was hard not to let her head fall back when touched her skin, but her gaze held his as he took the egg and pushed it inside of her.

"How does that feel? Tell me."

"It feels nice, Sir. It feels good." Small enough to be comfortable, but big enough to make its presence known. And then he turned it on. The slow vibrations made her clit throb from the inside. Armando stood, keeping his fingers on the outside of her cunt. He rubbed her lips, moving his fingers up to the height of her slit and back down again.

"Still have to watch out for that lipstick, don't I?"

"Yes, Sir," Nailah moaned.

"I'll guess we'll have to improvise." Just as the words left his mouth, Armando's lips brushed against her neck. Then his tongue. Then his lips again, firmer against her pulse. His fingers slipped back and forth.

They should skip the club. The bed was right there, so inviting. Or the floor, or the dresser. The shower and the tub in the bathroom could accommodate two people easily. But they stayed where they were, right beside the bed.

"I want you to have fun with your friends tonight," he whispered. "But just remember, I came here for you."

"I want you now. Sir."

"No, baby."

Nailah was prepared to beg, but she cried out, bracing her forehead against his shoulder as he turned up the speed on the egg. "Please, Sir."

He gently bit her neck. "No. Don't come. Not yet."

Every time before, things had been so fast, so intense. Armando knew tender. He knew soft, but he usually didn't do slow. Nailah didn't know if she could handle this. She was ready to burst.

He turned the egg off, then stepped back, holding her by the shoulders. "We have to save that for later, okay?"

"Yes, Sir."

"Good. Let's go meet your friends."

Nailah had never been so grateful for how oblivious her friends got when they were drinking. Otherwise, Shelly and Meena might have noticed that she could barely stand up anymore, even though she'd only had one glass of champagne. They might have also noticed the way she couldn't keep her hands off Armando, or maybe they would have asked about the dirty things he was saying in her ear. Shelly would have definitely noticed the huge erection in his pants, the one he continued to grind against her ass or her hip with every new song that vibrated through the packed club.

She'd asked for it, but it was cruel teasing her like this. The pain of the flogger or his bare hand created a different sensation throughout her body. She could focus on the pain, see it, feel it in a way that pushed the simple act of coming to the back of her mind.

But this constant teasing, the fluctuating of the rhythm between her legs, made it impossible to think of anything else. Armando knew exactly how to control the little toy too. He knew exactly how much she could take and exactly when to back off. She knew if she tried she could come right there in her high heels, but she didn't want to disobey him. He knew everything, damn him.

It was obvious in the way she begged. She wanted him to keep talking to her. She had no idea when he decided to start with the "sweetness" and the "baby", but she didn't hate it. She wanted this type of sweet torture to go on and on until she really couldn't take the frustration of it anymore, because she knew once they made it back up to his room he was going to fuck the shit out of her.

A little after midnight Daniel said he was going to meet his mom, since she'd just finished her shift at the Monte Carlo. As he faded into the crowd, Nailah looked up at Armando. The spiraling red and blue lights almost made her dizzy.

"Sir. Please," she said, as calmly as possible. Her patience was wearing extra fucking thin.

He stared back down at her. "Since you've been good. Come on."

Nailah got Shelly's attention and let her know she'd catch up with them in the morning. Shelly made some goofy face, like they were at a middle school dance and Nailah was slinking off for her first kiss. Although from the way Armando kissed, his lips and that slick tongue might be enough to trip off the orgasm she desperately needed.

They made it maybe three feet across the dance floor before he turned the vibrator to the highest setting. Nailah stopped in her tracks, almost stumbled as she held her hand to her stomach.

He took her other hand. "Uh-uh. Keep going."

She squeezed her eyes shut for a moment, then opened them as he led her out of the club to the elevators. A group of guys piled into the elevator with them. She was afraid they might be able to hear the vibrator, which echoed loud and clear inside her own ears, but their loud talking drowned out every other noise in the space, even the sound of her heavy breathing. Armando pulled her back against him, pushing his hard-on into her back. She wasn't going to make it to the room. There was no way.

When the group o'dudes unloaded on the fifteenth floor, Armando spun her around to face him. His hand came down on her ass with a hard smack. Instead of smacking her again, he gripped her ass cheek in his palm, digging his fingertips into her skin. The motion made everything inside her clench. "Oh my god! Fuck." Drool almost slipped from her mouth. She was going to come.

Armando gently took her by the chin, but practically growled in her ear. "Don't you dare. Not until I say." He smacked her ass again, then grabbed another handful. Nailah could barely breathe. She'd hold on, but only to find a way to make him pay for it later.

By some miracle they made it back to his room and as soon as the door closed behind them, he told her to strip as he started to undress himself. Simple, if that fucking egg wasn't still vibrating against the walls of her cunt at full speed.

"Did you bring the collar with you, Sir?" She had no clue what made her ask. The words just came out.

"I didn't, but next time, you'll wear it all night."

She ignored the odd sense of disappointment and focused on getting out of her underwear without driving the egg harder against her g-spot. She joined him on the bed, both of them completely naked. It must have been his magical Dom powers, acquired through years of study and discipline, but somehow, even with his hard cock pressed between them, Armando seemed completely calm. Nailah, on the other hand, thought she was going to pass out at any moment.

He turned off the vibrator, then reached between her legs and started tugging on the small plastic string at the base of the egg.

Nailah stopped him with her hand on his wrist. "No, leave it in. Sir."

"That'll make it a little difficult for me to get my dick in there."

Nailah moved off the bed and grabbed the lube off the dresser. "You said something before, about fucking me in my ass."

That got his attention. Armando sat up against the headboard, his huge cock bouncing against his stomach. "Are you sure? I wanted to take it slow with that."

Nailah reached down and rubbed her clit. Being wound up this tight? It was a first. This was as good a time as any. "I'm sure." She climbed back on the bed, between Armando's legs, and poured a generous amount of lube on his cock. It was her turn to tease him a bit. She leaned forward, not caring where her lipstick got now that they were in for the night. She kissed him deep, stroking his erection in her slick palm. It was his turn to groan, which he did, thrusting his tongue deeper into her mouth.

"Give me the lube," he said, almost out of breath. She handed it over and kept stroking him, up and down, as he slicked his fingers. "Come here, baby."

He pulled her closer with an arm around her waist. The pressure of his cock in front, rubbing up against her clit, and his thick fingers pushing against her at the back made her whimper and groan. And the egg—it was still there, filling her up.

He kissed her cheek, whispered against her skin. "Relax, baby. I'll go slow."

"You don't have to. I want you to fuck me."

"Nah, nah. We're going slow. And you forgot to call me sir."

"I'm sorry, Sir." Nailah's voice hitched as he slid one finger inside. He moved it slowly in and out, before he added another and then a third. There was a pinch of pain, but her body was so completely primed that the pain simply added to the urgency. She squirmed in his lap, driving herself hard down on his hand.

Armando pulled back just a little so he could look her in the eye. "You want to sit on it?"

She nodded quickly. "Yes. Yes, Sir."

He pulled his fingers out, then pushed just the head of his cock in. Then, the vibrations started up again. Nailah couldn't wait. She let out a deep breath, and then she sank down on his cock. She felt the girth of him all the way up to her chest, the sweet pressure filling her and stretching her out. There was pain, but it was a pain she wanted, something she craved. She knew she could handle more. Armando held her tighter, pumping in and out slowly. The speed, the rhythmic force of his hips dictating the way her lungs filled and then way her throat clenched.

The egg shook with double the force.

That was it for Nailah. She came, so hard all she could do was cling to her Sir as she screamed. He wasn't done with her, not even close. She held on as he continued to pump into her body, scoring his back with her nails, smearing what remained of her lipstick against his skin. She may have bit him. She couldn't be sure. But he continued to give her the pleasure she'd been begging for all night. He kept fucking her, hard the way she liked. Forceful, the way he needed. The egg amped up to full speed. She came again and again, shaking as sweat started to slick their skin where their bodies met.

He gripped her hair, pulling her head back so he could suck the spot just beside her lips.

"Are you my girl?" he asked, his voice straining. They both knew the answer, but maybe they both needed to hear it again.

"Yes," Nailah said before she kissed him. She could barely breathe. He hadn't slowed down one bit.

SEVEN

Nailah sat on the edge of the bed, looking at the pictures she'd just taken with her phone. She didn't want to delete them ,but knew she should, unless she showed them to Armando first. And she wasn't ready for that, not yet. She knew exactly why. These weren't "hey look I totally got laid last night" pics. They were "I might want to date this guy" pics.

Nailah knew she should delete them right then. She wasn't ready for that. She didn't want a relationship with anyone, even if there was an undeniable pull between her and this particular man. She wanted to build her business and maybe in a few years, when she was ready to think about moving out and finally settling down, she'd find someone. They wouldn't necessarily have to be Egyptian, but they would have to be Christian or okay with raising their children that way. And that was just the start of her long list.

Nailah squeezed her eyes shut then lay back against the pillow. She shouldn't be thinking about that. She should have been thinking about the night before. She should have been thinking about just how amazing Armando was in bed. She should have been thinking more about this whole submission thing.

Discovering this side of herself had been an eye-opening experience. She could give herself over to a guy, follow his every command and still get everything she wanted. She could be fucked clear into next Tuesday, in the dirtiest of ways, and know that, at least for that night, she would fall asleep in someone's arms. She'd know what it was like to feel cared for and treasured and...

Nailah dug the heels of her hands into her eyes and let out a groan. No, it was not the time for this. They'd come to an agreement. They'd worked out a perfectly good routine. Gym during the week with a sex chaser on the weekend. None of that needed to change. Not yet. And what if she wanted to explore things with other Doms down the road? She was just scratching the surface of this whole BDSM thing. She was pretty sure a boyfriend, even if he was a Dominant, would ruin that.

When Nailah opened her eyes, Armando was looking at her.

"Morning," he said before he stretched.

"It's actually almost twelve. We were both out cold. You want to meet my friends for lunch? We're heading back after that."

"Sure."

"Cool, I'll grab first shower."

Nailah started to get up, but then Armando had to go and ruin everything. "Before I forget, do you have anything going on next Sunday?" he asked.

"Sometimes I go to church with my family, but we're usually home by one. Why, what's up?"

"My dads are throwing a party-barbeque for my sister. It's her birthday. Just wanted to see if you wanted to come."

"Oh, uh..." *Why aren't you saying no?* she thought to herself. *Say no!*

"It's not a big thing. Just close family and friends. Figured you'd like to be my plus-one and then we could go to my place after."

"I—yeah!" She actually sounded a little on the manic side. She coughed and gave it another try, even though the very loud voice in her brain was screaming at her to reconsider. "I'll go."

"I can pick you up or we can meet at my place."

"Uh, we'll just meet at your place. That way you don't have to drive to Beverly Hills."

"My dads live in Beverly Hills."

"Oh. Well, we won't have to go far."

"Are you okay?"

Nailah looked down and saw that she was twisting the comforter between her fingers. Her knuckles were white. "Yeah I'm fine. I'm just going to shower."

"I think I should spank you first."

"Why?" Nailah asked like it was stupidest thing he'd ever said. It seemed like he ignored her tone though because he flashed her that sexy-as-fuck smile that seemed to quiet all her doubts.

"You messed up several times last night, cursing at me, forgetting how to address me. You even bit me." He motioned to the nice purple bruise starting to bloom where his shoulder met his neck. "I definitely think you need a reminder."

Nailah hesitated a moment. She wasn't in the fucking mood. She needed to get in the shower and get up the courage to reject his invitation to this party. She did not want to meet his family. They would ask questions and think she was his girlfriend and... No. Just no.

But then part of her thought of how much more she would enjoy lunch with her friends while thinking about her sore ass and how it had gotten that way. Actually, her ass was already sore from the serious pounding she'd received the night before, but she could always stand more. And maybe if she asked nicely, he'd finger her while he spanked her.

She peeled off the fluffy robe she'd snagged from the bathroom. "Make it quick, Sir. I'm hungry."

"Yeah, I bet you are. Get over here."

She was across his lap in a flash. Nailah tried not to smile when his hand came down with a loud smack.

*

When his parents split up, before his mom moved back to Texas, every Thursday night his dad would pick up Armando and his sisters. They'd spend the weekend at his apartment in Hollywood. The place was too small for four people, but his dad always made sure they had a good time. It was the highlight of his week, every week, so much so that he and Connie begged their mother to leave them in LA when she moved.

Most nights his dad would run late, and Maria and Connie would count the red cars driving by until their dad's red Ford pulled up. As they played their games, and when Armando wasn't trying to keep them from bumping into random pedestrians or stepping off the curb with their carelessness, he would think about all the stuff he was going to tell his dad after Connie and Maria had gone to bed. They'd have their father/son time in front of the TV and Armando would tell him about school, about baseball, about the girls he liked in his class. Sometimes, he'd make a list so he wouldn't forget.

That Sunday, Armando lived that anticipation all over again. For the first time since his junior prom, he actually wanted his family to meet someone he was dating. Not that he and Nailah were dating exactly, but he did care about her. He was falling for her. He wanted his family to know her.

He'd already checked himself in the mirror a half a dozen times. And then he got tired of waiting on the couch. He grabbed Maria's gift and decided to wait out front. He'd have to go out to meet her anyway when she arrived. Nailah had a lot going on, but she knew what time he was trying to leave. She was almost an hour late.

Two black sedans drove by before Connie hit up his phone.

> You coming? Dads and Maria keep asking where you are?

His phone lit up again before he could respond.

It rang too this time, but it wasn't Nailah. It was his step-dad.

"Hey Mark. I'm coming."

"Hey, where are you?" Mark asked. "You okay?"

"Sorry, yeah. I'm good. I was just waiting on my friend. I'll be over there soon."

"Okay. Grab some ice on the way. Javier forgot it."

"Got it. Ice. I'll be there in a few."

Armando hung up with Mark and flipped back over to his texts and told Connie he'd be over in a minute. Still nothing from Nailah. He wanted to wait for her, but he was never late when it came to his family. He couldn't leave Maria hanging like that. Not on her birthday.

He dialed Nailah's number. It rang twice then clicked over to her voicemail. He listened to her voice, sweetened by her professional demeanor. But Armando didn't want to speak to Nailah Shalaby of NSL Designs. He was wondering where the hell his girl, his Nailah, was and when she was going to show up.

"Hey, it's Armando. I have to get over to my dads' so let me know if you're just running late or planning on coming later. I'll shoot you the address. Later."

Armando stood there, looking down the street for a few more minutes. He knew he shouldn't wait, but that little kid in him, the hopeful optimist wanted to give her a little more time. She'd show up any moment.

Eventually, he gave up and headed to his truck. His phone vibrated in his pocket as he loaded Maria's gift into the passenger seat.

It was a text from Nailah.

> Can't make it. I'm on little cousin duty. But have fun with your family. I'll see you at the gym tomorrow.

Armando felt like he'd been punched in the gut, which made

no sense. It was just a barbecue. There would be plenty of barbecues. But still that pain was there, and not the good kind. Armando texted her back, something cool and unaffected. She was right, he'd see her at the gym the next day, anyway.

Nailah sat on the couch between Aziza and Abasi. They were fighting over the Xbox controller, even though Nailah had already decided to let Abasi watch his movie first. They'd be watching another fucking seven-hour marathon of *Frozen* in no time. Her phone hummed in her clenched hands.

Taking the coward's way out didn't begin to describe what she had done. She knew for sure, from the moment she flew out of Vegas, after the high from the sex and the spanking and that damn vibrating egg wore off... she knew she couldn't go through with it. She couldn't meet Armando's family. She had no idea how she felt about him in a real world, long term sense. But she knew how she felt about meeting parents.

Her father had said it a hundred times, even to her brothers. "I'm only interested in the people you're going to marry. Otherwise, you are wasting my time and their time." He usually ended that diatribe by wandering off and grunting to himself. The old man was being ridiculous and archaic, but Nailah saw the value in what he said.

When her family loved, they loved full out. Isra wasn't just Garai's wife. She wasn't just a sister-in-law. Nailah treated her like a lifelong sister. They would do anything for each other and Nailah knew that from the first time Garai brought her home. Why? Because she was precious to Garai. They'd done the work on their own terms, and by the time she showed up at the Shalabys' door, it was a done deal. Isra was already this new piece, this new addition to Garai's heart, which meant, automatically, she was a piece of Nailah's heart.

They drove each other crazy, but that's what Nailah's family meant to her. She loved and trusted her brothers that much. The idea of calling Armando family at this point was downright laughable. She liked him, but she barely knew him. He'd last two minutes under her dad's third degree. And what if they broke up? Garai and Haji would hunt Armando down just to get the how and why out of him.

Why would he want to put *her* through that? If Armando's family was so important to him why would he want to expose Nailah to that intense of a connection if they weren't even a couple?

Yeah, she had no business going to that party. Still, she felt bad. She didn't like canceling last minute. It was a classless move. She looked at his text.

Cool. See you tomorrow.

Sorry. she texted back, as if the shitty apology made up for her blowing him off. She didn't even call him back. If he didn't get that she wasn't the one for him, not in the real world sense, then she'd let him know for sure the next time she saw him. They needed to renegotiate if they wanted to keep seeing each other at all.

"Who are you texting?" Aziza asked.

"No one. Let's watch *The Expendables* and then we'll watch *Frozen* again..."

Abasi snatched the controller from his sister and started his two-hour action fest. Nailah's phone vibrated again, but she didn't check. She shoved it under her thigh and settled in to watch the movie.

Eight

Armando deserved an award for playing it cool. He endured an hour with Nailah. He was funny, encouraging, cheered her on as she tackled that target heart rate, and not once did he do anything even the slightest bit weird. He didn't cry. He didn't beg. *Why? Why didn't you come to my baby sister's birthday party? Why?* Which was particularly impressive since he had to deal with a solid hour of everyone at Maria's party, including Violet and Grant, asking where Nailah was. His dads were looking forward to meeting her. Connie and Maria were looking forward to hazing her into the family, and Violet had some questions about remodeling a rental.

His dad saw the disappointment in his eyes so he didn't bring it up again, but he did say Nailah had an open invitation to come by whenever she wanted.

She didn't even mention the party, even when they were done with their workout, so maybe twenty- four hours later was too soon to ask for a rain check.

He finished his day at the gym and then, instead of going home and sitting alone on his couch, he called Master Phillip and asked him to meet for a drink. Armando promised he wouldn't cry. Master Philip said he could cry all he wanted.

Nailah stood outside of Melrose Fitness, finishing her call with Mrs. Levitz. They were making some great progress on the house. Her daughter's room was nearly done, and they had finally come to a decision about what to do with her husband's office. Nailah offered to find a professional organizer to help her sort through Mr. Levitz's things, and then they would recreate the office into an art studio for her client. Mrs. Levitz had given up painting when they started their family, but now that her youngest was in high school she was ready to get back to her own hobbies. It made Nailah feel good to see the woman getting her groove back. She made a mental note never to let her own groove go.

After they hung up—Mrs. Levitz was telling her about some custom easel she'd found online—she headed into the gym. Armando had been completely normal during their last workout, so Nailah figured it was business as usual. They could plan a time for their next bang session after she gave those sumo squats another go.

Armando came from the back office just as she put her stuff in the cubby. She glanced over her shoulder at him. "I'm feeling pretty fucking buff today, so you might actually have to let me bench press the bar."

"Totally. We can do that. I have to talk to you about something first."

Nailah froze. Something in his voice didn't sound right. When she turned around she noticed a strange look on his face. She knew that look. He wanted to talk. And he knew she was about to bolt.

"I just want to get something off my chest," he said.

"What if I don't want to hear it?"

"I'm almost positive you *don't* want to hear it, but a big part of this, between girl and Sir, is communication. I have something to communicate to you and then you can do whatever you want with that information. I'm not expecting it to magically change anything, I just want to say it. That okay?"

Nailah squeezed her eyes closed. "Yeah, fine."

"You want to sit down?"

"No. We're already cutting into my hour. We don't need to make ourselves comfortable."

"Okay. Well, I'll just get on with it. I'm falling in love with you."

Nailah looked up at him, confused. "Okay?"

"I didn't think it would be a good idea for us to go on with our other activities without sharing that fact with you."

"Okay? Is that it?"

"Yeah, pretty much."

"So you're falling in love with me and that's it? Alright, cool. So what are we doing for a warm up today?"

"Nailah."

"What?"

"Come on. Say something."

"No. Fuck you. You said you wanted to tell me something. So you told me and then you said you were done. So, now, I'm done. It's not my fault you're a shitty communicator and can't figure out what you really want to say or clearly articulate what you want from me. Not that it would matter. I don't know what the other women you've dealt with were like, but just because a guy bum-rushes me with his feelings- splooge doesn't mean I have swallow it and like it. Or ask for more."

"I don't just go around telling every woman that I love them. You have to know that much about me by now."

"That's true, but I don't know much else. Is it sweet? Yeah? I guess it is? But you're giving me no real time to think or respond, so thanks, but no thanks. Can we please work out now?"

Armando's jaw clenched like he was working out what to say

next, but Nailah didn't have time for that shit. She went over to the treadmill and started her own warm up. She had to pull the plug on the sex. Clearly, he couldn't handle it. Unfortunately he was definitely the best trainer she'd ever worked with it. If he couldn't keep it together for sixty minutes, she would have to go looking for another instructor.

✶

Turns out, looking elsewhere wasn't necessary. They'd come to a new understanding. Armando would continue to train Nailah. She could tell he was upset as their session went on, but he didn't bring up his bizarre love for her again.

Now with her connections on kinklife and even her access to Master Philip, she didn't think it would be too hard to find a man to call Sir. When she was ready. If she was ready.

She needed to get Armando out of her mind first. She could start by erasing the pictures of him from her phone. That would probably keep her from lying in her bed in the middle of the night, looking at his sleeping face. He'd posted those pictures of her on his kinklife page. Their captions were simple: *First morning with N.*, but he hadn't tagged her. She tried not to think too hard about what any of that meant. Again, she scrolled through her phone and when it occurred to her that she actually wished she had more pictures of Armando, she knew she had a problem.

It was almost midnight, but her parents' door was always open. She grabbed a sweatshirt and her flip- flops then power walked across the pool deck to her parents' back door. She poked her head into the living room where Haji and Abasi were still up playing video games. Upstairs, her parents' bedroom door was cracked open.

"Om?" Nailah said quietly. Her mom didn't answer, but Nailah heard her getting out of bed and moving around the room.

A few moments later, she stepped into the hall wrapped in her silk robe.

"Okay?" her mom said.

"Yeah, I just wanted to talk."

"Okay, habebti. Let's get some tea."

Nailah followed her mom down to the kitchen. She hopped up on a stool at their marble topped island and waited while her mom boiled some water.

"What's troubling you, baby?"

"I may have developed feelings for a man, but I broke things off with him."

"Why, darling?" Her mom sounded genuinely confused.

"Things were moving too fast, you could say."

"Fast how? Stop being vague."

"We were hanging out and then he just got all serious, wanting me to meet his family and telling me he loved me and shit. And stuff, I mean. Sorry."

"You and your sailor mouth. What was wrong with him?"

"What do you mean?"

"You don't have to say I love you back. That's just silly if you don't feel that way, but you just told me you have feelings for him. Why did you break it off? What is wrong with him?"

Nailah looked down and ran her finger along the edge of the island. She didn't have a good answer.

"Are you having sex with him?"

Nailah hesitated, but she knew that her mom was asking a simple question. It wasn't like she would freak out like her father. "Yes."

"And the sex was good?"

"I'm not telling you that."

"Is he the one who made your butt sore?"

"Oh my god." Nailah covered her face and slumped against the counter.

"You aren't telling me anything. You have a man who loves you and dumped him because he wanted you to know his family. Tell me the real reason."

"I'm not ready for that. I'm so busy with my design work. I want my business to grow before I settle down."

"Did he propose to you?"

"No."

"Did he ask you to settle down?"

"No."

"So what is the problem? You are young. You are well. You have no children. Why not spend your free time with someone you care for?"

"What about Garai? What about Baba? They are so nosey. What if they don't like him?"

"Then don't tell them. How long were you seeing this man?"

"A month?"

"See? And they had no clue."

"You knew?"

"Of course I knew. I'm a mama. I know things."

"Why didn't you say anything about it?"

"Because I trust you. I trust your judgment. You have always been responsible and bright. I knew if it was nothing, you'd handle it and if it was something, you'd come to me eventually."

Her mom was completely right. It was the way their relationship worked. Even when she told her mom she was ready to open her company, she had zero follow-up questions. She just started making calls and lists to help get the ball rolling. She even told Garai to get Nailah a deal on available office space.

Her father was all about the rules and ideals that he assumed everyone was following. Her mother just wanted her to live her life on her own terms. Her mother just wanted her to be happy. And smart. It was important for Shalaby women to use their heads.

Nailah took the hot mug her mom handed her. "I think you are putting too much pressure on yourself. Does he have a job?"

"Yes. He owns my gym."

"Uch, you and these fitness men," her mother teased. "He loves his family. Are there other women?"

"No, mom. He's a good man"

Her mom shrugged. "If you don't like him then don't talk to him. But if you have feelings, I say, why not? Good man, good job. Sore butt. All sound like good things to me."

If Nailah was being completely honest with herself, when she was done being completely mortified, she couldn't find a good reason not to be with him at all.

NINE

Armando almost ate shit and fell on his face running to answer his phone. The fake hardwood in his condo offered nothing in the way of traction when he was bolting from the shower. He grabbed his cell off the kitchen counter and hit accept before his brain fully processed the name on the screen. His nerves were on edge in the split second it took him to raise his phone to his ear.

"Hey," he said, trying to keep it light.

"Did I catch you at a bad time?" And there was Nailah, straight and direct. She'd ended all communication with him outside of the gym so he had no idea what this call was about.

"No, just got out of the shower. What's up?"

"I had some things I wanted to communicate to you, if that's okay."

Armando had done everything he could to shut off his feelings for this woman. After he'd gotten ripping drunk on Egyptian wine and bitched to Grant and Violet about how much of an ass he'd made out of himself after Master Philip's encouragement to "tell Miss Shalaby how you really feel", he set about doing everything he could to keep every interaction he had with her from being awkward as hell. He knew he had to move on, and he would when he was ready, but it was hard to shut off some pretty intense feelings in a few days.

Hearing Nailah's voice, with all its bone deep dryness, destroyed all the healthy progress he'd made. He was just as hung up as ever. He adjusted his towel, then leaned against the counter. He chose his words carefully. "I am open to communication. What's on your mind?"

"First, do you now or have you ever gone to church? What's your religious situation?"

"Uh, I was raised Catholic by my mom, but haven't been much lately—gay dads and all—but I still have faith. Does that work?"

"Yes. Do you want children? If so..." And she went on like that for a solid ten minutes. It wasn't a conversation. It felt more like an interview or an interrogation. He told her more about his relationship with his sisters. How he and Grant met. He admitted that he cheated on one girlfriend, but at the time he was young and dumb and inconsiderate. He knew he'd never do it again. Finally he told her he thought it was very possible for a married couple to have a fulfilling monogamous relationship that included their kinks.

"Can I ask what this about?" Armando asked when she seemed like she was wrapping things up. "Are you planning on proposing to me?"

"Fuck no."

"Well, what—"

"Hey, I have to go. I have client call coming in."

"Nailah, hold on a sec. Tell me what's going on."

"We'll talk later. Calm down. Bye."

Confused and really fucking annoyed, Armando realized there was nothing he could do until she called him back.

He put on some boxers then settled in bed with his laptop. Emails were answered and he considered watching some porn, but first he went to his kinklife account. There were several alerts from Queen_ofTheNile asking him to approve all sorts of connections, confirming a new relationship status, including naming him as her Dominant. Clearly they needed to have a serious conversation, one he wasn't going to wait around for her to instigate. In the meantime, he hit accept on every single connection.

✳

"Someone is here to see you."

"What?" Nailah looked up from her computer at Maura, who was standing in her doorway with this goofy grin on her face. "Who? Why are you being weird?"

Armando stepped into the doorway behind her. He was holding a huge bouquet of pink and white flowers.

"Hi," he said.

"Hi." Nailah almost stood up, she was so surprised.

"Do you have a minute?"

"Yeah. Maura—"

"I'll go to Starbucks or something." Her assistant dashed out the door, her signature giggle echoing in her wake.

Nailah stood and walked around her desk. She saw Armando three times a week in his workout clothes. She loved the way his T-shirts and shorts showed off his body and his tattoos, but he looked so much sexier in a long sleeved shirt and a well-fitted pair of jeans. She tried not to eye his crotch.

"Do you have an appointment?" she asked.

"I confirmed a dozen different connections last night that made me feel like maybe I didn't need one." Nailah sat on the edge of her desk, then folded her arms. That worked until Armando closed in on her. It was impossible to keep from inviting him into her personal space when he was so close. When she wanted him this bad. Her fingers went to the belt loops on his jeans. With his free hand, he touched her face.

He lowered his voice a bit and talked to her in that way that always threatened to crush her resolve. "Tell me what's going on."

"I've never been in a relationship before. Ever."

"Okay."

"Okay? Well, I went from no boyfriend experience to being with you. That's a big jump from nothing to a whole lot of something."

"I'll take that as a compliment."

"You scared me."

"Why? Tell me."

"Because I didn't want to become someone that you just had a lot of intense fun with for a while, like the other women in those pictures. When I want something, I commit. I didn't think you were in that same headspace with me so I never let it enter my mind that you *could* be there with me. And then you said you loved me."

"What changed your mind?"

"My mom."

"You bailed on meeting my family, but you told your mom about me?"

"Don't be so smug. I can talk to my mom."

"You can talk to me too, you know?"

"I know, but she made me realize that being afraid of imaginary situations wasn't a good reason never to sleep with you again."

"So is that all this is?"

"Why? Will you take back the flowers if it is?"

"No, but I might want to return this." Armando pulled a long, slender white box out of his back pocket.

"What's that?"

"Tell me something first. Why all the questions last night? What do you want with me?"

Nailah sucked it up and told the truth. "I want to be with you at the gym. I want at home on the weekends and during appropriate social functions in between. I want you—"

"In a box? With socks? On a bagel with lox?"

"Shut up. I want to do the whole thing with you. I talked to a few submissives online. One was even married to her Dom so I figured, if things go that way, we can work it out. I just wanted to be ready."

"We can do whatever you want, whatever you need, when you're ready."

"But I'm not very good at this whole feelings thing. And I don't do well with maybes. When I'm in something, I'm in all the way."

"Do you think I want you to change?"

Nailah shot him a look that suggested he'd lost his mind. "Do you think I would?"

"Not for one second. That's what I love— Sorry." He corrected himself with a sarcastic smile. "That's what I find to be most appealing about you. You know who you are. Even if you're figuring out your next move, you don't give an inch on what's inside."

"It's bothered guys who wanted to date me before."

"Nah, not me. I love that shit."

Nailah nodded toward his hand. "What's in the box?"

"It's a dog collar with a little metal bone tag that says 'Armando's Bitch'."

"I'd kill you."

"Here."

Nailah took the box and opened it. Inside was an oblong-shaped emerald pendant on a gold chain.

"It's an egg. Get it?"

"In my birthstone. Very clever." She had to remember that Facebook stalking went both ways.

"We can get you a proper collar whenever you want, but you can wear this one all the time."

"And this means I'm your girl all the time?"

"I would say so."

Nailah handed the box back to Armando then turned around, gathering her hair off her neck. He slipped the necklace into place, rubbing her back when the clasp was secure. She turned back around and stepped into his arms.

"What do we do now, Sir?"

"I wanted to take you to lunch."

"It's a little early for lunch."

"We could christen your office. I have all sorts workplace role-play scenarios worked out for you."

The thought of fucking in her office seemed so unprofessional, but Nailah was the boss. She made the rules.

"That door doesn't have a lock."

Armando glanced at the fogged glass before he brushed her lips with his. "You think your assistant can take a hint?"

Nailah shimmied back on her desk and slid her skirt up her thighs. "I think she'll have to."

TEN

Nailah was familiar with long goodbyes. It took an hour to actually make an exit from any of her family events. It was no different when it came to dinner with Armando's dads. She and her Sir had been together for two and half months and finally she'd built up the courage to meet the family. Just the dads though. She was holding off on meeting his sisters, but she knew she would have to do it soon. They'd been asking about her.

After a delicious dinner that Javier prepared, there was more wine and dessert, and then more conversation before Armando announced it was time for them to go. But then, she and Mark started talking about changes he wanted to make in their den and the outdated fixtures in the bathroom. Before she knew it, they were walking through the whole house while Javier and Armando finished doing the dishes. Finally, Armando put his foot down and dragged her out the door.

"You were amazing tonight," Armando said, once he started his truck. His dads lived a five minute drive from her parents' house off Sunset, but she wasn't heading home tonight.

She looked over at his gorgeous face, lit up by the dashboard lights. "Was I?"

"Yes. I'm pretty sure they love you. And you went four whole hours without saying fuck."

Nailah would be lying if she said she wasn't pretty charmed by Armando's dads too. Javier was hilarious and Mark was one of the sweetest men she had ever met. She could see how Armando turned out the way he did.

He reached over and rubbed her thigh, just under her sundress. "Thank you for coming with me."

"I wanted to. I owed you for winning over my mom. I think she likes you more than I do."

"Should I buy her her own vibrating egg?"

"Do it. See what happens."

There was no way to keep her relationship with Armando a secret from her family. She saw him on a pretty regular basis, nights and weekends. Her family knew all her friends and there was no way she was spending that much time with Meena and Shelly, but with her mother's help, her dad and her brothers agreed to chill the fuck out until she was ready to invite Armando over to the house for a proper introduction.

Still, her mom wanted to meet him, in exchange for keeping the Shalaby men in line. Especially since her dad, who was so over-dramatically devastated that his little girl finally had a boyfriend, continued to pout about it almost every day. God help the man if he ever found out what they were really up to.

Nailah offered to take her mom to breakfast on a Saturday morning, and on the way they stopped by Melrose Fitness to see Armando between clients. All Armando had to do was flash that killer smile and her mom was done for. There was some playful interrogation, though, before she was completely satisfied.

"The night is still young. What do you want to do?" he asked, as he turned at the next stop sign.

Nailah squirmed in her seat. "Probably something about this plug in my ass."

"How does it feel?"

"You know how it feels."

"No, I don't," Armando said, with a cruel laugh. She'd been threatening to shove various things in his ass ever since they started her plug training. Every time they went up a size she gave him a piece of her mind, but by now Armando fully understood that when it came to him, she was all bark and no bite. Unless he actually stepped out of line.

He gave her thigh a gentle squeeze. "How does it feel? Tell me."

She moved a little closer, as close as the center console would allow her. "It feels too big, but I don't want to take it out."

"You want me to leave it in while I fuck you?" he asked, as his hand found its way into her underwear. "Fuck. Have you been this wet all night?"

Nailah picked her pendant up off her chest and ran the chain over her teeth. "Mhmm."

His hand moved up and a finger swirled around her clit. "You want me to pull over?"

"Yes, Sir."

He found a spot on the side of the street, between some streetlights, and threw his truck in park. As soon as the engine and their seatbelts were off, Nailah scrambled over the seat into Armando's lap. He reached for a condom in his glove box. The outdoor sex they had was becoming more frequent. They were always prepared.

He kissed her, that way only he knew how to kiss her, deep and slow, with his hand twisted in her hair. She went for his zipper, letting his cock out to play. He'd been good, keeping those three little words to himself until Nailah was ready to say them back. As he kissed her and pulled her panties to the side she knew she was getting closer to that day. She was nearly there. Just not yet.

. . .

The End

ADORED

Nailah checked her mascara for the fifth time before adding another coat of inky black. Tonight was going to be a big night, an important night. Dinner followed by hours of kink and debauchery. She'd been with Armando as his trained and collared submissive, and exclusive girlfriend for almost a year now. He'd told he loved her months ago. At the time it had pissed Nailah right the fuck off. She obviously wasn't there yet. Not even close mostly because they weren't even a couple, so she didn't said it back. Plus he'd dropped the l-bomb as a first-ditch attempt at conflict resolution instead of just talking to her like a normal person.

They were past that now and after all the time they'd spent together, getting to know each other, learning from each other and worshiping each other's bodies, Nailah had come to realize that Armando was it for her. She loved him deeply. She was not a sap. Far from it. Her cold exterior was one of the things that had turned him on. He'd learned to love her the way she wanted to be loved and never once asked her to change. Oh did she try, but it was hard not to fall for him. The amazing sex didn't hurt.

"Are you sure you don't want to at least split the room?" her best friend Shelly asked from her perch on the hotel bed. She absently flipped through one of the design magazines Nailah had brought for her to peruse. Nailah was still living at home in her parents' pool house and she would until she got married and moved out. Her mom had supported her relationship with Armando from the start, but her traditional father was still pretending his sweet daughter was single with a single minded focus on her career.

To Dr. Shalaby Armando was just some friend Nailah saw every weekend and at least twice during the week. Sometimes she said she was staying out with friends when it came to overnight situations, and tonight was no different. Tonight's date called for a sinful dress and some tall heels. Changing at a hotel and letting her friend keep the room overnight was better than trying to sneak across the pool deck, praying her father didn't see her in some tight ass black lace.

"No. Armando's got it. Don't worry."

"I like him," Shelly said, a smile in her voice. Nailah poked her head out of the bathroom and gave her friend a steely glare. "I mean I like him for you. I'm not trying to take your man."

"Good. Enjoy your night at the W courtesy of *my* man."

"Maybe I'll thank him with a deep kiss on the mouth." Shelly cackle echoed through the room as Nailah's tube of concealer whizzed by her head. "You know I'm joking. I love you two together. I'd never try to break up your happy home."

"Thanks. I like him too." Nailah hadn't told Shelly why the night was so important. Her friends knew Armando meant a lot to her mostly because Nailah was claiming him publicly, but she had to get the words out to Armando himself without vomiting or freaking out and jumping out the window before she confessed the depth of her feelings to her girls. Honestly she'd probably never say it out loud to her friends, but they'd figure it out when they got invitations to their wedding. A wedding that was still a long way off. She needed to focus on tonight.

She leaned back from the mirror and took in her newly

finished look. Her thick black hair was straightened perfectly and pulled back slick and tight. Armando loved her hair down for nice, casual situations, but for what she had in mind tonight she needed her hair out of the way. Her caramel-brown eyes framed with dark liner, her lips painted red. Nailah was born gorgeous and no one could tell her otherwise, but since she'd met Armando she felt like her perception of her own beauty had changed. She felt the shift from being seen to being appreciated in a way that made her feel incredibly sexy and in turn, somehow stronger. She was definitely in love.

She adjusted the emerald pendant resting on her chest, then turned and smoothed down her black dress over her ass. The thong she was wearing was doing the job it needed to do nicely. The old her wouldn't have given a single shit what a man thought about what she was wearing, but she knew Armando would be battling his better self in a race to get her naked, no matter how disciplined he was feeling.

"Babes, your phone is vibrating," Shelly said, rushing into the bathroom. "Oh, it's my man."

Nailah let out a low growl as she snatched the phone out of her hand. The name ARMANDO flashed across the top of the screen. She hit accept, fighting the smile that wanted to touch her voice.

"Hello," she said.

"Hey, baby." Nailah was not the type to sigh or swoon, but Armando knew just the sound of his voice did something to her. He'd told her once that her eyes and her lips give her away. Subtle twitches letting him know just how affected she was. Now, though, something in his tone immediately set off a wave of unease in her stomach.

"Everything okay?"

"Fuck no. I think it would be smart for me to cancel tonight. I know you wanted to play. You know I wanted to play, but I don't think it's a good idea."

Nailah let his words rush over of her again and once more as she registered how tight and off he sounded. She knew she shouldn't jump to conclusions, but this shitty voice in her head screamed out a loud and clear "I told you so!" Just when she realized how she felt, when she'd gotten up the nerve to tell him, Armando was ending things. Nailah locked down her temper, another thing she'd been working on, and decided to wait for an explanation before she started freaking out.

"Can you tell me why?"

"Yeah. Of course." Armando let out an angry sigh. "I just had to fire a client—well two clients— and shit got really messy and then it got racist. I'm pretty fucked up right now and I don't think I should Top you like this. Actually I know I can't. Philip would kick my ass if I did."

Nailah felt her eyes roll. She didn't give a fuck about Master Philip, Armando's mentor in kink. Yeah he taught Armando everything he knew about BDSM, but Armando and her had a relationship outside of that world. It annoyed her sometimes when The Club and the rules of their Dominant/submissive relationship got in the way. Still, she understood. Things needed to be done a certain way, for her safety and the integrity of their arrangement. She wasn't giving up that easily.

"So let's just have dinner," Nailah suggested.

"Babe," Armando said, the defeat in his voice followed by a long silence. Nailah's temper flared.

"What aren't you telling me?"

"A lot," he laughed mirthlessly. "Some really bad shit happened and I'm just trying to wrap my mind around it. I'd ruin dinner and I'd definitely ruin what comes after. Trust me."

"Okay fine. What are you going to do instead?"

"Sit in my house and stare at the wall while I try to think about this job, this gym, my whole life. I promise I'll make it up to you. I just really figure some shit out. Mostly I need to calm down."

And now Nailah felt bad. Armando wasn't quick to anger, but

his temper flared when the moment called for it. If he was this keyed up something very bad had happened at the gym.

"Do I need to beat someone up?" she asked.

Armando scoffed. "I might put my sisters on this one, but I appreciate the offer. I just—I haven't been this pissed in a long time." Nailah could hear it in his voice. He was telling the truth. "I really want to see you, but I need to cool off. I wasn't in the wrong, but I wasn't my best self tonight."

Nailah let out a sigh of her own, frustration and concern weighing on her equally. "Okay. I'll take a raincheck, but we better get up to some really filthy shit the next time I see you."

Armando's laugh was warmer this time. "I promise. Is Shelly still there?"

"Yeah."

"Why don't you two run up the room service. On me."

Nailah glanced out the bathroom door at her friend who was focused on the rerun of *Sex and the City* playing on the TV. She hated the feeling of disappointment that rushed over her. She really hated that she thought she might cry. She sniffed hard, instead, forcing her tears back.

"We can do that."

"Sorry. You know I want to be at my best for you."

"No, I understand. When am I gonna hear from you again?"

"Tomorrow, maybe even later tonight. I need to go for a long run I think and punch the air for a while."

"Okay." They agreed to talk later and then Nailah ended the call.

"Everything okay?" Shelly called out.

"No." Nailah padded back into the bedroom and sank down on the bed. She was pissed. Tonight was supposed to be their night. "Armando had to cancel. Some bad shit happened with a client."

"Aww babe, I'm sorry. Is he okay? Are you okay?"

"No." She had no clue who these asshole clients were, but she was considering calling Keira for details. She wouldn't do anything too crazy, but keying a car or two felt like the right move at the moment. Nailah sucked in a deep breath and shook off the dark cloud spreading over her. Armando was just asking for reasonable space for himself. She knew he had made the right call. Still, it hurt. And, no she wouldn't admit that out loud.

"You wanna hang out with me tonight?"

"Yeah, I guess," Nailah grumbled sarcastically.

Shelly brought up the guide on the TV and flashed her a big smile. "There's so much edited *Sex and the City* for us to watch."

Nailah sighed again, and looked at her phone clenched in her palm. Room service and girl time was a fine way to spend a Friday night, but she wanted to see her man. Even if it was just to talk. They watched Miranda discover she was pregnant with Steve's baby before Shelly hopped up and grabbed the room service menu.

"I think you need fries and ice cream."

The SATC theme started up again and Nailah felt like she was climbing out of her skin. She stood up, grabbed the extra room key off the desk and stepped into the heels she'd set next to her overnight bag.

"I'll be back. Maybe."

"Where are you going?"

"Over to Armando's. I need to talk to him."

"Okay. You want me to come?"

"No, I got it." Nailah didn't need a witness for what felt like a rising freak out. She did not like having plans canceled. She didn't like that it was some client who caused it and she liked even less that she was suddenly feeling so unsteady. She did not do unsteady. She was going to go over to Armando's. Obviously their plans had changed, but she didn't like being shelved like this. She grabbed her date night clutch and her black blazer then scanned the room one more time to make sure she wasn't forgetting anything. She left Shelly with firm instructions to go crazy on the room service and then headed down to get her car from the valet.

She knew there was a chance she was doing too much, but that didn't stop her from making the drive over to his condo. After she parked Nailah looked down at her phone. She could call him, or text him and give him a little warning, but she'd come this far, powered by her own raging annoyance with the situation. She had to see it through.

Nailah climbed out of the driver seat, her determination renewed, a solid plan formulating. Nothing petty, but they needed to figure something out. She couldn't come second to his clients, especially if they were treating him poorly. That wouldn't work. Nailah made it around the front of her car before she felt that electric familiarity in the air. She looked down the street just as a very sweaty Armando came running around the corner. Nailah swallowed and tried to not be distracted by how good he looked, his golden skin drenched in sweat glistening in the fading light of the setting sun.

He spotted her and slowed to a jog and then a walk until they were just a few inches apart. Nailah did her best not to groan with pleasure when the scent of him swept over her. Instead she took another deep breath through her nose and pushed her shoulders back.

"Hey," he said, pulling his earbuds out. He seemed shocked to see her, but not annoyed. And he did look tired, not in a freshly worked out sort of way. His face was red and there were stress lines under his eyes. Something was really bothering him. Nailah could work with that.

"Hello."

"Are you okay? I was still planning to call you later," he replied.

"As your submissive, I understand that you're upset and don't want to tie me up or paddle me, but you're also my boyfriend. If something is bothering you so much you feel like you can't dominate me physically, we can adjust our plans. But I don't think that should stop us from spending time with each other."

A smile bloomed over his gorgeous face as he wiped his face with his forearm. "You're right."

"I know I am."

"You want to come inside?"

"Yes, if you'll tell me what actually happened."

Another smile lifted his trimmed mustache. "I will if you promise not to go all vigilante on me. Not that they don't deserve it, but I don't want you to go to jail."

"I will promise no such thing. Let's go." Nailah turned and headed up the walkway. Her heart rate slowed a bit as she felt Armando fall into step behind her. Once they were inside Nailah helped herself to a glass of the chilled rosé he kept in his fridge for her and then she waited. She couldn't sit. She couldn't relax. She was waiting for Armando to tell her something that would truly set off and after seeing the stress etched across his face she was still debating if this was the right time to tell him how she felt.

He showered quickly and maybe five minutes after the water cut off, he came strolling into the kitchen in nothing but a loose pair of sweatpants. A bottle of lotion was tucked under his arm as he rubbed a generous amount over his face and chest.

"You want me to get your back?" she offered, her tone cool.

"Yes, please."

Nailah nodded toward the couch and took a seat behind him as he eased down to the floor. "So tell me what happened."

"Is it too late to tell you how beautiful you look?"

"No, it's not and thank you. I did in fact, wear this for you," she replied, easing her lotioned hands over his muscular shoulders.

"I'm seeing where I screwed up."

"You didn't screw up, but it did take me a long time to get ready. I'm glad you're experiencing it. Now talk."

Armando let out another deep breath and then he started talking. Nailah didn't keep up with all his clients. He taught classes and did individual sessions, but there was always a certain level of confidentiality. Every once in a while he'd tell her if a client said something funny or if he was frustrated with a fat shaming family member he hadn't met, but had just heard about. He'd mentioned Tiffany Palenti and her daughter Isabella months ago when they'd signed on, but he hadn't mentioned them since.

She wasn't so surprised to hear that both women were flirting with him. Armando was incredibly sexy and good at his job, but she didn't expect him to tell her that Tiffany had burst into a Isabella's session earlier into the day not only to confess her infatuation with him, but to demand that Armando choose.

"Choose what?" Nailah said, sitting back. Armando turned just enough to pull her foot into his lap. He took off her heel and started massaging the arch of her foot.

"Choose between them."

"Uh huh." Nailah forced herself to ignore the way his fingers were perfectly kneading her skin.

"It descended into chaos from there. They started fighting and Grant had to come in and help me break it up. I didn't really have a choice but to fire them as clients on the spot and that's when things got racist."

"I see," Nailah replied. She glanced over at her clutch. She only had to send a text or two and she was pretty sure she could find out exactly where Tiffany and Isabella lived.

"I don't want you to do anything," Armando said, his voice stern, his fingers on her still gentle.

"What? I was just thinking."

"Yeah, thinking about the best way to handle this without leaving any prints."

Nailah smoothed down her ponytail. "I don't know what you're talking about. Go on."

Another deep sigh from her man. "I reacted. Cussed them both out pretty good, said some pretty harsh things. They deserved it, but I felt shitty after. I hated that they pushed me that far. Grant said I was vibrating, I was so angry."

"How did you get rid of them?"

"Grant threw his white guy weight around a little and got them out of the gym, and dared them to try and come back. I don't think we'll be seeing them again."

Nailah chewed the inside of her lip, trying to keep her cool. She felt Armando's gaze on her and she wasn't sure if now was the right moment to hurdle over him and try to find his phone. He also texted his clients to confirm sessions. Or maybe it would be easier if she just waited and quietly tracked the mother and daughter down. No way they were gonna harass her man, hurl slurs at him and move on with their happy hateful lives. Not on her watch.

Slowly Armando rose to his knees and shifted so he was facing her, settled right between her legs. Their gazes locked for a moment before he gripped her hips and pulled her to the edge of the couch. Nailah almost forgot about those two racist hags as her pussy instantly started to swell with need. She wanted him so badly.

"I shouldn't have canceled our plans," Armando said, his gaze roaming over her face. "I just felt a little outside of myself, but I'm glad you came over."

"I'm glad I did too," Nailah said. She forced herself to look down at his chest because if she looked into his kind brown eyes she knew she would lose the nerve to say what she needed to say next. "I can't promise that some tires won't be 'accidentally' slashed in the next few weeks, but I am glad you told me what happened and I am sorry people who were trying to help were so evil to you. Of course I don't want anything like this to happen again, but I want to be there for you if it does. I want to be there for you the way you're always there for me."

"You already are," he said back.

"Well, I also have to be honest and admit that a part of me came over here for selfish reasons."

"Oh yeah?"

Nailah swallowed at the sudden heat that touched Armando's

voice. He was definitely focused on other things now, like her mouth. She glanced up at him and then back down at his chest.

"I mean I couldn't let some asshole stop you from seeing how good I look tonight."

"True," he chuckled.

"And I was going to tell you that I love you tonight. I was going to tell you how much you mean to me. And now I want to tell you that it hurts me to see you upset too. Slashing tires seems like the least I could do."

"Nailah," he breathed. She dared a look into his eyes suddenly unsteady again for different reasons. She'd never felt this way about anyone before. She never knew she could love someone so completely that the thought of not seeing them ruined her whole day.

"I do love you," she said, her voice uncharacteristically quiet. "I love you a lot."

Armando reached up and brushed her cheek. "I love you too."

"Good." Nailah couldn't wait any longer. She leaned forward and kissed the man she had grown to love very much. She let herself sag against him as he pulled her closer and kissed her right back. They didn't have to do anything kinky, but she needed this. She wanted to be with him at every possible moment. Relief rushed over her when he pulled away just enough to press a few more soft kisses to her face.

"Let me slash one tire," she whispered.

Her own body shook as Armando chuckled. "No."

SATED

No. 3 in the Fit Trilogy

About This Book

SATED
No. 3 in the Fit Trilogy
Nominee: 2015 Romantic Times Book Reviews Reviewers' Choice
Award Digital Erotic Romance

All Keira Kenney wants is her happy ending. Too bad she can never make it through a first date. Is a nice man who's into fitness and comics, with an extensive knowledge of everything science-fiction too much to ask for? Apparently, since Keira can't seem to find a partner who can simply tolerate her interests. Perhaps it's time for her to give up. She has her job at Melrose Fitness, a new season of her favorite space drama added to streaming, and hundreds of thousands of words worth of fan fiction all to keep her mind busy. Her heart will have to wait.

Pyrotechnics expert Daniel Song isn't looking for anything. He spends his days doing what he loves, and his nights and weekends participating in the kinky activities his body craves. Single life as sexual switch suits him perfectly, giving him the freedom to indulge the types of erotic adventures some people only dream of.

When a good friend asks Daniel if his co-worker, Keira can join him at a local sci-fi convention, neither of them expect any sort of fireworks to spark. After all, Keira's turned off by kink and Daniel can't live without with it. So naturally they both agree that an official first date would be a great idea.

With this new relationship fresh between them, Daniel shares what he can of himself without scaring Keira off, hiding his shock and growing infatuation as she rises to every sexual occasion with her silly, geek-girl personality. It's only a matter of time before they both have to face the truth; what he wants is the furtherest thing from what she needs. But in the meantime, pushing each other's sexual limits seems like a good plan. It's like not either of them is looking for love.

This story contains two massive nerds who can't keep their hands off each other. And fisting.

To Fangirls Everywhere!

ONE

Keira took the dessert menu even though she was full. She was determined to save this date.

"Everything looks good," she said, trying to sound cheerful. She glanced up at the man sitting across from her. Travis Humphrey, power forward for the LA Clippers. He was good-looking, on TV at least, but from the moment he'd met her outside the restaurant he became more and more unattractive with every word he spoke. He wasn't speaking anymore though. He was looking at his phone.

Why do I keep doing this to myself? Keira thought. *Oh, you know why.*

She did. She'd been single for almost two years and completely sex free for almost ten months. Being a massive dork, who enjoyed spending the majority of her time on fan-based blogs or in a movie theater alone, didn't make the quest for a life mate any easier. And this nagging need to find a man seemed that much worse when Keira stepped back and looked at how great her life was. She had plenty to be thankful for. A great job teaching kickboxing and doing a little personal training at Melrose Fitness, one of the best gyms in town. She had amazing parents who doted on her, and plenty of great friends. Keira had it all, except a date who could give her his undivided attention through an entire meal.

Before the evening even kicked off, all signs pointed to disaster. Keira picked out the perfect dress. Her cousin was sweet enough to come over and do her hair. Even the weather was just right. The day had been unusually hot for November, but by the time she'd stepped out of her North Hollywood apartment, things had cooled off to a perfect degree. Everything was in place as she drove to meet Travis at Más. Everything was too right. She was putting in too much effort for a guy she didn't even like. That's how desperate her situation had become.

The fact that Travis hadn't been the one to ask her out and she still said yes? That should have been the first red flag. His assistant did the legwork. Travis had seen her across the room at a charity function and sent the young kid over with his cell phone out and ready to receive some digits. Travis flashed her a smile when his assistant pointed him out to Keira.

It wasn't charming in the slightest, but when was the last time someone had asked her on a date without yelling the words "Eh girl!" from across the street or sending a message on DotCom-Cupid asking for nudes? She said sure and gave the assistant her number. Travis was courteous enough to call himself, but the conversation was short and filled with innuendo. He had one thing in mind. Keira wasn't sure she was going to give that one thing up, not on the first date. She wanted to see if there was any real chemistry between them.

There wasn't.

"You wanna split something?" Keira tried again.

"Nah, I'm not much on sweet. But I got you. Get whatever you want." He glanced up from his phone, finally, and flashed her that smile that must work wonders on other women. Who was she kidding? The smile had worked on her.

Keira put the menu down. It was time to wrap up this waste of an evening. "I think I'll pass too. You have plans for this weekend?"

"Flying down to Miami with my boys. Playing the Heat. But after the game we're always looking for more company."

"Oh," Keira tried to sound disappointed. "Thanks for the invitation, but I can't."

Travis leaned forward. He'd been doing that all night, arching an eyebrow and testing the support strength of the table legs. She was only two feet away. She could hear him just fine. But that didn't matter.

He had to get closer and take any chance he got to turn the conversation toward sex. That's when he was all interest, completely engaged, and probably at full attention. "What'd you have going on that's better than hitting South Beach?"

"I..." Keira had a day pass to Galaxi-Con, the annual convention for only her favorite show in the whole freaking universe. She'd already told her boss-buddies, Grant and Armando, they were going to have to cover her schedule at the gym. She had her cosplay outfit planned with two back-ups just in case the she wasn't up to full body makeup for a whole day. She almost told Travis about it, but something about the way he was glancing at his phone again, kind of waiting for her answer, mostly waiting to get her in the sack, made Keira think he wouldn't be interested.

Screw it, Keira thought. *Tell him.*

"I actually have tickets to Galaxi-Con. Do you watch *Galaxis*?"

"Nah. What is it?"

Oh, he really screwed up. Geek-mode, activated.

"It's this really cool show. It's basically about this girl, well this young woman, Orora. She's living on this Earth-like colony on the outskirts of the galaxy. Part human, part alien and totally orphaned, she finds out that she's actually the heir to this whole kingdom and she has to get back to Earth and stop the remaining humans from killing her mother's people."

Travis completely checked out, looking from his phone to his watch, to the women at the table just to Keira's left, but Keira kept talking, five seasons worth of nerdiness. She even dropped some bits about the fanfiction she'd been writing and how many friends she'd made online because of it. Travis could not be less interested.

Their server came back, all smiles. "Did we decide? Any dessert?"

Keira tried to smile back. "No, thank—"

"Nah, we're good." Keira could feel herself frowning as Travis reached into his wallet then threw a bunch of cash on the table before he moved to stand up. It was more than enough to cover the bill, but geez. Manners much?

"Ready?" he asked.

"Uh, yeah." Keira offered a quiet apology to their server then followed Travis out of the restaurant. As soon as they hit the door, she cut right for the valet stand. The street was swarming with paparazzi, but Travis didn't seem to mind.

"Yo, Travis! Yo, Travis! You on a date, man?"

"Nah, just out with some friends."

Keira felt the hot light from a camera turn toward her. She almost jumped behind a potted plant, but thought better of it. She raised her clutch instead and covered her face.

"Leave her alone, man. We're just friends."

"You sure, bro?"

"Positive."

Keira listened on as the pap started asking Travis about his watch and how he saw the rest of the season going. He sounded happier than he'd been all night. Good to know they'd *both* had a terrible time. Eventually he got tired of the lights and cameras and came over to join her. The valet attendant already had his car waiting.

"So you wanna come back to my place?" he asked, just as her car pulled up.

She walked around to the driver's side, putting her Dodge Challenger between them. He had no interest in anything she had to say, but she had a feeling he might go in for the kiss. A final attempt at persuasion.

"I'd love to, but I have a client early in the morning." Both lies rolled easily off her tongue.

"What do you do again?"

Keira glared at him for a moment. She'd told him about Melrose Fitness, at length. In the brief moment when he'd actually been paying attention, he'd teased her, in his not so charming way, about her kickboxing skills and how he was sure he could still take her.

"I'm a vet tech. Pit bull puppies first thing in the morning. Have to be alert to deal with that handful."

"Oh aight. Cool—"

Keira didn't wait for him to finish his sentence. She tipped the valet, then slid into her car. Before she turned the corner onto the next street, she caught a glimpse of Travis in her rear view mirror. Three women heading into the restaurant already had his attention. Keira made up her mind right then and there, she was never dating again.

The gym was quiet except for the sound of Keira's foot striking the bag. She was exhausted. Sweat poured down her face and her hip was starting to ache, but her feelings for Travis Humphrey were almost all worked out. Well, more like her non-feelings for Travis Humphrey. And that's what pissed her off so much. How could she be so upset over a guy that was clearly wrong for her? You could see how poorly matched they were from outer space. Still she couldn't help feeling as if she'd failed again; failed to live up to some weird standards she'd created for herself. Like she'd failed to be enough.

Her mother had always told her that her looks would only get her so far. From the time she could comprehend compliments, people had always told her how beautiful she was, but Keira took her mother's words directly to heart and made it her life's goal to not only develop her physical but her mental strength. When she wasn't in the gym, her face was buried in a book or a comic, or focused on the nearest screen playing her sci-fi favorites. Keira had crafted herself into the dream student, the model child, and the ideal athlete. And the most socially awkward human being ever.

No one cared about her favorite books and TV shows, no one except her friends online. And only Grant and Armando gave a crap about how many handstand push ups she could do. She got along great with Armando. He treated her like a little sister; a little sister he sort of put up with. She wasn't super close with Grant, even though he'd been the one to hire her. They were both super nice, but they were also her bosses, and they saw what she could bring to their gym as a female fitness instructor.

At the moment, both of them were gone. Armando was returning from a trip at some point that day and Grant had stepped out to join his girlfriend, Violet, for lunch. Keira had the gym to herself until he came back and the afternoon sessions with clients kicked up again. Keira knew she should chill out and mentally prepare to spend the rest of the day smiling at people, but she could not shake this funk. She worked her fists, punching the crap out of the bag for a few more minutes. Then Armando came bounding through the gym's frosted double doors.

"Well hello, Keira," he said cheerfully, as he walked by. "See the place didn't blow up while I was gone."

"Yeah, we managed," Keira mumbled. Armando popped into the back office. He reappeared a minute later, chest bare, carrying a Melrose Fitness shirt in his hand. Keira tried not to look. He was taken too, but a nice body was a nice body.

"What's going on?" he asked.

"Nothing." Keira delivered another hard kick. More sweat slicked down her back.

"You okay?"

"Peachy."

"Hey. What's going on?" Armando grabbed the bag and held it in place. That didn't stop Keira from throwing a few more punches. She glanced up at his face. He wasn't going to leave her alone until she talked. Keira sank to the floor and started pulling off her wraps.

"I went out with Travis Humphrey last night and it was terrible."

"What happened? Did he try any funny business?"

That made Keira laugh. "He hinted heavily at the funny business, but he didn't try anything. I just don't know why I bother. I go on so many first dates, but guys never seem to like me. Maybe I'm just too buff. Some guys don't do muscles." She playfully poked at her sweaty bicep.

"That's not it. You're too pretty."

She looked up at Armando, scowling. "Thanks?"

"Listen. Men are functional morons. We take everything at face value. We see a hot woman and we think about sex and nothing else until we actually speak to you. And then some of us, the assholes mainly, can't believe it when a woman comes with weird shit like a brain and her own personality. Look, it's stupid, but we have a hard time seeing past a pretty face sometimes. Shit, even I read you all wrong when we first met."

"You did?"

"Yeah, ask Grant. I was pissed when he hired you. I had to force myself not to ask you out."

"Cause you're my boss?"

"Pretty much. But then I got to know you and I realized—"

"You realized that we're such good friends. That I remind you of your little sister. I know, I know. Connie and I are practically personality twins."

"You are, but that's not it. I realized that we'd be terrible together."

Keira flopped onto her back. "You're not helping."

"Come on. You know I love you to death, but could you honestly see us together?"

"No." And it wasn't because he was her boss. Armando and Grant were both funny, sweet guys, but something about them always made Keira feel like they were on a different level of cool adultness. Didn't help that both of them were involved in some bondage club, freaky domination type stuff. It intrigued her, but she could never be on the receiving end of that kind of torture. And from what she's witnessed between Armando and his girl-friend, he was only into giving.

"Dude, you've met Nailah. You see how much I love her. Or look at Grant and Violet. He's a teddy bear and she's Miss Skepti-cal-Sarcasm."

Armando had a point. Nailah had a very cool demeanor that you had to chip away at. Once you got to know her though, she was sweet as pie. They weren't friends, exactly, but Keira liked Nailah a lot and seeing her with Armando, it was clear how good they were together. He was hot and she was cold. Keira herself was also hot, cheerful and outgoing, just like Armando and Grant. Their upbeat personalities made it so easy for them to get along, made it easy for the three of them to run the gym so smoothly, but there was nothing romantic there. It wouldn't make sense. Dating Grant or Armando would be like dating herself.

"Seems like opposites do attract, but it's not like Travis and I were too much alike."

"Something tells me that you and a guy like Travis Humphrey have nothing to connect on at all."

"And I don't even like him! Ugh, you're right, but what am I going to do? It's not like..." Keira let out a deep breath. "I know I don't *need* a man—"

"Keira, stop." Armando's tone was too serious. The sound of it made her look up again. "You need what you need and if you need someone in your life who cares about you that way, then there's nothing wrong with that. Just don't rush it. If you want the real thing, be patient. He'll come along."

"When did you get so insightful?"

"Blame Nailah. She makes me think about crap like feelings and shit."

"I'll have to thank her."

"You're going to that comic thing this weekend and you said your Internet buddies bailed, right?" It wasn't some comic thing, but Keira was too tired to correct him.

"Yeah."

"You should meet up with my buddy, Daniel. His brother is involved with the show. I'm sure he can hook you up with some behind-the-scenes perks. Help you take your mind off this dating crap."

Keira remembered meeting Daniel once and she only remembered because he was an intensely hot Asian guy who'd had one of his hands amputated. He also had a really deep voice that threw her off a bit. They hadn't said more than a hello to each other at Grant's last birthday party, but he was hard to forget.

"It would be nice not to walk around the convention alone." She had planned to meet up with a few friends from the *Galaxis* blogs but, for one reason or another, each of them was unable to make the trip to Los Angeles this year.

"Cool. I'll text him. I'm sure he has some sort of VIP access. You'll have fun."

Grant walked in then, face a little flushed, grinning from ear to ear. Lunch with Violet probably hadn't involved any food.

"Hey! What are we doing?" he asked as he lightly slapped the heavy bag still hanging near Armando's head.

"I was just telling Keira she should go to the that Con thing with Daniel. You know, let him show her around."

"Daniel Song?"

"Yep."

Grant's hesitation made Keira's stomach sink. They couldn't

even find people who wanted to spend an afternoon with her. "Bad idea?"

"No, no. Not at all," Grant said, cocking his head to the side. "I just realized you guys have never hung out. He's a cool guy. And I think his brother is big in the sci-fi TV world. You should have a good time with him."

"See? Forget about dating for a while. Just go to the comic con and have some fun." Armando patted Keira on the leg before he stood up and pulled on his shirt. Keira hoped this was a good idea. If not, she was fully prepared to ditch Daniel. She could geek out on her own.

Daniel stood in the middle of the arena floor, eying the stage. He hated last-minute jobs, but it kind of went against company policy at Fire In The Sky Pyrotechnics to leave a new client in the lurch.

Forty-eight hours prior, as his first nationwide tour kicked off in San Diego, "teen sensation" Blake Carlisle had to end the show when not one, but two of his pyro effects malfunctioned. The first caught the pants of a backup dancer on fire, but roadies were able to stop, drop, and roll her before any bodily damage was done. She was back for the next number, in new pants.

The fans to the left of the stage weren't so lucky when a flame tower tumbled into the audience. Two dozen concertgoers were sent to the ER with severe burns and other injuries. Blake's tour management had immediately fired the previous pyro team and stuck them with the legal problems, but the show had to go on. Daniel had a day to figure out how to fix or replace the stunts before the tour took up again at the Staples Center. He'd wished he'd brought earplugs though. They were doing a run-through of the whole show so Daniel could fix the issues, but the kid's music sucked.

"The stage is too small," Daniel said to his partner, Mike. Daniel gestured to the right side of the stage with his prosthesis. Sometimes it caused some discomfort, but he always wore it to work. Helped him manipulate the charges better and it scared newbies who thought you could fuck around with fire and not get burned. The body-powered beauty was black with a black hook attachment. He did like that it got people's attention. "And they based the tower right on that slope. I'm surprised it didn't take out more people."

"Should we kill the fire all together?" Mike asked.

"That's what I'm thinking." Daniel looked down as his phone vibrated in his palm. He expected his mother, checking in after her shift at the casino, but the number of a good friend of his, a buddy-in-kink, Armando Vasquez, lit up the screen instead. He'd known Armando and his business partner Grant for years. Daniel had taught them both a thing or two about wielding a flog. And dealing with male submissives.

He usually caught up with them a few times a month at the bondage club Daniel's close confidants and mentors owned. Master Philip's or "The Club" as it was also known, was where all three of them had come into their own as masters of their sexual needs and desires. He'd spent some of the best nights of his life in that refurbished warehouse, recovering, playing, growing as the man and switch he wanted to be. There was nothing on The Club calendar that coming weekend, but maybe Armando had something else in mind.

Blake was still mid-performance, but Daniel answered anyway. He had the gist of this shit-show.

"Vasquez, what's going on?" Daniel asked over the music.

"Not much. You busy?"

"Sort of. Just a last minute consult. What's up?"

"Question for you. You're still going to that convention this weekend, right?"

"Galaxi-Con? Yeah. Why? What's up?"

"You feel like some company?"

"You want to go?" Armando was cool and all, but conventions for popular sci-fi shows didn't seem like his thing. Fan conventions weren't really Daniel's thing either, but he'd promised his mom he would show up and support his brother.

"No, I had someone else in mind. I think you might know her."

Daniel listened as Armando laid out the particulars for what sounded like an adult play date with his co-worker, Keira. Daniel had only met her once, but she seemed like a nice girl and smoking fine, if his memory served him correctly. Armando was quick to explain that she was just looking for someone to hang out with while she took in the day's events. Apparently Keira was a hardcore fan of *Galaxis*, but none of her local friends shared her enthusiasm.

"Yeah, send me her number and I'll call her. I'll make sure she has a good time."

"Thanks, man. I appreciate it, but, uh, one more thing."

"What's that?"

"She's...not like us."

"What? A dude?"

"No, dick. She's vanilla. Very vanilla. She knows about Grant and I, but it totally weirds her out, so don't—"

"So don't ask her back to my place to make a spanking video. Don't worry. I'll keep the kink talk to myself."

"Thanks. I owe you one."

Daniel ended the call and turned his full attention back to the train wreck falsely labeled as entertainment playing out on the stage before him.

Two

Keira waited by the front doors of the LAX Westin. She'd decided against her Naymorian villager costume, which called for head-to-toe purple body paint, but only took one dedicated step down and dressed as Princess Orora from episode 1.16, "The Coronation". It took forever and some serious online searching, and maybe a YouTube tutorial or two, or five, but Keira managed to fashion Orora's teal gown and jeweled tiara.

The makeup was simple enough, just a series of silver dots placed across her face, over the bridge of her nose. The gown though was a showstopper, as was evident by the number of people who had already stopped to take pictures with her in the few short minutes she'd been waiting for her con companion for the day.

When she agreed to meet with Daniel, the conversation had been kind of quick. They were both busy with work and ended up ironing out the details over text. She wasn't sure what to expect when he showed up, but she just hoped he was ready to dive right in to all the *Galaxis* related fun.

A nerd through and through, she was going to gush over the actors during the afternoon panel. She was going to get in line and ask some questions. She was going to partake in the trivia games, and she was going to take pictures, and buy a t-shirt, hopefully some original art, and the only Orora figurines she was missing from her collection. And she was going to be as happy as a pig in poop doing it all. Hopefully Daniel could keep up.

"Keira?"

She swung around at the sound of a deep voice. There was Daniel, just stepping through the hotel doors. Keira blinked. She'd remembered that Daniel was attractive—Grant and Armando were allergic to having ugly friends—but she hadn't remembered him being quite so good-looking. And she'd forgotten just how resonant his voice was. She could feel it under her skin.

Keira watched him as he came closer, all six-plus feet of him. He was dressed plainly, in a white t-shirt, black jeans and black boots, but his clothes fit him so well. You could see the muscle definition through his shirt. He wore his hair kind of like Armando did, shaved on the sides and along the back, but thick black waves on top were styled in a 50's kind of way, with just a touch of hipster. It worked for him.

"It's nice to see you again," he said, reaching out with his left hand to greet her properly. Too busy staring at his face, Keira stuck out her right hand, which resulted in one of those awkward upside-down handshakes.

"Oh, sorry." She laughed nervously.

"It's okay." He smiled back.

"I didn't see you drive up."

"I got here earlier. Didn't know what the parking situation would be like."

"Understandable. I made sure I bought parking vouchers with my convention pass."

"Smart." He took a step back and looked her up and down. "I thought about dressing up, but I'm glad I didn't."

"Why?"

"I don't want to take focus off you. Armando told me you were going all out."

Just then a mother and her young daughter walked over. The little girl was also dressed in Princess Orora's coronation gown.

"Hi, sorry," the woman said. "Can we take a picture with you? You're the first cosplayer she's seen today."

"Of course!"

Keira posed for a few pictures with the little girl, then Daniel snapped a few so the mom could hop in the photos as well. When they were alone again, Keira glanced up to find Daniel staring at her with his striking brown eyes. She felt her face heat up.

"What?"

"Nothing," he said with a hint of a smile. "After you."

Keira ducked her head to hide her embarrassment. She wasn't used to guys looking at her like they were actually looking at her. That subtle smile still in place, Daniel guided her through the hotel doors with his hand gently touching her back, touching the skin exposed by the cut-outs in her Naymorian gown. She did her best to ignore the goose bumps that popped up all over her body.

Keira couldn't believe how much fun she was having. She couldn't believe how much fun she was having *with* Daniel. He stuck by her the whole day, as she bounced from vendor to vendor and panel to panel. He held the stuff she accumulated while she posed for dozens of pictures. He encouraged her to enter the costume contest being held before the main panel of the day. She didn't win, but she won an honorable mention prize, a replica of the pins the Galaxis fighters wore on their uniforms.

The highlight of her day came when it was time to head to the grand ballroom. The line was ridiculously long. Keira was afraid she wouldn't get in, let alone get near one of the mics for the Q&A, but that didn't matter. Daniel had an in. Turns out his brother's "involvement" in the show really meant that his brother was JD Song, who played Orora's love interest on *Galaxis*. A few words to the guys at the door got them to the front of the line and back to the green room after the Q&A.

It wasn't like she should have made the connection. It wasn't like everyone with the last name Song was related. Plus JD spent his whole run on the show in full Naymorian make-up, complete with a flattened nose and massively enlarged eyes. Also, he and Daniel didn't really look alike.

Still, it was great to meet him. JD introduced her to the rest of the cast, including Selia Monroe, the actress who played Princess Orora. She went on about Keira's costume and somehow Keira managed not to break down in crazed fangirly tears. There was a Naymorian ball that was meant to wrap up the day's events, but neither Keira or Daniel were in the mood to dance, so Daniel suggested they continue their evening at a diner up the street.

"I wish Armando had told me about your brother. I wouldn't have dragged you around with me all day. You could have spent time with him," Keira said, as they settled into the tiny booth. She felt bad for monopolizing Daniel's time, but she could not stop smiling.

"No, it's fine. We hung out last night and this morning."

"But you had to listen to me all day. Sorry I'm such a dork about the show."

Daniel shook his head at Keira's bashful smile. "Trust me, I enjoyed it. It's nice to meet someone so passionate about something my brother works on."

"You mean disturbingly obsessed?"

Daniel laughed and picked up his menu. "Maybe a little."

"I thought I was going to cry when he introduced me to Selia."

"I'm sure she's used to it. It's a popular show."

"It is."

Still smiling, Keira watched Daniel for a moment as he looked over their dinner options. He really was good-looking. And he was sweet, kind of soft-spoken—as soft-spoken as anyone could be with a voice like that—and witty. He only had nice things to say all day, even though Keira could tell he was having about an eighth of the fun she was. She liked him a lot so far, but she wanted to like him more. Which was good, right? Armando hadn't meant to "set them up" so to speak, but if the shoe looked like it worth trying on...

Keira squeezed her eyes closed and almost hid under the table. She'd really just compared Daniel to a shoe. At least she hadn't said the stupid words out loud. Just a quick second to clear her throat and she gave not sounding like a complete dummy a shot.

"We spent the whole day focused on me and my *Galaxis* problem. Tell me about you. What do you do? Armando never told me."

"Thank you for asking. I'm part owner of Fire in the Sky Pyrotechnics. Spend most of my time designing fireworks and fire displays."

"That's so cool. I was going ask you what you do in your free time, but—"

"But, what?"

"Actually, I'm sorry. I was about to say something super rude." See, this was the real reason Keira was single, her inappropriate verbal diarrhea. She did not know when to keep her mouth shut and that just plain turned guys off. Maybe if she buried her face in the menu Daniel would forget she was there.

No such luck. He nudged her foot under the table. "I can handle it. Tell me."

"Oh, geez. Okay. I was going to ask what you do in your free time, but I know you hang out with Armando and Grant. And I know what they do in their free time."

"Did they tell you all about it?"

"No...I just...know. They aren't rubbing anything in my face, but they aren't exactly hush-hush about it either. And Armando posts things on Facebook sometimes."

"And what do you think about it?"

Keira shrugged. "I don't really know."

"Do you know much about sadomasochistic practices and power exchange?"

Keira's mind blanked for a second. She had no idea what he was talking about, but she wasn't about to admit that. "I just know they like control or whatever. They like bossing Violet and Nailah around, telling them what to do. And then there's lots of sex involved. It's not really my thing."

That small smile touched the corner of his lips again. Keira wanted to be annoyed with him but she couldn't. And then she realized what she'd said.

"No! I like sex! I definitely like sex—"

"It's more than that, but I see what you're saying. It's not for everyone."

"I'll be honest. Most of what I know it, I learned from fanfiction."

Daniel's eyebrows shot up. "Really?"

He shouldn't have said that. Keira felt her geek mode activating again. "There's this AU fic where Orora— Are you sure you want to hear this?"

"After you tell me what the hell an AU fic is, yes I do."

"It means Alternate Universe. So Orora is a florist and she lives next door to JD's character, and he's a carpenter and he seduces her and ties her up and—"

"Okay, stop. I don't want to think about my brother seducing anyone or what follows."

"Right. Sorry."

"You liked the story though?"

"Yeah. I like reading it, but the stuff he made her do? Not my thing."

"Why's that? Not that I'm trying to persuade you."

"I don't like being told what to do, even if sex comes as a perk."

"I gotcha." Daniel let the subject drop and turned his attention to the menu, but then Keira's curiosity was piqued.

"What's the draw for you, if you don't mind me asking?"

"I don't mind, I just don't want to make you uncomfortable."

"I'm good. One hundred percent comfortable. Go."

"Alright. How can I put this? I may roll with Grant and Armando, but we're into different aspects of the lifestyle. They are Dominants, clear and easy. I'm what you would call a switch."

"I don't know what that is," Keira said.

"I like to play both sides. I can do what your boys do. Have a partner or partners who agree to follow my lead. I can act as Master and Dominant, give out the orders, take the control. And just as easily I can submit."

Keira swallowed as she felt her face heating up. She did not mean for the conversation to go anywhere near this direction, but now she was interested. And possibly picturing Daniel doing all sorts of things with his shirt off. "Which do you like more?"

"I'm most at peace when I'm submitting. What looks good to you?"

"Oh, ah. I think I'm going to get the waffles. I'm sorry. We don't have to talk about this. What are you going to get?"

"The waffles actually sound pretty good. We can talk about whatever you like. Armando mentioned to me that you weren't into kink. *You* just told me you weren't into kink, but I'll go on if you want to know more?"

"He wasn't wrong, but will I sound like a complete hypocrite if I say yes, I do want to know more? Armando and Grant are more like brothers. I can't really talk to them about sex."

"Nothing hypocritical about being curious. But before I get into it, let me tell you about some of my other interests."

"Oh yes. Please do."

"I enjoy puzzles and I love to bowl. And I try to go to the movies at least once a week."

"No, wait. Let's go back to the puzzles."

"I love puzzles." Daniel lifted his arm off the table a bit. "They helped me with my rehab and they've been a bit more of hobby ever since."

"Interesting. Do you mind me asking how...? Jesus. Never mind." Keira really, *really* needed to shut up, but Daniel just laughed her latest faux pas off.

"It was an accident on my first set. Our lead was an idiot, didn't check to see if I was clear of the blast zone and the effects went off."

"Oh my god."

"I'm on the mend, I promise you." That wink of his was too much.

"I see that. Um, back to your other interests. You said something about going to the movies. Would you...like to go with me some time?" Keira took the leap then instantly regretted it when Daniel practically froze behind his menu. "Sorry. I know this wasn't that kind of hang out. I just—"

"No. I would love to."

"Are you sure? You're not saying yes now to be nice, but then you're gonna call me sometime next week and tell me you can't?"

"No, no. How about this? Keira, would you like to go on date with me in the next seven days. Your schedule permitting, of course?"

"I would love that."

"Excellent. Now I say we see about these waffles and then I'll tell you more about my attempt at the jigsaw puzzle world record and how I was off by a full fifteen minutes."

Keira managed to hold back her laughter, but still she smiled.

✳

Keira plopped down on her couch with her laptop. As soon as she pulled it open, a chat box lit up the screen.

• • •

LoriNLynn+Twins: TELL ME EVERYTHING!!!

Keira snorted at her friend's enthusiasm. Lori was one of several online buddies who had to back out of the Con, and the person Keira missed the most. She lived in Milwaukee with her wife and their kids. Unfortunately wife and the kids came down with a horrible flu and Lori couldn't bear to leave them. Keira understood, but she was still bummed. Lori was her best fandom friend. They'd only met in person once, but they talked on the phone or online and texted every day.

ItsKeiraTime: How are the babies?

LoriNLynn+Twins: there is snot everywhere. i have kid snot in my fucking hair. and Sammy threw up on me this afternoon.

ItsKeiraTime: lol omg im so sorry.

LoriNLynn+Twins: tell me your day was better than mine. how was the con? send me all the pics. did you get to see Selia? was JD there? Did JD take off his shirt? did Selia take off her shirt? did they simulate a sex act on stage during the panel?

This was why Keira loved Lori; she was just as obsessed with everything *Galaxis* as Keira was.

ItsKeiraTime: no sex, but i think i got a date out of it.

. . .

LoriNLynn+Twins: what? SPILL!!!

Keira set about explaining how she met up with Daniel at the convention and how she'd ended up asking him out, even though their time together was only supposed to be a friend-type thing. Then she casually mentioned that Daniel was JD's brother.

LoriNLynn+Twins: WHAT THE FUCK!!! I feel awful for abandoning you and then you end up scoring a date with JD's brother??

ItsKeiraTime: i know. he introduced me to JD and Selia too.

LoriNLynn+Twins: Brb dying on the floor. i can't fucking believe this. should I ditch you more often?

ItsKeiraTime: maybe.

LoriNLynn+Twins: why don't you sound more psyched? you met JD and Selia and now you have a chance to pork JD's brother. I can feel it through the computer. you're not psyched.

Keira knew exactly what was bothering her. She'd had such a good time with Daniel, and he was so cute, but...

. . .

ItsKeiraTime: I think I might have spoke too soon. Jumped the gun in asking him out. He's into the bondage stuff.

She included a somewhat conflicted frowny face.

LoriNLynn+Twins: And?? Let him tie you up.

ItsKeiraTime: No!

ItsKeiraTime: He's the real deal, Lor.

Not that she actually knew for sure, but from the way he talked and the mere fact that he ran in the same circles as Grant and Armando? Yeah, they were pros. And Keira? She wasn't, nor did she want to be, any type of sexual professional.

LoriNLynn+Twins: What made you say yes, then? Did we not learn a lesson with Travis McLoser? Don't go out with guys you don't like.

ItsKeiraTime: I DO like him. That's the problem.

LoriNLynn+Twins: Afraid you'll let him do more than tie you up?

That was exactly what Keira was afraid of. What if she ended up really crushing on Daniel? What if he ended up being really good in bed and he turned her into some weirdo perverted sex addict who had to go to therapy because she'd been arrested for public indecency?

Keira's mind continued to run wild. Too many what-ifs. She wanted a boyfriend, but she wasn't so sure she wanted a boyfriend who was a freak.

ItsKeiraTime: He said he's a switch.

LoriNLynn+Twins: Oooh that means he goes both ways! You can tie him up.

ItsKeiraTime: How do you know all this?

LoriNLynn+Twins: google, honey. the internet is your friend. just do it. go out with him once. for me. i need this excitement.

ItsKeiraTime: aren't you gay?

LoriNLynn+Twin: kid. snot. in. my. hair. i need this excitement.

Keira leaned back against her couch, her laugh turning into a sigh. She wasn't going to back out of her date with Daniel, but she needed something. Some sort of reassurance that everything was going to be okay. She had to know more about Daniel. She had to know he could seriously be with someone like Keira, someone who wasn't into those kinky things. She had to talk to Armando and Grant.

✳

Two days later and Daniel's head was still all fucked up, clouded with different flavors of regret. He regretted not kissing Keira before they parted ways the night of the convention. He'd known a lot of people, fucked a lot of people, but as corny as the thought seemed, he'd never met anyone like Keira. Genuine was the best way to describe her; or maybe honest.

He was proud of JD and the career he'd made for himself. Hollywood was not an easy place for Korean actors to navigate, but his brother was doing it. *Galaxis* was his brother's livelihood and further proof that their mother had been right, encouraging them both to chase their dreams. But Daniel had only watched the show to support JD. He'd known fans of the material, but he'd never encountered a fan like Keira. He found her enthusiasm for the whole culture of the fictional world to be insanely attractive. He liked that she wasn't too shy to embrace her inner nerd in front of strangers. He loved that he got to see the real her the first time they met.

He got the feeling Keira wasn't one to hide any part of herself and he dug that. Problem was, she wasn't into kink, and that right there made him regret the hell out of taking her up on her invitation to spend more time together. Kink wasn't just something he was into in his free time, as Keira had suggested. Kink was his life.

He'd been into sadomasochism in some capacity since he was a kid. Along with setting things on fire, he started messing with bondage and pain play around the age of nine. Luckily his mom didn't discourage either. Scouts, and apprenticeships with some of the stage acts at the Bellagio had handled most of his curiosity, helped him perfect his knots, but it wasn't until he found Mistress

Evelyn that he'd come to understand exactly what was going on in his head.

He really only played with or even dated people he'd met through her and her husband, Master Philip. He'd become so accustomed to his life as a switch, so comfortable with other members of the community, that spending a romantic evening without some element of BD or SM didn't make a bit of sense. So why was he even considering seeing this girl again? Why had he asked her out?

Various reasons ran through his head. She's beautiful. She's smart. She blurts out exactly what's she's thinking and it's adorable as hell. Even with her dark brown skin, he could tell when she was blushing. He wanted to see that smile again. He wanted to see if he could push her buttons, in a good way. He wanted something different.

He'd drawn up a solution for Blake Carlisle's stage show, then sent a team out to finish the tour. He'd gotten word that things were going smoothly, but he couldn't think too much on it. He had other, more important projects coming down the line.

Yeah, he definitely should have kissed her, but something told him he should wait. He wanted her to make the first move or least tell him when she was ready for him to call the shots. She'd told him that he'd hear from her via text, her preferred mode of communication, but she hadn't reached out to him yet. He hoped she wasn't following that stupid three-day rule. He supposed he could text her first...

Daniel rolled his neck and clicked back into his email. The subject lines started to blur together for a moment before he shook his head and forced himself to focus. He had invoices to review before another meeting about the Super Bowl, the last massive event before Fourth of July madness turned the office upside down again. He glanced at his phone, reminding himself to sync his calendar, when he noticed a missed text from Armando.

Thanks for meeting up with Keira, man. She's
been smiles all morning.

That news made Daniel's day. He had no idea what the hell he
was doing with Keira, but this weird tightness in chest pulled even
tighter at the thought of making her happy. He shot Armando a
text back.

Not a problem. She's a great girl.

Just as he hit send, another text hit his phone, this one from
Keira. It must be break time at the gym. Daniel pictured Keira and
Armando standing around talking about him.

I Googled "switch".

That made him smile for sure.

Oh yeah? What did you find?

Naked people.

Is that all?

I got so caught up looking at all the naked
people it was time for me to go to bed before I
remembered my original plan.

Plan?

Daniel was definitely intrigued. What was Keira up to?

Not telling. You'll laugh me into next week.

I won't.

He wouldn't.

> Well you said a switch does both.

> I don't think I'd be good at submitting.

> I was looking up how to be a good mistress. I'll continue my research tonight.

> Let me know if you need any assistance.

> I will.

> Also I'm not saying that I'm going to dominate you or anything.

> I just like to know. I like to know things.

And now he was hard. He could imagine it so clearly, being under her control. It made him wonder though, what had changed, what had Keira suddenly considering domination and submission, any aspect of it, beyond her so-called quest for knowledge? Daniel adjusted the crotch of his jeans then started to text back, but Keira's next text beat him to it.

> Knowledge is power. 😁

Daniel snorted with laughter. He'd only known her a few days, but he could imagine Keira saying those exact words, and the smile that came with it. Would she still be smiling when she got to know him though? Daniel wondered what she would think of his video collection. The hours and hours of footage he had of himself engaged in erotica acts. Some he'd uploaded to the internet for educational purposes, sharing them with friends. Hell, Armando had shared a few of his clips with Nailah when she was getting into the game. No, Keira wasn't ready for that. There was a good chance she never would be.

Daniel had sworn to Keira that he wouldn't back out of their plans, but now that he was thinking of who he really was and what he really needed, and how things between then would probably end, jumping ship before things got complicated might be for the best.

Wait. You guys are going out again?

The text from Armando appeared at the top of the screen.

"What the fuck?" Daniel said out loud as he clicked over, reading the text again. He was not in the mood for this shit, not when he was this horny and frustrated. He pressed the little phone icon next to his friend's name. Armando answered right away.

"What's the problem, man?" Daniel said.

"Nothing. Hold on." Daniel waited while Armando probably took their conversation out of Keira's earshot. "I came in and she's talking to Grant about seeing you again and asking just how committed you are to kink and if she should date you and shit. What happened?"

"Nothing *happened*. We spent the day together and we had a good time. We want to see each other again."

"I just didn't think you guys would go out."

"I get that, but we are going out," Daniel said, his regret shifting somehow into determination.

"So what are you going to do, 'cause I just—"

"You just what?" Daniel laughed. He'd known Armando for years. He had always been a possessive Dom, but Keira wasn't his and Daniel wasn't his to push around either. He was not going to let this shit slide. "You know you have your own girlfriend right?"

"Fuck you. That's not what I was getting at. She's just vanilla, man. Extra strength vanilla. She's not ready for all of *you*."

"Let me be the judge of that. Shit, let her be the judge of that."

Daniel's phone beeped with another text from Keira. "I gotta go. Just be proud of the possible love connection you've helped facilitate."

This time Armando laughed. "Good luck, man. I hope you know what you're doing."

Yeah, me too, he almost said. How the fuck was this going to end well?

Three

Despite his freezing cold feet, and Armando's odd, yet completely justified behavior, Daniel managed to nail down a date and time to see Keira again. At first they'd planned to go to the movies and out for some dinner, but she'd texted him that morning begging off for a night in. When she quickly clarified that she wasn't in fact cancelling, they decided on a movie and pizza at her place. He was buying.

On his way to pick up some beers, he got a text from his buddy, Marcos. Nothing official was planned at The Club that night, but Marcos was always up for something.

You busy tonight? I got some new tails.

After his accident, Daniel had gone through a long recovery period, learning to do a number of things with his left hand while his right arm healed. In the decade since, he'd become perfectly adept at functioning with both arms, with or without his prosthesis. But beyond healing, he'd become obsessed with perfecting his skills with a flogger. With hours spent practicing with Master

Philip, he'd crafted himself into somewhat of a legend in the community.

He moved on to other implements; paddles, slappers, cat o' nine tails, bullwhips, canes. He'd taught classes and seminars, made plenty of videos, performed night after night at the club and in private for his Mistress and her Master. It was only natural for Marcos to reach out to Daniel when he'd acquired a new toy. Daniel was the best person to help him break it in.

Daniel read the backlit words again. Any other night he would have said yes. Had he made plans with any other girl he would have invited them along. But as curious as Keira was, what Marco had in mind would surely scare her off. A girl like Keira would need monogamy, for one. A girl like Keira would definitely need a little warm-up before he introduced her to his sexually fluid friends and their collection of whips and cat o' nine tails. He texted Marcos back.

> Can't tonight, man.
>
> I made plans.
>
> Thanks for thinking of me though.

Something else stirred in his chest. First time in years he'd turned down an invite.

> Always. Have a good night!

Oddly enough, even though he suspected their date would be vanilla and pretty tame, he had a feeling that spending a few hours just talking to Keira would make for a perfectly good night.

*

Keira had shown Daniel her nerdy side and clearly it hadn't

scared him off or he wouldn't have agreed to see her again. Now she had a chance to show him another real side of herself, the lazy bum who hated getting dressed up for anything other than conventions. Her hair was already flat ironed, but that stayed in its ponytail. When she finished in the shower she'd thrown on an oversized Melrose Fitness sweatshirt and a pair of workout shorts that really could have doubled as underwear. She put on under-wear too, including a bra, and she'd shaved her legs. She wasn't a complete heathen.

It was hard not to run for the door when the bell chimed through her apartment. She may have skipped though, and she did nothing to conceal the huge smile that hit her face when she opened the door for Daniel and the two large pizzas he carried.

"A veggie lovers and a meat lovers for the lady who does not like to mix the two."

Keira laughed as she let him in. "I'm sorry. I just like my meat separate."

"I'm sure you do. Here take these off my hands."

"Oh sure."

Daniel had a leather jacket on, but Keira realized that he was wearing a prosthetic arm with a blunted hook he was using to carry a six-pack of amber ales. She took the pizzas then led him to the living room so they could make themselves comfortable in front of her TV. After she put down the pizzas she looked up at him.

"When I see a movie for the first time I demand silence, so I figured we could revisit some classics and let the running commentary flow. Dates should involve conversation, after all."

"I couldn't agree more." Daniel put down the beers and shed his leather jacket. "What?" he asked, with a slight grin.

"Sorry. I didn't mean to stare." Which she totally was. "It's just nice to see you."

"It is?"

"Yeah. I haven't really looked forward to seeing a guy in a while. It's nice."

"Well, here I am, in the flesh," he said with his gorgeous smile. "I hope tonight lives up to pleasant expectations."

Right then, Keira wanted to kiss him, but five minutes into their first date was all kinds of too soon. When they sat down she figured cuddling was off the table too. Ignoring the fact that cuddling had even entered her mind, she made herself comfortable on the other side of the couch with her feet tucked under her butt. Did a guy like Daniel even cuddle? Or if she wanted to get close to him would she have to get on the floor and play human footstool? Cuddling bondage style.

She really needed to get out of her head. "How does *Terminator 2* sound?" she asked.

"One of my favorites. Let's do it."

Keira found the movie in the queue on her streaming service, then hit play. They dug into the pizza and polished off two beers each, sharing light conversation about work and the upcoming Terminator movie before resting back to actually watch the film. It was hard to take her eyes off Daniel, but as soon as the T-1000 popped on the screen she was back in nerd mode, reliving the excitement of the first time her aunt let her sneak and watch T2 on VHS with her cousins.

"Do you mind if I take this off? I've had it on all day." Keira looked over as Daniel started shrugging out of the straps that secured his prosthesis to his shoulders.

"Sure. Here." Keira hopped up and cleared a spot off the trunk behind her couch. Daniel stood and took the arm off, and then the white stocking that covered the healed area where his wrist should have been. Keira smiled as he let out a sigh that turned into groan as he rubbed his skin. It was strained relief, but to Keira it was an oddly pleasurable sound.

"Does it hurt? To wear the arm?" she asked when they sat back down.

"It doesn't hurt, but it likes to remind you that it's there. All the time. I usually only wear it to work or if I need to around the house. Uhh, that feels better and now I can do this."

Keira let out a little squeak when Daniel reached down and grabbed her legs. The squeak was followed almost immediately by a moan as he started rubbing her feet. Daniel worked the top of her foot and toes with his left hand and used his right arm to massage the arch and her heel. It wasn't a cuddling, but it was something.

"You have no idea how good that feels." Keira moaned as she slid down into the couch cushions.

"You're on your feet all day. I'm sure you could use a good rub down."

"Obviously. You don't have to stop at the feet. Really. I won't be mad if you want to do my whole body."

"You sure about that?"

"You know what I mean, pervert."

"How 'bout you just let me know when you're ready for me to go a little higher?"

"Oh, I will," Keira replied, almost so softly she wasn't entirely sure Daniel had heard her. She watched him for a few more moments out of the corner of her eye. He was wearing another simple t- shirt that was snug enough to show off the definition in his chest and his biceps, but somehow the perfect article of dark cotton didn't look tight. It made him look...delicious.

Keira spoke again on impulse. "What's your favorite thing, switch-wise?"

"Switch-wise?"

"What's your favorite 'activity'?"

"That's right. You never did tell me the results of your research. Is this a part of your Mistress plan? Slowly pull the information out of me after I'm fed and completely relaxed?"

Keira scoffed as she squirmed some more on her end of the couch. "At least one of us is relaxed."

Daniel immediately stopped the movements of his fingers. "Am I hurting your feet?"

"No, that's no—No. You can keep going with the foot thing. I was just wondering what you like. The stuff I found that was... sexual seemed to appeal to the general masses and then there were other things that just looked like something you would do to someone during an interrogation."

He kept on with her foot, but tilted his head back and looked thoughtfully at the ceiling. "Hmm, my favorite activity. That's a tough question. Sometimes it depends who I'm with, what they want, what kind of mood I'm in, what kind of mood they're in. With some people, it's been the same thing each time."

"Ah, I see." Keira needed to shut up. She was glad Daniel had come over, and he was aces with the whole foot rub thing, but no amount of internet research would prepare her for his other extracurricular activities. What she needed to do was enjoy her time with him. Enjoy the foot rub, enjoy the movie. Yes, she was curious. She'd been curious all week, but thinking about the freaky things Daniel liked to do for days on end was different from participating in those things with him. She was *not* ready, so why bring those freaky things up?

Damn right you're not ready, she told herself. Just watch the movie.

"With you?" Daniel said.

Keira's eyes opened wide the second she realized what he was getting at. Just as quickly she closed them and covered her ears. "No. Don't tell me. Please."

Daniel's deep laugh vibrated up her legs. "Why not? We're just talking. It's all hypotheticals."

"Because—" Keira lowered her hands. "Actually, no. Tell me."

"See, I can already tell that your thirst for knowledge will betray you every time. But let me think. With you, being the generous, thorough Mistress I know you can be, I think possibly a little edging, or some prostate milking. I'd have to be gagged though. And tied down."

"I understood about three-quarters of what you just said. What the heck is edging?"

"It's a way of being stimulated for a long period of time, without coming."

"How long are we talkin'?"

"Depends how much time you have? Schedule permitting, I've had sessions go all day."

"Wait someone played with your... your dick all day long? Like for a whole day and you didn't come?"

"I came eventually, but yes. We were at it for basically the whole day."

"Yeah, no. I don't think I could do that. My arms would get tired."

"There are ways to get creative. You don't have to use your hands at all."

Keira's brain almost broke as she tried to picture it. Daniel naked. Trying not to come. She coughed. "So you like edging, while being tied up and gagged. That's your favorite thing?"

"When I'm submitting, yeah."

"And when you're not?"

"Oh, I don't know. I love to eat pussy. I mean, I guess I like to do that when I'm submitting too, but if you were under me, I'd eat your pussy until you couldn't walk anymore and then I'd fuck you to sleep."

Keira swallowed in an attempt to calm her jumping nerves. This time when she squirmed, her feet shifted in Daniel's lap, right against what appeared to be his growing erection. She shouldn't have looked directly at his crotch, but she couldn't help it. She wasn't thinking clearly. When she looked up, Daniel was staring back at her. She had no idea what made her so bold but she moved her foot again, this time with meaning.

"All this, just from talking about it?" she asked.

"Mhmm. And thinking about you. You have to tell me now. What do you like?"

Keira realized she was wet now. She could feel the wet patch forming between her legs. "What do you mean?"

"I know you're not well versed in bondage or submission, but you've had sex and I'm guessing you masturbate. What's your sexual act of choice?"

Thinking of an answer was the distraction she needed. Daniel was still rubbing her foot, but now there was the matter of his hard-on and how the thickness of it was pressed against the side of her arch. She balled her fists in her sweatshirt to keep from slipping her own fingers a little farther down her body.

"I don't know. I just like sex."

"Sex covers a lot ground. Let's be more specific. What's a top fantasy of yours?"

"Ha. Finding a guy who's willing to sit through a Twilight Zone marathon with me at least three times a year."

"I'm sitting right here. Try again."

Keira rolled her eyes, but answered anyway. "I don't know. More foreplay, maybe. Every guy I've ever been with? We've done all sorts of positions, but we always get right to the sex. There's never any build up. Just, *Bam!* Doin' it.

"I was with one guy who didn't even kiss me. He just threw me on the bed and pulled my underwear off. I want, like, more— what's the word I'm looking for? I want more play, more fun. I want it to last longer, before it even gets started. I am making no sense."

"No, you're making complete sense. What's one thing you've always wanted to do with a partner that you haven't?"

"I'm going to tell you, but I want you to know it's super embarrassing to say all this out loud."

"There's no reason to be embarrassed. How can you get what you want if you don't share the details? Out with it."

"True. Okay. I really like watching guys jerk off. It's like the only porn I watch, when I watch porn." Keira said the words so fast it was like they all ran together.

"What do you like about watching guys jerk off?"

"I just think it's hot. I mean, porn's a mess, but when it's just one person it just seems more real. Less forced. A little less ridiculous. I've always thought it. would be fun to watch a guy masturbate before or even after we have sex. He can watch me too, but yeah."

"So you like watching guys come?"

"You make it sound like I have a hole drilled in a men's locker room wall somewhere."

"Hey, I don't know what you do when you're at work. Excuse me." Daniel gently lifted her feet and placed them back on the couch. Then he reached for his zipper and started undoing his pants. It wasn't until his hand was all the way inside his boxers that Keira realized what he was doing.

"Oh my gosh, no! Don't!"

"You sure?" Daniel asked, his hand still in his boxers.

"No. Yes. I don't know! Do you usually whip it out on first dates?"

Daniel dropped his chin, giving her a telling look. "It's happened."

"Oh gosh. Okay. Okay. Do it. No! Do it."

"Okay. I'm gonna do it, but from now on if you really, genuinely don't want me to do something, say 'pizza'."

"Is that our safeword?"

Daniel's smile should be illegal in every state. "So you did do your homework."

"A little bit. Okay, pizza. That'll be your word too so I don't get confused. Not that you'll get anywhere near using it. I just— yeah. Okay. Do it. Oh my gosh. What we doing? There's still pizza left!" Keira blurted out the last bit just before she covered her eyes again. He was lifting his hips to give himself more room to pull his boxers and his jeans all the way down. She couldn't watch, but she had to. When Keira dared to peek between her fingers knew she had to stop him again.

"Wait! Kiss me first. Just real quick. If we're going to do anything close to sex, you have to kiss me. Makes it more personal, less... back room of the saloon."

"You're weird, but I like it. Here I come. I'm gonna kiss the shit out of you."

He wasn't kidding either. Daniel went for it, climbing over her, digging his fingers into her hair as he lightly caressed her cheek and then her neck with the healed skin on his arm.

Goose bumps had already spread out all over her body, but now her goose bumps had caught some sort of fever. His lips were so soft and he knew how to use the right amount of tongue at the right moment. Just a hint brushed against her own tongue, and then a little more.

He was pulling away before she knew it, back on the other end of the sofa with his jeans halfway down his thighs before she could tell him she wasn't done yet, but then his hand was in his boxers and he was pulling out his cock.

Keira was almost humiliated by how much it fascinated her. It was nice looking, as dicks go. Long and thick, which wasn't unfamiliar to Keira. She'd been with well-endowed guys before but, as Daniel started to stroke himself, it really hit Keira just how one note her sex life had been. If she could count the seconds, from kiss to the moments that followed—if it wasn't suggested that Keira enthusiastically give her partner some head—she never got a moment to appreciate a man's body.

If Daniel was anything like her last boyfriend, he'd already have her bent over the arm of the couch, going at her doggy-style and coming before she could even get close to her finish. Like clockwork, he'd go down on her afterward, but if she came, or if she faked it, he'd head to her room to pass out or take off for his own place before she could get her wits back. Her last boyfriend sucked.

But as she watched Daniel, his long fingers gliding over his skin, squeezing and tugging, she wanted to sleep with him, she wanted to take things further, but this was her fantasy, witnessing this filthy, private act. Why had it taken so long for her to find someone she could share her fantasies with?

"Can you take off your shirt?" she asked suddenly. "And your pants? All the way. Please."

"Yes, ma'am." His tone was light, but sincere. He stood up and started to shed his clothes. Keira almost asked if he needed a hand, but thought better of it. He deftly undressed one-handed and, even if he hadn't been able to manage, Keira got the feeling he would ask for help if he needed it.

When he sat back down, a look of concentration came over his face, like before maybe he had been teasing her, seeing how far he could go before she pizza'd their night to an early conclusion. Now the game was on.

"You have to tell me if you want me to stop, or if you want me to come," he said.

Keira pulled her knees up to her chest. "Definitely don't stop. I'll...I'll tell you when to come."

Daniel just nodded and kept on stroking.

The movie had long since faded into the background, but the sounds of the gunshots and motorcycle chases and explosions gave Keira something in the distance to focus on. She needed something tangible, an anchor to keep her from going wild as she watched him. She didn't want to think about what more she could want from this scenario, because Keira had no doubt in her mind that Daniel would give it to her.

She had no clue what he was talking about half the time they discussed anything sexual. She could come to him with the wildest, most off the wall idea and she knew he would have no problem meeting her demands. She was still playing in the minors, but guys like Daniel had invented the game, crafted the whole rulebook. Her most outrageous request would seem like child's play to him and that scared her.

"How do you do it when you're alone?" she managed to ask.

"Just like this, no alteration to the show."

"I mean what do you think about?"

"I think about how good it feels, touching my own cock. Or I think about something else that would make me come." Daniel's voice was strained in the sexiest way. Keira had a feeling he was getting close, but he would wait for her to say it was okay.

"Like what? What kinds of things make you come?"

"Right now? I'm thinking about you and if you enjoy watching me."

"I do. It's really hot."

"Then that's enough—Fuck." Daniel let his head fall back as he stroked himself faster. "Thinking about how much you like this is enough to make me go off."

Without really thinking, Keira braced herself on the couch and slid closer to Daniel, so close her knees were now pressed against his bare thigh. His head was still tilted back, but he cracked his eyes open just a bit to look at her. He licked his lips.

Kiera leaned in a little more. "Can I touch you?"

"You don't have to ask."

"Yes, I do. Don't stop." Keira meant to lead with her hands, but her mouth took charge. She kissed Daniel on his shoulder, leaning a little closer so her lips could make the journey along his neck. He smelled so good. Something clean, but warm and fresh, like fabric softener and the hint of a perfect cologne. His arm brushed against her breasts as his hand kept on moving up and down his shaft.

He turned his head just enough and their lips met, but Keira pulled away. Before, it had been clear that she wanted the kissing portion of the night to go on and on, but now she knew what would happen if they kept kissing and she wanted to save that for another time.

Daniel seemed to understand. He slowed his movements down again, squeezing his cock in his palm, alternating his grip, upside and then down, probably to keep himself from coming before she said it was okay. Keira laid her head on the back of the couch and continued to watch. Her knees were still pressed against his thigh.

After a few minutes of listening to his harsh breathing and occasional groans, Keira couldn't take anymore.

"You should come now," she said, her voice near a whisper.

It didn't even take a second suggestion or a couple more pumps of his fist. Come erupted out of Daniel's cock and onto his stomach. It came in several jets, a creamy white, painting his lightly honeyed skin. The sounds that came out of him were just as erotic as the sight of his fingers urging the last drops from his swollen head. He continued to touch himself until he was completely finished, but Keira knew she was still in charge. She still owned the moment. In her fantasy, in some of the better clips she'd watched, this had always been her favorite part.

"I like it when guys spread it around."

"Like this?" Daniel said, using his fingertips to move what he'd spilled on his stomach across his defined abs and up the center of his chest.

"Lower."

Daniel followed orders and spread what was left farther down, up the length of his penis and around his balls. He was still breathing a little heavy, but Keira could tell he wanted more. It would be wrong for her to pretend that she didn't too, but there was no clear direction for her to go. Her own body was still tingling. She'd soaked through her underwear and there was no doubt in her mind that if she slid her hand between her legs she'd find that her shorts were wet too.

But part of her wanted to hold on to that tight, swollen sensation, the heat. It would be easy to tell him to go down on her, or to tell him to rally up another hard-on so they could have sex. Either of those things could happen, or both, but she was practically high off the control, off of her own arousal. An orgasm would ruin that for her.

"Tell me what you want."

Keira thought about it for a moment before she answered. "Can you spend the night, just like this? No clean up?"

"Okay."

"Do you want to finish watching this in my room?"

"That would be nice."

"Wait here one sec." Keira grabbed the remote and turned off the TV, then put away the rest of the pizza. Then she told Daniel to follow her down the hall. She glanced back at him as they went. His cock was softening, but it still had some life to it. In her bedroom, she pulled back the sheets and invited him to lie down. She could feel his eyes on her as she set about getting ready for bed. She ditched her sweatshirt and her shorts, and grabbed her laptop before she climbed between the sheets with him in just her bra and underwear.

"You want me just like this?" he asked.

Keira looked back over her shoulder at him, realizing that no one had pizza'd. She was still in charge. He was lying in the same spot, back against her pillows, legs slightly spread.

Rolling over, she considering him for a minute. Was there more to the fantasy? What did she really want?

"Um, how do you feel about spooning?"

"It's something I enjoy."

"Okay, you be the big spoon please."

Daniel didn't hesitate to scoot closer and wrap his arm around Keira's stomach. She moved back and down a little as well, pressing her ass against his crotch as she loaded the video streaming to the spot where they'd left off. It didn't take long before he was hard again.

It was difficult not to wonder what would happen on their second date.

Four

"Was last night weird?"

Daniel looked up at Keira, who was still cozy in her bed. It was early as hell, still dark out, but work called. Still, he couldn't help but smile as he slung his harness and arm into place. "That wasn't even close to weird. That was hot. I will happily jerk off for you any time."

"Not the jerking off part. I mean everything else."

Daniel had to admit, Keira had surprised him. Coming for her was a breeze, but he hadn't expected the rest, her wanting him in her bed, on her fresh sheets, covered in his own jizz. Some of it got on her back when she asked him to spoon her, but that wasn't the last of it.

As they watched the rest of the movie, she started to rub her soft ass against his hard cock. He'd held still, letting her wiggle and grind against him as she pleased, thinking maybe this was her way of getting off, but that wasn't the case. Eventually she asked him if he could come again, just from rubbing up his cock along her ass. Of course he could and he told her as much, but he still waited until she told him to rub himself off again, using only her ass for friction. The idea alone brought his hard-on completely back to life and, in seconds, he had her small, tight body pulled flush against him as he rotated his hips.

This time she let him touch her, guiding his hand up over her breasts. He pulled the thin cotton of her bra aside and teased her puckered nipples until she told him to climax again. Which he did, all over her back and ass. He could have sworn he heard her moan and knew he felt her shiver a bit, but he knew there was more. Still, she just wanted him to hold her, no reciprocation, no clean up.

Had someone asked him where he saw their night going, his answer would not have included him lying naked in her bed after she'd exhibited a bit of a jizz fetish, but, on the scale of a little off to this chick needs help, what Keira wanted from him fell right on par with normal. She liked what she liked and Daniel was honored to be the one she'd opened up to.

"If you're looking for someone to judge you, you're looking at the wrong guy. Nothing we did last night was weird. If we step outside of my comfort zone, I will tell you. And I hope you'll do the same."

"Good to know."

It was beyond time for him to go. He had a ton of shit to do to prepare for the wedding that night. A wealthy groom wanted to end the couple's exchange of vows with a two minute fireworks display. He insisted that Daniel be there to oversee the crew, even though his team was more than capable. Either way, the client was always right and he had to be at the venue early.

That didn't change the fact Daniel wasn't quite ready to leave Keira yet. He grabbed his jacket, but climbed back onto the bed. His slid his hand under the covers and up her bare thigh. Her skin was so soft, so smooth. "Are you sure you don't want me to take care of you?"

"I'm sure. Maybe I want you to work for it," Keira said with a smile.

"I like the sound of that. When can I see you again?"

"Whenever you want. My schedule's busy, but it's pretty regular. Yours seems more action packed."

"How about I call you?"

"And I'll text you in the meantime?"

"You better." And then, like it was almost an automatic response, Daniel closed the small space between them and kissed Keira one last time.

"I'll see you," he said. And then he kissed her again.

"'Kay."

Daniel had to force himself off the bed and out the door. He was still pretty high from the orgasms he had the night before, not to mention waking up with Keira still in his arms. He walked out to his SUV, checking his cell as he hit the curb. He'd missed a couple calls and there were a few texts. The calls and messages were from Mike. Just a few reminders about the day, a message asking if Daniel had walked off with his favorite socket wrench, and a final message saying he found it. Mike really needed to learn to utilize the text feature on his cell.

The texts were all from Mistress Evelyn.

> Hey Honey. You free later?
>
> Meegan earned a reward.
>
> I was hoping you could come over and help me treat her.

The texts tripped Daniel up in the most unexpected way. He climbed behind the wheel and stared at his phone. The regret was back. Seeing Keira again, spending the night with her, that all felt right, but he hadn't given any thought to what would happen after. He hadn't considered what the fuck he should do when his life came calling. Or texting, in this case.

Any other time, his response to Mistress Evelyn would be an automatic yes, but his fingers refused to type out that simple word. He was starting to feel something for Keira and the idea of being with someone else without her knowing, even if there was nothing romantic about it, didn't sit well with him. He had a feeling it wouldn't sit well with Keira either.

> Actually I don't think I can make it.

Daniel texted back. Mistress Evelyn was an early riser. She'd probably been up since 4:30, embracing the quiet as she got her day started. She sent a text right back.

> Something up?

> You never miss a chance to play with me and the girls.

This wasn't the conversation to have over text. Daniel hit the little phone icon next to Mistress Evelyn's name.

"Hey, sweetheart. What's going on?"

He got right to the point. "I've kind of just started seeing someone and she's not in the community."

"Oh." Daniel wasn't quite sure how to read her shock, but her tone quickly became more pleasant, less what-the-fuck. "I'm sorry, honey. I wasn't expecting you to say that. Tell me about her."

Daniel told her pretty much everything that had happened since he and Keira had met on more official terms. He didn't realize he was rambling on about her laugh and her smile and the blunt, yet innocent and honest ways she carried on conversations until he heard Mistress Evelyn's laugh through his phone.

"What?"

"Nothing. It's just—you two sound like me and Philip when we first met. We didn't have all the text messaging back then, but he proposed to me after a week."

"Well, we aren't even close to that. I just like her."

"I know honey, but it's been a short time and it sounds like she's already changing you. And not in a bad way."

"Changing me how?" Daniel didn't like the way that sounded.

"Well, when was the last time you told me no? And I've never heard you go on about anyone like this. About things, yes, but never people. I just never—"

"Pictured me dating a vanilla girl?"

"Not exactly. I just didn't know if you would ever want to settle down."

Daniel closed his eyes. "We're not settling down. We're hanging out. I just I think she needs monogamy right now."

"What do you need?"

The honest answer to that question scared the shit out of him, so for the first time ever, he lied to Mistress Evelyn.

"I don't know. Time to think?"

"Well, you take all the time you need. Philip and I will always be here for you."

"Yeah, I know," Daniel said, feeling like a complete asshole. "I know."

✳

Keira's last cardio kickboxing class was going down in slow flames. Saturday mornings were always the best. Everyone who had slacked during the week, or just didn't have time, showed up in droves for Armando's first yoga session and Grant's boot camp. She had her a.m. regulars, but 5:30pm on Saturdays were where workouts went to die. She often had to cancel her last class, but one of her clients decided to show up with three of her friends, who actually had no interest in working out. Keira had to push them though. It was her job.

"Hands up, ladies. There you go. Keep going," she called out over the music. "And five. Four. Three. Two. One. Now step. And punch. Good! Step. And punch." She'd punch herself in the face of she could. Before she could manage it, the front doors eased open and Daniel poked his head in. Keira almost lost her count.

She smiled like a fool though, so big that Jan, the one putting in the least amount of effort, actually stopped her stepping and punching to see what she was looking at.

"Come on, Jan. Stay with us. Five. Four..."

Keira nodded toward the back and mouthed "Armando." Daniel got the drift and made his way back to the office where Armando was probably busy sexting his girlfriend.

The last ten minutes of the class dragged on forever. Finally she wrapped things up and sent Jan and company off to no doubt complain about what a horrible mistake they'd made taking her class. Once they were gone, Keira darted to the back office.

"Hey! What happened to the wedding?" she asked Daniel. He was leaning against the wall in the packed space.

"Bride left the groom at the altar."

"Ouch." Armando grimaced.

"Oh my god," Keira added.

"Yeah, we offered to stay for the guests, but they pulled the plug on the whole thing. So here I am."

"You're free tonight?" Keira asked, as she bounced on her heels. It had barely been twelve hours since she'd last seen him, but when he left her place that morning she was convinced it would be another week before she actually got to see him again. She couldn't hide her excitement. Daniel time was A+ quality time.

"It seems so. Would you like to go out?"

"Yes. Oh, I know. Let's go play some skee-ball. There's this place called The Alley Way—"

"That doesn't sound suspect at all," Daniel said with a smile. Then he motioned her closer. "Come here."

"I'm kinda sweaty."

"I don't care."

Keira walked into his arms and stood up on her tiptoes so she could kiss this man that she was suddenly dying to call her boyfriend. Their smooch lasted just long enough for it to be awkward with another person in the room. When they broke apart, Keira looked over to see Armando staring at them in the most bizarre way.

"What's that look?" she asked.

Armando fixed his face and tried to play it off like he hadn't just looked completely disgusted. "Ah—nothing. I—"

But Daniel wasn't letting him off that easily. "He thinks me showing up here is a sign that we're moving too fast."

"Well, then he shouldn't have introduced us. Two dates in two nights too out of control for you, Mando?" Keira laughed. She turned around in Daniel's arms and made herself comfortable. He pulled her closer and Keira could have sworn she saw Armando cringe.

"Nope, not at all," Armando said. "I didn't say a word."

"What are you and Nailah doing tonight? You want to come with us?" Daniel suggested.

"Yeah, you can chaperone. Make sure things don't get too out of hand in the fun department," Keira added.

"Can't. I promised her a thing."

"I'm sure you did." Keira looked over her shoulder. "Just us tonight?"

Daniel hugged her tighter. "Just us."

In forty short minutes they were kicked out of The Alley Way. When they arrived, Keira headed right for the skee-ball machines, and everything was going smoothly until Daniel decided to show Keira the way he and JD used to cheat. She knew the methods, but he insisted it was the fastest way to win her a giant stuffed panda that looked like it had been sitting behind the counter since the place opened in 1978.

They were in good shape when Daniel was just standing near the top of the ramp feeding balls into the 50 point hole, but the manager was about done when Daniel actually climbed up the ramp and made a dramatic show of slam-dunking their last ball into the hole while screaming "Ah yeah!" at the stop of his lungs.

Keira could not stop laughing. Even after they were closed in Daniel's SUV, they were both still cracking up. She had tears running down her face.

"I don't know what the fuck his problem was. He didn't have to be so pissed." The mock outrage in Daniel's tone made Keira laugh even harder.

"I know! Even after we gave all our tickets to those kids." Keira wiped her face. "Oh, my gosh, he's gonna ban me for life. What do we do now? It's not even 8:30."

"It's your call, sweetheart."

"I don't know. Let's just go back to your place." Keira was half laughing when she said it. It took a few seconds for her to notice that Daniel wasn't laughing anymore. He was just looking at her. "Or...we don't have to?"

Daniel shook his head a little. "No, sorry. I think I just heard you the wrong way. Actually that's not right. Old habits run deep or however you want to say it. Usually when I have people to my place, things go a certain way. You saying we should go there, it triggered something."

Keira's case of the giggles was definitely gone. "What way is a certain way?"

"If we go back to my place you're agreeing to submit to me. For the night."

"I have to do whatever you want?"

"No. We'll talk about what I want to do to you and what I want you to do with me and if we both agree, then we will spend the night doing those thing."

Keira was confused. That sounded like regular consensual sex. "I don't get it."

"This isn't about me just bossing you around. You relinquish control, trusting that I'm going to give you exactly what you need. At the same time, your desire to please me, if you have that desire, will naturally lead to you doing things that please me."

"Like what?"

"Like letting me taste you. Letting me find out what you feel like inside. I'm also going to come on your tits. That's definitely gonna happen."

"Those sound like things that would please me."

"Hmm," was all Daniel said.

"What? What did I say wrong?"

"You didn't say anything wrong. I'm just getting a clearer picture of what you think is happening here. It is possible for me to find pleasure in pleasuring you. We can want the same things. It wasn't like that with your exes, I'm guessing."

"No, you're right. It was always this sort of tit for tat thing. I always had to hope and bargain and beg—"

"And you were still left unsatisfied."

"Yeah."

"I think we need to change that. You still want to go to my place?"

Keira didn't hesitate. Her answer was yes. The night before had been nothing like any first date she'd ever experienced, but she wouldn't change a thing about it. She liked Daniel. She trusted him. It might be fun to see what it was like if the tables were turned.

"Let's get out of here, then. I'd rather not fuck you in my car."

"What if it pleases me though?"

"Well, if you insist." Keira practically screeched with laughter as Daniel started undoing his fly and climbing over the center console in almost the same motion.

"Oh my gosh! Can't you wait?"

Daniel settled back in his seat and looked over at her. "I'm just following orders."

"That wasn't an order. It was a... a question."

"Sorry."

Keira glared back at him "No you aren't."

"Forgive me?"

"Only if we stop and get ice cream before we go back to your place."

"Deal. Let's go." Keira watched as Daniel hit the PUSH START button with the side of his smooth hook. Butterflies started a full dance party in her stomach as they pulled out into traffic. What had she just agreed to?

FIVE

They pulled up to a brand-new, modern style house in Atwater Village. Keira asked Daniel about the neighborhood and he told her when he'd decided to buy instead of renting, as she followed him through the side door into the kitchen. Daniel put the two pints of ice cream—vanilla for comfort and cinnamon bun just in case they were feeling adventurous—in the freezer. Then he turned toward her.

"Okay." Keira bounced on the balls of her feet. As if it wasn't obvious enough that she was nervous. "What do I do first?"

"I want you to take off your clothes. Everything."

"Are you going to watch?"

"Mhmm."

"Okay. Here goes. I'm getting naked. Can I talk while I get naked?"

"Mhmm."

"Good, 'cause I'm not very good at not talking," she said, as she pulled off her jacket.

"I know."

"Jerk." Her boots and socks were next.

"Keep going."

"I'm going." Her thin sweater and her shirt hit the floor. Then her jeans. "They added the latest season of *Galaxis* online. I'm going to do a re-watch sometime next week. You in?"

"Yes. If you take off your underwear, yes."

"Here. Underwear's off." Her bra and panties joined the pile.

"Thank you. I'll be right back."

Daniel left Keira standing naked in the middle of his kitchen. She glanced around, but there wasn't all that much to see. The place was so new, it looked barely lived in. Or maybe Daniel didn't spend a whole lot of time in the kitchen. There was nothing on the walls, not even a reminder hanging on the fridge. The only thing that stuck out was a half-finished puzzle that seemed to dominate the kitchen table, what looked like a millions pieces that would eventually come together to make a depiction of a stained glass window featuring the Virgin Mary and Baby Jesus.

Daniel came back just as Keira was about to pick up one of the loose pieces. She spun around, caught in the act. "Sorry."

"It's okay. I've done that one a few times."

"So you weren't joking about the puzzles?" Keira said with a smile. This was the side of Daniel she wanted to get to know. She knew the man who liked to play with fire, literally, but it almost made her giggle to think of him settling in with a warm cup of tea to unwind with a one of his favorite puzzles.

"Not exactly. I had to learn how to use my left hand after my accident. The puzzles helped with my dexterity. I'll show you my drafting table later. I've become quite the left handed calligrapher."

"Ooh, I want to see that now."

"No. I want to play with you now."

Keira made a dramatic show of frowning at him, but that only lasted the few seconds it took for her to remember that she was butt naked and Daniel was going to show her what it was like to submit for him, on his terms.

He had a roll of red shiny tape hanging off his prosthetic hook. "Do you know what this is?"

"Festive duct tape?"

"It's called bondage tape."

"I'm probably ruining the mood, not being serious."

"No. You like to be silly and I like that about you."

"Oh."

"I'm going to bind you, wrists and feet. I'm going to cover your mouth and then I'm going to take you into my bedroom and we're going to have some fun."

"Promise you won't kill me."

"Keira."

"Promise."

Daniel leaned down and looked her right in the eyes. "I'm not going to kill you, I promise."

"I'm just saying, this is how horror movies start. I appreciate a bit of reassurance."

"I'm pretty sure Grant and Armando would be a little upset with me if didn't send you back to the gym happy and whole."

"That's true."

"Anyway. Can you snap?"

"My fingers? Yeah." Keira demonstrated, making a show of doing a little jig while she snapped both her fingers.

"Good. Instead of a safe word you're gonna snap. Place your hands behind your back, wrists crossed." He said the last bit as he circled her body. "And I want your feet together. Good, just like that." He made quick work securing her hands, then came back around to her front and got on his knees to secure her feet.

Keira tried to keep quiet and just observe as Daniel bound her ankles with the tape, but she was too nervous to stand there in silence. "I'm nervous," she blurted out.

Daniel glanced up at her, giving her the brief instance of reassurance she needed. "Why are you nervous?"

"Why shouldn't I be?"

"Because you're with me and I think you know I would never

do anything to hurt you. I think you can infer that I'm not the type to hurt anyone."

"It's not that. I just, I'm not good at this."

"At what, Keira?"

Keira let out a deep sigh as Daniel finished with her feet. The way she felt didn't make any sense. She wanted to sleep with Daniel, even though she wasn't exactly sure sex itself was on the menu, but she wanted to be with him again. She was already naked and she did trust him. In the short time they'd spent together, Daniel had already proved to be one of the sweetest men she had ever met. She felt totally safe with him. And he might have been a little impulsive, trying to drop his pants at the slightest suggestion, but he always backed off, even if she wasn't completely sure she wanted him to stop. Plus she could always snap or pizza her way out of the situation. It wasn't Daniel, it was something else she couldn't put into words, but it made her nervous as hell.

He stood and gently stroked her cheek. "Talk to me. What's wrong?"

"I'm scared."

"You're not used to being this vulnerable?"

"No, I'm not." The problem was Keira didn't hate it. She liked being naked for Daniel and she wanted to see what he had planned for the rest of the night. But that didn't change the fact that her heart felt like it was going to beat right through her chest. And she didn't like the idea of not being able to touch him. And, on the other hand, she didn't want him to untie her. Why was submitting so freaking confusing?

Daniel leaned down and kissed her. That cleared up some of the confusion. "Do you want to stop? We don't have to do this."

"No. I want this. I'm sorry. I'm just..."

"Let's try it for two minutes and after two minutes I'll check in with you and we'll see how you feel. No pressure to snap or anything."

"And you're still going to gag me? Cause you don't want me to talk the whole time?"

"I'm going to gag you because I want you to see what it feels like to experience something without being able to comment until it's finished. So what do you say? You want to try?"

Keira nodded, then added, "Yes." She wasn't sure what else she could say. She wanted to be with Daniel and she wanted to try something new. Fear came with the unknown sometimes and she was just going to have to deal.

Daniel wound a strip around Keira's face once, covering her mouth, then dipped down and threw her over his shoulder. For some weird reason as he carried her down the hall to his room, Keira started to pretend that she was being kidnapped. And for some even weirder reason it was the idea of being kidnapped—not being naked, not Daniel's kiss, but the thought of being taken by force, to be used by some strange man—that made her wet. She closed her eyes and pretended to accept her fate, stifling a small giggle as they made their way down the hall.

✱

Daniel had taken the whole ride from the arcade to get his mind right, but Keira had tripped him up with all her chatter. Most of the submissives he'd played with had been trained by Master Philip and Mistress Evelyn. A few had been whipped into shape by Armando. They were all different. All had their quirks, but none of them talked as much as Keira. He didn't mind all her talking, not at all.

The problem was that listening to Keira talk took him out of his headspace, because when he should have been handling business he just wanted her to keep on jabbering. Her ridiculousness had made him laugh, it kept him guessing. He loved her energy. He could easily sit around talking to her all night, but he really, really wanted to have sex with her. At the very least he had to make her come.

When they reached his bedroom he made a decision. He initially considered taking things easy on Keira. She was already bound, wrists and ankles. Her mouth was covered so she couldn't say a word. In some ways that might be enough for her first night playing the role of submissive, but he had to give her more. He wasn't going to go nuts and take things all the way to the edge, but he needed to push her a little more, see if he could reach a place where he could at least see the edge far off in the distance. He gently laid Keira on the bed on her side. She was breathing normally, if not a little heavier than usual. He took a moment to remove his arm. It helped with the tape, and he'd had submissives ask for some of his other attachments, but *he* wanted full skin-to-skin contact.

Once he had everything he needed in place, he sat on the bed beside his captive, right in the curve her stomach created as her body bowed forward. He picked up the shears he had on the nightstand. Keira's eyes bulged wide.

"Emergency precaution if we need to get the tape off quickly." Her shoulders sagged and she nodded. Daniel shook his head as he put the scissors back. It was time to get down to business.

Daniel knelt beside the bed but, just as he was about to pull Keira close, she started thrashing and making a noise that sound like his name. For a moment he thought she'd forgotten about her snap signal, but there was something a little too mischievous about the glint in her eye. And then it looked like she was trying to smile.

"Jesus Fucking Christ." It took a second, but he got Keira upright on her knees, then unwound the tape around her mouth. "What?"

"I don't care what you say. My father doesn't negotiate with terrorists," Keira said dramatically, before she bit the inside of her lips and made this little snorting noise.

"Nope. No way."

"Why?"

"My house, my rules. We can do your whole kidnapping, Stockholm syndrome fantasy at your place. Right now we're going to do things my way."

"I want to argue about this some more, but when you're firm like that it makes me really horny."

"Good. Tape's going back on." Daniel ignored her pouting, pushing her over on the bed as soon as the tape was back in place. He had planned to start with her tits, suck on them a while, just to help her get her mind focused on what was actually happening, but that wasn't going to work. She was distracting herself *and* him. Daniel was done wasting time. He dropped down on the bed and was not gentle about pulling Keira over his lap.

"I'm going to spank you now. Snap once if you want me to stop."

Keira's back rose and fell as she let out a deep breath, but her fingers remained still.

"Excellent. If you squirm I'm only going to make this worse."

Famous last words.

The spanking started off well enough. Not to say that anything went particularly wrong. It was just that, once again, Keira reacted in a way Daniel had not expected. He got in one, maybe two licks and then she started to squirm in his lap. She wasn't in pain, he could tell, and she wasn't even close to signaling out of the scene. It was the warning he'd given her.

He'd taken away her fantasy so she was going to get a certain level of manhandling out of him by testing to see if his warnings were actually idle threats. He hadn't expected her to go there, but he was ready. He gave her ten hard licks, pausing briefly a few times to rub and grope at her luscious ass cheeks and thighs. She continued to squirm and moan, and squirmed and moaned some more when he stopped and slid his hand between her legs.

She was wet, coating his hand with her slickness as he pushed two fingers nice and deep.

"You want me to stop?" She shook her head wildly.

"Good cause you're gonna have to beg me to stop."

Another moan, more desperate and pleading.

The spanking had worked for her, Daniel thought. He knew she could take more.

Daniel pulled his fingers out of Keira's soaked cunt, then dropped her back onto the bed. More groans and moans, but she rolled into the exact position he needed her in, on her side. He kneeled beside the bed and got her ponytail in the tight hold of his fist.

"How are we doing?" he said in a harsh voice. His promised check-in was a few minutes late. She glanced at him, but didn't make a noise. Air puffed out of her nose. "Do you want me to stop?"

She shook her head as much as he would allow. "Very good. I hope you're comfortable. You're gonna be like that for a while."

Keira made a little squeaking noise, but Daniel ignored her and went right for her nipple. He'd touched her breasts the night before, but he wanted a chance to really admire her body. Her breasts were perfect. A perfect handful with dark tips that been hard since the moment he told her to strip. He stroked over one tip with his tongue before pulling it between his lips. She squirmed again, but he still had a good grip on her hair. He looked up at her face. Little wisps of dark brown were starting to curl around her forehead.

"Are you trying to get away?" Dammit, Daniel thought. He'd played into her little game. Oh well. He was enjoying himself too much to stop. He lightly tugged her hair again. "Are you?"

Another shake of her head.

"I know what you need." Daniel stood unzipped his fly. "Maybe you'll hold still after I give you what you really want." He pulled out his cock and gripped it as he stepped closer to the bed. "Get on your back, now."

Keira groaned, but she maneuvered her way into the perfect

position for Daniel to straddle her stomach. The act of lying on her bound arms thrust her chest up. Still, it gave her a perfect view of his dick. He pulled up his shirt and tucked it under his chin, then started beating off.

Keira writhed, trying to arch closer to him. "Open your eyes," Daniel barked. That got her attention. From then on she kept her eyes open, though she continued to struggle against the tape. He should have recorded this. He hadn't told Keira about his cinematic hobbies yet, but he wanted more than the memory of this night to recall. He wanted to watch it again and again in stark color. He wanted to see it from a different angle.

See himself on top of this beautiful woman, see the way her well defined muscles corded under her beautiful brown skin as she ached for the come he was about to give her. They'd do this again, Daniel thought. He made up his mind about it, but the next time he'd bind her ankles to her thighs, strap her upper arms back, not just her wrists. He'd skip the gag though, the next time he was definitely coming in her mouth.

That made him go off; the sound of her moans, the look in her eyes, and the thought of him leaving a white trail along her pink tongue.

He managed to stay upright as he shot his load all over her stomach and her tits. Keira lost it, started thrashing about. She wanted to participate. She wanted to touch him, she wanted to spread his jizz around, but that wasn't part of Daniel's game. He squeezed the last bit of come out of his cock, the head red and swollen in his fist. Then he hopped off the bed and rolled Keira back onto her side so she was nearly teetering on edge of the mattress.

She was so far gone, forgetting his instructions the moment he shoved his fingers back between her legs. Two fingers deep in her wet cunt and his thumb pressing against her clit. "Look at me, baby. You're gonna come for me."

Keira shook her head. There were tears lining her eyes, but

there was also desperation. She needed to see this scene to its completion.

Daniel leaned down and made a show of licking a bit of come off her nipple. He made sure she saw the white drops before he pulled them into his mouth and licked his lips.

"I'm gonna clean you up and you're gonna come for me."

Another wild moan as she squeezed her eyes shut, but he knew she couldn't stand to miss the show. He made his way down her chest and up again, licking and sucking up every trace of the mess he'd made. Daniel was no stranger to his own flavor, but he knew this was a first for Keira. When he glanced up she was watching him intently. He shook his fingers inside her and pressed harder on her clit. Her body was clenching around him, wanting so badly to just reach that peak, but Keira was fighting it and she would until she physically couldn't stand any more. That was fine with Daniel. He could wait. He had all the time and forearm strength in the world.

But it didn't take all that. Something in Keira snapped and she stopped fighting. Her whole body went tight, her legs straightening out on the bed, trapping his hand between her thighs as her head and her neck arched back. The sound she made came from her chest, maybe even deep in her stomach. She held it for a few long seconds before she sagged limply on the bed. But Daniel wasn't done. His slid in another finger, then the fourth. Her body opened up for him. He saw the muscles on her stomach flutter. Her eyes blinked open.

"Do you want me to stop?"

She shook her head no, even though tears were leaking from her eyes. Daniel knew that feeling. She'd found her space, the sub space they called it. There were all sorts of psychological ways of explaining it, but Daniel knew it as the point where he could finally let go, the moment where he found his safety wrapped in euphoria and it was no longer necessary for him to keep up the barriers and walls necessary to keep him safe in everyday life. Keira was there with him. She'd succumbed to all the sensations. She'd given in to the act of submission and now all she had to do was sit back and enjoy. Daniel had everything in hand, quite literally.

His thumb was the last to enter her warm cunt. He held still for a moment as she swirled her hips, feeling her muscles squeeze down on his fingers before they relaxed then tensed again.

Daniel moved his hand, his whole arm, with deep, pumping thrusts. His right arm, with its healed scars, traced over the skin of her breasts and nipples. Keira met him at every beat, harder and harder as her strength came back to her, until she climaxed again. It was different this time, not one hard explosion, but a series of mini eruptions. She lay trembling on her side as liquid leaked from between her thighs and onto the sheets. The sight of it, the watery proof of her pleasure, almost made Daniel come in his jeans.

Eventually he slid his fingers free. He went to the kitchen and, when he returned with a bottle of water, he quickly unwrapped the tape from Keira's mouth and cut the tape from her wrists and ankles. He wiped her face with a damp cloth he had waiting, then pulled her onto his lap and helped her take a sip of the water.

She looked up at him, the tears flowing more freely. It had been an intense hour.

"How are you feeling?" he asked.

"No small talk. Where's the ice cream?"

"Yes small talk. That's how this works. How are you feeling?"

Keira looked down and grabbed onto his t-shirt. "Is it okay if I can't put it into words? I feel a lot, or I felt a lot, but I don't know how to explain it."

"Yeah, that's very okay. Are you hurt anywhere?" She'd be sore in the morning just from struggling against the bindings, but he needed to know if he'd hurt her.

Keira took another sip of water then settled against his body. "I feel great. My brain is like pudding, but my body feels... I can't explain it."

"I get it."

"Good. Now ice cream. I need it."

"If I didn't love you so much I'd drop your ass on the floor right now."

"I know it's tough," Keira said, playing off his ill- timed declaration. "I love me too."

Daniel rolled his eyes, but gently moved her over to the pillows. He'd think about what he'd just let slip later. Much later. Way after ice cream.

✶

"Daniel. Daniel."

He knew he wasn't alone. In fact he knew he'd fallen asleep with this perfect woman resting in his arms. Daniel just wasn't sure if he was dreaming or if Keira was really saying his name. He felt a little nudge to his ribs. "Dan."

"Yeah, babe."

"Do you have any condoms?"

"Yeah, I—"

She interrupted his sleepy groan. "I want to have sex with you."

He was still half asleep, but that was all his body needed to hear. He stood up and found the condoms in his dresser with his eyes nearly closed. Slid one on in an automatic motion. He was between her thighs next, feeling his way in the dark until his cock was exactly where in it needed to be. Keira bore down on him with a whimper, taking his whole length at once. He groaned in kind. She was so warm. Welcoming. There was no rush to come, just the slow, lazy motion of their bodies moving together. Daniel wanted it to last forever. He buried his face in the curve of her neck, praying it would.

Six

Daniel set his menu down the moment he saw Mistress Evelyn glide into the restaurant. As she got closer he did what he been taught to do for the last ten years. He stood and pulled out her chair. She smiled and kissed him on the cheek.

"Hello, sweetheart. It's good to finally see you."

"Likewise." It had only been three weeks, but that was a long time when it came to being away from The Club and The Family.

Daniel took his seat, feeling his face heat for a few different reasons. It was always something to be around Evelyn. And Philip. But his Mistress definitely had a way about her that made you aware of everything. It was her voice, the light and smooth, delicate way of it, and the fact that she was easily six feet tall. She was over sixty, but black women age in that way that had most people convinced she wasn't a day over forty. She was beautiful, with her salt-and- pepper hair shaved close to her head. And all Daniel could think of was Keira. He looked down at his glass of water.

"Do we bother with the pleasantries or should we just talk?"

Daniel smiled. She knew him too well. "Whatever pleases you."

"Oh stop it. Tell me about her."

"I don't think I can." That was the only way to put it. Talking to Mistress Evelyn was always an easy thing to do. She'd been with him since the beginning. Seen him through rehab and physical therapy. She'd flown his mother down so she could be there when he was fitted for his first prosthesis. If he could confide in anyone, it was Mistress Evelyn Baker. But there was some sort of block when it came to Keira.

He didn't like talking about her to anyone. It had nothing to do with shame. He loved her. He had admitted that to himself days ago. It was something closer to privacy. Something inside of him just didn't want to go there. But Mistress Evelyn wasn't giving up. She reached out and took Daniel's hand.

"Try. I want to know about this woman who's kept you away from us for so long."

Daniel gave up and pulled out his phone, going right to one of the many, many pictures of Keira he now had on it. A selfie she'd taken of them together the night before when she was sitting on his lap, live tweeting *Galaxis*. He handed his phone over.

"I thought you would have met her before at one of Grant or Armando's things, but I'm sure you would both remember each other."

"You told her about me?" she asked.

"Not exactly." More like not at all.

Mistress Evelyn just laughed. She was a stern, challenging Dominant, but also a kind, lighthearted, wonderful friend and Daniel was being an ass.

"Oh, she's beautiful. Such a sweet face, but I want to know, what's got you scared?" she asked. Their server appeared then and Mistress Evelyn ordered for them both without glancing at the menu. Again, his mind flashed to Keira.

"She doesn't know the extent...of all this," he said, once their server was gone.

"But clearly she's giving you what you need or you'd have come running back to The Club already." She wasn't wrong. They'd been taking turns Topping and bottoming, kind of. He topped her and she sorted through various fantasies she had stored in her imagination. And Daniel followed through with those fantasies, no matter how ridiculous.

The nights they'd spent at his place she'd been okay with, and then enthusiastic about him moving from bare hand spankings to the flogger. She didn't care much for the paddles. There was regular vanilla sex. Lots of that; more than Daniel was used to, but he couldn't bring himself to mind. He felt himself getting hard thinking about it. Sometimes after a long day at work, retreating to her apartment and falling into her bed, just to make love to her, was the best part of his day.

"I don't think she's ready for The Club."

"Or you're not ready to bring her to The Club. Which is it?" Mistress Evelyn asked.

"Possibly a little bit of both. How long before I'm banned?"

Daniel smiled again at Evelyn's laugh. He knew he sounded ridiculous, but he was only half joking. How long could he stay away, self-marooned on the Isle of Keira before his Friends-in-Kink stopped sending lifeboats? There had been texts from Marcos, calls from Meegan. Philip had even sent him an invite to a kink exposé in San Francisco at the start of the New Year. People had expectations of him. At some point he was going to have to show up.

"We would never ban you. Ever. We were hoping The Club would be yours one day, if you want me to be completely honest." Mistress Evelyn said the words so casually it made Daniel blink.

"I—excuse me?"

"You don't think Philip and I have talked about it?"

"Well I don't particularly like thinking about you two not being around for The Club *not* to be yours."

"It's going to happen one day, sweetheart. And even before then we'd like to retire from everything. Well, from the responsibility. We want to be around to see the place given into the right hands."

"But I couldn't even afford the space and everything else—"

"That's what the membership is for."

Daniel had almost forgotten. Membership to The Club came with several caveats, one being that you paid a sum to be invited to one of the most exclusive bondage establishments on this side of the country, but Daniel had never paid a dime. Master Philip wouldn't let him.

"I'm flattered, but what about Meegan, or Shane, or the boys?" Wouldn't their sons want dibs on such a valuable piece of downtown LA real estate?

"Meegan's not right for it. Jordy and Ray have their trust. You don't think we're making the right decision?"

"No. I just...I don't know what to say."

"Say you'll think about it. Say you'll consider it a gift from us to you."

"And Keira? You want to know how serious I am about her? How she plays into all this?"

Evelyn frowned. "No. Why would you think that? I just want to know more about this girl who has you so wrapped up. Nothing beyond that."

"I'm sorry, I didn't mean to say that—"

"Sweetheart, if you're still working things out with her, take your time. Relationships develop and play out in the way they're meant to. No matter what happens, we're here for you, and Keira for that matter. If she needs us."

"Thank you. I appreciate that."

"Can you bring her to the Christmas party? It'll be more cookies and punch than kink anyway. She'll have a great time."

Daniel didn't doubt that for a minute, but still...

"Give me more news. How are things at the fireworks factory? How's Mama?"

The change of subject actually helped. Work and family Daniel could talk about with ease. He wasn't exactly sure what his problem was when it came to Keira and The Club, but he needed to figure it out.

Keira's glance flicked to the clock at the top of her computer screen. Daniel would be there any moment. She was still sitting on her bed, forcing herself to breathe. Everything was going to be fine.

ItsKeiraTime: I'm going to chicken out.

LoriNLynn+Twins: don't you dare. you said he said he loved you. you've been hanging out AND sleeping together for weeks!

ItsKeiraTime: but it was a like a post sex buddy-buddy "i love you, buddy" kind of i love you.

LoriNLynn+Twins: whatever. guys dont accidentally say i love you. nobody does.

Keira wasn't exactly sure she believed that, considering Daniel hadn't said it again since that night at his place, but she knew there was something serious between them. They spent all their free time together and when they weren't together they were texting each other.

LoriNLynn+Twins: just ask him and if he says no then you know where you stand with him.

· · ·

ItsKeiraTime: no you're right.

As Keira hit 'send', her doorbell rang.

ItsKeiraTime: he's here. gotta jet.

LoriNLynn+Twins: Good luck! Lynn says good luck too!

Keira sent two kissy faces and an XOXO before signing out of her email. Part of her plan included her laptop, but she didn't want chat boxes and alerts popping up while she was trying to focus. She set down her computer and went to the door. Daniel was there, looking all perfectly handsome and beautiful and hot. He'd just gotten a haircut, the sides of his head practically buzzed clean. Keira actually bit her lip as she looked at him. *God, please let him say yes.*

He held up the bag in his hand. "Chicken fried rice and just chicken fried rice."

"You kept asking what else I wanted. I just wanted the rice. But thank you. Come in."

He slid by her, kissing her forehead as he headed toward the couch. "You okay?" Was it that obvious? Her nerves were so twisted up she was practically vibrating.

"Yeah I'm fine," she said, even though her voice nearly cracked. She watched Daniel as he made himself comfortable and he watched her as she stood by the door like it wasn't her apartment, like they hadn't made plans that involved them actually being on the same side of the room.

"Actually, no. Well yeah. I wanted to ask you something."

"Okay..." He slowly eased back into the couch cushions, a look of dread clouding his face.

"Gosh, I should have just said 'Daniel, we need to talk.'"

"Yeah, that's how it sounds."

"It's not bad. I swear. Okay." Keira rushed over to the couch and made a space on the coffee table in front of him. "So tonight I had two plans, but one plan depends on what you say to the thing I have to ask you. Okay?"

"Okay, shoot."

"I really like you and I really like all the time we've been spending together and I love that you will watch *Galaxis* with me and cartoons, and all the other silly stuff I like. And you indulge my weirdly specific food requests. You're awesome. I like you. But I also know that we're kinda different.

"I'm more traditional, you could say, and I thought about it, being a hip woman, keeping up with the times who can be with someone and sleep with someone who's seeing other people, but I'm not really. Not that I think you're seeing other people. I don't know when you'd find the time, but yeah. I was wondering what you thought about possibly being exclusive. Like you being my boyfriend."

"You're asking me if I want to be your boyfriend?"

Keira wanted to throw up. "Yeah."

Daniel looked at her for a moment, his expression completely blank. The silence would be perfectly filled with the sound of her barfing. And it would be if he didn't say or do something soon.

"You can say no. I mean of course you know you can say no. But if you said no I would understand. I'm a weirdo fangirl sci-fi geek who talks too much. I'm not sure I'd want to date me either. I just thought I'd ask."

Daniel slid forward and took her hand. His fingers were so warm. She thought of how they felt trailing down her back as she fell asleep in his arms and she wondered if that was over. If he was soothing her one last time before he walked out of her life.

"You know you might be my first real girlfriend since high school?"

"Really?"

"Yup. You know me, living that wild bachelor life."

"Oh, I just figured... You're so hot though."

Daniel's laugh made Keira bite the inside of her lip again. "Well not quite as beautiful as you, but I'll take that as a compliment."

"Can I take the fact that you didn't just jump out my window as a sign that you're saying yes?"

"Yes, baby. I'm saying yes."

Keira let out a huge sigh, letting her whole body sag forward. But that was just the first part.

"What sort of plans for the evening come with a yes?" Daniel asked.

"Well, you can pick. One second."

Keira jumped up and ran to her room. She'd prepared everything she needed and put it into a Melrose Fitness tote for easy transport to the other end of her apartment. Daniel hadn't made a break for it while she was gone, confirming that the yes still stood.

"So there's a Twilight Zone marathon on tonight and I thought we could play a combination drinking/stripping game to the repetitive themes. Or... I was hoping you'd let me try that edging thing you told me about."

Daniel's eyebrow went up. "What's in the bag?"

Keira reached down and started pulling out the pieces of plan B. "I got this ball gag cause you said you wanted to be gagged. And then I was going to get handcuffs, but no—'cause, duh. I did some research and this rope was highly recommended. The store only had this length in neon green. I hope that's okay."

"Green's fine."

"Then I got this oil that shouldn't stain the couch or clothes, and then I got this. The man at the store said this was the best one, besides a full kit." She handed Daniel the box enema. When she looked up, his expression had gone from pleasantly surprised to pure shock.

"Is this too much? You can tell me if I'm doing it wrong. All the edging stuff I looked up seemed to be better for the guy if some prostate stimulation was involved. I got these cool black rubber gloves too. He said some people like them. They look sexy, I guess," she added with a shrug. They were pretty neat.

"No, this isn't too much at all. Why don't we throw on the Twilight Zone and then we'll put all this into play."

"Great. I did a lot of reading. I'm kinda aching to apply my knowledge."

"I bet you are. Come here," Daniel said as he slid even farther to the edge of the couch. Keira met him halfway, brushing her lips against his until he leaned in a little more. Then his arms were around her and they were both standing, lost in the kiss. She was so glad she hadn't chickened out. If she had, she wouldn't be the proud, new owner of this awesome boyfriend who also happened to be the best kisser on Earth. She couldn't wait to tell Lori.

Daniel took his time getting ready. Not that he wasn't familiar with this sort of preparation, but he needed a few moments to think. It wasn't a matter of what he had just done, what he'd just agreed to. Keira was great, she was perfect. Any man would be lucky to have her and she'd decided that she wanted him to be that man. And that was all well and good for tonight, but at some point he was going to have to make the tough call. He was going to have choose between Keira and The Club and these people he'd come to know as his family.

He hadn't seen anyone from his kinky life in weeks. There had been plenty of texts and calls, but after he got a message from Marcos saying that Mistress Evelyn had mentioned he was some seeing someone, a fact he confirmed, the texts and calls stopped. He knew they were being respectful and giving him space, but there was a sense on everyone's part, even his own, that he would be back. It was just a matter of time.

But now the decision had been made for him. Keira had said it out loud, plain and clear. She wanted him to herself. Daniel was pretty sure tag-teaming various submissives with Master Philip was out of the question. He could kiss his amateur porn-making days goodbye. And if he really wanted to see this relationship with Keira through, it would probably be a good idea to decline Mistress Evelyn's offer to take over The Club.

But he figured he could worry about all of that another time, at least after the weekend. He finished up in the bathroom, stashing the towel he'd used after his shower in the hamper. He could hear Keira talking to herself as he came down the hall.

"Gosh, I hope I don't screw this up. He needs his circulation."

Daniel was just about to ask what she was talking about when he turned the corner and saw what she was wearing. She stood as soon as she saw him, gripping the length of rope in her hand. She glanced down when she realized he wasn't staring at her face.

"Oh, I—ah—I figured I should wear something dominatrix-y, but this was all I could come up with." Daniel looked her up and down, taking in the black push-up top that came with ribbons that she'd criss-crossed down her torso. There were black thigh-high socks with white stripes that added to the overall sexiness of the situation. What he couldn't take his eyes off of was the pair of lace panties she was wearing that appeared to be crotchless.

Daniel swallowed. "I think it'll work just fine. Turn around a sec."

"Um, excuse me. I think I'm in charge tonight."

"Just humor me."

"Fine." Keira spun around with a sigh, bending over a bit to give Daniel the view he was clearly looking for.

Definitely crotchless. Somehow he managed to keep his hand

to himself, but his erection, which had started to rise during his preparations, now showed up for the full occasion. It was just as difficult to keep his hand off his dick.

"Good?" Keira asked, still slightly bent over.

"Yeah we're good."

"Excellent. Please come to the couch, but remain standing. Please."

Daniel followed orders, coming to stand in front of the couch, where Keira had put down a thick towel to cover the cushions. Her laptop was open on the coffee table. A video he'd watched a while ago, a rope tutorial by Madam May, an amazing bondage expert, was queued up.

"Also, excuse the laptop and the video. I want to make sure I get this right. Just bear with me."

"I'm bearing."

Daniel stood patiently as Keira began binding his arms to his sides. She talked to herself the entire time, but she barely glanced at the screen as the knots and loops came together down the length of his torso. He wondered how many times she's practiced. And on whom. After a few short moments she stood back to admire her work.

"Is it too tight?"

Daniel moved his arms, just a fraction of an inch. "Perfect."

"Great," she said with the enthusiasm he'd loved about her from day one. "Can you snap?"

Daniel responded with a loud snap of his fingers.

"Excellent."

He had to laugh at the huge smile on Keira's face and the way she bounced up on the balls of her feet, but she had every right to be proud of herself. This was a night of firsts for her and so far she was knocking every bit of it out of the park.

"Would you like me to sit?" he asked.

"Yes, please. I must administer the ball gag."

Daniel sat, shaking his head at her silliness. She carefully secured the gag in his mouth, then gave him a light shove. It wasn't enough to move him, but he still flopped back against the couch.

Keira slid onto the floor between his legs. "K, here I go. Snap if the pleasure is just too much for you."

All Daniel could do was nod.

He channeled years of training, years of patience, as he watched her grab the bottle of massage oil and proceed to pour the slick liquid all over his dick. He watched her face as she watched the warm liquid run down his balls. She added more, then wasted no time spreading it around his sac.

"This stuff is safe for me to swallow. Not saying that I'm going to be putting anything in my mouth, but just in case you wanted to know."

Daniel let out a rough breath through his nose, his sign that he understood.

Keira started on his balls, massaging them slowly. He thought about closing his eyes, shutting everything out so he could focus on the feel of Keira's hands and the sound of her voice, and not how badly he wanted to lay her out of the floor and fuck her sense-less. But he had to watch her, to look at her beautiful face when she tilted her head to the side and gave his scrotum and ass a thor-ough inspection.

"Your skin is so soft. It's so weird how soft taint skin is."

Daniel snorted because this was his girlfriend now, his Keira, talking so matter-of-factly about the softness of his taint, and instead of turning him off it just made him want her more. He wouldn't change her ability to keep every moment they spent together light and full of humor for anything. He slid a little farther down on the couch and spread his legs a little wider.

Keira really started in on him then, using one hand to slowly stroke his cock while she massaged his balls. So slowly he knew it would be a breeze to hold off until she was ready for him to come. The only frustration came from not being able to touch her, not being able to kiss her. Those thoughts had him staring at her more carefully as she touched him. He started to memorize the features of her face, the way her straightened hair looked pulled back. Her lips.

She took him into her mouth after a while, talking to him and teasing him as she slurred up and down his shaft. She knew he wouldn't come and she knew he couldn't talk, but still she asked him how good it felt, if he wanted her to keep going. He groaned and grunted in the affirmative. Her tongue was enough to make him want to cover those, soft plump lips with his come.

The teasing didn't last forever though. She started sucking him in earnest, not for his pleasure, but for her own. Sitting up on her knees, she leaned over his lap and started going to town. For a moment, Daniel lost himself, actually let himself forget that he was supposed to be holding off. He snapped three times sharply. When Keira looked up he shook his head. Her lips were all slick and glossy.

"Do I need to stop? Are you close?"

He nodded with another grunt.

"Okay. I'll back off. This is easier than I thought." The wink she threw him was unnecessary. He was already coming to terms with how hard this was going to be. Daniel loved edging. He loved the tension it created all over his body, and the inevitable release that was always worth the wait, but he didn't want to wait. No. Not tonight. He wanted Keira, now. It was too soon though. He already agreed to her terms. Unless he wanted to end the scene altogether, he would just have to suck it up and wait 'til the moment where he could take her properly.

More oil then, along his shaft and all over his lap. She massaged his hips and his stomach before making her way down his thighs. The lack of direct stimulation helped a bit, but not for long because she was soon back on his cock, with her hand this time, while her other fingers started toying with his ass.

"Do you want the gloves?"

Daniel nodded. He'd already pictured her snapping the black

latex into place. She paused long enough to do just that and Daniel's cock jumped at the sound.

One finger then two gently probed his ass. The intrusion was too much and still not enough. He was groaning and close to thrashing on the couch, but his hips were the only thing that moved; his hips and the heaving of his chest, until he snapped again. He was gonna come.

"You really like that don't you?" she asked, before she went at him with just her tongue. Her mouth was everywhere, licking and kissing and sucking. She asked him again and again if she was doing things right. More groans and grunts and pumping of his hips as her head turned this way and that.

She brought him to the edge again, taking turns between using her mouth and her hands, stroking his cock, and fucking his ass with her slender fingers. Daniel didn't expect her to be so good at this. He'd never enjoyed this so much, not with anyone else.

Keira stood up and tugged off the latex gloves. "I'm sorry. I have to do something a little selfish."

As long as you keep touching me, you can be as selfish as you want. She did one better. She straddled his lap and sat on his dick.

He was already slick from the oil and her mouth, but her pussy was so wet and so warm, he could only squeeze his eyes shut to keep himself from ejaculating. It was his only way to claw at some sense of self-control. She felt too good. Daniel automatically thrust his hips up, burying himself as deep as she could take him. Keira cried out, falling forward to brace herself on his shoulders. He moved his hips again, pumping into her until she begged him to stop.

"Wait, wait. Hold on," she said, practically panting. "Just let me ride you."

Daniel groaned his disapproval, but gave in, settling in the couch so she could set the pace. He watched her as she got herself off, wishing she'd lose the strappy bra top so he could watch her nipples. It would have been even better if her nipples were in his mouth. He didn't care if this was her night. As soon as she untied him, he was taking over.

Keira came, slowing the vicious rocking of her pelvis long enough to draw out her orgasm. Daniel held off, focusing all his energy on not coming inside of her tight, throbbing pussy. But she didn't savor it, not the way he was hoping she would. She hopped off him, rubbing her clit as she retreated to the far end of the couch.

"Come," she said with a breathy sigh. Her fingers were still busy with their exploration. "Come now."

The only words Daniel's body wanted to hear. He gave in, letting all the sensations and built up frustration take control. Come shot out of his cock and up his chest in thick jets. Keira came back to him and started to tug off the gag. Jizz was still leaking from his swollen tip. He had two more nuts in him in, at least. She was in such deep shit once he got out of this rope.

As soon as the gag was off, she went for his stomach, licking up whatever she could find on his skin and in between the ropes. And then she kissed him.

"Go get the condoms out of my jacket," Daniel said when he had a moment to breathe and swallow the come she'd just put in his mouth. "And then I want you to untie me."

"But we're not done yet. You haven't pizza'd yet." Keira's attempt at arguing was cute, considering she was already reaching for his coat. She dropped the condoms on the coffee table and then made quick work of the ropes binding his arms.

"Is it bad that I set a timer?" she asked as she untangled the final knots.

"I wouldn't expect anything else from you. How'd we do?"

Keira glance at her computer then back at him with this toothy grin. "Two hours and twenty-three minutes. You think we can beat it next time?"

Daniel stood then pulled her closer, kissing her face. "I'm sure we can. Put a condom on me."

"You ready again?" she asked, even though she was already reaching for a rubber. He didn't even bother to answer because she was already sliding it over his cock. But he did ask her, "Are you worn out?"

"No," she replied, a hint of bashfulness coloring her voice. She wasn't used to being this greedy.

"We'll have to do something about that." Daniel kissed her once more. And then he turned her around and bent her over the couch.

Seven

Keira didn't know it was possible to smile for two days straight, but when she woke up Monday morning, way before the sun, she was still grinning like an idiot. Her first two clients even noticed she was perkier than usual, but she didn't think it would be professional to tell them that she had a new man. It would be extra unprofessional to go into the explicit details of how they spent their first weekend coupled up, but thinking about those explicit things just made her smile even more. Yeah, this kind of happy was something she could get used to.

When she came back to the gym with her lunch, Grant finally asked what had her on cloud eleven, even after she'd spent part of the morning in a one-on-one with her least favorite client.

Armando came into the office just as she was about to spill the beans. She figured she should tell them both.

"Well, Daniel and I are a couple now."

"Oh yeah?" Grant's face lit up with pleasant surprise. Armando, on the other hand... Keira tried not to be bothered by the look of horror spreading across his face. She did a double take before she turned her attention back to Grant.

"Yeah. I uh, I asked him if he wanted to go steady. You know, be exclusive 'cause I'm in high school and I need to define my commitment."

Grant shrugged that last bit off. "Nah. Violet asked me to be her boyfriend. Shit, it was good for me. I think it's fine to define a relationship when it gets to that point. And you guys have been hanging for what? Like a month?"

Thirty-three and a half days. "Yeah, something like that."

"Well, there you go. I'm happy for you guys."

"Thank you," Keira said and she meant it, but she was slightly distracted by the fact that Armando's eye looked like it was about to start twitching at any moment. "Are you okay?"

"Yeah. Yeah. I'm happy for you guys. I'll be right back." He turned on his sneakers and walked right out of the office.

"What is going on with him?" Keira asked.

Grant shrugged. "Who knows? So, I guess you'll be coming to the Christmas party at Master Philip's."

"Oh, I don't know. Daniel hasn't mentioned it yet."

"I'm sure he will. It's this weekend. Violet had to keep reminding me."

"Oh. I'll be back." She didn't mean to be so dismissive, especially since Grant was being supportive, but she had to know what Armando's deal was.

Keira wandered back out to the gym and saw Armando through the frosted front doors, talking on his phone. She marched outside, catching him off guard.

"She *is* my business, man! She's my friend! I—" He cut himself off when he realized he wasn't alone.

"Are you talking to Daniel?"

Armando's face fell. "Ah—"

Keira held out her hand. "Let me talk to him."

"Uh...here."

Keira took the phone, but kept her eyes firmly on Armando. What the heck was going on? "Hey, it's me."

"Hey." Daniel did not sound happy.

"Is everything okay?"

"Yeah, Armando's just worried about you. He doesn't trust me."

"Is there a reason he shouldn't?" Keira asked around the sudden sour taste in her mouth.

"No, not at all. He's just paranoid because I'm a pervert and he thinks I'll corrupt you, but I think we both know it's a little late for that."

"Yeah, I think so," Keira replied. Her smile was back. "Oh, Grant said something about a Christmas party this weekend? Do I need a dress?"

"Uh, yeah. I completely forgot about that." Daniel was quiet for a second before he went on. "It's at The Club, as in the bondage club. Are you sure you want to go?"

"Do I have to bondage with strangers?" Daniel's laugh made it easier for her to ignore Armando while he stood there watching her.

"No, you don't, babe. Unless you want to."

"I think I'm good. I have a client soon. Do you want to talk to Armando again?"

"No, I don't. I'll text you later, aight?"

"'Kay." Keira said her goodbyes then hit END on the screen. Then she turned on Armando. "What gives?"

"I've just never known Daniel to have a girlfriend. I don't want you to be the guinea pig, if it ends badly."

"That kinda sucks, Mando. I mean, that's a crappy thing to say," Keira said, despite the sudden tightness in her throat. "He's been great to me and I really like him. And *you* introduced us. I know you didn't think we would hook up, but isn't it better that we found each other?"

"I—No, you're right."

"You can have two single, unhappy friends, or two friends that are happy together."

"You're right, you're right. I'm sorry." Armando let out an uneasy laugh and then pulled Keira into his arms, a familiar hug they'd shared dozens of times. "You know how protective I am of my sisters."

"Well, I'm not one of your sisters and you're not the boss of me. Well actually you are, but you get what I mean." Keira stepped back and handed Armando his phone. He seemed to relax.

"You sound like Daniel. He basically said the same thing."

"Good. Stop being bossy and just be happy for us."

"Alright, alright. Let's get back in here. I've got a client soon. And your lunch is probably getting cold." Keira followed Armando inside. She appreciated that he cared about her so much, but everything with Daniel was going to be fine. Better than fine. Great.

During another meeting about the Super Bowl, Daniel decided the Christmas party would be the last function he attended at The Club. If he wanted to be with Keira, he couldn't share his life with all these other people who thought he was nothing but his kinks. He didn't know how he was going to break the news to Miss Evelyn, or Philip, but he would think of something. After the party.

Keira reached over and took Daniel's arm. He looked so sexy in his dress shirt and perfectly tailored vest. They were on their way to a party. A fancy, kinkified Christmas party with Daniel's fancy, kinky friends. And Grant and Armando. They were fancy too, but Keira was interested in meeting the rest of these mysterious people Daniel rarely mentioned. He said something about his mentors owning the place, the way he described them seemed way too clinical to be the truth. You own a freaking kinky club? You have to be an interesting character. Keira couldn't wait to meet them and the rest of the people they deemed worthy to include on the guest list.

Still, Keira's excitement wasn't enough to distract from the fact that Daniel was acting really strange.

He'd been oddly distant the last few days. He told her he was fine a bunch of times, but Keira was picking up all kinds of not-fine vibes. Daniel was an honest man, and pretty straightforward. If something was bugging him she just had to trust he would tell her when he was ready.

"So when the party's over, your place or mine?" Keira asked, code for do you want top me tonight or not?

Daniel glanced over at her, a small smile finally touching his lips. "We'll go to my place. I think it's finally time we tie you up properly with some rope." Keira's pussy clenched at the thought. She liked when he bound her with the bondage tape, but the rope would be fun.

Daniel pulled his SUV down an alley between two warehouses to where a valet stand and velvet rope had been set up at the door. Daniel handed off his key and helped Keira out of the car.

"Is it okay for me to be nervous?" she asked, as she took his hand.

"There's nothing to be nervous about. Come on." They took a short hall to a freight elevator that took them down one floor. It opened to a small receiving area where a bouncer sat on a stool. The short white guy lit up when he saw Daniel.

"Hey man! Where have you been? It's been weeks." They did that dude hug thing with the slap on the back.

"Just been busy."

"We thought we'd lost you." As the bouncer spoke he glanced at Keira in a peculiar way. Half way between curious and annoyed. She tried not to frown when he introduced himself as Trent, the club security.

Trent opened the door for them and Daniel led her inside. The party was already in full swing, people and things filling up the massive space. Christmas music was playing over the sound system and there were Christmas decorations up everywhere. Some people were dressed in regular party attire, like Daniel and herself, but there were a fair bit of people in leather bondage gear, accented with Santa hats of course.

Daniel leaned toward her and pointed to a large window that ran along the wall about twenty feet above their heads. It was tinted so you couldn't see through. "Mast— Philip and Evelyn use the top floor as a home away from home and this functions as the club proper."

Keira just nodded, her anxiousness overtaken by sheer curiosity and shock. She looked at the various contraptions around the room. A set of medieval stocks, this large wooden X thing, a giant bird cage that looked big enough to hold three people. There was a stage and two smaller stages with stripper poles. Small tables with chairs filled the middle of the floor, but each little nook and cranny that ran along the outer walls housed a different device and a perfectly positioned leather couch or love seat, for spectators Keira assumed.

Nothing was being used though. Everyone was just milling about the space, socializing. There was more, Keira could see as she looked around, but Daniel veered her over to the bar area where Violet and Nailah were standing. They were fully dressed.

"Where are your boys?" Daniel asked as he and Keira hugged them both hello.

Nailah rolled her eyes and pointed up toward the window. "They got recruited to be Santa's elves."

"Is it okay if you hang with the ladies for a moment? I have to go talk to Philip." Daniel asked Keira. Maybe it had to do with whatever was bugging him.

"Yeah, sure."

"We'll take care of her," Violet said with a smile.

Daniel kissed her on the cheek. "I'll be right back."

"Yeah," Keira said. She hoped their talk fixed things.

"Everything okay?" Violet asked when he took off across the room.

"Don't worry," Nailah said. "Armando ditched me the first time we came here too. It's like they don't know how to act when their worlds collide." Maybe she was onto something.

"Yeah, things are cool. I think. I think he's just having a bad day."

"Well just hang with us."

"Yeah, he'll be back."

Keira ordered herself a soda and stood by as Nailah and Violet tried to give her the skinny on the people in their line of sight. People they didn't know, Nailah started making up mean, gossipy stories about. Keira tried not to laugh, but Nailah had a way with words.

Soon a tall, younger-looking white girl came over to them and offered them raffle tickets. She had on a set of felt reindeer ears and not much else beyond the red paint on the tip of her nose. A red leather body harness wove its way down her torso, but it did nothing to cover her nipples or the glossy slit between her legs. Whoever had dressed her had gotten her nice and wound up. Looking at her made Keira even more excited to get back to Daniel's place.

The girl handed her a ticket. "What are these for?" Keira asked.

"For when Santa arrives," the girl said cheerfully.

"Meegan, this Daniel's girlfriend, Keira." The second Nailah made the introduction, Meegan's expression dropped, shock then pain hitting her eyes. "Keira, Meegan belongs to Master Philip and Mistress Evelyn."

Meegan swallowed, her eyes darting to the floor. "If you'll excuse me." She bolted to the next group of people and kept handing out tickets, looking like she was fighting the urge to cry.

"What the heck was that all about?" Keira asked. Violet glanced at Nailah, but, being less coy and tactful, Nailah just spit out the truth.

"Meegan has the hots for Daniel. She probably didn't think he'd show up with a date, let alone a girlfriend."

"But if she belongs to—"

"It's not like that. Philip and Evelyn are married. They own Meegan as a pet and a plaything. She's not allowed to be dominated by anyone but them, but she can date other submissives. I mean get it, but you'd think Daniel would have asked her out by now if he was interested."

"Nailah, Jesus," Violet said.

A strange kind of heat flashed over Keira's body and her stomach started to flip. She looked over to see Violet rubbing her face, annoyed.

"I'm sorry," Nailah said. "I'm working on not being so insensitive. Daniel's here with you. That's what matters."

Keira had no idea why she was so upset, other than the fact that she hated confrontation. Nailah was right. Daniel was here with her. Daniel was *her* boyfriend, but why did this Meegan girl seemed so shocked to hear it, especially if she and Daniel were any kind of close? Maybe he hadn't told her yet. Or maybe he wasn't planning to tell her anything.

Violet handed Keira a small bottle of ice water. The large gulp she took only made her feel a little better because, really, Daniel wasn't with her. She couldn't see him anywhere.

✳

Daniel headed back down to the floor just as conflicted as before. For someone so determined to make up his mind, he was getting nowhere. He loved Keira and he wanted to be with her for the long haul, but he needed The Club and his kink community too.

They were a part of his life and such an integral part of who he had become as a man, and a switch.

He'd had an interesting talk with Master Philip. Grant and Armando, who had been in the room and done their best to listen and not comment, only added that whatever he decided to do, he better not hurt Keira in the process. That right there was the tricky part. If he took over The Club someday, he would want Keira by his side. If she was by his side, he was going to marry her. If they planned to see this through, if he finally got up the guts to propose to her, she had to become a member of The Club. But he had no idea how to approach her about peer counseling and proper training. He had to make her see that he could be involved and still be faithful to her.

Daniel found Keira right where he'd left her, at the bar chatting with the girls.

"How's it going?" he asked, as he pulled Keira into his arms. It didn't go unnoticed that she was a little stiff.

"Had a pleasant run-in with Meegan," Nailah said, giving him a look that said there was a sixty percent chance he'd be going home alone tonight. Just then Anthony, a Dominant he'd played with numerous times, came over to say hello. Everything was going fine until...

"All this time you've been away, I hope you and Keira have at least made some new clips. Your adoring public is waiting for new material." A statement innocent enough, but... "Actually I was hoping you'd recreate the one you made with Pamela. You know, we talked about the quality and the angles. Keira would be perfect for that."

Daniel tried to ignore the fact that Anthony glanced at the roundness of Keira's ass as he made the comment. "No, you're right, but we haven't gotten around to that yet."

"Oh that's a shame. Keira, I'm sure you've seen Daniel's handiwork. You have a favorite video yet?"

She looked over her shoulder at him, so much subtle murder in her eyes. "Um, I'm not sure I've seen them all." She hadn't seen any.

"We made some good ones, didn't we, Dan?" Anthony meant well, but he needed to shut up. Luckily the sound of sleigh bells signified the start of the festivities. Anthony excused himself and found a seat.

Daniel pulled Keira closer and whispered in her ear. "I promise I'll explain later."

"I bet."

Master Philip entered and took center stage with Grant and Armando at his side, each with sacks of unwrapped kink toys to be raffled off and exchanged. Daniel usually put himself into the raffle, but this year he put in a gift certificate for an erotic massage. The effort was lackluster at best, but no one would know it was from him. That was the point.

Things kicked off all in good fun. Keira's number was called third and she went to the front of the room to claim a pair furry handcuffs and edible panties from Grant. They shared a good laugh and some words Daniel couldn't make out from across the room.

"These are both for you to wear," Keira said when she made her way back to the bar.

He took the box of panties out of her hand. "That means you're going to have to eat them." He laughed when Keira turned up her nose, and with good reason. He'd eaten those thin pieces of flavored plastic before. Keira stepped back into his arms and continued fiddling with the furry cuffs as they watched the rest of the ridiculous spectacle.

When Keira settled against his chest, laughing, asking questions, sharing appropriately snarky comments with Violet and Nailah, he figured whatever had happened with Meegan and the awkwardness with Anthony had been forgotten or, at least, tabled for a calm, rational discussion. Yeah everything was going just fine, until Marcos went up to the stage. Just fine, even as Armando handed Marcos a heavy-duty leather flogger. Just fine, even as Marcos turned around and started scanning the room. Just fine, until his gaze fell on Daniel.

"I'm accepting this gift under one condition," Marcos called out.

"And what is that, little boy?" Philip replied in his best Santa voice.

"I want Daniel Song to flog me with it tonight. He hasn't been here in over a month and I think he owes me a little something, plus owing you fine people a show."

To Daniel's expected horror, several people around the room joined in with similar complaints and jabs about his absence. He did his best to laugh all their comments off.

"I'm sorry, Marcos. Not tonight," he called back.

"Oh come on. I'm sure Keira will let you play with us. Come on." And that's where shit really went south.

"Oh, so she's your Mistress now?" Meegan said, loud enough for everyone in the whole place to hear.

Meegan was quickly admonished by a sharp look from Mistress Evelyn, but the damage was done.

Keira looked up at him. "You can play with whoever you want. Really, I don't care."

She didn't mean it, not by a long shot. It was written all over her face, but then was not the time or the place to discuss the real issue at hand.

Daniel tried to play it cool. "I don't think so. Maybe one of Santa's elves wants to help you out."

"Um no. *I* don't think so." Everyone laughed at Nailah's outraged rebuttal. She'd staked clear monogamous claim on Armando the moment she'd joined the club.

"Don't worry, my little Marcos. Santa and Mrs. Claus will treat you to something special before we tuck you in," Mistress Evelyn said, finally ending the debate.

Marcos jumped off the stage with a "Yippee!" bringing the

focus back to the front of the room and away from Daniel. And Keira. She was tense in his arms again. He knew he had to talk to her, but he didn't know where to start, which fuck up to try to fix first.

The night went on, more gifts, more absurdity. A performance or two. Daniel continued to introduce Keira around with mixed results. Some, like his good friend Anna and her submissive Caitlin, were kind and gracious, welcoming her to The Club, and others teased her as the wet blanket, keeping Daniel away from them for too long. Keira took it in stride, but Daniel could tell she was growing more and more uncomfortable. He asked her twice if she wanted to leave, but each time she said no, that she was having fun.

Near midnight, Daniel was ready to go. He made his rounds saying his goodbyes and explaining himself in as few words as possible. He was just another member for Christ's sake, but he was being treated like some sort of prodigal, as if The Club had stopped functioning in his absence, which he knew was far from the truth. He finally made his way back to Keira as Armando was handing her and Nailah their coats. He took Keira's and helped her into it. Then she turned to him, fluffing out her hair. "I'm actually going to get a ride with Armando and Nailah. You stay. Hang out some more." The smile she flashed him was sour as hell.

Daniel glanced up at Armando, who met his gaze with the same type of look. Annoyed. Completely unimpressed. A little pissed. If Daniel wanted to stop Keira leaving with Armando and Nailah, he would have to go through Armando. This was not the time or the place.

"At least let me walk you out."

"Really, you don't—"

"Daniel. Let it go," Armando said.

Keira stepped between them and put her hand on Daniel's chest. Her touch did something to him. He wanted to pull her close, and please her for as long as she would let him, but that look was still in her eyes. She was leaving without him. "We'll talk later."

Knowing there was nothing else he could do, Daniel watched Keira walk out of The Club. He just hoped, with everything that had happened during this awkward as shit night, Keira wasn't walking out of his life.

EIGHT

Keira could hear Armando yelling when she came into the gym. She realized what or who he was talking about when he said a certain someone's name.

"Fucking Daniel, man. I don't know what the fuck he was thinking. I told him to take it easy with her. I told him The Club wasn't her scene and then he brings her in there totally unprepared."

She couldn't make out what Grant said in response, but she could hear the muffled tone of his voice.

She walked right into the office, not wanting herself or her non-relationship with a certain someone to be topic of conversation for another minute. They both looked up when she came around the corner.

"Morning boys." She almost sounded cheerful, but the anger still radiating off Armando and Grant's hang-dog expression ruined any chance of her work day starting off on a light note. She'd already cried all weekend. Paced and cried and put away laundry in a huff and complained to Lori on chat. She'd spent more than enough time being upset about what had happened at the party. But Grant and Armando seemed to be just warming up.

"How you doing, Keir?" Armando said.

"Ugh, I'm fine." Keira tossed her bag on the floor and sank against the door jam.

"You talk to your boy?" Grant asked.

"No. He's been calling and stuff, but I only texted him back to let him know I didn't want to talk."

"Keira, listen. This is my fault. You told me you weren't into BDSM, and I know I didn't set you guys up, but I *know* Daniel. I put you in the mix with someone real fucking deep in the game. I knew better. We both did." She looked from Armando to Grant, who nodded in agreement.

Keira swallowed as the tears rose in her eyes. This was exactly what she didn't want. She already felt like an idiot, like an imposter who thought they could waltz right into their world of kinky fun and just adapt. She didn't need Grant and Armando to tell her that it was obvious to them too, obvious that she had no business at the club that night and even more obvious that she had no business being with Daniel.

"I'll be back." She went right to the ladies' locker room and sat down against the concrete wall. Daniel was at work, but she knew he would answer her texts. He always did.

> I'm really mad at you.

Not even ten seconds went by before her phone chimed.

> I know. I'm sorry.

> Seriously. what was that all about?

> I can't explain it over text.

> I don't know if I want to see you.

> You made me feel so weird.

Keira's throat tightened even more as she hit send.

> Weird how? I'm so sorry.

> Weird like an idiot.

> Can I please come see you tonight?

> I have more than a lot of explaining to do.

> I understand if you don't want to be with me anymore.

> Just want to talk to you.

That was the problem. Keira didn't know what she wanted. The Daniel she'd gotten to know, she was falling in love with. Actually, she was already there. And that's why his behavior the night of the party and everyone's reaction to him, to them, made her feel so uncomfortable.

Who the heck was this other Daniel and why had he hidden what seemed to be such an important part of himself from her? She had questions for sure, and she wanted answers, face to face. She was just terrified of which version of Daniel was going to show up. The last thing she wanted to was to be sweet talked into forgiving and then falling completely in love with a man who was okay with making her look like a fool.

Her fingers flew across her screen and she hit send without thinking.

> Are you fucking that Meegan chick?

> NO.

> I haven't been with anyone since we met.

That didn't exactly make her feel better, but she needed to get the question off her chest. Meegan looked like she wanted to kill

Keira the moment she found out who she'd shown up with. There was more than jealousy in her eyes. There was possession, and Keira did not sign up for a catfight.

Great, Kiera thought. But was *everything* something she wanted to know?

*

Daniel closed his eyes as he heard Keira undoing the lock to her front door. This was his chance. His one chance to unfuck the mess his personal life had become. He had one chance to tell Keira the whole truth, because he knew she didn't deserve anything less. She wouldn't stand for it. They wouldn't make it as a couple without it.

He tried not to smile when she opened the door. She was standing there in those microscopic shorts, and a *Galaxis* hoodie. Her hair was up and she had no make-up on, but her toenails were painted black. He'd painted them red for her the day of the party. The last time he'd seen her. She looked just as beautiful and adorable as ever. Daniel wanted to pull her into his arms or fall on his knees at her feet, but the look on her face suggested both would be a dumbassed idea. Her eyebrows were drawn so tight together it looked like her anger and frustration with him was giving her a headache.

Daniel cleared his throat. "Keira."

"You can come in, but you are not staying."

"That's fair."

"I know it is. Come in."

Daniel followed her to the living room and sat beside her on the couch.

"No. Sit over there." She pointed to the armchair on the other side of the room.

He made the mistake of laughing as he went to his assigned seat. "Don't want to be near me?"

"This isn't funny. I don't like the way you're making me feel right now and I don't want to be fooled into thinking this is all okay if you touch me."

"Fair enough."

"So, what the heck is your deal? I knew you were acting strange before we went to the party, but I still don't get what happened. Half the people in that room, actually everyone in that room, seemed to see me as some sort of enormous cock block. Which I guess I was, considering I'm or was kinda your girlfriend. But I want to know what you told them?"

His one chance.

"I didn't tell them anything and that was part of the problem. The other part was that I didn't tell you anything either. I lied to you, Keira."

She swallowed and pulled her legs up to her chest. "About how many things?"

"A few, but a few is too many. Especially when I take into account how I feel about you and how I hope you feel about me. I'm not Grant and I'm not Armando."

"I know that."

"I know you do, baby. Sorry. Keira. But when we met I think you thought in a lot of ways I was just like them. Grant and Armando are proper Dominants and the three of us belong to the same club and we run with the same crowd, but I'm part of what is called a Family. Grant and Armando aren't involved in this."

She seemed to be following so he kept going. "Master Philip and Mistress Evelyn trained me in all things BDSM, but when my training was done they stayed a major part of my life and my sex life. Meegan is also a part of that family. As is Marcos."

"And you've had sex with all of these people?"

"Yes, I have, with the exception of Master Philip. But I have submitted to him. How do you feel about that?"

"I don't—I don't mind. I just wish you'd told me. I basically went into a room with all of these people you're involved with and you never told me. Can you imagine if I'd invited you to a party with all my exes or people I was still with, let them say all this stuff to you, but didn't explain it at all?"

"I'd be pissed. Like you are now. But you see how this makes me different from your boys?"

"Yes, I do. So what does this mean? Philip and Evelyn own you and you were just taking a break with me? Grant and Armando are free to date, but you have to go back to your family?"

"And that was where I started to fuck up."

"What?"

"That's what I thought—that I had to choose between you and the Family. I owe them my life, Master Philip and Mistress Evelyn. After my accident they were there for me in ways I can't even explain to you, Keira. I love them."

"Okay."

"When I met you I had no idea what was going to happen. I didn't even think about what Armando was asking me to do. It was a favor. A simple favor. Meet up with his friend for an afternoon, but..."

"But what?"

"But you. Do you have any idea how amazing you are? How bright and sunny and wonderful and smart? And you're an absolute freak even though you refuse to use swear words, which I think is the cutest shit ever.

"I didn't think I'd fall for you like this, but I did. But you only wanted part of me. You didn't want what Armando and Grant were into. I definitely didn't think you wanted The Club or this community we belong to, so I gave you what I could, on your terms, so I didn't scare you off."

"So it's my fault?"

"No. I could have walked away, but I didn't."

"And you lied to me?"

"I did, and other people I care about. I couldn't keep it up though. Philip and Evelyn want to give The Club to me when they're ready to retire. I would be the head of my own Family and the owner of The Club and I realized then that there was no way I could do that without you, so I went to Philip to ask him how to fix things between us and what I should say when I finally got up the nerve to propose to—"

"What?!" Keira sprang up right on the couch. "You were gonna ask me to marry you?! What the heck? Do it! Do it now!"

Her enthusiasm changed the whole climate of the room. Daniel practically snorted when he tried to hide his smile, but he wasn't finished.

"I can't, because you don't know everything. You only know one part of me. After we started hanging out, I started to feel like —I thought a lot of people were using me at The Club. They love to see me perform, put on a show, and I was okay with that, until I met you. With you I started to see that something was missing. I thought kink and companionship were all I needed, but that's not true. I needed love, someone to be in love with. Someone to be in love with me."

Daniel pulled the flash drive out of his pocket and moved back over to the couch. Keira took the drive from his fingers when he offered it to her.

"That's everything I have. Every video I made. This will give you an idea of what you're really dealing with, with me. If you can watch this and still be with me then..."

"Then we'll get married and run a sex club and be swingers with Marcos and Meegan, and Grant and Armando and Nailah and Violet will come by and watch sometimes."

Daniel shook his head. "It doesn't have to be that. But it has to be something."

Keira chewed the inside of her lip for a moment as she rotated the drive in her hand. "Is there an expiration date on this? You're giving me a lot to think about."

"No expiration date." Daniel meant it. He wanted to be with Keira. He would wait.

"Okay. Well, you should go."

Daniel didn't want to push things, so he headed for the door. Keira followed so she could lock up behind him. He turned to her one last time.

"And the proposal? That's what Meegan was mad about. I've been single for over ten years. She knew if I started seeing someone it would be serious. She thought when I made the move it would be to her, but it wasn't. You're my queen, Keira. My princess. Only you."

"Okay, you have to leave." Keira shoved him out the door and slammed it in his face. But she was almost smiling when she did it.

"I love you," Daniel said through the door.

"Bye," Keira shouted back.

"I love you!"

"Go home!"

Enough was enough. Daniel walked out to his car, thinking maybe the two of them had a chance.

✷

Keira plugged the drive into her computer, but it took her forever to actually slide that little arrow over the first video. She watched the clip through fifteen minutes of a younger Daniel with Mistress Evelyn and another young man. It was interesting. Interesting enough for her to click the next and the next.

A couple hours later, when she finally had to take a break, two things were obvious. One, Keira was really wet and she was definitely going to have to masturbate. And the other surprised her a little. She'd seen Daniel in almost a dozen clips of different lengths, with almost two dozen people, and it didn't bother her. The opposite. It turned her on.

He was right, they'd only scratched the surface of what they could do sexually, what Daniel was capable of doing with his various toys. And what he was capable of having done to him. Instead of making her want to take the drive and flush it down the toilet, or call Daniel and tell him to never contact her again, what Keira had seen had made her want to act.

She had to say something, do something, but she wasn't ready to talk to Daniel yet. Something she couldn't quite name had to be done first. She decided to sleep on it, think on it some more. Maybe she'd even confide in Armando and Nailah. He always looked out for her and Nailah always gave it to her straight. She watched a few more clips, ya know, just to be sure, then headed to bed with her vibrator.

In the morning Keira realized that she needed to figure out exactly what she wanted, and if she wanted all the details on Daniel and his kink crew, the person she really needed to speak with was Mistress Evelyn.

Nine

"Crap. Crapcrapcrapcrapcrap." Keira wasn't even close to being ready, but Daniel was on his way up to her apartment. She'd given herself plenty of time, but a new video of the cast of *Galaxis* went up online right as she got out of the shower. The panel was only an hour, but then Selia did a bunch of interviews with JD. They were so funny together. There was also a little bit in the b-roll where she saw herself in her Princess Orora costume. She had to roll that part of the video back ten or fifteen times.

Then she remembered that she had to be over at the Bakers' for a little New Year's Eve dinner. The festivities at The Club wouldn't kick off until ten. It was so kind of Evelyn to include her at their small dinner party. Keira didn't want to be late.

She'd actually gotten pretty close with Evelyn in the last couple of weeks. She liked Philip too, but she and Evelyn really clicked.

With a little help from Armando, she'd met up with Evelyn for brunch. Evelyn told her all sorts of stories about how she'd met Philip and the way they'd started and grown The Club and their Family. She'd also shared her unique perspective in being a black woman in the BDSM community.

After, they'd had a pretty serious heart-to-heart about Daniel and all his bonehead moves. And then they'd talked at length about what Keira wanted, what she needed and what scared the crap out of her. They continued to talk on the phone and over text and planned to meet up again soon. No matter what happened with Daniel, Keira definitely felt like she'd made a great friend. Evelyn was awesome.

So yeah, Keira did not want to be late.

With her hair only a quarter straightened, Keira flung the door open just as Daniel rang the bell. She tried to ignore how good he looked in his tailored slacks and suit jacket. He had a simple white t-shirt on underneath, but he still looked delicious. Keira put her eyes back into her head.

"Thanks for agreeing to see me again," he said.

"I'm late as crap. Come into the bathroom and we'll talk while I finish getting ready."

"Okay."

She talked as they walked. "Have you talked to Evelyn lately?"

"Yeah we talked this morning," he said hesitantly. "Why?"

"No reason. We've just been talking a lot lately."

"I see."

"Sit on the toilet. Tub's still wet."

Keira bit the inside of her lip when he did as she suggested. This gorgeous six-foot Korean man sitting on her closed toilet seat. In a suit. She grabbed her flat iron and went back to work.

"We talked about you a little."

"Oh?"

"Yup, and The Club and stuff. She's a great lady."

"She is. What else did you two talk about?"

"Well, I told her about some of my misconceptions about BDSM and she cleared a lot of stuff up. Which was good. She also got Meegan to apologize to me. Meegan and I had a good talk too." Even if Keira could tell that the girl was still kind of bitter.

"You've done a lot of talking lately. Talking's good."

"Yup and she explained to me that you can be a part of their kink family and still be collared by someone outside of the family or someone who's planning to join."

Keira glanced at Daniel. He was squinting at her, confused as all get out. He also looked like he was turning a little red.

"She told me I could be any kind of Mistress that I want to be. That I don't ever have to wear leather. And she said I don't have to be mean or cruel. I can just be me. But she did say that I should go through some training so I understand how to treat all submissives the right way. I have to learn more about limits and negotiations and also what I need for the dominant part of myself and the submissive side. I thought that sounded pretty cool. Right?"

"All very cool. What else did you talk about?"

"Hold on. Crap. I hate doing the back." Keira sucked her nearly singed fingertip before she went on. "We talked about you some more. I told her how I went out of my way to be myself with you. That so many guys didn't want the real me and after all that it was *you* who was holding back."

"Yeah? I fucked that up."

"But we figured that out, talked about why and what—"

"And what I need to do to get you back?"

"More like what you need to do to keep me."

Daniel swallowed, running his fingers through his hair. "Can I have the details?"

"Well, for one, you have to understand that I'm not Evelyn or Philip. I'm me and I like that. So I can't change to emulate what they are to you."

"I wouldn't want you to do that."

"I didn't think so, but I had to say it."

"Okay. What else?"

"Say you're sorry one more time."

"I'm sorry, love." Keira didn't move when he reached over and rubbed the bit of bare skin on her back. "I'll never lie to you again."

"You promise?"

"I promise." When he stood up Keira let him kiss her, but he wasn't completely off the hook yet.

"Good. Sit."

He obeyed immediately, dropping back down onto the toilet seat. "So what's the occasion tonight? Are you coming to The Club later?"

"After dinner at the Bakers'."

"Oh yeah?"

"Yup. You're my plus one."

"Am I?"

"Yup."

"Does this mean we're dating again?"

"Possibly."

"Then I have to do something first."

Keira froze when Daniel took the flat iron out of her hand and placed it on the counter. She stayed frozen in that same spot as he pulled a little ring box out of his pocket and showed her the sparkling ring inside. She let him slip it onto her finger. What other choice did she have?

Keira glanced up into Daniel's deep brown eyes before she looked back down at the aquamarine stone surrounded by diamonds. An embarrassing snort came out of her mouth.

"What, you don't like it?"

"No, no. I love it. I just—I'm just thinking about this AU fic I wrote and Orora totally gets an engagement ring like this."

"I asked Selia what ring would suit Orora best and she suggested this."

"Oh my god. That is so cool. Selia picked out my freaking ring. Lori is going to die."

"I thought a super fan like you would enjoy that." Daniel leaned down and kissed her again. "Should I still ask? I will if you want me to."

Keira shook her head. "No. We should probably meet each

other's parents at some point, though, that kind of stuff, but you don't need to ask. And you already know my answer. Evelyn told me she and Philip got engaged after two weeks of knowing each other."

"We've known each other for over six weeks. We're practically ready for grandkids."

"True."

"When you know, you know."

"I agree."

"Do you need help getting ready?"

"Nope, but you can keep me company while I finish my hair."

"Done."

Keira watched Daniel out of the corner of her eye as he sat back on the toilet and made himself comfortable. This was her man alright, she thought, as she held in another snort. And it was somewhat of a relief. She'd never have to go on another bad first date again.

Ten

Keira slipped off her shoes and flopped onto her couch. Daniel didn't waste any time removing his prosthesis and getting undressed. It was her night to Top, but she needed a few minutes to get the stars out of her eyes. Daniel had taken her to an honest to goodness Golden Globes party. *Galaxis* wasn't up for anything, but JD was invited to a bunch of parties and asked Keira and Daniel if they wanted to tag along.

They'd made it till one a.m. when JD subtly hinted that he was trying to take off with his own date. Keira didn't blame him. She was perfectly tipsy on champagne and she couldn't wait to get Daniel home and naked. Booze and fangirling made her extra horny.

"Would it be weird if I hung pictures of me and Selia around the apartment?" They'd taken about twenty of Keira showing her favorite actress the perfect ring she'd helped Daniel pick out.

"I don't think it would be weird at all, but they'll only be hanging up for another few months."

He had a point. In few months her lease would be up and she'd be moving to his house in Atwater Village. They weren't getting married for another year, but the planning had begun. His mother's schedule at the casino was wonky so Keira, her mother, and Ms. Song had started discussing details over the phone. Daniel's mother was amazing. Loud and funny, but so sweet. It was like JD and Daniel had each taken the best parts of her. Keira would be proud to call her mom-in-law. Next month they were all flying up to meet her in person. Keira's parents had already met Daniel and they loved him, just like she knew they would.

A year from now they'd be joining their families at a small ceremony in Malibu And until then...

Daniel sank to the floor between her feet and rested his hand and his healed arm on his thighs.

Keira leaned forward and stroked his hair. "You want to record this?"

"Yes, my Princess."

Keira smiled. Princess was what she asked him to call her. She liked it better than Mistress.

"Go get my laptop then. And grab the lube and one of the dildos from my closet."

"Yes, Princess."

"Good boy."

When he came back they'd do the best to make a mess out of the little black dress she still wore and then off to bed. She made him lean down before she ordered him across her lap. She gripped his chin and kissed him.

"You're gonna come all over my lap and then you're going to lick it up. You'll enjoy that won't you?"

"Yes, Princess. You know I will."

"Good." Keira gave his ass a good slap before she sat back and guided him into position. When he was settled, she reached for the laptop and hit record. Keira couldn't wait for them to watch the playback, together.

The End

BLESSED

"Luuuuucy! I'm home!"

Violet looked up from her tablet as her boyfriend/Dominant bounded through the door, his arms loaded with bags. She didn't exactly look at him, she glared. She was not in the mood for Grant's cheery bullshit. Christmas was two days away, but the Christmas spirit had been sucked right out of her.

She'd broken her ankle in the stupidest way, dancing on the stairs at her latest wrap party. Producing *Chef Masters* had been an absolute nightmare. So many divas, so many problems, little and huge, but it was the holidays. They'd wrapped under budget and her boss had suggested they throw a huge party for all the crew and production staff that had worked for them throughout the year. It was Violet's time to cut loose.

In line with her plan to drop some weight, she'd cut back significantly on her junk food and alcohol intake. She'd lost a few pounds and turned herself into a lightweight who could barely handle more than two drinks. Another thing she hadn't planned on? Landing herself a new man in the form of her personal trainer.

Things had changed a lot between them in the last eight months, professionally and personally. Grant still trained her, free of charge of course, but their relationship had grown intense. He introduced her to his kinks and the world of BDSM, shown her a true submissive side of herself that had been laying dormant, waiting for the right man to tap into her needs and wants. She loved Grant with all her heart as her boyfriend and Dominant and that's why she was so bummed when he couldn't make it to her wrap party.

He had to fly home to help his parents with something that turned out to be minor. But Violet still sulked and drank herself stupid. So stupid she danced herself right off a flight of stairs and broke her ankle. A girl her size had no business walking in heels that high and definitely no business dancing in them like a drunken burlesque girl.

She'd planned to spend Christmas in Los Angeles with Grant instead of back home in Connecticut with her family. What she didn't plan for was spending her whole hiatus in Grant's condo with her leg in cast.

Poor Grant was trying his best though. He went out and bought a huge tree. Decorated seventy percent of it by himself when Violet got tired of standing with her crutches. Every morning when she woke up she found a couple more presents under said tree, meaning he'd wrapped them while she'd been asleep and just the idea of that made her want to cry, it was so cute.

He'd even gotten festive collars for his dog, Max and his cat, Bill. Whenever the TV wasn't on, Christmas music was playing through his surround system. He actually had pretty thorough and varied collection, but Violet couldn't find herself in the Christmas mood. She had something to tell Grant. Something she'd discovered while she was being tended to in the ER. Only her best friend Faye knew, but she had to tell him soon.

Grant dumped the bags on the counter and the floor then stood in all his Scandinavian god glory and smiled at her. "Don't you all get up at once."

Violet ignored the way that smile made her pussy clench and

glanced at Max on the couch beside her. The massive Rottweiler gave Grant a cursory look then went back to sleep. Bill was probably asleep on the bed.

"I think everyone's in chill mode."

"I'm seeing that, Miss Ryan."

She watched as he crossed the room. He was too gorgeous. Tall and blond with a thick gold and red beard, and muscles and muscles for days. Oh and the tattoos. Violet ignored the skip her heart beat tried to pull and set down her tablet. She wasn't too cranky to tilt up her head when he leaned down to kiss her.

"How are you feeling?" he asked when their lips parted. Another shiver to ignore as he stroked her hair.

"Okay. Just a little achy. I feel like my ass is spreading out mostly."

"You're not gonna get any complaints from me in that department." Violet had lost around thirty pounds since they met. She had a lot more to go, but Grant always made it clear that her loved her body in whatever state it was in. Even if she had a bum leg.

He kissed her again before going back to the kitchen. "I got my mom's Christmas cookie recipe so I'm baking today, girlfriend. And I got few other surprises for you too."

"Oh yeah? You fix that time machine so I can go back and unbreak this ankle?"

"Not even close, but I think you'll like it. You want your one of your surprises now?"

Violet shrugged. "Sure."

"Okay. I'll be right back." He grabbed one of the bigger bags off the floor and walked toward the bedroom, singing along with the Stevie Wonder song that was playing through speakers. That made Violet smile. He had a voice like an angel.

She tried to get back into her e-book, but now that Grant was home she was too restless to focus. She stood and hobbled to the kitchen and started putting away the groceries. She was almost finished when the sound of Grant stomping back into the room forced her to look up.

"HO HO HO! How do I look?"

Her boyfriend was standing there in a full Santa costume complete with a fake beard and a huge bulk of padding around his middle. Violet almost choked.

"Um, you look festive. And oddly sexy. Am I supposed to be attracted to Santa?"

"I don't see why not. He's a big, strapping man. Cares about kids, knows how to direct an army of elves. A lot of women find that type of power attractive."

Violet held on to the counter as she looked him up and down. He'd included Santa's signature white gloves. "So is this for me or...?"

"It's for you. You said you missed your window to get your picture taken at the mall with Santa."

"Yeah, I'm not battling a sea of kids and stressed out parents in this cast."

"So take pictures with your own private Santa." Grant came toward her, slipping a large hand under the hem of her shirt. It was a challenge to keep her eyes open. "And I thought we could do a little roleplaying. You can tell Santa how nice and how naughty you've been, and Santa can dole out presents or punishments accordingly."

Violet was definitely wet now. They hadn't had sex since he'd gotten back from Florida. She was still shaken up from her tumble and he was just worried about her getting better. Sex hadn't come up, until now.

"What do you say?" Grant asked.

"Yes."

"Tell me your safe words."

Violet *did* close her eyes then as a shiver rippled over her body. She had no clue how Grant did it, slipped so easily from being this sweet, silly doof of a guy to being one of the sexiest, commanding men she'd ever met. But every time all it took was a simple change in his voice, a look, a touch or a few simple words, and she was right there with him, ready to go and more than willing to submit.

She looked back up into his deep blue eyes. "Yellow if I need you to pull back and Red if I need you to stop."

"Good girl. Now, why don't you step into Santa's workshop."

Violet shrieked as Grant scooped her up and carried her over to his oversized rocking chair beside the couch. At first Violet thought it was a weird thing for a single man to have in his living room, but the piece of furniture had worked its way into a lot of their games. It might get a lot of use in other ways, down the road.

When they were situated Grant pulled out his phone and started snapping pictures of the two of them. Some were intentionally sweet. He pulled down the beard for a few so you could actually see his face and then they took a couple silly shots. Violet stuck her finger up his nose in one and her tongue in his mouth for another. Her favorites ended up being of the one of them sharing a simple kiss and the one where Grant was licking her face.

"So tell me, Violet. What do you want for Christmas?"

Violet let out a light sigh even though her mind was racing. *I want to stop being a scared ass and just tell you. I want you to be happy. I want you to tell me you want this because I think I do. I want you to tell me it's going to be okay, that I'm not ruining my career. That this will work.*

"I think I just want you, Santa."

"You think?"

"I know."

"You should show me."

"Switch seats with me, please."

"Not a problem." Grant stood and gently deposited Violet into the rocking chair. She went right for the large belt. Grant caught on and tossed the pillow he had against his stomach then started unbuttoning the jacket, revealing his tight abs under his tank top.

Violet pulled his huge cock out of his boxers and went right to sucking it. She loved the taste of him, the feel of him in her mouth and between her fingers. He rocked his hips in time with the bobbing of her head, stroking her hair and murmuring nasty, sweet nothings until his came down her throat.

"Was that good enough for Santa?" she asked between final licks over the head of his cock.

"Oh yeah." Grant squeezed his eyes shut, something he always did after he came, but wasn't done playing with her yet. Proof was the intense look on his face when he started pulling off the white gloves. He dropped to his knees and slowly started working Violet's pajama pants and underwear down her thighs. He was careful pulling both over her cast and more careful as he spread her legs apart. He slid his fingers into her waiting cunt, making Violet whimper. He used his other hand to grip the back of her head.

"I want you to come for me."

"Yes. Oh god, I will."

Grant did that thing he did, read her perfectly, did exactly the right thing. Sometimes she needed it soft and sweet and a little slow, but not today. She wanted it rough. He stood up straighter, pressing their foreheads together as he delivered the finger fucking of a lifetime. Violet couldn't stop thinking about how good it felt, how badly she was wanted to come. How much she loved him. She just blurted it out.

"Oh god! Fuck. Grant, I'm pregnant!" Grant froze, then yanked his fingers back. Violet let out a laugh that sounded a little manic. "You weren't hurting me."

"Are–are you sure? I–I" He smoothed his hands over her thighs, checking to make sure he hadn't broken anything on her suddenly delicate body.

"Yes, I'm sure and yes, I am pregnant."

"How? I mean–" Grant sat back on his knees and shook his head. "When?"

"I'm about seven weeks."

"That night of the Halloween party."

Violet smiled, nodding. "Yeah." She'd been on the pill and they used condoms frequently, but not always. And it only took one time, that one percent of ineffectiveness. They'd gone to a costume party at the bondage club Grant belonged to and fucked until sun up in one of the private rooms. Condom free.

"Is this okay?" Violet had already made up her mind. They had passing conversations about kids and family, but they hadn't discussed marriage or kids of their own. Still, Grant looked surprised at her question.

"Yes! Of course it's okay," he blurted back. And now Violet was crying, happy tears though. Grant kissed her, wiping her face. "I would have asked you to marry me months ago if I thought you would say yes."

He had a point. Violet had a feeling that Grant had made up his mind about her, that he wanted to be with her forever. She wanted that too, but she wanted to spend more time just being with him. They could take things slowly, move in together first. After a year or two, talk about getting engaged and she wanted to give her career more time before she thought about kids, but none of that had happened and now there was another human being on the way.

"How do you feel about it?" he asked.

Her hand went to her stomach. She'd been doing that a lot lately. "Good. Scared shitless, but good. There's a lot I'm unpacking about being adopted and having my own kid, but I want her or him. And you."

"Can I be a little selfish and say this is the best Christmas present you could have ever given me?"

"You're never selfish." And that was the truth.

"Or maybe all my selfishness just involves loving you." Grant kissed her one more time, a kissed that morphed into more, a declaration or a pact and then proof that Violet desperately still wanted to come. She took his hand and guided back it between her legs.

"I'll be gentle," he whispered against her lips.

"You don't have to." Violet gripped his wrist and rocked a little closer. "I need you."

Grant looked her in the eye and she knew he meant it when he said "I need you too."

WRAPPED

A FIT Adjacent Christmas Novella

About This Book

WRAPPED
A FIT Adjacent Christmas Novella

Following a painful divorce, all pastry chef Shae Kenney wants for Christmas is one good date that doesn't end in disaster. When Aidan Meyer, a smoking hot hunk from her past, matches with her on a dating app, Shae asks Santa for the strength not to screw it up. But when one perfect date with Aidan rolls into a second date, then a third and a fourth, Shae's fear of heartbreak might just sabotage one of the best gifts she's ever received—real love.

This sweet Christmas novella features a slightly anxious plus-size beauty who is a master of all things cupcakes and tarts, and a bespectacled tech guy who just wants to sweep her off her feet.

DEDICATION

For everyone with anxiety, out there trying to make their way through the dating scene.
I believe in you. And so do Santa and Mrs. Claus.

ONE

ear Santa, Save me from another awful man...

Shae Kenney on the porch of her cousin's place in Atwater Village, freezing her ass off. Thanks to good old climate change it had been between eighty and one hundred degrees in Los Angeles clear through the end of November. A few days ago, though, the temperature had dropped and they were back to the cool winter nights a Mediterranean climate called for. She thought her trench coat would be enough. But the drive over to Keira's house was so short it took the whole ride for the heat to really kick in and then it was time for her to head right back out into the cold.

"Fuck." She shivered and hit the doorbell again.

"Coming!" she heard her cousin yell inside. The door flew open and Shae was bathed in the smell of Italian food and the sound of Christmas music.

"Hi!" Keira beamed in her usual chipper way, a common trait amongst most Kenney women.

"Hey!" Shae met her smile and stepped inside. She couldn't help eyeing the Christmas decorations that hung from nearly every square inch of available space. "It's so Christmasy in here! You two weren't playing when you said you were going to do it up this year."

"Thanks. There's mistletoe in every room." Keira shrugged, sticking out her tongue. "All the spontaneous smooching helps keep my mind off the wedding."

"Aren't you excited?"

"I am, but I think Mom and Mrs. Song are a little more excited than Daniel and I combined. They just asked if they could sing a duet at the reception." Her cousin's wedding was just a few weeks away. It would definitely make for a memorable New Year's Eve, but what had started out as a small, intimate ceremony had ballooned into a full blown *thing*.

"A duet of what?!"

"They haven't decided yet, but they've been bonding over karaoke and realized they missed their calling as the next hot thing in girl groups. I just want my man to whisk me away from all this," Keira whined.

"You two are so cute. It's ridiculous. Everything will be fine. Just tell them no to the singing and let them do an extra toast."

"Oh, good call. I saw your text about the shoes. I'm glad they came."

"Oh I'm all ready, baby. Ugh, you guys are really making me feel like I need to decorate. I might just get a fake tree this year. I should do something." This was the first year in a long time where Shae actually felt like celebrating the holidays. Hopefully she could rise to the occasion and inject some Christmas cheer back into her own life. Being inside Santa's Village, otherwise known as her cousin's house, might help.

"I brought your favorite, the vanilla mousse filled, and I slipped two of the salted caramel in there for Daniel when he gets back." She handed over the plastic container filled with her gourmet cupcakes. The plan was to rotate who was responsible for which parts of the menu for their weekly *PRINCE CHARMING: New Zealand* viewing parties.

Shae always handled dessert. It had taken a few years, but her bakery Sweet Creams was finally making a nice little profit. Never understatement the power of refined recipes and social media.

"Oh, thanks. I'll put these on the table."

"Don't worry. I made extra for Meegan," Shae said as she followed Keira to their open concept living and dining room. It looked like Mrs. Claus had gone on a decorating bender. Shae loved it. The doorbell rang again before she could shed her jacket.

"It's me!" their friend Meegan called through the door.

"I'll grab that." Keira slipped around her and headed back to the front of the house.

Shae dropped her jacket on the back of a chair and made herself comfortable on their sectional. She could hear Meegan and Keira talking down the hallway, but she was too lazy to get up. She was pooped. She'd been working her ass off all weekend and this upcoming week was looking pretty packed as well.

She had to do all the regular baking for her storefront and she had orders for office parties, two birthdays and a regular customer that liked to have her own personal stash on hand when she wanted to hide from her kids. Shae caught her brain running through the rest of her schedule and had to force herself to stop. This was her night off. Instead of thinking about cupcakes and tarts, she pulled out her phone and opened MATCHED, the dating app her friends had convinced her to join.

After her divorce from Harvin, Shae knew it wouldn't be easy to get back into the dating scene. Extra hard considering she and Harvin had gotten married almost right out of high school and she'd never actually been in the real dating scene before that. She just didn't think it would be this difficult to find a halfway decent guy to enjoy her free time with. So far she'd been on two okay dates, five miserable dates, and one date with a guy she was convinced should be serving a lengthy prison sentence. She'd also been stood up twice. Needless to say she was still on the hunt.

"I brought salad!" Meegan announced as she came into the room. Shae looked over her shoulder. Keira was carrying the salad in question while Meegan pumped her fists in the air above her head. She collapsed on the couch next to Shae and lightly swatted her thigh. "What's up? We didn't see you last week."

"I know. I had to bake a bajillion cupcakes for a wedding, but I got paaaaid."

"Oh good. Did you bring more cupcakes tonight?" Meegan asked as she cupped her hands under her chin and batted her eyelashes.

"Yes, she did," Keira laughed. "You can relax."

"Oh! Where are they?"

Keira came over and sunk down on Shae's other side. "On the table. Patience."

"I'm going to grab one right now. Excuse me." Shae laughed as Meegan jumped up and rushed over to the dining room table. She tore open the plasticware and went right for the goods.

"Save two for my man!" Keira yelled.

"I will!" Meegan said as she came back to the couch, double fisting salted caramel cupcakes. "Okay. Go on. What else is new? Besides all the baking in the world."

"Nothing much. Had a date last week that tanked in the first five minutes. I may have said I was going to the bathroom then bolted out the front door," Shae admitted with a wince.

"What happened?"

"He spent the first five minutes talking about how much he loved big girls, but vehemently denying that he was a chubby chaser. I still don't know what was more off-putting—that dudes are still using the phrase 'chubby chaser' or if he thought I should find any of what he was saying to be flattering."

Keira made a face. "Ew."

"Okay. Give me your phone." Meegan held out her hand.

"Why?"

"I'm gonna swipe for you."

Shae glanced at Keira, who just shrugged. Right. She met her fiance the old fashioned way. Through friends. The doorbell rang and Keira jumped up to answer it, leaving Shae alone with Meegan and her itchy swiping finger. Shae gave in and handed over her phone. A few moments later, Erica, Sarah and Joanna came walking into the room, their arms loaded down with more sides and lots and lots of booze.

"Holy Christmas!" Erica said. "It looks amazing in here. How are you girlie?" Erica leaned over the couch and kissed Meegan on the forehead.

"Finding Shae a new lubber."

"Oh, let me! Let me! I'm a master swiper," Erica said.

"She's right," Sarah said. "She swiped on Angelo for me." Shae had to admit that was a pretty good vote of confidence. Sarah and Angelo had been together for about six months and things seemed to be going pretty well. Angelo was a total sweetheart. Shae could handle starting over with a guy that nice and cute.

"Meegan. Give her the phone."

"Whatever. I could have found you someone good. Take it." She moved over so Erica could sit between them, then handed her the phone.

"You ladies swipe while we eat. Dinner's ready." That's all Keira had to say to get them all to swarm the table, piling their plates high with food and emptying not one, but two, bottles of wine in the first go.

Once they were all settled back on the couch, ready to stuff their faces, Keira asked as she grabbed the Apple TV remote, "Okay. It's time. Are you ready for Prince Charming?"

There were YEAH's all around. Keira turned off the rendition of "Santa Baby" coming through the speakers, then pressed play on episode four. They all had their money on Jenna getting eliminated this week, if her shenanigans from the week before were an indicator. Erica started swiping. Shae wanted to know who Jenna was going to start shit on in this week's episode, but she was more interested in Erica's plan of attack. She watched her closely as she swiped right and left on several guys. Erica was onto something. Every guy she swiped right on seemed to be right up Shae's alley.

"Do you have a method you use or…?" she whispered. On the flat screen, Chad was talking about his upcoming one-on-one date with April-Jane.

"Oh, I have a method, but I can't tell you," Erica replied. "It'll ruin the magic. Don't worry, we'll Hallmark movie you right into a honey for the holidays."

"Ha! That would make a good movie," Keira giggled.

Shae smiled and turned her attention to the TV for a moment before she looked back at her phone.

"Oh, this guy's hot," Erica said.

"Oh my god, I know him." On her phone was the picture of Aidan Meyer, one of the hottest guys she'd ever had the pleasure of knowing in real life.

"Yeah, see those little dots? You guys have mutual friends. How do you know him?"

"Work. We used to work together at Allight. He was our head IT guy."

"Well he is hot and his bio isn't awful."

Shae took her phone back and actually read the words below what looked like a recent company headshot. He looked even better than she remembered. Cute white guy with dark red hair and a red-brown beard. He'd changed his hair a little. The cut was a bit sharper than the way he used to wear it and she could have sworn he had different glasses, but it was definitely Aidan. And his bio wasn't too terrible.

Just your average IT guy with a start up. Ladies have to do most of the work on this app.
If we match, I'll do my best to shoulder the rest.

Didn't mean to rhyme, but it's too late to change it.

Short, sweet, nothing offensive or misogynistic. She flipped through all of his pictures. Everything seemed in order there too. No pictures of him holding an assault rifle or posing with young girls in foreign countries, and yes, that was definitely a pattern she'd seen on dating apps and it creeped her the fuck out.

"Okay, you've been looking at his profile for like five minutes?

"Lemme see," Meegan asked.

"No!" Erica reached over and gently peeled the phone out of Shae's hand. "Let's make a decision first. Then we swipe. Then we hand off the phone. When the swipe is up for consideration like this, you can't make any sudden movements or you might miss the swipe."

"I'm friends with him on Facebook," Shae said. "I can always message him if we lose the swipe."

"Just let me handle this. Okay?"

"You're the master," Shae said, putting her hands up in surrender. "Please proceed."

"Okay. So you know him. You've been around him a little. You've talked a time or two."

"Yeah, we worked together for a while. He was kinda quiet, really nice though. Super polite. He always made sure to thank me personally whenever I brought in dessert. I think he was dessert deprived though, so it might have just been the sugar going to his head. He was very professional, which couldn't be said about a lot of the guys there."

"Okay, so he passes that not-shitty test."

"Yes."

"Would you go out with him?"

"Truthfully, yes. Look how hot he is!"

"Hey, you're no slouch," Sarah said.

"Yeah, Shae. You're sexy," Meegan said with a wink and she knew Meegan meant it. She often commented on Shae's sexiness.

"I say swipe. At the very least, sleep with him. If he turns out to be a social dud, you can politely step aside and wish him the best," Erica said.

"Or ghost on him," Meegan said with a grunt and a thrust of her hips.

"Uh, ghosting doesn't involve any motions of the pelvis," Shae replied.

"Make this your Christmas wish." Joanna held her hands up and started praying out loud in her low monotone voice. "Dear Santa and his badass wife, Mrs. Claus. Please let the super hot guy from Shae's old job sweep her off her feet and give her the dicking of a lifetime, just in time for Christmas. In Frosty's name, amen." She dropped her hands and looked back over at Shae. "That should do the trick.'"

"Well, I guess you have to swipe on him now. Joanna blessed our union, just in time for Christmas."

"Okay. I'm swiping."

Shae glanced at the TV as April-Jane tripped and fell as she was walking with Chad toward their helicopter date. There was some giggling and talk of how she was afraid of heights, even from five feet off the ground.

"Uuuuummmmm..." Erica nudged her arm.

"What?" Shae looked back down at her phone. At first she didn't believe what she was seeing. Her face in a heart. Aidan's face in a heart and little sparking flames bouncing around them.

Shae grabbed the phone from Erica's hand. "Oh shit. What do I do?"

"What? What happened?" Keira asked.

"We matched." Shae held up the phone so her cousin could see. Her heart was thumping. It was all so stupid. She was actually excited over something that would most certainly turn out to be nothing in the next thirty seconds.

"What do I do?"

"You wait," Erica said. "You gotta wait. Some guys swipe on

everyone. Wait until the show is over and then message him if he hasn't unmatched yet."

"Okay, I can do that."

"Actually, give me your phone so you won't be tempted," Erica said, holding out her hand. "Watch Jeanna try and sabotage Lauren B. on this group date coming up after the commercial break."

"Okay. That's a good idea." Shae let out a deep breath, then handed her phone back to Erica. She picked up her fork and decided to focus on the bizarre mating ritual unfolding on the TV screen in front of her instead of her own pathetic love life.

Thank to the shit show that was *Prince Charming: New Zealand*, Shae managed to pretend that she wasn't thinking about what was happening inside her phone for the rest of the night. Or at least until she got in bed a few hours later. She turned off her bedside lamp and lay under her covers, staring at her phone. It had been two hours, and she and Aidan were still matched.

The words MESSAGE AIDAN taunted her. She looked at his pictures again instead. He was really cute. The worst that could happen was him ignoring her and her feeling a little embarrassed for a few hours. The truth was, she had nothing to lose. And Joanna did pray to Santa and Mrs. Claus.

Just message him, she told herself. Shae clicked the little menu on the side of his profile and brought up the empty chat box between them.

> Hey! Looks like we have a match.

She typed quickly, adding the smiling emoji with its tongue sticking out, then hit send before she could stop herself. Then she set her phone back on her bedside table. She knew what would happen next. He'd either see her message and immediately unmatch with her, realizing he'd swiped right on someone he had a first hand non-attraction to, or he'd message her back something crazy like his lax opinions on gun control or our need for border walls. Then she'd have to block him and delete the app for at least a week to recover from the knowledge that yet another man had turned out to be a disappointment.

And honestly, that's where she went wrong—getting prematurely invested in anything that could leave her feeling disappointed.

"Turn the hopes down a little there, boo," she said to herself as she rolled over to face the wall.

Five minutes later, her phone vibrated. Shae's eyes popped open. She was mimicking sleep to encourage her body to relax, but the buzz of the notification had her alert as ever. She grabbed her phone and looked at the screen.

"Okay. Chill out. Just chill out. He's probably just saying hello." Shae sat up and unlocked her phone, opening the MATCHED app. There was definitely a response from Aidan.

> Hey! I thought you were married.

Shae's eye twitched as she started typing her response. She wished people just knew she'd gotten a divorce so she didn't have to talk about it anymore. Hopefully Aidan wouldn't have any follow up questions once she clarified.

> Was. Married no more.

Shae stared at her phone for a minute and just when she realized he might not be sitting in bed hanging on her every word, those three little bubbles popped up.

> I'm really sorry to hear that.

Unless it's a good thing.

Definitely a good thing.

Glad to be back out there.

Kinda.

This app is terrible.

Have to agree.

Present company excluded.

Of course.

Of course.

Shae typed back. And then her mind froze. This was the point where things usually got weird for her. She could go the small talk route. Something felt off about that though. Should she just straight up ask him out? Then they could do the awkward face to face. Did she even want to go out with Aidan?

Um, dude? her brain chimed in. *How many times did you and the other women in your office talk about how sexy and sweet Aidan was?* The answer was literally every time they saw him. Should I ask the dumb question? Of course she should. She wanted to know the answer.

What brings you to Matched?

Looking for love?

The sex?

Hiking partner?

Cosplay partner?

Aidan answered right away this time.

The classic fear of dying alone.

Ah, that old chestnut.

I guess I shouldn't feel so special about your swipe than.

Since you're desperate and all. 

I wanted to see if you were still baking.

I still dream about that chocolate caramel crunch thing you made for the office.

You wanna come over and taste my sweets? She started to type, but she couldn't hit send. Aidan knew her. Not really well, but enough for that kind of cheap come on to come off as weird. She knew exactly how he'd respond. He'd say "as a matter of fact, yes" and then they'd sext until things got weird or they'd actually set up a booty call and then things would get weird. She was tired of things getting weird, but she knew it was already too late for things not to get weird.

Things got weird with every guy she'd talked to on the app. Also, as hot as Aidan was and no matter how much she'd seriously considered sleeping with him in the last few hours, she wasn't sure if she was ready to go through with it in real life. She needed to be sure. Shae deleted her cheesy come on and started to type something more sensible, like *Well it was nice talking to you again...* Before she could hit send another message from Aidan popped up.

Let's get off this app for one night.

Shae instantly felt hot all over. Was he asking her out?

What do you have in mind?

Lady's choice, my treat.

Bowling. Dinner and movie out.

Dinner and a movie in.

People watching at the Grove.

We could be real creepy and go people watch from some shrubs at Griffith Park.

How about this?

Why don't you plan a date that doesn't involve hiking or any other outdoor activity that makes me sweat and I'm game.

I think I can handle that.

Not a big fan of hiking myself.

What's your schedule like?

I'm free most nights, but I go into work early so I turn into a pumpkin by 10 pm.

You're up late tonight.

The eleven-fifteen at the top of Shae's phone was taunting her. It didn't stop her from smiling as she responded though.

I got a match.

Who can sleep through that?

Ha. True. You sleep.

We'll reconvene tomorrow.

You might laugh, but I have to ask.

> Does this mean we're going on a date?

> Or is this like a friend hang?

I'd love for it to be a date, but if you'd rather meet up as friends, I'm cool with that.

We haven't seen each other in a while.

We can catch up.

Shae had plenty of friends. She didn't need more, not like this.

> Let's call it a date.

Okay. It's a date.

> Well since we have that settled I should head to bed.

> See you soon?

"Yes, definitely time for bed. Don't want to fuck this up by saying anything else," she said out loud.

Absolutely.

Goodnight, Shae.

> Goodnight Aidan.

Shae locked her phone and put it back on its charger. Then she flopped on her stomach and took a deep breath before screaming into her pillow.

"Dear God," she said out loud. "No, scratch that. You're actually busy with illness and genocide and things. I hope. Dear Santa. Please let this go reasonably well. Please don't let him be low key dickhead. Or a knife-wielding collector of women's ears. I just want one good date. Or many good dates. Yeah, many good dates with this super hot guy that I know you sent my way because I have been such a good girl this year. Okay, that sounded really gross. To the republic for which it stands, in Mrs. Claus's name. I really appreciate it."

Shae rolled on to her back and stared at her ceiling. This was really happening. She really had a date with Aidan Meyer. She picked up her phone again and jumped on the group text she had with the girls.

Holy shit.

I'm going on a date with Aidan.

Joanna responded first.

Praise Frosty!

Two

"What are you looking at?"

Aidan glanced over his shoulder as his business partner, Matt, passed behind his desk. Then he looked back at his screen. He'd been researching events around Los Angeles all morning.

"Gotta date coming up. I volunteered to plan it."

"What kind of date? A bang 'em and bounce date, or a real date?" Matt flopped down in his chair and let it skid backwards a few feet across the hardwood floor. They were alone in their office. As usual. They were the only full-time employees. Aidan watched as Matt stopped his backward progression with the heels of his sneakers, then started spinning himself slowly around in the chair. One day their company, PrimedRealty.com, would expand and they'd have to act like mature adults in front of what Aidan hoped turned out to be many future employees. For now, he turned down the music they were blasting so he could hear Matt a little better.

"Real date. Met her on MATCHED. Actually, that's not true. We used to work together and I ran into her again on MATCHED. I'm gotta find someplace nice to take her."

"Got a picture?"

"Yeah." As Matt scooted his chair back to their desks, Aidan picked up his phone and brought up his Facebook account. He wouldn't admit it, but he'd spent most of his night and part of his morning looking at Shae's pictures on her Facebook profile. When she popped up in his MATCHED feed, he admittedly swiped on her out of curiosity. He'd always had a bit of a crush on her. At first for juvenile reasons.

Shae had the body of an old school pin up—large breasts, large hips and an ass to match. She wore a dress to work every day and no matter how she switched up her look, she always managed to pull off this vibe that was a mix between comfortable, classy and sexy as fuck, while still professional. And then there was the baking. Shae could bake her ass off and she baked all the time. Their CEO had approved a small budget that allowed Shae to bake for employee birthdays and most holidays. That's how good she was in the kitchen.

As Aidan got to know her, he got to see that she was more than a body and baked goods. She was pretty damn thoughtful and considerate, and she had this great, upbeat personality. Once he found her crying in one of the back stairwells and when he asked if she was okay, she managed to make them both laugh. All that had turned his crush into legitimate attraction, but there was the small issue of her husband. Aidan had seen the guy once in the parking lot of their office building and now he was out of the picture. Pictures he'd been looking at all day.

Aidan remembered what had really sent him over to full crush territory—her smile. Every time he walked down to the payroll department to ask them a question or request paperwork for someone on his team, she'd always greeted him with a warm smile. He wasn't sure if she was just a master of customer service or what, but after a few months and various company functions, he knew that upbeat demeanor was just Shae. A few times he may have told himself she only smiled like that for him. That was a lie. He wasn't anyone special in her bright sunny, world. Now that they'd matched, though, maybe that would change.

"Oh." Matt tilted his head to the side. "She's hot. You ever date a black girl before? Not that you shouldn't. I just—"

"Once in high school for ten minutes, the whole football player/cheerleader thing, but her dad made us break up so she could make honor roll."

"Where's that girl now?"

"Crystal? Pretty sure she's a research scientist."

"Good call on the dad's part. Good luck with this one." Matt laughed as he handed back the phone.

"What?"

"Nothing. From the looks of her profile, she has her shit together and she's good looking. I know nothing about her, but I'm pretty sure she's too good for you."

"You are probably right." Aidan felt himself swallow as he looked at his phone as Matt rolled back to his desk. He knew he had some pretty good qualities to bring to the table. Still, this was kind of the girl of his dreams.

"What does this one do? What's her name?"

"Her name's Shae. And she's a baker now. She owns Sweet Creams over—"

"That bakery, by Platform!?"

"I don't know. Is that bakery called Sweet Creams over by Platform?" The block of new construction was only five years old, but had just started bringing in a lot of business in the last year, or so Matt had told him. Aidan never went over there because parking was bullshit, but there was some Korean BBQ /Mexican fusion place over there another buddy of his swore by.

"Fuck yeah, there's a bakery over there called Sweet Creams! Dude. I don't give a fuck what people say about Confettis. That place tastes like dog crap compared to Sweet Creams." Matt jumped out of his chair and started putting on his jacket. "Let's go over there now."

"What? No. Sit down. I'm not going over there."

"Fine. I'll go without you. It's almost lunch time, and Adam and Chelsea won't be reporting back on their mission to Tarzana for at least another three hours." Matt had a point. They ran out to get lunch all the time. They could stop by the Korean spot and get some food, and then stop in and say hello to Shae. "We're going to her place of business to purchase items she sells. We're not sneaking into her sorority house."

"Alright fine." Aidan stood and grabbed his own plaid bomber jacket. "But you're driving."

✳

Sweet Creams was packed. The space wasn't all that big, just a few tables, the display cases, a table off to the side with cream and sugar and napkins, and the cash register. The tables were all taken, though and there was a line zigzagging in front of the cases of desserts. Christmas music was playing through the speakers above the door. It was only the second full week of December.

Aidan usually settled into the spirit of the holiday season sometime around eleven forty-five p.m. on December twenty-fourth, but he didn't mind the festive jams at the moment. It was fitting for the whole scene. Nothing said rich sweets like "Santa Baby".

"What can I get for you guys?" one of the girls behind the counter asked.

"We're going to get two of everything. Shit. Give me one more second," Matt replied.

The girl laughed like she knew what kind of dilemma Matt was going through, then turned her attention to Aidan. "And for you?"

"Uh—" He jerked back as Matt elbowed him in the stomach. "Um, is Shae in?"

"Oh. Yeah. She's in the back. And you are?" the girl asked.

"Oh, sorry. Totally understand if she's busy."

"Tell her Aidan Meyer is here. They have a date this week," Matt said in a loud as fuck stage whisper. A bit of pink flashed up the girl's light brown cheeks as she chuckled a bit.

"She doesn't have to come out here. I just wanted to say hello," Aidan said, trying to wave her off, but she was already backing toward the swinging door to the kitchen. She held up her finger to the customers behind them, flashing the "I'll be right back" nod, then disappeared.

"Fuck." Aidan ran his fingers through his hair, then shoved his hands in his pockets. This was a big mistake.

"Relax and pick out a cupcake."

"You fucking relax," Aidan grumbled. A moment later, the girl came back through the door.

"She'll be right out. She's just rinsing her hands."

"Thanks," Aidan replied. He tried to focus on the desserts in front of him and not the sense of doom that was making his heart pound behind his ears.

"You have to try the salted caramel cupcakes. They—" Matt was still talking, but Aidan wasn't listening. The door to the kitchen opened and out walked Shae. She looked better than Aidan remembered. It was definitely the smile. Her long curls were piled on top of her head and she was wearing a pink apron splattered with frosting and flour. Still, she looked like a million bucks.

"Hi!" she said cheerfully. "Did I miss a MATCHED message or does our date start now?" she laughed, but Aidan could hear the nerves in her voice. He'd fucked up.

"I'm sorry. It—"

"I made him come. I'm Matt," his asshole friend said, reaching his hand over the top of the display case. Shae laughed and shook Matt's hand.

"Nice to meet you, Matt. I'm Shae. Welcome to Sweet Creams."

"Oh, I'm all about Sweet Creams. I Postmates you guys at least once a week."

"Oh, you're *that* Matt. Nice to put a face to a name. You're quite the loyal customer." Aidan's eyes roamed Shae's gorgeous face as her full lips turned down in an impressed smirk. Okay, maybe he didn't regret coming to see her. Unfortunately Matt would not stop talking.

"He was planning your date in the office while he should have been working."

"You were?" Her eyes narrowed in shock. "And now you're here."

"We're on lunch," Aidan said with a shrug. "And this seemed like a nice small business to support."

"Well, we appreciate it. Matt, you want to pick out a few cupcakes, on the house of course, while Aidan and I step outside for a second?"

"Deal," Matt said, licking his lips like an addict about to get his hands on the best crank he'd ever had in his whole life. Aidan followed Shae down the length of the counter, weaving through patient customers, then waited by the door as Shae came around the cash register.

"Come on," she said, walking out the door. Aidan followed her outside and around the corner. There were a few benches, but they were all taken. Instead they sat down on the concrete ledge near the steps that led out to the street.

"Good thing it's cool out today. That heat was killing me. So how are you?" Shae crossed her thick thighs and turned toward him. She rested her chin in her hand and flashed him the sexiest smile.

"I'm sorry about this. I know you were trying to work—trying to run a business. We shouldn't have shown up like that."

"No! It's totally fine. I was actually kind of having a weird day. I didn't sleep well last night. I was up late thinking about this guy."

That caught Aidan off guard. He didn't remember Shae being such a bold flirt. It was pretty hot. Aidan managed not to trip over his tongue when he responded. "I see. Thinking good thoughts, I hope."

"They were good thoughts, but like, nervous thoughts."

"What kind of nervous thoughts?"

"Oh, just the usual. I wonder if he'll like me. I wonder if I'll like him."

"I think at least one of those things you won't have to worry about. I just left my office in the middle of the day to get cupcakes for lunch."

"That's true. So you were researching our date? Come to any decisions yet?"

"Along with every single tourist trap in LA and Orange County, the internet encouraged couples to check out the tree lighting at the Grove and Universal City walk."

"Mhmm, go on."

"We could also hit the Petersen Automotive Museum."

"Are you into cars?"

"Not at all."

"Okay," Shae snorted, then covered her mouth to hide the sound. She didn't need to though. It was anything but a turn off. "*I* need a Christmas tree. I've kinda dropped the ball on the holidays the last couple of years."

"Seems pretty Christmasy inside your store. Didn't I catch candy cane shaped cookies for sale?"

"Maybe?" Shae scrunched up her nose in this adorable sign of guilt and Aidan almost leaned over and kissed her. "I'm dropping the ball at home though. Do you want to get a tree with me? And then maybe we can wander around Target because I have no Christmas decorations to put on the tree? Or does that sound like a horrible date?"

"That sounds like a great date," Aidan replied. And he meant it. "When do you want to go?"

"Do you have plans tonight? Or is that way too soon?"

"No. I'm free. I usually leave the office around five."

"Oh, perfect. I usually leave around four. That'll give me plenty of time to go home and change."

They swapped cell numbers and decided that Aidan would swing by her house and pick her up at six-thirty. She assured him that Home Depot was actually the best place to get a tree and not a Christmas tree lot. After they hit Home Depot and Target, they'd find some place to get takeout.

"This sounds like a pretty solid plan," Shae said with a smile. Aidan definitely wanted to kiss her. "Let me get back inside. I have some stuff to finish before my big date with this cute guy tonight."

"I should go stop Matt from annoying the shit out of everyone in your store." Aidan stood. "After you."

"Thanks."

They walked back into the shop and Aidan found Matt standing in the corner with two boxes big enough to carry a dozen cupcakes each.

"Oh you're all set up, aren't you?" Shae asked as she made her way back behind the counter.

"These should last me the ride home."

"Anything for you?" Shae asked Aidan.

"Are these all for you?!" Aidan asked Matt.

"Uh, yeah. I told you. This is my spot. These should last me through the weekend. And I didn't get all this on the house. I paid for them."

"I told you. He's *that* Matt," Shae insisted. "Would you like anything, Aidan? It will be on the house since Matt just paid my rent."

"Actually, I was hoping you would have that layered cake crunch thing you made for the office."

"Oh, the caramel brownie trifle! Yeah, I don't make that here, for sale. I can make that...later." There was a little bit of hopeful suggestion They were talking about desserts and Aidan was definitely getting a hard on.

"We can do that."

"Okay. Well I'll see you tonight. Matt, share at least one cupcake with him."

"Yeah, sure. Okay."

"I'll talk to you later," Aidan said as he held the door open for Matt. Their first date was still hours away, but Aidan was determined not to blow it. He wanted to get closer to Shae.

*

Aidan was late picking up Shae. He had a real excuse. A call with one of their investors had run late. He thought he had enough time to go back to his place, shower and change, but construction on the way to Shae's sent him on a nice detour that put him in the center of a shitload of rush hour traffic. Luckily she wasn't finished getting dressed when he got to her place. Shae opened the door in a robe with her hair up in this silk shower cap. After she let him in, she tasked Aidan with finding a new place for them to grab takeout when they came back from their Christmas tree mission.

Shae's apartment was small, but he was impressed by how put together it was. Her place looked like a showroom, fully furnished with real adult furniture. Pieces that Aidan had never really considered owning, like a wall clock. She had real plants that she managed to keep alive and pictures of her family hanging on the walls along with other pieces of real art. Aidan's sister had helped him get his place somewhat in order, but Shae's place felt like a home.

When Shae finally emerged from her bedroom Aidan was tempted to ask her if they could kick off their date in her bedroom. She was wearing a simple button down striped shirt that fell to her thighs, a pair of tight black pants and some boots, and it made her body look amazing. He managed to keep his sexual propositions to himself though and they headed out to Home Depot.

Shae was right. Aidan had been to some shitty Christmas tree lots, but Home Depot had some prime cuts of Douglas fir. Aidan got to show off a bit, hoisting a large tree up and strapping it to the roof of his car on his own. When he finished his exhibition of full body strength, they headed over to Target, which was oddly packed.

He followed Shae as she weaved through the aisles with the cart. She apologized for grabbing more than Christmas decorations.

"I've been so busy, I figured I should grab a few things while we're here. You don't mind, do you?"

"Don't mind at all. Here." Aidan grabbed the closest item as they made their way toward the back of the store and tossed it into the cart. "I was running low on Centrum Silver."

"That two pack should last you at least a few days."

"Two max," Aidan joked. "I like my vitamins.

They were in Target for over an hour, and Aidan realized as they finally reached the Christmas section that he was having a great time. In the back of his mind, he knew there was a chance his memories of Shae had been clouded by his intense physical attraction to her and her baking skills.

Shae was still as sweet as he remembered, but he hadn't seen this funny as fuck or flirty side of her before. Probably because they'd only known each other at work. And she'd been married. As she schooled him in cheat codes for finding her way around any Target, no matter the lay out, he realized he definitely wanted this date to go on.

They bought a small fortune's worth of ornaments and decorations, including two different holiday wreaths. "I just like to have options," Shae said with this cute smile. "I like to switch it up." Before they headed back to her place, stopping to pick up Indian food on the way. After they secured the tree in its brand new stand, Shae led Aidan over to her couch.

"We'll eat and then we can decorate, if you want to." Shae said as she passed the naan over to him. "You've already put in a lot of manual labor tonight."

"Nah, I can help. Especially with getting the lights up to the top. That's always a two-person job. Also I don't think tapping out this early in the night will bode well for my chances at a date number two."

"Oh, are the kids fucking after two dates now?" she said, laughing. Aidan choked more than laughed, but managed to clear the rice he'd just swallowed from his wind pipe before he really started coughing.

"You know us Millennials. Always coming up with their own rules. You're a Millennial too right?" Aidan had heard the phrase "Black Don't Crack" and he suddenly realized he had no clue how old Shae was. She didn't look much older than twenty-four, but she carried herself with a certain maturity. He had no clue.

"Yeah, we're the same age. I'm thirty-two."

"How'd you—"

"I had to process your payroll, remember? Not in a creepy way, but I just noticed that we were the same age. Once. A long time ago."

"It's okay to say you were stalking me, Shae. I won't hold it against you."

"Yeah, thanks." God, her smile was infectious. Aidan could still feel his own smile lingering as Shae cleared her throat and sobered her expression. "Okay. I want to know. Why are you single? You had a girlfriend when we were working together right?"

"Part of the time. We broke up about a year ago."

"What happened there? If you don't mind me asking."

"Classic 'we just grew apart' thing," Aidan replied with a shrug. "How about you?"

"Okay. I'm going to overshare, 'cause why the hell not. Better to get it all out there, right? And then you can run for the hills when you see my baggage usually arrives via cargo plane."

"Nah, I'm not running anywhere. Unless your ex-husband is obsessed with you and well armed. Then I might power walk in the other direction."

"I wouldn't blame you if that was the case. No. Um..." Shae paused and started moving her rice around her plate. "It was kid stuff actually—fertility stuff. Are you sure you want to hear all this? It's not pretty, first date chatter."

"Not if you don't want to talk about it. I'm not trying to make you upset."

She waved him off. "No, I'm fine. Okay, so he has this huge family. He's one of six, both his parents have a ton of brothers and sisters and all his siblings are working on their, like, third and fourth kids now. We started trying and trying and trying and trying, but of course I wasn't getting pregnant. I asked him if he wanted to go get checked out together and then we could check out our options."

"There's always adoption too."

"Exactly. I suggested that too, but he wasn't having it. I went to go get checked out on my own and my doctors told me I was completely fine."

"It was him."

Shae nodded, pursing her lips. "Pretty sure. We got into an argument about it and he said something I don't want to repeat because that *will* make me upset. Things kinda fell apart after that and I knew I would be happier on my own."

"That sucks. I'm sorry that, you know..."

"Thank you. It was for the best. I'm—things aren't perfect, but I'm definitely happier now. Also, I quit Allight. That place fucking sucked."

Aidan let out a burst of laughter. "It was a pretty shitty place to work. And now you just need to find the right guy."

"Uh huh. Scouring the world of dating apps to find Mr. Right."

"And what does Mr. Right look like to you?" Aidan didn't know what made him ask, but the second the words left his mouth he realized he really wanted to know if he had a chance.

"He's about six-two, with red hair and glasses, pretty buff."

"So you're saying we don't even have to wait until the second date."

Shae laughed some more and reached for her glass of water. "Okay, I'll give you the real wish list that's in my head."

"Let's hear it."

"I want someone I can have fun with. I want someone who wants to go on adventures with me. Like midnight runs to In-N-Out adventures and spur of the moment road trip adventures to Vegas."

"Seems reasonable."

"I want someone I can send nudes to," she said, scrunching up her nose like she'd confessed her darkest secret. "I've never sent a nude before."

"Hmm. Neither have I, now that I think of it."

"What about you? What does Mrs. Right look like to you?"

"She can bake her ass off, for starters," Aidan said, his chest warming at the sound of Shae's laugh. He couldn't get enough of it.

"Fine baked goods are a must. What else?"

"Someone who wants to send me nudes," Aidan heard himself say. He immediately wanted to tell Shae he was joking, but he wasn't.

THREE

D*ear Santa, What was I thinking...?*

Shae watched Aidan watching her as she tried to process the words he'd just said. Was he sweating as bad as she was? Was his stomach turning over too? She was flirting too much. She knew it and she was being too honest. Another trait of Kenney women. Light, hilarious, yet blunt honesty. Shae could always rely on her own honesty, but it was truly a crapshoot when it came to how others responded to it. Harvin had loved that part of her personality at first, until it came time for him to deal with his own truth. Shae mentally shook off the unpleasant thoughts of her unpleasant ex-husband and turned her focus back to the issue at hand. Aidan wanted nudes. Her nudes.

"I'm sorry," he said a second later. "I didn't mean it—"

"No, don't apologize. I have a question about the nudes though."

"How can you have a question for me? The nudes were your idea," Aidan laughed.

"I know! But say I wanted to send you nudes. Like if I wanted to send them to you specifically."

"Right. Okay. You're sending me nudes. What's the question?"

"Would you send nudes back?"

Aidan tilted his chin up a bit and let out a "Hmmmm..."

"See! This is why I have follow-up questions. I'd be out here sending nudes and getting 'Hmmmms' in return," Shae joked. Kinda.

She was definitely sweating, not on her forehead or anything. She was just hot all over from nerves. She took another swig of her drink. In over her head didn't even describe it. Agreeing to this date was a bad idea. She was not ready to be out in the playing field or whatever you call it.

"I was just thinking of how to frame my response so I didn't come off like a complete dirtbag," Aidan replied. "If you were sending me nudes, I would be happy to send you nudes in return, if you wanted nudes from me. I know women don't like unsolicited dick pics."

"That is true. So if we decided, like mutually, to send each other nudes—"

"Mhmm. Go on." His eyes narrowed behind his thick framed glasses. Shae didn't know what to make of it, so she just kept talking.

"Right. So we're adults and shit, right? And we *can* decide to send each other nudes. Is that something that you could possibly be interested in doing?"

"Yes," he replied calmly.

"Okay."

"If that's something you're interested in doing."

"Can I be honest? If I had known it was this easy to get naked pictures of you, I would have asked years ago." Shae smiled as a burst of laughter erupted from Aidan.

"Well, I think timing is an important factor here. I think your marriage would have ended for completely different reasons if I was sending you nudes years ago. Can I ask you one thing? Before we get back to the nudes, I mean."

"Please." *I need to stop talking anyway*, she almost added.

"Would you like to go out on a second date with me?"

"Yes. I would and this time you can actually plan it. And I'll make sure I run my errands beforehand."

"Fair enough. But I don't mind if you need to stop into CVS for something."

"I'll make a list before you pick me up."

"Deal. Before we get back to the nudes, there's one more thing I have been wanting to do for a few years."

"What's that?" Shae asked. A second later it clicked. Shae froze as Aidan moved the plates between them and slid to the middle of the couch. His green eyes scanned over her features before settling on her lips. She regretted picking out a long-wear matte lipstick. It made her lips look amazing, but she wasn't sure if it made them kissably soft. Would matte cosmetics ruin this kiss for them both?

Shae's eyes slid closed as Aidan's lips pressed against hers. The matte was definitely not a problem. It all started off pretty tame. Just lips on lips, Aidan's hand sliding around the curve of her neck. Her own fingers went to the front of his shirt, toying with the hem of the soft cotton as their tongues entered the equation. Just when Shae thought to take things a little further, Aidan pulled away. Shae's eyes blinked open. If her skin wasn't a dark brown, she knew she's be sporting the same red blush that now covered Aidan's face. She cleared her throat, then bit the inside of her cheek.

"You've wanted to kiss me for a few years?"

Aidan nodded. "Yeah, I have."

Shae wanted to press him for details, see if he was really telling the truth about this hidden desire, but she knew she'd ruin the moment. Instead she said, "That was a very good kiss."

"I have to agree with you."

They finished the meal and Shae was so relieved by how easily the conversation flowed. They talked more about their old co-workers. It seemed like they both had only kept in touch with a few people. He told her more about his start-up, which helped buyers find houses that specifically needed renovations. In this real estate climate in this part of California, the whole concept of Primed-Realty seemed like a great idea. After they got the tree about seventy-five percent perfect, Shae had to send Aidan on his way.

"I have to get to work early. Otherwise I'd ask you to stay. Not like the whole night, but longer. Or the whole night. Whatever."

"I get it. I'll call you and we can figure out date number two."

"I'd like that." Shae walked him to the door and was not at all disappointed when he kissed her again. This time it was just as good, but different. There was some real heat behind this kiss, not just a sense of curiosity asking to be fulfilled. This second kiss was a promise of naked things to come, if Shae let them.

"I'll talk to you soon," Aidan said as he stepped backward out her front door.

"Wait!"

"Yeah?"

"About the nudes?"

She almost melted at the smile that flashed across his lips. "Right, the nudes. What's on your mind?"

"Well we need Nude Rules right?"

"Rules are good. What are you thinking?"

"Well, I wouldn't want one of my girls at the bakery to accidentally see your dangle, so maybe we don't send nudes during office hours."

"Yeah. We should keep my dangle between us. And I definitely don't want Matt to see any part of you."

"Oh yeah, no. He might be one of our best customers, but he's not that good." They both laughed and Shae knew she was dangerously close to asking him to come back inside. "Okay. You have to go."

"I'm leaving. Goodnight." He turned quickly and walked down the hall to the elevator.

"You can send me nudes tonight if you want." Shae called after him. He just laughed.

Shae couldn't sleep. She lay in bed, playing out her night with Aidan over and over in her mind. She'd really gone on a date with IT Aidan and the date was good. The kissing was great. Still, she felt like she'd made a huge ass out of herself. She reached for her phone again and opened her group chat with the girls. She knew they were waiting on an update. Meegan and Keira were talking about a Twilight Zone reboot that was in the works. Shae didn't feel bad interrupting.

> Hi. I'm back

Meegan: How did it go?

Keira: OMG yeah what happened?

> He asked me what I wanted in a relationship and I said someone that I can send nudes to.

> WHAT IS WRONG WITH ME?

Meegan: UM NOTHING! That's amazing.

Keira: What did he say?

> Oh he was on board, but for like a nudes exchange.

> Which is all fine and good, but what the hell kind of first date move is that?

> I give him twenty-four hours before he decides I'm a complete weirdo and ghosts me.

> Joanna: He's not going to ghost you. Just relax. What else happened?

> We went to Target and got decorations and then he helped me set up my tree.

> Keira: That's so cute.

> Meegan: Did you let him smash?

Shae wanted to answer, but she couldn't seem to get over whatever was eating at her. Instead of replying to Meegan, she pulled up her text conversation with Aidan. She could feel herself really blowing it now, saying way too much or just enough, the exact right thing to turn Aidan off forever. Holy shit, dating was the worst.

> Was the nudes thing weird?

Just as she was about to switch back to her conversation with the girls, the little text bubble popped up in the bottom left of her screen.

> Not at all. I was shocked.

> In a good way, not weirded out.

> Do you want me to break the ice?

> You really want to send me nudes, don't you?

Shae, listen.

Every man lives for the moment when a beautiful woman says she wants awkwardly framed, poorly lit pictures of his junk sent to her phone.

Shae laughed to herself and immediately started typing back.

No! Send artsy nudes! I want quality photographs I can brag to my friends about, but of course not show them.

Of course.

I thought you were going to sleep.

I tried to, but I'm wide awake.

You're thinking about the nudes.

I'm going to put you out of your misery.

Shae stared at her phone a full minute and those three little dots still hadn't popped on Aidan's side of their text conversation. She clicked back over to her group chat with the girls.

Omg I think he's sending me a dick pic right now.

Meegan: Sweet lord. Please show us.

I can't!

That's like privacy violation #1

Meegan: Okay well tell us what his junk looks like in graphic detail.

And then show us anyway.

Joanna: Don't show us!

Keira: Yeah please don't. I'm good. LOL

Before Shae could respond, a picture message popped up at the top of her screen. The little square on the right hand side was so tiny. Still, the sight of lightly tanned skinned covered in freckles was unmistakable. Shae was pretty sure her heart stopped.

Omg he sent pics! I can't do this.

I cannot do this.

Keira: Can't do what? What's wrong?

I DON'T KNOW! I'M FREAKING OUT!

Joanna: Take a deep breath.

Keira: Do you want me to come over?

No. You don't need to witness my freak out firsthand.

Meegan: Also she's about to jerk off to hot ginger nudes.

Keira: Alright! Stop.

I'm okay, just give me one sec.

That was a lie. Shae was used to being honest and sometimes too straightforward, but it rarely led to things she actually wanted, especially from guys she actually wanted to sleep with. So no, she was not okay. Shae was overwhelmed, if it was possible to be over-whelmed by a good thing. Yeah, she was definitely overwhelmed, but not too overwhelmed to look at the pictures.

> Okay I'm going to take fifteen minutes to carefully analyze these pictures.

> I'll be back.

Shae saw Meegan typing, but she didn't stick around for her next colorful comment. Instead she took a deep breath, then clicked out of her group chat. The red little notifications bubble above her text message icon taunted her. There were four texts now. Four texts from Aidan containing pictures of what she was convinced was a rocking bod. She let out the deep breath and pulled another one in.

"Okay," she said out loud. "This is no big deal. You've seen a naked man before. You've seen hot naked men before. None this hot in real life, but you're an adult. You can handle this. Okay. Dear Santa, give me the strength I need."

Shae pressed her thumb to the little green icon, then moved over Aidan's name at the top of her message list. She was wrong. She wasn't ready and holy shit, it was a big deal. In the first two pictures, Aidan had snapped two selfies in the mirror, from his chest down to the dark red curls just below a perfectly defined V of muscle at the top of his equally muscular thighs. The bright lights of his bathroom showed off every muscle, every freckle.

He still had his dark frame glasses on, which made Shae wonder how strong his prescription was for a second before she moved on to the next picture. Aidan had moved things to his bed. He had held his phone somewhere down around his thigh and captured a picture that featured both his face and his erection grasped in his other hand. The last photo was similar but from a slightly different angle.

Shae's body was now hot all over. This time it wasn't from

nerves. She couldn't remember the last time she'd been this turned on. Her head felt tight and tingly, and her pussy was starting to throb. Shae swallowed the drool pooling in her mouth. As she was turning her head to analyze every inch of his cock, Aidan sent another text.

> I'm open to constructive criticism.

> Can't change the equipment, but please let me know if I can step up the lighting and composition.

A burst of laughter slipped out of Shae, releasing some of the lustful tension that was building in her chest. Criticism? How could she criticize perfection? Thank Santa, Frosty, and Rudolph that she was already lying down, because otherwise she would have fainted. Swiping through the pictures, she wasn't sure she hadn't bumped her head. Aidan's body was...there were no words.

> Sorry. I need a minute.

She added the emoji with sweat dripping off its forehead and hit send. Then she went back to the last picture. Shae had seen big cocks before—the internet was busting with them—but she never seen a cock this thick around. Aidan's hands weren't small and his penis looked large in his fingers. Shae's pussy throbbed at the thought of what it would feel like to have that thing filling her from the inside. She had to respond, but she didn't know what to say. She clicked back over to her group chat. Erica and Sarah had jumped back in.

> Okay. He definitely sent nudes and they are definitely impressive.

> What do I do?

Meegan: Go over there and mount up.

Keira: No. Don't do that. Unless you want to.

Erica: I say if you wanna get with him tonight, go for it. Just make sure expectations are clear.

I don't know what I want to do!

Zero expectations here.

Okay, so she did want to sleep with him. It was too soon though. Definitely too soon and she still had those antiquated notions buried deep in her head that if she gave away the custard for free, the farmer would never come back to the market or some shit. She knew it wasn't true. But truth and reason didn't stop her from panicking. This was definitely a bad idea.

Another text from Aidan popped up.

Too much?

Shit he's texting me.

Let me talk to him.

I'll report back.

Keira: Don't do anything you're not comfortable with!

Shae sent a heart emoji to the group that was mostly meant just for her lovely, caring cousin who would absolutely come right over to talk her off the ledge. Her fingers were more interested in typing to Aidan though. She went back over to their conversation.

I'm thinking. This is a lot to process.

What are you thinking about?

> What I want to do next?

> Hmmm. What are the options you're weighing?

Shae tried to think of something cute and clever, but her brain and her thumbs just wouldn't cooperate. The truth came tumbling out.

> Option 1: Send equally impressive pictures back. If I can match your expert lighting situation.

> Option 2: Ask you if you want me to come over, like right now.

> I'm fine with either option, but now I do feel bad because I know you have to get up early for work.

> What's the best option that involves you getting the best night's sleep?

Shae felt herself grinning like an idiot. How could a guy be this cute and sweet while sexting?

> Well a good orgasm does usually put me to sleep.

> But by the time I got over there…

> Right. We'd be blowing your full night of sleep plan to smithereens.

> How do you feel about FaceTime?

> You can see me. I can see you.

> Not exactly sex, but the next best thing.

> It seems like a reasonable Option 3.

If it will help you sleep, that is.

Give me a few minutes.

Shae didn't wait for him to respond. She tossed her phone on her bed, then jumped up and ran into her bathroom. There was no shame in her bonnet game, but she needed to sleep with Aidan at least once in real life before she exposed him to the world of Black women's night time protective style routines. She unwrapped her hair as quickly she could, fluffing it along its natural part before she dug up her best fuck-me lip gloss.

She gave herself one last look in the mirror and realized that should do the trick. As soon as she changed out of her t-shirt and sweats. She ran back into her room and dug up this lacy nightgown she'd splurged on after her she'd moved out of her parents' house in Baldwin Hills and into her own place. She'd worn it for more than five minutes exactly no times.

Shae slipped it on and it actually fit better than when she'd first tried it. No panties felt like a safe go-to move. She flopped back down on her bed and grabbed her phone, pressing the video chat icon under Aidan's profile before she could talk herself out of it. Aidan picked up right away. Shae had literally just seen pictures of him completely naked. Seeing his face and the upper part of his bare chest on her phone should not have come as such a shock. Still, just looking at him reclining against his pillows had sent a fresh wave of heat all over her.

"Can you see me?" she asked. Her bedside lamp was on, but it was really dim.

"Yeah, I can see you just fine."

"Or would it be better if I took this out to my living room and turned the Christmas lights back on?" Shae teased, but as soon as she made the suggestion it was clear Aidan was thinking it over.

"I mean, that wouldn't be the worst idea. I've never had holiday themed phone sex before."

"Okay. You're coming with me." Shae hopped off her bed and went back out to her dark living room. It took her a second to find the plug to the lights, but the moment the tree lit up, she knew she'd made a good choice. She grabbed her throw blanket and flopped down on the couch.

"Hi."

"Hey."

"Your voice sounds deeper," she said. She could see herself smiling like a dope in the small rectangle on her screen.

"Does it?"

"Yeah. It's kinda hot."

"I'll work on making it completely hot."

"No, it's working," Shae said and then she actually giggled. Her heart was pounding so fast. "You should have just stayed over."

"Next time, all you have to do is ask."

"I'll keep that in mind." She let out a deep breath and tried to focus. "So. We were going to work on getting me to sleep. The fun way."

"Yeah. I don't want to ruin your day tomorrow. I know it's important to get a good night's sleep."

"It's very true. Even with coffee, I can be an unpleasant kind of cranky."

"We should get to it then. You have to tell me what you like."

Ignoring the lump that started to wedge itself in her throat, Shae slid her hand between her legs. She was pretty damn wet. "Why don't you tell me what you would do to me right now if you were here and we can do some team building work from there."

Aidan let out a burst of laughter. "Team building, huh? Well I would definitely start by kissing you again. Are you wearing one of those nighty things?"

"Oh yeah. You want to see?"

"Yeah, I do." Shae shivered at the way his voice seemed to drop even more. She could get used to dealing with aroused Aidan. She crossed the room and set up her phone on the kitchen counter, then stepped back a bit.

"How's that?"

"Fuck, Shae. I definitely should have stayed." Hearing Aidan curse sent another odd thrill right between her legs. They definitely needed to have sex soon. It had been too long.

"I don't wear stuff like this very often." The last time she'd rocked any fancy lingerie it had been her wedding night, but that memory had no place in this conversation.

"I like it," Aidan said as she picked up her phone again and walked back to the couch. "Is that the only one you have?"

"Yeah. I guess I should buy a couple more. Now that I'm doing sexy stuff like sending nudes and cybersexing."

"Shae." The tone of Aidan's voice wiped the doofy smile right off Shae's face. His voice meant business.

"Yeah?"

"You've seen me and now I want to see you. I want to watch you touch yourself."

"Okay." Shae rigged up a little stack of her coffee table books and leaned her phone against it. When she was sure Aidan was getting a good view, she spread her legs and then spread her lips.

FOUR

*D**ear Santa, There's no need to panic...*

Aidan couldn't stop thinking about Shae. He'd woken up the next morning after their little video chat run-in and he was still naked. They hadn't slept together, but watching Shae fuck herself on his phone screen was definitely the next best thing. He'd been thinking with his dick when he sent her those naked pictures of himself. He could freely admit that. After the kisses they shared, he was kicking himself for not at least staying long enough to fuck Shae to sleep.

He wanted to be a gentleman and respect her space and her time, and her need for sleep. She was running her own business and Aidan didn't think it would be too safe to be groggy around hot ovens and other kitchen equipment. None of that stopped him from fantasizing about Shae on his drive home. He was half hard by the time he walked into his apartment and dead set on jerking off the moment he got in bed.

Even though Shae had asked for dick pics, Aidan knew she'd been half joking. It was a bit of arrogance on his part, actually sending the pictures. He knew what he was working with and maybe if Shae had gotten a peek of what he had to offer, she'd... He didn't know what a glimpse of his dick would make Shae want. He just hoped she'd want more of him.

What he got was a hell of a show. Anyone could see that Shae had an amazing body. Those curves were fucking killer and the little bit he'd gotten to touch when they kissed on her couch made him want to explore every inch of her body. Seeing her fingers pump in and out of her wet pussy had been something else. Something so fucking hot he'd nutted twice before he finally went to sleep just playing the image of it and the sounds Shae made over and over again in his head. All of it was much better than any naked picture he could have gotten from her in return.

The video mutual masturbating had been the icing on their night together. He had an idea that he was going to enjoy himself with Shae. He just never anticipated he would enjoy spending time with her so much. Their date had definitely been different from every other first date he'd been on, but he realized that was one of the things he was starting to like about Shae.

In the least cliched way possible, she was different from other women he'd dated before and he could get used to that. He tried to shake her from his mind. Didn't work. Even after hitting the weights at the gym, thoughts of Shae came flooding into his head. So many thoughts, so many possibilities of what they could do when they saw each other again, that he had to stop himself before he got a hard-on in the gym showers.

Avoiding a public erection was the best he could manage. He gave in to his pathetic infatuation and stopped on his way into the office and picked up the most alive looking bouquet of grocery store wildflowers he could find. Then he headed over to Sweet Creams. He thought he'd have to have another awkward conversation with the girl behind the counter, one of those conversations that had her asking Shae the moment he left if that weird creep who kept popping up was bothering her. Luckily Shae was in the front of the shop refilling the creamers when he walked in the door.

"Excuse me, ma'am?" he said as he walked closer. Shae spun around, her face lighting up the moment she saw him. She didn't hesitate to rush to his side.

"Hey! Are these for me?"

"Yeah. For last night." Aidan couldn't stop himself. He reached up and smoothed a small bit of Shae's hair behind her ear. She froze for a second before this hint of something Aidan liked came to her eyes. She smiled a little, then bit the inside of her lip.

"Yeah. Last night. Thank you. I've never done anything like that on a first date before," she said quietly. "Or ever."

"It was a first for me too."

"Really?"

"Yeah," Aidan said, laughing a little. What kind of player did she think he was? "A night of firsts."

"So we're both feeling sufficiently awkward."

"But not bad, right? You don't feel bad about last night?" he asked.

"No! Definitely not bad. Just pleasantly surprised."

"And these are for the whole night. Not just the extra stuff at the end. I mean, I would have brought you flowers anyway. Not just because you—"

"I get it. These are very sweet." She smelled them again. "Thank you. Are you on your way to work?"

"Uh, yeah. We have a call with one of our investors in a little while. Just...wanted to see you first," Aidan admitted.

"Fortify yourself by gazing upon my beautiful face before you face the day?"

"Something like that."

"How about a few donuts on the house?"

"Sure. I'll buy some more pastries too," Aidan said, following her back to the display cases. He picked out a half dozen tarts and another half dozen donuts. "I'm sure Matt made sweet love to those cupcakes last night, but I know he'll try to fight me if he finds out I came in here and didn't get him anything."

"He really is keeping us in business."

"At least he's good for something." Aidan took out his wallet, then paused. There was something he had to ask Shae. "So this weekend they have the ice rink set up at LA Live. Is that something you could be interested in?"

"Oh, you should go!" The girl at the register said. "I go with my sister every year. It's so much fun."

"I'm terrible at skating," Shae replied.

"So? Are you looking at his arms? I'm sure he can hold you up."

"I can," Aidan said.

"Thanks, Darby. Ah, yeah sure. Let's do it. Sunday is better. It's kinda crazy here on Saturday and Monday I have off. I can stay out past my curfew on Sunday nights."

"Great. Let me know a good time and I'll come pick you up. We can have dinner right downtown."

"Sounds perfect."

Aidan didn't know if they were at this stage of whatever was going on between them yet. He took a risk and leaned down, kissing her lightly on the lips. Shae was smiling and maybe blushing a bit when he stepped away. Aidan took that as a good sign.

"I'll call you," Shae said, her voice sounding all breathy. Aidan didn't take that as a bad sign either. He decided to quit while he was ahead and turned for the door, carrying enough baked goods to keep Matt happy until lunch time.

✻

Shae couldn't breathe. As soon as Aidan disappeared around

the corner, she casually excused herself from Darby. She needed to put the beautiful flowers Aidan had bought her in water. As soon as she was alone, the wheezing started and she felt like she was going to cry. She knew she needed to talk to someone. She could call her mom, but then her mom would leave the hospital and come over just to check her out.

The last thing she needed was Dr. Kenney with her medical gear bursting through the door, scaring the shit out of Darby and her customers. She grabbed her phone out of her apron pocket and started at the top of her "most likely to calm me down" phone tree.

It was a crapshoot whether or not her cousin would be with a client or teaching a workout class, but Keira answered after a few rings.

"Hey boo. How was last night?"

"Fine. It was great actually. I think I'm having a panic attack."

"What's wrong?"

"Aidan just stopped by the shop again—"

"Oh no. Is he being creepy? I have a client in ten, but I can ask Daniel to have a little 'check yourself' chat with him."

"No. That's not it at all."

"Oh right, he sent you scandalous pictures last night. What happened there?"

"The pictures led to more...adult stuff."

"Okay. You have to tell me why you're panicking."

"I don't know! We kinda totally had phone sex last night, with a video component, and then this morning he came by the shop with flowers and asked me out on a second date."

"Do you not want to go out with him? 'Cause you don't have to. Even if the video intercourse was good."

Keira's silliness was helping. Shae's heart slowed down enough to let her laugh. "I do want to see him again. I think I'm nervous. Like really, really nervous."

"Ah okay. I'm just going to say this. I get why you're nervous."

"You do?" Shae leaned against the edge of her stainless steel counter and tilted her head back. She should have never let Erica near her phone.

"Yes. I was a mess when Daniel and I started dating. A bumbling mess and now look at us."

"Right, but then you and Daniel got engaged forty-five minutes later." It had actually been something like three weeks, but it was pretty close. "I'm not trying to marry Aidan. We literally just started dating. I don't even know if we are dating. We might just be hanging out or whatever the youths are calling it these days. We haven't even had sex yet."

Oh now you're just filling yourself with shit, that voice in her head said. *As if you showing him every inch of your minora and majora didn't count as something.*

"Okay, so you don't want to rush into things. You don't want to label it yet. That's fine. Don't. Just tell him that you want things to go slow."

"But I don't know if I want things to go slow. Ugh," Shae groaned. "What is wrong with me? I want to spend more time with him. I definitely want to sleep with him. But every time I see him, it's like my brain stops working."

"Shae, you're dating for the first time since high school. You've been out of the game for over fifteen years. It's okay to be kind of confused. It's okay to be a lot confused. And I know it doesn't help that he's super hot. I had the same problem with Daniel. I used to just stare at him. Heck, I still do! I mean, we're both hot, but it's weird to be matched with so much hotness."

"Yes! Thank you. It has nothing to do with the way I look. It's him. He's so damn hot!" Shae said with bit of hysterical laughter.

Keira was laughing on her end too. "Trust me, I get it. There are cute guys and there are guys who stop traffic. Aidan is a darn crossing guard. Just promise me something."

Shae's laughter died. Keira was about to deliver some tough love. She knew it. "Yeah, sure."

"Promise me you'll take it easy on yourself. Be confused, that's fine. He's just gonna have to deal with that. Like, don't jerk him around. Be honest that you're confused and if he's not okay with that, then move it along to the next one. Or spend more time making delicious baked goods until you figure out what you do want. Harvin did a number on you. It's okay to be a little gun shy with the boys. Especially the really cute ones that set off fantasy rockets in your dreams."

Shae smiled again. "You are such a dork and I love you."

"I love you too. I'm secretly praying my client cancels because I can't stop thinking about wedding stuff."

"What's going on?"

"Nothing. I just want to get it over with, in a non-jerky way. Was it this bad for you?"

"Yes. Remember, I had to deal with my mom and then every woman in Harvin's family telling me they knew better than I did since I was such a young bride."

"Ugh, yeah. I remember." She'd cried to Keira more than once about how Harvin's family had ruined parts of their special day for her. If there was ever an omen of things to come...

"Let me know how I can help and I'll try to take some of the stress off your plate."

"Just unavoidable bride blues, I think. Daniel's back tonight, so I'll smooch him under our many mistletoes until I feel better."

"That sounds like a great plan," Shae said just as her timer dinged. "I have to pull some cookies out of the oven. I'll text you later?"

"Yes. And call me if you're having another freak out."

"I'll just focus on the baking. That usually helps." She said her goodbyes to Keira and then forced herself to get back to work. After she pulled the second batch of brownies out of the oven, she felt much better. Calm enough to text Aidan again.

I hope you're alone.

> I have something naughty to show you.

She leaned over and took a picture of her mouth agape, right next to two huge sheets of fresh brownies. Her phone chimed in her hand before she could send them.

> Definitely not alone.
>
> DO NOT SEND NUDES.
>
> I REPEAT DO NOT SEND NUDES!

Shae's snort of laughter filled the kitchen as she sent the picture of the fresh baked goods.

> I'm adding your favorite to the menu.
>
> Chocolate Brownie Caramel Crunch Trifle and Candy Cane Crunch for the holidays.

This was actually one of Shae's favorite desserts. There was no reason not to add it to the menu.

> Okay now that is just unfair.
>
> New rules. No nudes at work and no tempting me with desserts I've been dreaming about for years.

> Oh come on.
>
> I have to tempt you with something.

See. She could do this. She was a perfectly good flirt.

> Fine. Are you making the caramel from scratch?
>
> Please say yes and describe it to me slowly.

Oh yeah baby.

You know it.

He sent back a drooling emoji that made Shae chuckle as she set down her phone. Keira was right. All she had to do was be honest with herself about what she wanted and everything would be okay. And for now she wanted to flirt with Aidan via text while she baked the afternoon away.

＊

Something was bothering Shae, Aidan could tell. They'd been texting the last few days. Their texts mostly involved her sending him pictures of everything she was baking and the occasional late night nipple shot, which he very much appreciated, but when he'd shown up at her house to pick her up for their skating date, she'd barely looked him in the eye. Even when he kissed her hello, she seemed like she was holding back.

She held up her end of the conversation in the car, telling Aidan about the rest of her work week and letting him fill her in on the two properties they'd found for their website. He was about to mention that he found a house that he was considering renovating himself, but he kept that to himself.

LA Live was packed when they finally battled their way through the weekend traffic and made it to the heart of downtown LA. As soon as they emerged from the underground garage, Aidan was hit with the full spirit of Christmas. The whole outdoor plaza was decorated with lights and garland. Stevie Wonder's voice came through the massive PA system.

As they turned the corner, the massive tree and outdoor skating rink came into view. It was as close to the tree at Rockefeller Center as Southern California was going to get. Aidan made a bold choice and reached for Shae's hand as they moved through the crowd of people. She gave him a half-hearted smile and wove their fingers together. He wasn't sure what to make of that. Didn't stop him from holding on to her for as long as he could, though.

Aidan wasn't one to beat around the bush, so as soon as they sat down to strap on their skates he asked. "Are you okay? You seem kind of tense?"

"Actually, I'm not sure." Shae finally turned and looked at him. Aidan knew the signs. She was about to friendzone his ass hard. Not that there was a problem with them being just friends, but he'd be lying if he said he didn't want more. He swallowed and prepared himself to handle the rejection like an adult.

"What's going on?" he asked.

"Remember the other day when we were talking about a night of firsts?"

"Yeah."

"Well I know we are literally at the start of our second date, which might actually be our first because I did drag you to Target the first time—anyway." She stopped herself with a wave of her hand and seemed to regroup around her original train of thought. "I feel like everything I'm saying and doing is silly."

"What do you mean?"

"Aidan, you asked me what I wanted in a relationship and I said pornographic photos."

"Were you lying?"

"Hell no. If it wouldn't be really weird, I'd frame the pictures you sent the other night and show them to guests."

That made Aidan laugh and finally relax a bit. "Please don't do that."

"I won't, but I just—I don't know what I'm doing."

"Neither do I. I'm spending every second thinking of one of two things," Aidan said, making a confession of his own.

"What two things?"

"Well, since we're being honest I'll just go ahead and embarrass myself. I'm either thinking about when I can see you again and when I can bring up the subject of us having sex in person without sounding like a total dick. I also think about you baking naked, which I know is completely unsafe."

Shae's laughter put him at ease. Finally she seemed to relax next to him. "Okay. That makes me feel a little better."

"The other night I was just asking. Just trying to break the ice—"

"I know."

"I wasn't trying to put any pressure on you. I didn't exactly hate it either."

"What? My super weird first date confession?"

"It wasn't weird and yeah that. Tell me what else you want in a relationship. Go ahead. Whatever comes to mind. Nothing can shock me," Aidan said.

"Don't say that. I might seem like a sweet, horny baker, but there's some wild stuff going on up here," she said, tapping her temple with her finger.

"Give it a try. What do you want right now?"

"I want to have fun with you tonight."

"We can definitely make that happen." Aidan's smile dropped, though, the second Shae leaned closer and lowered her voice.

"Also, I do really want to see your dick up close in real life and then maybe ask you questions about it because booooy, I have questions."

Aidan swung his arm around Shae's shoulder as he burst out laughing. Then he kissed her forehead. "After dinner, you decide—your place or mine. You can have an in-depth, person to package interview with my dick."

"Deal." Aidan held still as Shae leaned up and kissed him on the mouth. When they came up for air, he took a few extra minutes lacing up his skates. There were children around and he and his dick were in no condition to take to the ice. Not just yet.

★

Shae figured out how to deal with her crippling Aidan-related anxiety. All she had to do was spend every waking moment with him for the rest of her life. After they finally dealt with the elephant in the room, she had a blast during the skating portion of their date. Turned out Aidan was an amazing skater. He left out the part where he started playing hockey when he was eight and sometimes felt more comfortable in his worn out Bauers (Shae no clue what the fuck those were) than he did in regular shoes.

Shae, on the other hand, was a terrible ice skater. She put in one hell of an effort and that resulted in her at least staying upright a good portion of the time. It also gave her an excuse to hang on to Aidan's muscular bicep for the bulk of the evening.

When she was with him, she realized she didn't feel nervous at all. Aidan was so very sweet and very attentive. Shae could feel that she had all of his attention, even when other women were trying to catch his eye as they made their way around the rink. He didn't even seem to notice. They kissed a few times on the ice and then again when Aidan was helping her take off her skates.

She realized she could get used it, smooching a really hot, nice guy. The thought of getting used to it had the anxiety creeping back, but the moment he took her hand and led her around the corner to the Yard House, she let those tight feelings go. This was just their second date and, as far as second dates went, Aidan made for excellent company. All she had to do was enjoy his company and everything would be fine.

The sprawling brewery style restaurant was really crowded, packed with patrons watching football, basketball and even rugby on the large mounted televisions. It was so loud they decided to eat quickly and then head back to Shae's apartment to watch a movie. And by watch a movie, Shae hoped Aidan meant put on a movie in the background while they got completely naked and did it in front of her Christmas tree.

As Aidan was paying the check, Shae may have mentioned that she had a fresh caramel brownie trifle back at her apartment. She thought he was going to pull her arm out of its socket rushing her back to the car.

"You can't tease me like this, Shae!" He yelled as he weaved through all the people blocking his exit from the plaza.

"It'll still be there when we get to my place," she reminded him as he gallantly opened her door and almost shoved her inside. Tears of laughter were nearly running down her face as he started cursing an elderly couple who were taking their time exiting the parking garage ahead of them.

"You can take the whole thing home with you. The whole trifle."

"Don't play with my emotions. I've been thinking about that crunchy sweet goodness for years!"

"I made some at the store the other day and you never came by."

"I'm a working man, Shae! I thought you would save me some but you were sold out every day before I could get over there—Will you hurry the fuck up!!!" he shouted in this hilarious, over the top shriek. Good thing the windows were up. Shae could not stop laughing. As soon as they got back to her apartment, she made him sit on the couch and then she grabbed two wooden spoons and set the whole trifle down on the coffee table.

"Go at it, big guy."

"Thank you."

Shae kicked off her shoes and made herself comfortable as Aidan slid to the edge of the couch and pushed up his sleeves. He grabbed one of the spoons and then turned to her. "Are you going to want any of this, because..."

Shae bit her lip to hold in her chuckle. "I might have one bite, but this one definitely has your name all over it."

"Great." He picked up the whole bowl and started going to town. Shae watched the side of his face for a moment, trying hard not to laugh at the moaning sounds he was making with each bite. After a minute, Shae turned on the TV and found the romantic

Christmas movies section on Netflix.

"*Twelves Loves of Christmas* work for you?" she asked. He answered with a nod and another groan.

FIVE

*D*ear Santa, Please let it fit…

Shae tried to enjoy the holiday romance unfolding on her TV screen. Instead, she couldn't help watching Aidan out of the corner of her eye as he put in a serious effort to destroy the whole trifle. He only made it halfway through the bowl though, and that included the occasional spoonfuls he fed to Shae before even she had to tap out. Shae glanced at him as he sat back on the couch, rubbing his belly for a few moments. After a bit, he turned to her.

"I have a question," he said.

"Please, go ahead."

"How are they both suddenly in Europe when he said he didn't have a passport?"

"I didn't even think you were listening. There was so much moaning coming from that side of the couch."

"Oh, no. I'm invested, just confused."

"The spirit of Christmas got it expedited to him overnight.

You're not accounting for the magic of the season or the power of overnight shipping."

"Oh, okay. Well I'm glad he made it to Prague. He has some serious groveling to do."

"He really does. It's gonna be over in a little while. After that, we can watch one of your holiday movie selections. Or we can watch something that has nothing to do with Christmas. I feel like I'm shoving my need to feel jolly and bright down your throat," Shae said with a nervous laugh.

"No, this is amazing. I usually just head home for Christmas and those few days are as festive as it gets. We can watch all the holiday movies you want."

But I want to have sex! Shae almost blurted out. Instead she said something less weird. "Um, are you going home for Christmas this year?"

"Nah. My dad surprised my mom with a trip to Spain, so they're doing that, and my sister and her husband are taking their kids to Disney World. Matt's Jewish and he and his sister and a few of their friends invited me to hang out with them on Christmas day."

"Well, we host a big friend Christmas Eve dinner thing if you want to come. With a gift swap and everything."

"Count me in."

"I will. I'll tell my cousin to add you to the RSVP list."

"You just made that face again," Aidan said suddenly.

"What face?" And of course now she was definitely making a face because she wanted to know what the heck he was talking about.

"The same face you were making earlier when you were talking about being nervous. Are you nervous again?"

Shae thought for a moment and tried her best to choose her words wisely. "I'm not nervous. I'm...filled with nervous anticipation. Like 'sixth grade hanging out with your crush' anticipation. But also working up the courage to tell you I don't really care about any holiday movie right now because I'm thinking about how we can segue from making out to doing more interesting naked things. Or just skipping the confession and going right to making the first move."

Aidan leaned back with a hand pressed to his chest in mock surprise. "Who says I wasn't going to make a move?"

"No, I didn't mean it like that. I just know—I know you can't read my mind, so clearly I'd have to make it obvious that sex was something I wanted like right now, but of course I don't want you to just pounce on me. Or maybe I do. I don't know. How about I stop talking and we just see how these two find their happily ever after and we can pretend I never brought this up."

"Yeah, that's no good."

Before Shae could blink, Aidan was on top of her, their lips pressing together in the most perfect way. Shae sighed against his mouth, sinking deeper into the couch cushions as he moved his body over hers. She moved her arms from between their chests and wrapped them around Aidan's shoulders.

The tips of her fingers found the soft shaved hair at the base of his neck as his hands started moving down her sides, over her hips. She could still taste the sweetness of the dessert she'd made on his lips, the chocolate and the whipped cream, and oh god it was nice.

A soft whimper escaped her lips as his knee gently nudged her thighs apart. A moment later, his hand slid between her legs. Shae couldn't remember the last time she'd been touched like this, over her clothes. She'd forgotten how good it felt, in the strangest way. Her hips started moving on their own, brazenly pushing her clit harder and harder against his fingers through the layers of her clothes. Her underwear had been wet since the moment he kissed her before they stepped on the ice. Now her arousal was seeping from her pussy, easing that particular ache and making it so much worse.

She made a desperate noise and silently promised to make

Aidan all the desserts he wanted when his hand slipped past the waistband of her thick leggings and into her underwear.

"Shit, Shae," he groaned on a whisper as soon as he touched the slick wetness coating Shae's clit. He was right back to kissing her then, his tongue feeling so, so good against hers. Shae let him feel her, finding his way to her entrance and then back to her clit before pressing two fingers inside of her. Shae broke the kiss and pressed her head back into the throw pillow. The most pathetic noise came out of her mouth and she didn't care one bit. There was an orgasm just out of her reach, she could feel it. Aidan's fingers were pure magic, but she wasn't ready yet.

"Aidan. Aidan, wait."

"Yeah?" He pulled back a little, propping his elbow up on the back of the cushions. His other hand was still in her pants.

"I love what you're doing here. I like it a lot, but I want to switch gears before I come all over your hand."

"Yeah, sure, sure." Shae realized how worked up Aidan was when he removed his hand and sat back. The light from the TV showed just how red he was turning and he was a little out of breath.

Shae sat up as well, adjusting her shirt. "How about I take off my clothes, you take off your clothes, you tell me you definitely brought condoms with you and then we reunite somewhere in the middle. Of the couch."

"We can do that."

"Okay."

Like complete fools, they both jumped up and rushed to opposite ends of the couch and started pulling off their clothes. Shae didn't realize they were racing until they both started laughing. She finished first, then grabbed her throw blanket off the back of the couch and spread it down the cushions. She was about to sit and tease Aidan for taking so long when he turned around to face her and reached for his pants, which he'd kicked under the coffee table.

That's when she caught sight of his erection. She'd felt and seen the bulge in his jeans when they were kissing just moments before. She'd *seen* it on her phone at the beginning of the week, but there was a big—*BIG*—difference between seeing a penis that size on her phone and being a few feet away from it in real life.

"Wait. Hold on," Shae blurted out. She waved her hands in the air, driving her request home. Aidan stood up straight and then froze. He had something in his hand, probably condoms.

"What?"

Shae sunk down on the couch, her mouth hanging open. "Come here. I want to look at your—if you don't mind. The pictures just—"

"No, I don't mind."

Aidan came closer, standing with this leg pressed against Shae's knee as she reached up to take what she could of him in her hand. His dick was actually very nice, aside from the massive size. Nice even coloring, prominently displayed veins down its length, but not in a scary way. She thought she might stroke him a little bit, if only she could wrap her fingers around his considerable girth.

She just held onto him, running her thumb over the head of his cock. Shae looked up at Aidan as he let out a deep breath through his nose. He still had his glasses on. It was too dark to see just how green his eyes were. That didn't stop her from melting as he gazed back at her.

"Aidan. Jesus Christ—I'm sorry. I just—" He reached up and smoothed a piece of her hair behind her ear. She nearly shivered at his touch.

"We don't have to—"

"No! No! I want to!" Shae said, nodding her head like she's just been gifted the greatest toy ever and then asked if she wanted to give it away. "I definitely want to. I'm just shocked." Her focus was back on his erection as she gently released him, then ran her fingertip down the length of him to the dark red curls at the base of his hips.

"I know I'm not small."

Shae looked up at the thick sound clouding his voice. "God, I'm making you uncomfortable. I'm such an ass. Sorry."

Instead of packing it in for the night and telling Shae to call him when she was done being so socially awkward, Aidan responded with a soft laugh. Shae's gaze held his as he lightly gripped her chin and leaned down to kiss her on the mouth. Her nerves settled again as soon as their lips touched. She felt like she was floating when he finally pulled away.

"Shae, trust me. You're not being an ass. Whatever you're thinking right now, just know that I will tell you if you're making me feel any kind of uncool. You're not."

"Okay. I've just never seen a penis this big before in real life. It's a little alarming, in a good way." Her voice came out steady that time, even though she was ridiculously embarrassed by the whole truth behind that confession. Yes, she'd seen other penises before, but Harvin had been her first and only. She'd been so concerned with not ending up with another asshole or a murderer that she hadn't really given any thought to moving on to bigger and possibly better in the penis department.

"Without...sounding like too much of a sleaze," Aidan said slowly. "It's probably best if we go at your pace." He sunk down on the carpet between Shae's legs. He was so tall, even on his knees they were almost eye to eye. Shae held back another shiver as he ran his thumb across her lower lip.

"You want me to level the playing field a little?"

"Sure, yeah," Shae said with a nervous laugh of her own. She watched Aidan closely as he gently took her breasts in his palms. He held her gaze as he dipped his head and ran his tongue over each of her nipples.

"Your body is the most impressive I've ever seen in real life."

Shae decided to take the compliment for what it was worth and just enjoy the feel of Aidan's extremely capable hands playing with her breasts. He leaned down again and took her right nipple into his mouth. She was already so turned on, the sensation quickly became too much. She threaded her fingers through his hair and pulled him closer. Aidan continued to kiss his way up her chest to her neck. One of his thumbs was still having its way with her nipple, but the other hand gently curved around the side of her neck. He placed another soft kiss to her lips.

"Tell me what you want," he said quietly. On the screen behind his head, the movie was ending, the happy couple united on Christmas morning, kissing passionately in the middle of an inexplicably empty New York City street. Shae knew he couldn't give her that movie kind of love. And she wasn't even sure she was looking for that level of romance.

"I just want it to be good," she said.

"I think we can manage that." He tilted his head up and kissed her again. "I've been told that it's, uh, easy from behind. Not in the ass!" he said, course correcting with the most hilarious look of horror on his face.

She couldn't control her laughter. "I know what you mean."

"Or on top. It'll give you better control."

"Watch out." Shae waited until Aidan moved out of the way and then moved the coffee table out of the way. Out of the corner of her eye, she saw Aidan ease the condom down his shaft. Shae turned back to the couch and moved the throw blanket to the floor between her feet. She smoothed it out because no one likes carpet burn, then moved to her knees facing the cushions. She glanced over her shoulder and saw Aidan watching her. He was still standing a few feet away, gazing at her with this dark heat in his eyes.

"Come here," she said.

Shae closed her eyes as Aidan moved behind her. She waited to feel the head of his cock pressing into her entrance, but it was Aidan's lips moving over her back as his hand eased over her stomach that had her moaning. His hand continued to explore her lush body, moving back up to her breasts. She'd never begged before. She'd never had to. She begged now. She needed to come and she wanted to come with Aidan's impressive cock inside of her.

"Aidan, please."

He didn't respond. Still, Shae could feel his weight shifting and then she felt the tip of him nudging at her pussy lips. She slid down a little, arching her back and spreading her thighs to give him better access. That seemed to do the trick. He didn't slip inside with ease, not even close. The angle was good though, the position perfect. Shae took him little by little, the slow back and forth of her hips helping him stretch her just right, getting him just to the edge of that deliciously sensitive spot. Her throat contracted, forcing her to swallow the drool that was pooling in her mouth. It had never felt this good. It had never been this slow.

She stopped moving altogether, taking in the feeling of Aidan's hands resting on her waist and the weight of his thick cock throbbing inside her. Her pussy clenched on its own, wanting so much more. He started moving again, but at an excruciatingly slow pace. Shae knew there was at least six more of inches of Aidan's erection to go before she had taken him all the way. She couldn't help herself though. Her hand slipped between her legs and found her clit. She started teasing herself, lightly stroking over the explosive bundle of nerves. A moment too late, she felt that surge of lightning spreading out all over her body.

"Aidan. I'm gonna come—shit." The orgasm slammed into her as she dropped her forehead down on her arm. Shae squeezed her clit between her fingers, drawing her orgasm out and at that moment, Aidan started slowly pumping his hips. Another cry of pleasure slipped from Shae's lips as the sensation doubled down on itself, sending more and more ripples of pleasure all over her body. When she finally felt like she was back on Earth, Aidan had his arms wrapped around her and his lips were pressed against her throat. And every inch of his dick was seated inside of her. Shae let out another deep breath, trying to process how it was possible for him to fit and for it to feel so damn good. She braved the slightest movement and another tremor of delight rolled over her body as her pussy clenched around him again.

"God," she moaned.

"Okay?" Aidan kissed her cheek.

"Yeah. Oh my god. Yes. That was smart. Very smart move." This was what she wanted, for him to touch her without her having to think too much about the how or when or if it would be a good experience. She turned her head just enough so their lips could meet and then Aidan took over, slowly pressing his hips tightly against her ass before withdrawing just a little bit.

After a few minutes, he started to move a little faster, in this amazing deep grinding motion, not the senseless pounding that Shae had become accustomed to. She realized then, as the sound of Aidan's quiet grunts and groans started to fill her ears, that he'd been completely silent as she took the time she needed to adjust to him.

She liked these sounds. She liked hearing him moan. She focused on both their pleasure. His hand cupping her breast and the feeling of his breath on her neck, and she came again. Her body was spent for now, but she wanted Aidan to come too. He'd earned it. She leaned forward on the couch and pressed back on him.

"Shae," he said on a deep grunt and then she felt his dick pulsing inside of her. They stayed pressed together for a few long moments, his chest and stomach and muscular thighs cupping her whole body in a hot embrace.

"If I don't move soon, I might stay like this forever," he said quietly, his voice still strained.

Shae let out a huff of laughter. "Do what you must."

Aidan slowly withdrew and somehow Shae made it onto the couch. Her whole body was liquid, she could barely move. She watched Aidan as he walked into the kitchen and got rid of the condom. When he came back toward the couch, Shae couldn't believe how big his dick was, even semi-erect. She forced herself to stop looking at it and focused on Aidan's face. He stopped next to the coffee table and picked up the spoon that was sticking out of the trifle bowl.

"Do you want to stay the night?" Shae asked as he licked a dollop of chocolate pudding and whipped cream.

"I'll have to leave really early for work, but I'm totally into spending the night. Especially if we watch another Christmas movie."

"You can pick this one."

"Fuck yeah." He took another bite of the trifle, then knelt on the floor beside the couch. Shae was hoping he would kiss her again, but his eyes just wandered over her face as he kept the small distance between their lips. "Was that good?"

"It was very good."

"I'm gonna eat that whole thing," Aidan said, glancing over his shoulder at the remains of the sweet dessert. Shae snorted, then reached up and pushed his glasses a fraction of an inch back up his nose.

✷

Aidan's alarm went off early as fuck, but when he sat up to keep the thing from waking Shae he was shocked to find himself in an empty bed. The rest of their night had been pretty fucking great. He picked out some movie about this woman falling in love with Santa's son who was due to inherit the Claus empire. It was actually a pretty good movie that dealt with some intense themes like parental expectations and fear of failure. Aidan was impressed. They spent another couple of hours naked together on the couch, then moved their party of two to Shae's bed. They both passed out after they realized that Shae could take every inch of his cock in two more positions.

He woke up a few times in the middle of the night, the result of sleeping in a different bed with another person for the first time in a while, and every time he opened his eyes, there was Shae pressed against him, curled up in his arms. They'd known each other for years, but they had only been seeing each other for a week. Didn't change the way Aidan knew he was started to feel. He was falling for Shae.

He hopped out of bed and went looking for his clothes. He found them and Shae in her living room. She was sitting on the couch with a fresh cup of tea in her hand. She was dressed again, wearing some cute pajama pants with cupcakes on them and a Raiders sweatshirt. She greeted him with a warm smile and a good morning as soon as he came around the couch.

"It's pretty early for your day off," he said, stepping into his boxers.

"My sleep cycle is set in stone. I wake up early, enjoy the quiet for a few hours, then go back to bed until noon. It's a good way to spend a day off. Do you want some breakfast? I have bacon and eggs and croissants." Aidan thought back to that massive bowl of brownies and whipped creamed he'd destroyed the night before.

"I usually have breakfast after I work out. I'm gonna head to the gym, then grab breakfast on the way in. I have the shittiest metabolism ever. I skip a day and this all starts going to shit," he said, patting his flat abs that stopped being so flat the minute he quit playing sports.

"Ah, I see. You did work off a good bit of that trifle last night."

"It was totally worth it."

He finished getting dressed, then leaned over the couch to kiss Shae. If he had morning breath, she didn't say anything about it.

"When can I see you again?" he asked.

"I have a standing engagement with my friends and my cousin tonight and I'm gonna be slammed this Friday and Saturday—"

"And Sunday is your Christmas Eve get together."

"Yeah and you should definitely come to that. My cousin's fiancé is a fireworks expert. He'll probably blow up something cool."

"Sounds like a plan," Aidan replied, chuckling a little.

Christmas wasn't exactly a fireworks holiday. "Wednesday night sound good? You can come to my place and I'll make you the one thing I'm sure I won't burn."

"That sounds great."

"Bring a change of clothes just in case."

"Oh. Sure." Shae stood and walked Aidan to the door when he turned to her one last time.

"I had a great time last night, even though you're a terrible ice skater," he joked.

"Hey! I kinda got the hang of it."

"I'll see you." He leaned and kissed her one last time before walking toward the elevator. Lovesick punk that he was, he couldn't help but turn around to just take the sight of her in one last time before he had to get on with his day. Aidan didn't know what he expected when he turned to get a glimpse of her, but he caught something before her million-watt smile spread across her cheeks and she tossed up her hand in a little wave. Shae had that look on her face again. Something was bothering her again. Something was holding her back.

Six

ear Santa, Am I doing this right...?

Aidan slammed the door to his car shut, then switched his phone to his other hand so he could get a better grip on the box of bagels he was carrying. His sister, Emily, answered with her typical cheery greeting.

"'Sup punk. It's early for you, isn't it?"

"Hey. You're not busy, are you? I need advice. About a girl. A woman. This woman I started seeing." Aidan had made it through his workout and miles of bullshit Los Angeles traffic just fine. That didn't keep the image of Shae's anxious face from playing over and over in his head. He'd had such a great night with her, he should have been skipping and whistling his way out of Shae's apartment building.

He could have sworn she'd had just as good a time, but that tell-tale look was there and he couldn't ignore it. Yeah, it felt too early in whatever was going on between them to look for problems. It was also never early enough to take notice of something, a tiny red flag that Aidan knew could turn into a full-on disaster zone surrounded by lights and sirens if it went unchecked.

"Oh, seeing a *woman*? We're maturing. Well done, Aid."

"Shut up."

"I'm just messing with you," Emily laughed. They were only three years apart, but she'd taken the plunge into aspects of adulthood that he couldn't wrap his mind around when he was still in college. Now she was a working mom with three kids and a husband who she actually communicated with really well. If there was anyone he could get relationship advice from, it was his sister. "Okay, what's the deal?"

"Her name's Shae. She owns a pretty successful bakery," he said with a bit of pride that he had absolutely no claim to. "We used to work together. She was married, now she's divorced and we ran into each other on MATCHED."

"Okay. What seems to be the problem—shit!" his sister yelped.

"You okay?"

"Yeah. I just stepped on a lego and then stubbed my toe. Shit." Aidan waited, trying not to laugh as his sister rattled off another string of curses, mumbling to herself about his slob of a nephew. "If you ever have kids, make cleaning up their toys a part of their play time. At least once a week, I almost break my neck stepping on something or tripping over something else."

"I need to get past a third date before I consider what to do about my future children, but I will keep that in mind."

"Sorry. Woman troubles. You have them. Go on."

"Not exactly troubles. I just don't know how to handle a situation, if it is a situation. She's very funny. Very sweet. But sometimes out of nowhere, she just kind of shuts down or—it feels like she's keeping stuff from me because she thinks I'm going to reject her in some way. She usually opens up about whatever it is with a little encouragement, but—I don't know. I feel she's holding back something and making assumptions about me and how I'm going to react to her all at the same time. That's the best way I can describe it." Hopefully he was making some sense.

"You said she was divorced?"

"Yeah."

"Could be stuff with her ex. Divorces aren't like regular break ups and she's dating again? If Dave and I split up, I don't even know how I'd get back into dating again. Do you know anything about the ex or why they broke up?"

"Yeah. Without going into too much detail, he blamed her for some shit she had no control over and then they got divorced."

"Ah, okay. So the ex was a dick. Yeah, she's probably still a little wounded in the heart department. She might be having rejection issues, which is totally understandable, especially if her ex was a dick."

Aidan didn't like the sound of that. "She did say they kind of had a rough split, over some rough stuff." Aidan and his ex-girl-friend had been pretty serious, but they weren't close to getting married and they definitely had never fought over bringing chil-dren into the world. He had no idea what that must have been like for Shae.

"I mean, I'm saying this knowing the small bit of information you've given me."

"Yeah."

"My advice? If you want to keep hanging out with her—"

"I do! I like her a lot." Aidan almost shocked himself with how true those words were. He'd been hanging on to some sort of feel-ings for Shae for a long time. The short time they'd spent together only confirmed his suspicions. Shae was someone he could defi-nitely seem himself with.

"Okay, well just keep hanging out with her. Let her know she can always talk to you about what she's feeling."

Aidan laughed as he leaned against the wall next to the eleva-tor. "That won't be a problem. She's honest and so vocal with that honesty that I think she's embarrassing herself."

Emily's own chuckle came back through the phone. "Well if she's awkward and dealing with baggage, be extra nice to her."

"I will."

"Don't worry, Aid. Things will work themselves out. Be good to her and if it feels like it's not working out romantically it's okay to step away too, without being a dick to her of course. There should be two happy people in a relationship."

"Good point." Not that Aidan was considering bailing on Shae because of her clear hesitations. His sister did have a point though. "I'm going to head up to my office."

"Okay cool. Should I call you back later and you can ask me how my day is going, you little shit?"

Aidan let out a burst of laughter as he turned and pressed the up button with his elbow. The thing usually took forever. For once the door sprang open. Aidan stuck his foot over the threshold to keep it from closing.

"How's your day doing, dude?"

"Well as soon as my toe stops throbbing, I think it'll be right on track. Got three orders in this morning, so that'll keep me busy for the week."

"Oh nice." His sister and Shae had more in common than he realized. Emily also owned her own small business making custom jewelry.

"Yeah, I love marriage proposal season. Maybe one day I'll make something for one of your women friends."

"Yeah, maybe. On that note."

"Yeah, yeah. I'll talk to you soon."

After he made sure to include hellos to Dave and the kids, he ended the call and stepped into the elevator. His sister was right. He just needed to treat Shae right and let her be herself. Hopefully in time she would see that there wasn't a single thing about her that he found to be weird or strange or even remotely unattractive. He'd already brought her flowers, so more might be overkill. Maybe there was another way to show how he was feeling about her. He left the elevator, brainstorming ways to further woo her. He made it two feet into the office before Matt was on him, almost knocking the box of bagels out of his hands.

"Tell me you went to Sweet Creams."

"No man, get off me. I got bagels. They're closed on Mondays anyway."

Matt backed off, with this sour look on his face like Aidan had just crushed his wildest dreams. "What's the point of you dating this chick if you don't bring in the highest quality of baked good every day?"

Aidan set the bagels and his messenger bag down on his desk, then adjusted his glasses and leveled Matt with a serious stare. "Are you out there dating women just for free food? Are ya, buddy?"

"You say it like that's a bad idea. The girl likes you. The girl likes to bake. And I personally think I should benefit from these truths in your budding relationship."

"How about you enjoy the bagels I'm not going to ask you to pay me back for and we never again talk about any woman I'm dating in terms of how they might benefit you."

"You're going to get me banned from Sweet Creams if I don't stop talking about this, aren't you?" Matt said, his face going slack.

"Hadn't thought of that, but now that you mention it..."

Matt put up his hands in surrender and started backing toward their office's small kitchen. "Hey man, I know when to stop rocking the boat."

"Thanks."

Aidan didn't realize he kind of wanted to punch Matt in the face until he had to relax to dig up his phone. Sometime in the seconds between the elevator and Matt's ambush, he'd missed a text from Shae.

See. Back in bed.

Aidan felt himself smile as he looked at the pictures she'd

texted him. She was back in bed with the covers pulled up to her chin, flashing a huge smile. She had her hair wrapped up in a shiny, black bandana with some of her curls springing out of the top.

> Looking good.

> Enjoy your day off.

Oh I will.

I still have the nudes you sent me.

When Shae sent a Boomerang gif of herself biting her lip and waggling her eyebrows, Aidan's laugh echoed through their office

> Just promise me you won't hurt yourself.

I'll do my best.

"What's so funny?" Matt asked as he came back to their desks. "Nothing. Eat your bagel."

✳

Shae needed keys to Keira and Daniel's house, just for the winter. It was another freezing cold Monday night, standing on their porch waiting for Keira to answer the door. Okay, maybe Shae was cranky as hell for some unexplainable reason and she was taking it out on the thirty extra seconds it was taking one of them to respond to the sound of their doorbell.

She'd spent the whole day bouncing between feeling pure elation and gut-wrenching dread. Spending time Aidan was great. Sex with Aidan was even better. Between the ice skating, his adorable commentary during not one, but two different Christmas romance flicks and the sex—Shae had to keep the sex in mind because it was that good— she wanted to smile whenever she thought about him.

But for some unknown shitty reason, the butterflies in her stomach would suddenly turn into rabid zombie reindeer, pummeling her already rattled nerves. She'd spent most of the day trying to figure out why and all she could think about was Harvin and that just made her feel worse. And thinking about thinking about Harvin made her feel even worse.

She took a break from the shitty feelings to bake some massive cookies and that had helped a little. Still, she wasn't able to shake the icky feelings that had almost ruined her day off. The only thing that had saved it was the texts she'd exchanged with Aidan. And the nudes she still had of him on her phone. The nudes she might have referred to before she got in the shower.

She might have been thinking of one of the better shots on her phone when Keira's front door finally opened. Her fiancé, Daniel, who looked like a male supermodel on a bad day, stood on the other side of the threshold.

"Hey Shae. Come on in."

"Hey." Shae stepped inside and gave her cousin-in-law-to-be a quick hug. "Did you get your cupcakes? We had to wrestle Meegan away from them."

"I did," Daniel said with his handsome smile. He reached out with his prosthesis and took the bag containing this week's desserts out of her hand. "They were great. You ever think about selling them?"

"Ha! Good one. Keira's marrying a natural born comedian," Shae said, shaking her head. She shrugged off her jacket and followed him into the kitchen where Keira was stirring what smelled like chili. The house was still decorated to accommodate Santa and his whole village, but some Guns N' Roses song was playing over their stereo system.

"Hey!" Keira set down her wooden spoon and crossed the kitchen to give Shae a hug.

"I'll be in the bedroom." Daniel leaned between them and kissed them each on the forehead before handing Keira the bag Shae had brought with her.

"Thanks, baby."

"Yeah, thanks babe," Shae added.

"No problem." He winked at Keira and disappeared down the hallway. Shae almost asked him to come back. She could ask him some questions about his recent work trip. Get the latest updates from the world of pyrotechnics. Anything to stop the inevitable conversation she knew she was going to have with Keira and then with the rest of the girls when they showed up. Of course, Keira dove right in.

"So? How are you feeling?"

Shae sighed and let her shoulders drop. "I don't even know."

"Well, two dates in a week is pretty good, so clearly you don't hate him." She set down the bag on the table and surveyed its contents, her face lighting up.

"Yeah, chocolate chip cookie sundaes. A crowd favorite," Shae said.

"Your cookies are the best. I know that sounds gross, but I stand by my statement."

"I am good at what I do."

"Okay, so talk to me. You were panicking the other day. You saw him last night and I'm assuming you didn't kick him to the curb," Keira said as she shoved the vanilla ice cream in their already packed freezer.

"No. Absolutely not. I like him a lot."

"But...?"

The sound of the doorbell saved Shae from having to answer.

"Let me grab that."

"'Kay." Shae hung tight while Keira went to open the front door. Part of her wanted to text Aidan just to see what he was up to. Which should have made complete sense. She did like him, a lot. When you like someone, you can text them whenever. She reached into her back pocket to pull out her phone right as Erica, Sarah, Joanna and Meegan all came spilling into the room. Shae was swallowed up with hugs and hellos and repeated confirmations that she had indeed brought a fresh baked dessert.

Erica was complaining about her boss's perfume and Shae was totally on board with that thread of conversation, but Sarah—the traitor—turned to her, eyes bright with excitement.

"Erica, I care. I really do, but Shae is now dating a super hot dude and I want details." She spun around and grabbed Shae by the shoulders. "Okay, let's hear it. You. The hot boy. Let's hear it."

"Yeah. Dish, dish, dish," Joanna said.

"And then show us the nudes," Meegan added.

"Um, no. Let's see. We've been on two dates since last I've seen you all. Both dates were very fun. He's very sweet. I told you he dropped by the store with flowers."

"But have you fucked him yet?!" Meegan whined.

"We had adult intercourse last night. It was great. I'm not saying anything more than that and no, I'm not showing you the nudes. I already deleted them." Which was a lie.

"Ah, man!" Meegan and Erica both said.

"We're going out again this week." She didn't mention that she'd invited Aidan to Friendsmas Eve 'cause she knew they'd take that as a sign that she was developing feelings she wasn't sure of yet. She'd casually mention it in the group chat a couple days before. "Enough about me. Someone's getting married in less than two weeks." She turned to Keira and flashed her a bright smile. "Let's focus on the bride."

"Eeeee!" Meegan squealed. "Are you excited?"

"Yeah, I—"

"Oh um, I still haven't found a dress," Erica confessed. Keira only asked that the bridal party wear silver, but the plus-size selection in silver formal wear ranged from something close to a skintight mini dress to clearly-mother-of-the-bride matronly. Luckily Shae knew just where to shop.

"Here. I got you covered." She pulled up her phone and brought up the XXI And UP website. "They have three similar styles in silver. I got this one." She showed Erica a long sleeve, knee length sequin dress. Then clicked over to a similar floor length dress with spaghetti straps and a sexy slit that rose to mid thigh. "Get this one."

Erica grabbed Shae's phone out of her hand. "Oh my god, that's perfect. I'm texting this to myself right now."

As the wedding chatter continued, Shae filled her chili bowl and faded into the background. Keira's upcoming nuptials were important. Shae's confounding stress about Aidan was not. She just had to sort out the butterflies from the rabid zombie reindeer and once she did, she knew everything would be fine.

✳

Santa or Frosty or whoever was just fucking with her. All Shae had to do was go to work and bake. That's all she had to do, but no. The rapid reindeer had relocated from her stomach to her brain. How could someone worry so much about texting a guy? Hours, she'd spent literally hours, getting herself worked up about wanting to text Aidan and not texting Aidan too much. Shae got herself so worked up that she ruined at least two batches of chocolate and three batches of caramel just thinking and waiting for Aidan's "well this has been fun, but you're kind of annoying me" text that never came.

Every time one of them had a free second, they were asking each other about their day. Aidan felt bad about the ruined confections even though he had no idea why Shae had let them go to shit. And then she'd ask him how things were going in the world of online real estate. He sounded stressed, but happy. Shae completely understood. Starting your own business was no joke. She'd had her own adventure finding a storefront she could afford, even with a healthy loan from her parents and her grandmother.

One afternoon when Aidan sent her a picture of their newest listing, she knew he'd been bitten by that independent business bug. It was a simple craftsman with smoke damage and bad plumbing and electric, exactly the sort of listing they needed for their site. Shae felt herself smiling as she looked through the interior shots, thinking of the first batch of cupcakes she'd made in her very own professional kitchen. She hoped that PrimeRealty lived up to the dreams Aidan had for it.

The few nights they were apart, texting with him seemed like the easiest thing to do after a long day. Easier when those texts quickly turned to sexts and Shae found herself getting off to the simple, but ridiculously hot messages from this ridiculously hot guy she was seeing. The next morning it would start all over again. Aidan doing laps through her head, on the back of one of those rapid zombie reindeers, flustering Shae to the point where she knew all she could do was breathe and bake. She had to do something about it and she would. Soon. As soon as she saw Aidan one more time.

Date night arrived, and now that she was standing across from him she realized what the problem was. Shae liked Aidan. A lot and not in the way that made her feel light and fluffy and good, like the economy was suddenly going to bounce back and nations around the globe would start to practice the true meaning of democracy.

No, her feelings for Aidan made her feel completely out of her element and out of control. When she got to his apartment she assured herself it was just butterflies. That worked until she laid eyes on Aidan standing in his doorway, still in a dress shirt, sleeves rolled up and an actual "Kiss the Cook" apron draped around his neck. Shae held up a brown Sweet Creams bag in her hand.

"I brought lemon bars."

"Hey. Come on in."

"It smells great in here," she said, setting down the sweets she'd made just for their night together.

"Not sure I've had those before—don't take off your coat just yet." Shae froze and shrugged her jacket back onto her shoulders.

"I thought I was a slow cooking genius, but my stew needs another hour," he said as he closed the door behind her, then led her into his small galley kitchen that looked like it had seen better days. There was evidence of his culinary skills all over the counter. Bits of red potatoes, the ends of carrots and celery, and the fat that had been trimmed off of a whole lot of beef. Shae smiled as she glimpsed an unopened can of biscuits on the edge of the counter near the fridge.

"Are we going somewhere in that hour?" Shae asked and then almost fainted when she turned and saw the way Aidan's face lit up at her question.

"Yeah. There's something I want to show you."

"Okay."

Shae waited while Aidan shed his apron and grabbed his own coat, then pulled out his phone. "Let me just set a timer. O...kay. You ready?"

Shae swallowed and forced herself to smile. "Yeah, let's go." Her whole body warmed as Aidan took her hand and led her down to the parking garage where his car was waiting. After they pulled out on the road, he reached over and took her hand again. Shae looked at his face as he explained where they were going and all she could think about was the feeling of his fingers intertwined with hers. Then all she could think about was kissing him. Shae wanted Aidan so bad she knew nothing good could come from it.

SEVEN

D*ear Santa, Please save me from myself...*

If things kept up this way, Shae was going to let Aidan plan the rest of their dates for the rest of their lives. Not that they would be together for the rest of their lives, but she didn't hate the way he seemed to know exactly how to dial up the romance and splendor. There were several places to view over-the-top residential holiday decorations, Candy Cane Lane in Torrance being the most well-known in the county, but Aidan took Shae to this small cluster of houses in Beverlywood that had really outdone itself.

There were a few other looky-loos cruising the neighborhood. Luckily it was a Thursday night and they were able to drive around unencumbered to check out the elaborate red, white and blue theme that stretched from one end of the block to the other. Aidan explained that during the weekend the house in the center blasted a few holiday favorites early in the evening and the lights on each house blinked to the beat. Shae only knew two of her neighbors. She couldn't imagine coordinating something that spectacular with so many people.

Aidan held onto her hand the whole time she stared out the window in awe. Thousands and thousands of lights. Thanks to traffic, they couldn't spend too long taking it all in, but Shae didn't care. The neighborhood was so beautiful.

She'd driven around Los Angeles plenty of times with her family over the years to check out the lights. Harvin had killed the tradition, choosing instead to spend time at her ex-brother-in-law's house watching football and talking basketball. Not that Shae had anything against sports. Her ex just had a certain way of making the holidays...not fun.

When Aidan's thumb gently stroked over hers, she forced her mind back to the present, pushing Harvin and his bullshit to the dark pit in the corner of her thoughts where he belonged.

"What do you think?" Aidan asked.

"It's amazing."

"One day I'm going to buy a house. One that needs extensive renovations," he laughed. Shae joined him with a smile. "And then I'll figure out how to hang enough lights that you can see the place from orbit. Also, there will be enough room in the backyard for a bouncy castle."

"I'm sure your kids will love that," Shae teased.

"Who said anything about kids? Have you been in a bouncy castle lately?"

"Have you?"

Aidan nodded with a sort of hilarious cockiness. "Oh yeah. Last summer at my nephew's birthday party. Time of my fucking life."

"Well, you get that house and your lights and your bouncy castle. I'll stop by with cookies and lemonade and make sure you haven't twisted your ankle."

"Never. I'm all about bouncy castle safety." Suddenly Aidan leaned over and kissed Shae on the mouth. She returned the kiss, pressing closer to him for just a moment. Her eyes blinked opened when he pulled away.

"Let's head back. I have to check on my roast."

Shae snorted. "Okay."

When they got back to his place, Aidan insisted that Shae let him serve her. He didn't have a dining table so they ate the delicious beef stew at a loosely constructed coffee table made of plywood and cinder blocks in front of his television. Aidan pulled up his Netflix account and selected "Fireplace for Your Home S1 : E1 Crackling Yule Log Fireplace," the scene perfect for a romantic evening in. They ate in silence for the most part, enjoying the sounds of the Christmas instrumentals and the crackling fire.

When Shae was done, she set down her plate and turned to face Aidan. He was still working on his large second helping.

"Do you have any plans for New Year's Eve?" she asked.

He swallowed and then set down his plate. "Not yet. What do you have going on?"

"A wedding, actually. My cousin Keira is getting married."

"Oh, cool. Where are they having it?"

"Malibu. Brother of the groom is a big actor. He's on that show *Galaxis*. J.D. Song?"

"Oh, I know him. He just got cast in some superhero movie."

"Yeah. He arranged the venue and everything. We'll be spending the night out there."

"That sounds like it'll be a good time."

"Yeah, it should be fun." Shae bit her lip, toying with the idea of cashing in her last minute plus one that Keira would sure grant her, but she chickened out. "So, dinner was great."

"That's some high praise I'll hold on to."

"Well, slow down now. I know you didn't make the biscuits from scratch. Pull that off and I'll hand you the blue ribbon."

"I'll have to get back in the kitchen and practice."

"I'll be waiting patiently for your presentation."

He winked at her as he reached for their plates, grabbing and taking them back to the kitchen. "You want anything else to drink?"

Shae eyed her half-empty glass of wine. "I'm fine. I, uh—um, I have a bag in my car. An overnight bag, if you would like me to stay overnight."

She watched Aidan as he froze for a moment, then slowly set the plates down in the sink. He turned around and ducked to look at her over the small kitchen peninsula. "I would like that very much. You want me to walk down to your car with you? We can grab it now."

"Yeah, let's do that." Shae reached into her purse, grabbed her keys and met Aidan by the door.

"And when we get back, I found something called a Very Merry Christmas." He grabbed his own keys off a handy hook next to the jamb, then held the door open for her.

"You're hooked on the holiday cheesiness, aren't you?"

"I am and it's all your fault." Aidan took her hand and let her lead him out to the street where she left her car.

As they walked, they talked about the weird, fluctuating weather and she mentioned that his work buddy Matt had ordered from Sweet Creams twice in the last two days. She laughed, trying to hide her nerves when Aidan told her that Matt had thought their newfound relationship meant he was getting free and frequent baked goods. Shae almost slipped and said that she only baked for free for people she loved, but she managed to swallow the words, laughing instead at the idea that she would trade Matt's money for his good graces.

When they stepped back into Aidan's apartment, Shae made for the couch to settle in for another romantic Christmas instant classic. She made it maybe two feet before she felt Aidan's fingers gently wrap around her wrist.

She turned quickly. "What's up..." The words died in her mouth when she saw the look on Aidan's face. She went to him without question, her arms going around his shoulders as his hand went to her ass, pulling her closer, their lips coming together perfectly. Soon she was kissing him deeper, begging his tongue to tease hers, which he pleasantly obliged. Shae knew she could spend all night like this, just standing in his kitchen, kissing and kissing and kissing until she couldn't breathe.

"I'm sorry. I've been wanting to do that all week. You wanna watch the movie?"

"No."

Shae watched him carefully as his gaze roamed over her face. She didn't miss the way his eyes lingered on her lips. He reached up and lightly smoothed the hair at her temple away from her face. "Do you want to take this to my bedroom?"

"Yes."

"Come on." Shae followed Aidan to the back of the apartment. His bedroom was simple, but clean and it smelled like freshly washed clothes. Just his bed on a high metal frame, no headboard, a dresser and an armchair draped with a pair of jeans and gym shorts. He had nothing on the walls except a Michigan license plate she saw hanging over his door when she turned back to face him. Aidan was already unbuttoning his shirt.

Shae figured she should follow suit. Sinking down on his bed, she reached down and started unlacing her boots. Next time, maybe next time, they'd get to the real down and dirty foreplay. She'd see how much of him she could fit in her mouth and he'd return the favor. Now though, Shae just wanted pure sex. She wanted Aidan inside of her. She kicked off her boots and yanked down her leggings and underwear.

By the time she got her shirt and bra off, Aidan had slid a condom into place. In perfect sync, Aidan climbed on top of her, kissing her lips just as Shae shuffled back into the center of the bed. For now, kissing and feeling his muscular bare chest pressing against her swollen nipples was foreplay enough. Shae was already soaking wet. With skill, Aidan's finger slipped between her legs. She was more than ready for him. Her hand slid onto his, pushing his fingers deeper inside her pussy, grinding the heel of his hand harder against her clit. A pathetic whimper moved from her parted lips to his as they kissed and kissed.

Shae's other hand found its way between their bodies, brushing Aidan's arm as she wrapped her fingers around his thick erection. She was so close to guiding him inside of her and letting him take control as he moved on top of her, but there was something she wanted more. Shae pulled back a bit, breaking their kiss and watching Aidan's face as his eyes opened. He was in the same trance she was, drunk on lust, warmed from the inside out. Or at least she liked to think he was.

"What's up?" he said, his breath a little out of sync.

Shae smiled and kissed him one more time. "I want to be on top."

"We can do that," he said. "We can definitely do that." Fingers let slip and they then untangled their limbs from one another, giving Shae the space she needed to move. She crawled to the foot of the bed, out of the way so Aidan had plenty of space to roll onto his back and stretch out. Shae crawled over her him, pausing just long enough to run her tongue up the length of his erection. She didn't care much for the taste of the rubber, but even through the sheath she could feel the heat of Aidan's cock, matched by the heat in his gaze as he looked down at her. His hand gently cupped her cheek. It was such a tender touch, Shae couldn't stop herself from turning her head and brushing a soft kiss to his palm.

He kept his hand on her skin as she moved up his body. When her hips were hovering perfectly above his, Shae watched Aidan as he moved his hand lower. She felt his knuckles brush her inner thigh and then she felt the head of his cock teasing her entrance. The wet proof of her arousal was more than enough to help ease the first inch or so of him in. He released his dick and looked into Shae's eyes.

"Go as slow as you need to."

"Okay," she replied. She'd barely moved, but she already felt out of breath. The anticipation had her heart racing. Bracing herself with her hand just above Aidan's shoulders, Shae gently pressed her hips back. Her body instantly began to shiver. He was so big, but the slow stretch of her pussy around his girth felt so damn good. Shae closed her eyes and turned off her mind, letting her body chase the pleasure it desperately craved. The position was perfect. After a few slow moments, she'd taken every inch of him. Grinding her hips against his, Shae rode him hard and slow.

"Is it good?" Shae knew he wasn't being arrogant. He genuinely wanted to know, she could hear it in his voice. He wanted her to enjoy this.

"Yes." There was no question of whether or not she was going to come, it was just a matter of how long she could hold off before an orgasm overcame her. The harder she tried to put it off, the more her hips moved. Tiny tremors started to ripple over her body and she knew she was a goner. Her eyes opened at the feeling of Aidan's fingers brushing over her breast. He looked into her eyes as his tongue jutted out and teased her nipple. He did it twice more, flicking a trail of slippery wetness over the brown tip, before drawing it into his mouth and sucking gently.

The short hairs in his mustache tickled her skin for a brief moment before he opened his lips wider and sucked a little harder. That was all it took. Shae's hips ground down hard against his pelvis, driving his cock in a perfectly firm press against the walls of her cunt. She came hard, pressing her forehead against Aidan's. His arms wrapped around her body, holding her close as she rode out her orgasm.

When she could breathe a little again, he started to move.

✴

Shae couldn't sleep. Aidan was awake too, probably for different reasons though. They both lay awake in his bed, looking at the ceiling with their bodies still intertwined. Aidan ran his fingers down Shae's side. She had a little roll that sometimes made her self-conscious, but she didn't mind when Aidan touched her there. Her fingers trailed the soft hair on his stomach. Her anxiety was at bay for a moment, but Shae felt like she was watching the clock, just counting down the seconds until she'd used her peace and calm all up.

"So you have your nudes. You have a man who can wield a slow cooker like no other. What else do you want in a relationship?"

And there it was. Shae suddenly felt her eyes stinging. This is exactly what she *didn't* want, to have to think about her feelings, especially when she was with Aidan. It was too much, too overwhelming to try and wrap her mind around. She swallowed, stopping the tears from touching the corners of her eyes.

"I don't know." Her body was vibrating with anxious tension. She quickly sat up. "I am wide awake."

"I'm surprised," Aidan chuckled as his hand slipped over her thigh. "You did say a good orgasm usually knocked you out. Either I'm doing a terrible job—"

"No! No. You did a great job. A great job. I mean, that was some good stuff. Trust me, I am a terrible liar. If it was bad, I would have rolled off you and army crawled out of here naked just to get away." The sound of Aidan's burst of laughter calmed her nerves. They just needed to keep talking about things that had nothing to do with their actual feelings and she would be fine.

"Good to know a rejection from you will be really in your face. There's no ambiguity with naked army crawl escape."

"Yeah, you'd know." She toyed with the edge of the sheet, that sourness in her stomach rising again. Why couldn't she just enjoy this?

"Hey," Aidan said softly. "You okay?"

"Yeah, I'm okay. I'm good. Actually..." Shae gave him a half-hearted smile, then tapped her temple. "A lot going on up here. Cursed with an overactive mind."

"Is there any way I can help calm it?"

"I mean, you could go down on me," Shae said. She was joking of course. Aidan chose to ignore her sarcastic quip though. He shot her a sinful look and then gently nudged her on her back. "Aidan, no—I was kidding."

He looked up at her, his head inches away from going under the covers. She froze at the intent in his eyes. He was not playing around.

"Do you want me to stop?" Shae shook her head. She'd be a fool to turn him down. "Just relax," he said. Seconds later, his head and shoulders were between her legs and his tongue was slowly moving over her clit.

Shae managed to will her body to settle into the sheets and just enjoy the magical way his mouth worked, but in the back of her head Shae knew one day this thing between them would end. Aidan would eventually come to some unfavorable conclusion about her and he would walk. She knew it, but that didn't stop her from thinking of how used to all this she could get. She could be with Aidan Meyer, really be with him, and that scared the shit out of her.

★

Shae needed to get a fucking grip. On edge was the only way she could describe the way she'd been feeling since she told the girls that Aidan would be coming to their Friendmas Eve celebration. They were all so excited to meet him. Shae knew it would be fine. Aidan was incredibly sweet and an absolute people person. She knew he'd charm the pants off her friends and Keira. Didn't help her relax one bit. It had been so long since she'd introduced anyone she liked to her inner circle. Surely that was reason enough for her heart rate to be up somewhere around one million beats per second.

She'd been the first to arrive at her cousin's house. Filled with too much anxious energy to sit home and wait until the party actually started, she headed over early and baked an extra batch of cookies in Keira and Daniel's kitchen while they finished setting up the backyard. Now the party was in full swing. The girls were all there, Daniel's buddies from Fire in the Sky Pyrotechnics. Keira's friends from work, Grant and Armando and their girlfriends Violet and Nailah. Darby's husband had to work a final shift with FedEx, so she'd decided to tag along.

When Aidan arrived, she did her best not to hide in the bathroom. Introducing him around had been a special kind of agony. She's tripped over her words a few times, but Aidan graciously threw her a life preserver and started introducing himself, leaving their relationship perfectly grey with the simple words "I'm here with Shae."

Aidan hadn't left her side all night. At every opportunity he was touching her in some way. Holding her hand, resting his arm around her shoulder. During the White Elephant gift exchange, he'd gamed Daniel's friend Mike into giving him the light-up toy microphone Shae wanted just so he could slip it to her once the festivities ended. Aidan was the perfect holiday party date and while she was enjoying her time with him, something still felt off and she knew he could feel it too.

Finally he pulled her out to the front foyer. It was darker and quieter there and Shae finally felt like she could think. "How are you holding up?" he asked with a kind smile.

"Oh, fine." And then for the first time in ages she lied. "Keira's wedding is literally in a week and we still have a ton more to to do."

"Are you handling the cake?"

"Yeah, but it's just a little one tier set up for them to cut during the pictures. We're doing a dessert bar. Most big cakes go to waste once they're cut up."

"There's so much to dessert management that I have to learn."

"You will, in time."

"I'd just like to point out that we are under the mistletoe," he said. Shae looked up and sure enough a little bunch of green leaves clustered with little white berries tied in a red ribbon hung above their heads.

"You'll go to jail if you don't kiss me," she teased, trying to lighten her own mood.

"Yeah, that wouldn't do." Aidan closed the distance between them and a second later their lips met. Shae sighed, her eyes slipping closed as she soaked in the softness of his mouth. A second too late, Shae could feel that they were no longer alone by the front door. Her eyes still closed, Shae could hear telltale clicking sounds from a camera phone.

"So cute!" Erica said as Shae broke the kiss and stepped away, her hand still on Aidan's chest. "See." Erica turned her phone so they could take a look. It was a sickeningly sweet picture. Romance and the spirit of the season captured in one perfect image. Their outfits even looked nice. Shae felt like her whole body was starting to vibrate from the inside out.

"Hey, can you send that to me?" Aidan said.

"Yeah, sure! Here." Shae watched Erica hand him her phone. "Text it to yourself."

"Thanks." Aidan pressed the necessary buttons on the screen and then handed the phone back to Erica. A second later he said, "I sent it to you too."

"Thanks."

"I'll leave you two love birds to it."

"I'm actually going to take off," Aidan told Shae.

"Okay." The party usually went late into the night. Shae would make her way over to her folks' place sometime in the wee hours of the morning and try to catch enough sleep before her mom and grandmother woke her up to help with breakfast. She didn't expect Aidan to hold out that long.

"I just gotta grab my coat."

Shae made the rounds with him again as he said his goodbyes. Daniel and Grant made plans to catch up with him again. There was talk of a group guy outing to a Kings' game at the start of the new year. The girls were very sweet, telling Aidan how happy they were to meet him and how they hoped they would see him again soon. Meegan managed to only waggle her eyebrows behind his back.

He grabbed his jacket and they made their way out to the front porch, closing the sounds of the party out as the door clicked shut. Aidan shrugged into his coat, then smiled down at Shae. Shae wanted to smile back. She couldn't though. That vibrating sensation had just gotten worse with each kind word and compliment about them as a couple that her friends had shared with her and Aidan as they made their way to the door.

She couldn't smile because her lips were numb from the way she was tensing.

"This was great. I'll text you tomorrow."

She'd love nothing more than a Merry Christmas text from him, but she realized then that she couldn't drag this out any longer. "Aidan I—I think we should take a little step back."

"Oh...okay." The shock on his face was clear and that made her feel even worse.

Shae groaned and rubbed her forehead. "It is absolutely not you. It is one hundred percent me. I've—I've been a divorced a few years, but I'm still new to the dating game and this is just too much for me right now," she blurted out.

"Oh. Yah," he stammered, but then he cleared his throat and seemed to recover a little bit. "No, I—yeah, I get it. I've never been divorced, but it doesn't sound easy. Or fun."

"I wish I could be one of those people who is just easy—"

"Listen. It's okay. We gave it a good try. Timing's just bad."

Shae swallowed the massive lump in her throat. "Yeah. I want to be less difficult with all this, but I'm not there." Shae looked up as eight different emotions danced across Aidan's features. His lips settled into a soft, understanding smile, but that didn't stop Shae from catching the look of pity that flashed through his eyes. He reached out and just barely touched the side of her hand before letting his fingers drop.

"Hey, at least we got off the app for a couple of weeks."

"We did and I enjoyed it. Sorry I wasn't a...sure thing or whatever. I'll—um, I'll make sure I delete those pictures you sent me. I should have already."

"Yeah, whatever you want. I wasn't worried about you having them."

Shae clammed up. There was nothing more she could say and if she tried to make things better by talking more, she was confident she would just make them worse. Thank god, Aidan took the hint. He knew their time was up.

"Well, I guess I should head out."

"Bye, Aidan."

"Bye, Shae." She hoped he would walk away and never look back. Instead, he stepped closer and wrapped his strong arms around her. She knew exactly what he was doing the moment his chin rested against the top of her head. He was taking her in one last time. She did the same, wrapping her arms around his waist, hugging him tight. She buried her face against his chest. The tears were so dangerously close to the surface, she nearly pushed him away just to get them to stop.

"Scram. Get on out of here before I do something extra stupid and make it impossible for us to run into each other in public one day," she said.

"I'm going, I'm going." This time it was for real. Shae watched him as he walked down the front steps and out of Keira and Daniel's yard. When he was down the block and out view, she went back inside and hid in Daniel's office and let herself fall apart. She liked Aidan so much, but no matter how silly it sounded when she repeated it back to herself, she knew she was no good for him. Aidan was the perfect guy and he needed someone who could be good for him. Not some neurotic bundle of nerves that was constantly waiting for the other shoe to drop.

As soon as she stopped crying, she'd rejoin the party. While she waited for her emotions to get their shit together, Shae pulled out her phone and deleted the MATCHED app. She'd meant what she said. She was not ready to date again and it was time to stop pretending she was.

EIGHT

Dear Santa, What the heck man?! Help me out here...

Being dumped on Christmas Eve wasn't something Aidan had experienced before and it was not something he would recommend. It had been a long time since he'd cried real tears, and even though no tears actually leaked out, he felt them stinging the backs of his eyes the whole drive back to his place. He did not want things to end with Shae.

When he got back to his apartment, he did his best not to get too down on himself before he went to bed. Purposely skipping over the bottles of booze lining the top of his fridge, he queued up episodes of a new cartoon on Netflix to keep his mind off the fact that he was now alone and pretty heartbroken. Shae didn't need space. She need to *not* be with him. It wasn't hard to get that message.

He understood. He really did. She'd been in a rough relationship and it had ended badly, but Aidan also knew what she wasn't saying. He knew what the problem really was. He had fallen for Shae, hard, and he didn't think she missed the effort he was putting in to make her happy and comfortable. He was pretty sure that's what sent her heading for the hills. He'd come on too strong, made himself too comfortable with her friends and family. They hadn't even discussed any relationship terms and he was in full boyfriend mode.

He knew it was a big deal to introduce someone new to the people closest to you and Aidan should have asked Shae how she wanted to handle it before he was all hands on at the party. He was drawn to Shae. He loved being near her, he loved touching her, but like his sister said, two people need to be happy in a relationship. Shae had been tense all night and instead of checking with her early on, he waited until the last second to see if she was okay. He got it. He'd fucked up. Shae wasn't ready to go where he wanted to take the relationship and he needed to accept that. It still fucking sucked. He was missing her already.

When he woke up in the morning, he was glad to find that his gym was actually open. He went to work out and then grabbed a big breakfast. He powered through video chats with his sister's family and his parents, grateful as fuck that his sister was too caught up in carting kids around an amusement park to ask about Shae. He thought he was doing okay until he met up with Matt outside the movie theater later that day.

"Ho ho ho, homie. Merry Christmas," Matt said as they briefly clasped hands and went in for the one-armed back pat.

"Thanks. Merry Christmas"

"Tiff will be here in a few. She's parking."

"Cool."

"How's my favorite baker doing?"

"Ah, good I guess," Aidan said with a shrug. "She kinda dumped me last night."

"Shit man, what happened?"

Aidan shook his head. "Don't really want to get into it because

I'm pretty fucked up about it. We're just not really doing the whole 'us' thing anymore. She called it off."

"Sorry, bro. I'll boycott Sweet Creams for two weeks."

"I appreciate that loyalty and dedication," Aidan said with an empty chuckle. "You don't have to boycott Sweet Creams at all. She's doing what's best for her and I think your business keeps their lights on."

"Okay, good. Two weeks is too long. Still sucks though. You haven't been this into anyone since Heather and you were pretty into her. I could tell you liked this girl. I saw you texting her all the time."

"Yeah, I'm pretty into her. I'll get over it. Don't really have a choice." Aidan looked over at his buddy as he gave him a firm pat on the shoulder.

"I am sorry."

"Thanks, man."

Just then, the top of Tiff appeared as she rode up the escalator.

"Are you boys ready to Star Wars?" she said, bobbing her head to the left and right. She walked right into Matt's arms and gave him a quick hug then moved over to Aidan.

"Aidan got dumped. We gotta cheer him up."

"Oh no!" Tiff said as she stepped back. "Are strip clubs open on Christmas day?"

"I'm not going to a strip club with you!" Matt said.

"Who said you were invited?" Tiff joked. "Come on, Aidan. All the candy and popcorn you can handle, on us." She looped her arm through his and tugged him toward the theater entrance. He didn't feel any better about losing Shae as they settled in to watch the interplanetary battle between good and evil, but at least he wasn't alone. He just hoped that, in time, he'd get over Shae and move on.

✳

Shae had survived Christmas day, just barely. Her parents' house was packed with her brothers and their wives and children, cousins and their children, aunts and uncles, including Daniel and Keira and her parents. She hadn't told Keira what happened with Aidan. After she stopped weeping in Daniel's office, she'd cleaned herself up and came up with the pathetic excuse that she had to head out to help her mom get a jump on desserts. Keira knew something was wrong, but she didn't press.

That morning she'd texted asking Keira not to breathe a word about Aidan in front of her parents. She'd explain later. Keira understood as was evident by the zipped lip emoji she'd sent back. Shae made it through the opening of a ton of presents, two and a half meals and an impromptu kitchen dance party. Now she was sprawled out on her childhood bed, hiding from the noise downstairs. She stared at the plastic stars on the ceiling that had stopped glowing in the dark years ago.

She didn't make a sound, but fat tears wouldn't stop running down the sides of her face.

"Shae?" Keira's voice was accompanied by a knock on the door. "It's just me."

"Yeah, come on in." She cleared her throat, then sat up as Keira cracked open the door. She came inside and started looking around in awe. The room was a bit of a late nineties time capsule. "What's going on downstairs?"

"Same old. Our dads are teaching Daniel how to play Spades."

"Oh god."

"Yeah it's gonna be a mess. I love that your room is exactly the same. My mom keeps telling me to come pick up my crap."

"Well duh, she needs a karaoke room."

Keira laughed and made herself comfortable at the foot of the bed. She grabbed an old stuffed panda of Shae's and pulled it into her lap. "Do you want to talk about it?"

She looked at the ceiling again for a moment, trying to will herself to not cry even harder. It didn't work. She swallowed a few times so she could at least talk. "I broke up with Aidan last night."

"I figured something happened."

Shae pulled out her phone and pulled up the picture Erica had taken of them under the mistletoe. She handed it over to Keira.

"Oh my god, this is so cute. What happened?"

"Well, I had another panic attack and I figure if I'm having so many Aidan-related panic attacks, that can't be good."

Keira winced and Shae could tell she was picking her next words carefully. "Do you know what exactly is triggering the panic attacks?"

"Yeah," Shae finally admitted out loud. "I was really starting to like him."

"What's wrong with that?"

"The last time I liked someone they—"

"Oh man. Come here." Keira shuffled to the middle of the bed and pulled Shae into her arms.

"When Harvin and I split, I remember Mom asked me one day what I wanted her to do with our wedding photos and there was just—there was something in her voice and I know she didn't mean it, but it made me feel like she was so disappointed me. Like I had it all and I somehow blew it. I know I didn't. That was all Harvin's fault—"

"Darn tootin'!" Keira said and they both started laughing. Shae pulled back and wiped her face. "Harvin...messed up a good thing. He messed it up real bad."

"When I got on MATCHED, all I was thinking about was just getting back out there. Test the waters, try some guys out. See what I even like in a guy who isn't Harvin. I wasn't expecting Aidan. I mean, I may have prayed to Santa and Frosty and Mrs. Claus for a good guy, but I didn't expect them to deliver someone so right on the nose, wrapped up in a perfect ginger bow. God, he's hot."

"Did he do anything—"

"Nope." Another massive lump lodged in Shae's throat. It

forced even more tears to stream down her face. "He was great. Sweet, attentive, patient. Fantastic in bed. He loves my baking. His coworker pumps a quarter of a million dollars into Sweet Creams weekly. I just—I freaked out. When Erica took that picture of us last night all I could think about was how it was all going to end and I was going to have to get rid of more pictures of yet another guy that I couldn't hold on to."

"So you pulled the old 'dump him before he can dump you' move."

"Oh god. I really did."

Keira reached out and took Shae's hand. "Listen, you can't stop someone from being a jerk. But it doesn't sound like Aidan's a jerk. He sounds pretty great and like he likes you a whole lot. I mean, we only hung out with him last night, but he looks at you like he's caught each and every feeling for you. And he is pretty darn nice. Daniel and I both really liked him."

"I like him so much, Keira. I think about him all the time. I want to text him all the time and that makes me so anxious. There's no way he likes me that much. No way. I just can't picture it."

"Shae. You've met me. You've met Daniel. Sometimes really sweet, hot guys just like weird girls like us. They can't help it. We're so cute."

"We are pretty cute."

"What do you want to do? Do you want another chance with him?"

"Yeah, I think I do. I'll take a few days and maybe after the wedding I'll text him and pray he doesn't hate me. I just—I have to get this Harvin baggage out of my head. It's like weeds growing on everything."

"I'll help you in any way I can. Bring my emotional weedwacker and everything."

Shae finally smiled. "Thank you."

"Can we stay up here for at least another hour?"

"Um, yeah."

"Good. If one more person gives me one more suggestion about what I should do about a wedding that is literally six days away, I'm going to elope."

"It's always an option."

"Yeah and have my and Daniel's moms lose their minds? No thank you. Maybe after the wedding we'll both find some peace."

"Seriously. Dear Santa, make it so."

Shae was exhausted. Finally, Keira and Daniel were married. Vows and rings exchanged, toasts raised, dinner served, cake cut and now the dance floor was packed to the brim with family and friends moving to the latest pop and R&B hits. Everything had gone off without a hitch. Everyone was on time, the food was delicious and Keira looked amazing in her custom wedding gown. Most importantly, Daniel and Keira were husband and wife.

Shae was exhausted, but she was finally starting to feel a little bit like herself again. Shae didn't realize how much residual anxiety she'd been carrying about the wedding. The only girls of the Kenney bunch, she and Keira had been best friends since they could walk. She knew that Daniel was the perfect guy for her cousin, but she wanted everything about their day to be perfect too. It was a lot to carry around that kind of emotion for weeks on end. They'd reached the finish line and everyone could finally relax. And tomorrow Shae could finally face the one thing she'd been putting off all week. Tomorrow.

Shae stood off to the side of the dance floor, champagne glass in her hand, swaying to the music. She didn't realize she'd been thinking about Aidan again, wondering what he was doing at that exact moment until she saw him coming down the stone steps of the venue, Erica by his side. He looked amazing in a fresh navy blue suit and dark tan dress shoes. His hair was combed back from his face and those damn glasses finished off his red-headed Clark Kent look. Erica motioned toward Shae and even after Aidan looked right at her and their eyes met, she still didn't want to believe he was actually there.

Their eyes held as he made his way around the outside of the tent over to where she stood.

"Hi," she said, her voice barely above a whisper.

"Wow—just wow. You look amazing, Shae." She looked down at herself. She forgot her hair and makeup were professionally done and that her curvaceous body was covered wrist to thigh in silver sequins.

"Thank you. You look pretty handsome yourself. What are you doing here?"

"If you want me to go, I'll leave right now. Keira invited me and Erica was my contact on the ground. She still had my number in her phone."

"Oh." The sound that left Shae's lungs was fueled by pure awe. Shae had stuck to her guns to wait until after the wedding to contact him. She'd hoped she wouldn't fumble explaining her feelings so badly that he realized it would be less of a headache to just avoid her forever—if he even agreed to see her. She definitely wasn't expecting him to show up deep along the shores of Malibu, tonight of all nights. She'd deal with her nosey friends later. Or thank them.

"Do you want to go somewhere and talk?" he asked.

"Sure. Yeah." Shae put down her glass and headed into the shadows outside of the tent. She'd scoped out different paths to the beach earlier just in case she needed a break from her family. Now seemed like the perfect time to take advantage of them. She slipped off her heels and carefully picked her way down the path. She could feel Aidan's hand on the small of her back the whole way and god, had she missed him. They passed by two of Daniel's guests who had just left one of the still blazing fire pits available. Shae sat on the stone bench just out of reach of the flames.

"This is a really nice place," Aidan said, looking out at the crashing waves bathed in moonlight.

"Yeah. JD really came through."

"Did you have a nice Christmas?"

"Yeah, I did. Thank you for asking. Um, I don't hate this small talk, I really don't, but did you come here to tell me something?" Shae asked.

"I did. I wanted to say that I'm sorry for coming on too strong. Me being here right now might be a little much—"

Shae's whole body turned toward Aidan so fast she was shocked she didn't pull something. "You think I dumped you because you came on too strong?"

"Yeah...didn't you?"

"No, Aidan. Oh my god. That wasn't it at all. I..." She hadn't fully rehearsed her speech yet. She thought she there was still time to figure out exactly how to phrase what she wanted to say. "Oh man, I screwed this up."

"What? Tell me."

"Okay. Here goes. I'll just tell you. I like you. I like you so much. Like, so so so much. I didn't think I would. Not that I didn't think you were a good guy, but you run into some hot guy from your old job on a dating app, you don't expect him to turn out to be real-thing good."

"I get it."

"I felt myself falling for you so fast that I got scared. My divorce affected me in ways I didn't realize until we started hanging out and I finally see that I am actually scared to fall for someone again. I am terrified, but it wasn't about you. You didn't do anything wrong. I just kept thinking about how I couldn't stop thinking about you pretty much every second of every day and I knew I was doomed. Have you ever felt like—"

"Shae," Aidan said, sliding his hand over her knee. The perfect feeling of his familiar gentle touch shut her right up. "Can I tell you something?"

"Yeah. Sorry I've been rambling. You go."

"You don't have to apologize for telling me how you feel. Okay?" It wasn't a rhetorical question. He paused and waited to see if Shae really understood him. He was right. She had nothing to be sorry for.

"I—yes. I have feelings. Lots of them. Okay. Please go on."

He smiled and closed the space between them. She almost melted as he gently swept her loose curls off her shoulder.

"I like you, Shae. A lot. I have liked you for years. You're dealing with a lot. I get it, but I like you. I know some guys are terrible at shit like this, but I'm telling you that I am here and I don't want to go anywhere. When you're ready you can tell me more about your ex and maybe I can help with some of the divorce related stuff you're going through. I might not understand it all, but I can be a shoulder or something."

"You want me to talk about Harvin?"

"If it helps you feel better, yes. Absolutely. And if it helps me be a better boyfriend to you, then fuck yes."

She laughed through the tears that suddenly sprang up out of nowhere. "You want to be my boyfriend? Good lord, I sound fifteen."

"Yeah. Maybe I should have mentioned that earlier. I got the feeling it might scare you off," he teased. Then he kissed Shae's forehead. "I would love to be your boyfriend and, as your boyfriend, I want you to be yourself. If that means getting shit about your ex off your chest from time to time, woman, I am game. I also hope it means we build our own memories together."

"I'd like that a lot. All of it. I got it pretty bad for you."

"Thank god. 'Cause if you weren't willing to give this a chance, I was going to ask you for that brownie crunch recipe and force the next girl to make it and that would be real fucking awkward."

"Oh my god!" Shae laughed and lightly swatted at his arm.

"I'm kidding! Come here."

The next thing Shae knew, they were kissing. All of Shae's fears didn't magically float away, but in those moments as their lips moved together, music from the dance floor at their backs, Shae felt like finally, her love life was moving in a good direction. Praise Santa.

The End

SNATCHED

Daniel waited by the front entrance of the condo for his friend to let him in. He looked down one more time, smoothing his tie and straightening his jacket. He wanted to look good for his date. A few seconds later the door swung open.

"Hey, man," Grant said. "Come on in. She's almost ready."

"Thanks." They crossed the courtyard and went up the few steps to the unit Grant shared with his girlfriend and baby mama, Violet. Daniel and Keira had sprinted to the altar exactly one year after they met, but Grant and Violet were doing things their way, taking their time in some respects and barreling over their friends in others, if their kid wasn't enough proof of their progress into real adulthood. Daniel was just glad they were home on Valentine's night so he could give his wife the gift she wanted, the way she wanted it.

Daniel followed Grant inside, and joined him on the couch. The Lakers were playing on the flat screen TV.

"Jack got his little pudgy hooks in her and I had to remind her that you were still coming to pick her up."

Daniel laughed. "Thanks man. She's easily distracted, but it's part of her charm. You guys gonna do anything tonight?"

"Nope. I ordered Italian from this place Violet loves. They should be here in a bit, but we're just staying in, praying for four consecutive hours of sleep."

"Man, I feel like such a dick. We could have given you guys the night off. We would have stayed with Jack."

"Never woulda happened," Grant said just as Violet came walking into the room with their four month old son snoozing on her chest. "Babe, Daniel offered to babysit."

Violet let out a snort of laughter. "Yeah, no. Nice try buddy."

"What?" Grant said with his own shock of laughter. "He offered."

"With Keira, of course," Daniel added. "I'm not really that good with kids."

"Neither am I," Grant said. Daniel wasn't sure if he was joking.

Violet opened the fridge and took out a bottle of water. "Give me a few more months, when this lunatic level of separation anxiety goes away. Then we'll ditch you with our kid at least once a month."

"I'm holding you to that," Daniel said.

Violet held out the bottle of water for Grant open. He stood instead. "Vi, you've been holding him for hours. Give yourself break."

She didn't hesitate, but Daniel saw something dark cross over her face as she handed the baby to Grant.

"Daniel, would you like anything to drink?" she asked, rolling her shoulders.

"Nah, I'm okay. Thank you."

"Let me go see if I can help move Keira along." Violet disappeared back down the hall toward their bedroom. Grant sat back on the couch, moving Jack on to his back across his lap. Jack stirred a bit, but settled immediately as Grant gave him a few rhythmic, gentle pats. Daniel watched as Grant's massive hand dwarfed the child's tiny body.

"She's thinks she's going to screw him up if she's not Super Mom every second of every day."

Daniel felt bad. He couldn't imagine the stress of parenthood. He and Keira were just enjoying each other.

"So you got Trent to help out tonight?" Grant asked.

"Yeah, I owe him big."

"Nice," Grant said. "She's gonna love it."

Just then Daniel heard Keira's voice and the sound of her heels clicking down the hall. He almost lost his breath when he saw her.

She stopped the second she laid eyes on him then did a little spin in place. The tiny royal blue dress looked great on her toned body. "How do I look?"

"You're right. I shouldn't have picked you up at home."

"See? I mean we live together. It's not a date date if you pick me up where we both live. But I look good, right?"

His wife spent most of her time working at the gym, in spandex and sweats. She claimed she hated dressing up unless it was cosplay, but he could tell she knew she looked great.

"You look amazing, baby. Let's get going." They said goodbye to their friends and headed out to Daniel's car.

As soon as they walked out the door, Keira grabbed Daniel's hand between both her palms. She was practically bouncing as they walked back out to the street. "So we're both dressed up. You look so hot, oh my god. I love that suit. Where are we going?"

"I made us reservations at Samba."

"Oh, that steakhouse?"

"The very one. I know you wanted to check it out."

"And after?"

"You'll just have to see."

Keira had turned into an top-notch switch, complementing Daniel's need to submit and dominate perfectly, but tonight was his night to top and he was going to do it right.

They drove across town, toward the beach, and Daniel listened as Keira told him about her day with her clients at the gym in her typical animated fashion. Daniel barely said a word, but he felt himself smiling as he snuck glimpses of her beautiful face. He had his prosthetic arm on so he couldn't touch her skin to skin while he drove, but she made up for it, rubbing his thigh over his suit pants. He'd deal with his slowly growing erection once they got to the valet stand.

Dinner was delicious and his date, the perfect company. He vented a little about stress at work and he listened as she talked about some online drama she and her friend, Lori had had with racist women in their fandom. It never crossed his mind that he might fall for someone who was so passionate about science fiction and the characters she found in the genres many mediums, but he loved how involved she got in every aspect of her favorite shows and comics. He was married to a thorough geek and he wouldn't have it any other way.

His chest warmed when she opened the gift he picked up the week before, an aquamarine pendant to match her engagement ring and a copy of the most recent companion book for her favorite television show, *Galaxis*. Thanks to his brother being *on* the show, the whole cast had signed it.

After he opened the custom six thousand piece puzzle she'd had made— a giant selfie of the two of them redrawn by one of her favorite comic book artists—he was ready to get on with the rest of their night.

"I'm going to hit the restroom and then we'll go," he said, rubbing his lips along Keira's knuckles. It was dark in the restaurant, but he knew her cheeks were heating under his intense stare.

"Okay," she said bashfully, the sound of her voice making his cock rise. He was going to fuck her so good.

He stood and leaned over to kiss her lips and then he whispered their key word in her ear. "Quality Assurance."

Daniel felt her tense and he knew she'd gotten the green light message he was trying to send her. Their scene had started. He left

Keira at the table, weaving his way through dinning couples. He'd told Trent exactly what to say and exactly what to do. He'd wait until Daniel paid the bill by the bar and exited the restaurant. Then Trent would find Keira alone at the table. She knew Trent well and Daniel knew she'd be happy to see him. He worked the door at The Club and Keira had grown close to him during their chats every time they arrived.

But Trent wasn't her friend tonight. He was Daniel's henchman and Keira's kidnapper, part of the fantasy Daniel had been denying Keira for months. He'd tell her not to make a scene, to gather their things and not ask any questions. Daniel pulled his car up outside of the restaurant, all fears that Keira had already foiled his scene dissipating when he saw Trent ushering her out the front door with a firm hand on her arm. The limo was waiting and Daniel watched as they both climbed inside.

In the few minutes it took for the limo to leave the curb, he knew Trent had followed his instructions, blindfolding Keira and binding her hands. Daniel would gag her himself later. They drove for about fifteen to the location he'd selected and Trent had helped him stage. He stepped out of his car. Just as the rear door to the limo opened. Her heard Keira's desperate voice.

"Where are we? I demand you let me go."

"I thought I told you to shut up," Trent growled before he turned to Daniel and flashed him a huge grin complete with a thumbs up.

Trent carefully pulled Keira out of the back seat and hoisted her over his shoulder. She struggled a little bit, but went still when Daniel gripped her elegant curls.

"If you want to live, I suggest you cooperate."

Kiera was quiet for a second or two as she lifted her head like she was trying to pinpoint exactly where Daniel was standing.

"Calhoune," she hissed between her teeth. "I should have known it was you."

"Quiet," Daniel barked at her.

"Who the fuck is Calhoune?" Trent mouthed. Daniel shrugged, then nodded for Trent to take her inside. The room had been cleared of everything but a sturdy metal bed frame, a bare mattress, and a few other essentials he needed for their evening.

Once Keira was settled upright it was time for Trent to go. Daniel offered him a silent thanks and waited for him to leave before he started forcefully undressing his wife. She put up a bit of a fight, but in no time he had her completely naked and bound spread eagle to the bed.

Daniel slid on this fake eye patch he'd picked up at the dollar store, then grabbed the stool and pulled it right up to the edge of the bed. Then he ripped off Keira's blindfold.

He watched as she blinked a few times, her eyes adjusting to the single bare light bulb that left him mostly in the shadows. If only he'd picked up some cigarettes that would have really added to the dramatics of it all.

"I'm warning you. People will be looking for me. Let me go."

"I don't think so, Miss Merrywether." Since they were going with made up names. "You have to give me what I want."

"I don't owe you anything. Your father made his choice. He got the land and my father got the diamonds. They're mine!"

"I'm so sorry you feel that way because we both know that isn't true. You father was a thief and I've come to take back what's mine."

"I'll never tell you where they are." Keira thrashed her head to the side in the most ridiculous way and it took everything Daniel had in him not to laugh. She was always so over the top.

"I've been trying playing nice with you. I tried to leave you out of this. I didn't want to hurt you, but you're leaving me no choice." Daniel stood and walked around the foot of the bed, giving Keira a better view of him. He slowly pulled off his suit jacket and set it aside.

"I like the eye patch and you wore your stainless steel hook?"

Daniel looked down at his prosthetic attachment which was usually a matte black hook.

"You look so Bond-villainy," she added with a giggle.

With any other submissive Daniel would have been annoyed. Keira slipped in and out of scene like it was nobody's business, but he knew a surefire way to keep her focused.

He leaned over the bed until his face was only an inch or so above hers. Then he took her pussy in his firm grip. She let out a little yelp, arching against him as her slick juices slid between his fingers.

"I'm glad you find this so amusing," Daniel said harshly. "I'm sure you'll change your tune after we spend a few hours getting to know each other a little better."

"I'll never tell," she said one last time, her voice near a whisper. "You can't make me."

"Oh, but I think I can."

Daniel pressed his lips to hers, demanding her body respond to his with every probing swipe of his tongue. She resisted again, trying to turn her head this way and that, but he wouldn't let up until she finally succumb to his violent attention. She relented with a pained groan and kissed him back.

Daniel let out a cruel chuckle, but didn't break the contact as he continued to squeeze and rub her wet slit with his fingers. He was gentle when he drew his rounded hook down her side, then back up to trace her nipple. The light whimper she let out against his mouth only made his erection throb harder in his slacks.

He pulled away, looking Keira in the eye as she tried to refocus on his face. She licked her lips.

"Tell me where the diamonds are," he insisted one more time.

"Never."

"Then I'll take what's mine."

Daniel stepped away from the bed and started to undress. He set aside his prosthesis and kicked off his dress shoes.

"No!" Keira cried out, thrashing some more.

"I gave you plenty of chances," Daniel said as he unbuttoned his shirt. "I'm going to fuck you senseless, and then you're going to give me what's rightfully mine."

Once he was completely naked he undid the ties around Keira's ankles. She flailed about, carrying on with her dramatic protest, but she was careful not to kick him by accident. Daniel joined her on the bed, gently pushing thighs apart so he could climb between her legs.

"Either way, I'm getting what's mine," he said one more time, just to drive his point home. He took her by the chin and kissed her with the same force as before. And she fought him again, pretending not to like the perfect way their mouths fix together—until the head of his cock entered her warm cunt. Her whole body arched off the bed, her legs spreading, her lips parting, giving Daniel all the access he could ever need. He fucked her deep and hard, kissing her deep and rough, driving both their bodies into the mattress, making the the bed frame clank against the wall. Keira cries drove him wild, only spurring him on.

"Daniel," she begged breathlessly. "Untie me, please."

Their scene wasn't over, but he knew what she wanted. She wanted to touch him while they made love and he wanted the same. He stayed buried deep inside of her as he made quick work of the ties at the top of the bed. She'd have some marks on her wrist for a day or so, but no crazy bruises. As soon as she was free she looped her arms around his shoulders, using the new leverage she had fuck herself harder on his cock.

Keira came, an urgent, but choked, "Oh my gosh, oh gosh, frick," coming from her lips. But Daniel kept going. He knew she had more to give. He continued to fuck her, making her come again and again until his balls swelled up on themselves and he filled her with his come. But still he wasn't done.

Keira had coined it the Nasty Finish, and he wouldn't end

their scene until he'd gone through with it. He slid out of her body and rolled her so she was spooned against his chest, then he reached down and shoved three fingers into her pussy, coating his hand with his jizz. The swirling of his digits made her body contract and pulse around him again. Daniel groaned as he felt the final tiny orgasms shiver over her body. He pulled his fingers out and shoved them into Keira's mouth. She licked and sucked at them, holding on to his wrist until she left his hand completely clean. She collapsed against his chest. Daniel held her, kissing her shoulder, giving them both a chance to catch their breath.

"Pizza." She groaned out their safe word as she stretched her toned legs against his, signifying that she was done with the scene, which was fine with Daniel. He'd been sufficiently drained of all his fluids. He smoothed the loose hairs that had escaped away from her face, then kissed her temple.

"How did that work for you?" he asked. She'd been after this kidnapping scenario for months, but he wanted to wait for a special occasion.

"It was perfect. Thank you, baby. Where are we?" Keira asked in sleepy haze.

"Our house. Come on." Daniel helped her up and opened the door to his home office that led out to the hallway.

"Where'd you put all your stuff?" she asked as she looked back into the mostly empty room that usually housed Daniel's drafting tables and his video equipment. He and Trent had even blacked out the window.

"Garage. I wanted you to be right at home when we finished." They walked into the kitchen, where Daniel had left the gifts they'd exchanged on the counter. He kissed her again then went over to the fridge to get her some water.

"You want some ice cream?" he asked. He'd already stocked the freezer with her favorite after sex treat.

"No, thank you. I just want you." Keira took a deep chug then handed Daniel the glass. He finished it off then pulled her into his arms.

"I love you, Miss Merrywether."

"Back at you, Calhoune," she said as she gave his ass an affection squeeze.

The End, for real. That's it.

Acknowledgments

To the following people who supported me through the various stages of this series:
Meghan O'Brien
Emma Petersen
Tecora Arnold
Heidi Belleau
Felice Fox
Summer Youngblood
Angel Lawson
KB Alan
Anya Richards
KM Jackson
Farrah Rochon
Bree Bridges
Minx Malone
Vivienne Westlake
Whitney
Leyla
Solace Ames
Angel Lawson
Alyssa Cole
Shelly Ellis
Thank you.

About the Author

After years of meddling in her friends' love lives, multi award-winning author Rebekah Weatherspoon turned to writing romance to get her fix. Raised in Southern New Hampshire, Rebekah now lives in Southern California where she will remain forever because she hates moving.

With over twenty-four titles under her belt, Rebekah has covered subgenres including extremely sexy and equally dark romantic suspense, paranormal romance, steamy romantic comedies on horseback, and now young adult romance. With everything going on in the world she still believes in love, the fluffier the better.

You can find praise for Rebekah's books in The New York Times, Entertainment Weekly, Book Riot, Oprah Magazine, TIME Magazine, and on a segment from The Today Show that is definitely pinned at the top of her Instagram page.

To stay up to date on Rebekah's most recent work and events, subscribe to her newsletter at https://rebekahweatherspoon.com/newsletter/